CARDINAL MAZARIN
First Minister of France—his grand scheme
is to capture the great British prize of
Bermuda, but one man stands in his way.

RICHARD DUNSTABLE
The young American patriot risks
his life on an explosive mission
of secrecy, deception, and death.

ELIZA DUNSTABLE
His young lovely wife, horrified to
discover the incredible but true identity
of her stepmother, Celeste Burrows.

CELESTE BURROWS
Beautiful, bright, and wily bride
of Eliza's father, finally forced to reveal
she is Mazarin's spymaster for America.

COLONEL ADAM BURROWS
Eliza's father and proud husband of the
exquisite Celeste, he is a rich shipowner and
bold leader of the colonies' militia.

(. . . and more)

ADMIRAL ANTOINE DE BOSQUETTE
A clever, suave, seafaring man, determined to find a way to accomplish his dangerous mission.

GENERAL ETIENNE DE CLUNY
A gruff, hearty, no-nonsense soldier, bewildered by the impossible order he has received—to wrest Bermuda from the British.

MARK PRESCOTT
Owner of Bermuda's largest tobacco plantation, a grizzled man called the Major, steadfast head of the island's militia.

ADELLA PRESCOTT
Mark's sister and housekeeper, a hardworking, courageous, pretty red-haired girl, considerably his junior.

ZWINGLI
A giant Bantu Chief, endowed with prodigious strength and fiercely loyal to Adella, his protectress.

CAPTAIN ROGER STEPHENS
The leader of the buccaneers, promised
a huge sum of gold for a bold assault
on a valuable English prize.

THE BUCCANEERS
The pirate captain's wild and bloodthirsty
crew, ready for a new and dangerous
voyage—wherever it may lead.

GABRIELLE
Half-French, half-English, a rude,
violent, flirtatious vixen.

WEE WILLIE WALKER
Like Zwingli, a brave giant
of enormous physical prowess.

ROARING WOLF
Richard's courageous Indian friend,
a boon companion in risky enterprise.

THE AMERICAN PATRIOT SERIES
Published by Ballantine Books:

THE NEW BREED

THE GREAT DECEPTION

BOLD DESTINY

THE **AMERICAN PATRIOT** SERIES

BOOK III

BOLD DESTINY

Douglass Elliot

BALLANTINE BOOKS • NEW YORK

Library of Congress Catalog Card Number: 82-91199

ISBN 0-345-29824-1

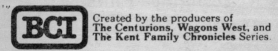

Created by the producers of
The Centurions, Wagons West, and
The Kent Family Chronicles Series.

Executive Producer: Lyle Kenyon Engel

Manufactured in the United States of America

First Edition: August 1983

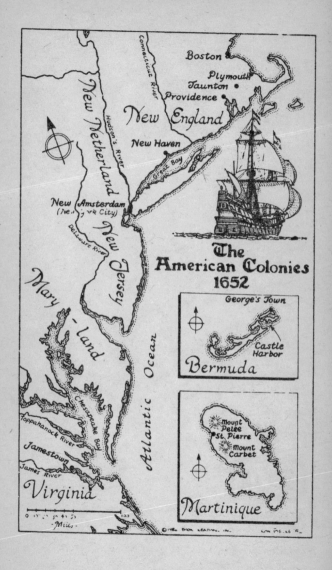

The
American Colonies
1652

Connecticut River

Boston
Plymouth
Taunton
Providence
New England
New Haven
Great Bay

New Netherland

Hudson's River

New Amsterdam
(New York City)

New Jersey

Delaware River

Atlantic Ocean

Mary-Land

Chesapeake Bay

Toppahanock River
Jamestown
James River
Virginia

0 10 20 30 40 50   100
Miles

George's Town
Castle Harbor
Bermuda

Mount Pelée
St. Pierre
Mount Carbet
Martinique

PROLOGUE

A GENERATION after the Pilgrims had first stepped ashore in Plymouth harbor, and nearly half a century after the founding of Jamestown in Virginia, the English North American colonies had far outstripped their neighbors in the New World.

In the north, New England boasted vigorous, bustling young towns, among them Boston, Providence, and New Haven, rivaling and threatening to overrun the strategic Dutch outpost of New Netherland. And in the south, Virginia, though less densely populated, each year spread its prospering tobacco plantations farther up the tidal rivers around the Chesapeake Bay and inland toward the foothills of the Blue Ridge.

Even the tiny group of islands known as Bermuda, clustered alone hundreds of miles off the Virginia coast, boasted a thriving English settlement.

But at home in England, a shadow had fallen over the land ever since King Charles had lost his head to the executioner's ax in 1649. After a series of bloody battles, the Puritan general, Oliver Cromwell, had seized power, and for the first time in centuries, it appeared as though no king or queen would again sit on the English throne.

All the while, England's enemies did not sleep. The never-ending political upheaval in Europe, fueled to new intensity by economic wars and religious rivalries, now erupted into near chaos. Alliances shifted, civil wars threatened, and espionage and intrigue were rife. The stakes included the New World; and the four great maritime powers—the Spanish, the Dutch, the French, and the English—lost no time in carrying their quarrels across the Atlantic. No ship was safe, and commerce soon degenerated into a bitter naval free-for-all—the beginning of the golden age of piracy.

The English colonies, largely abandoned by the beleaguered Oliver Cromwell, were forced to shift for themselves as best they could. Relatively isolated, the settlers there had already breathed the air of freedom, and life in the wilderness had taught them much. The quarrels of the Old World seemed distant and hard to understand, and other, more pressing dangers, such as Indian attacks, diverted their attention.

The English colonies, however, were too rich a prize to be passed over, and although Europe lay thousands of miles and an ocean away, the disputes of the Old World could not be ignored for long—not without dire consequences.

I

THE colonial brig *Eliza*, built in 1651, was only a year old but had already proved its seaworthiness on the crossing to France.

Now the white sails snapped in the gusting wind as the vessel sliced through the green-blue mid-Atlantic, and the stout hull rose and fell gracefully, rhythmically, rolling and pitching only slightly.

The *Eliza* was the pride of Colonel Adam Burrows, half owner of a New Haven company of shipowners and traders. As he often said, he had good reason to feel that this vessel was something special: It had been made to his personal specifications in the best shipyard in New England and had been christened in honor of his only child.

Eliza Dunstable herself stood with her husband, Richard, at the brig's port rail, and although she, too, had good reason to be pleased with her namesake's sailing abilities, her blue eyes were deeply troubled. She raised a hand to brush back a strand of her long, pale blond hair flying in the sea breeze, and as she did, she shivered slightly. Celebrated in her native

New Haven for her charm as well as her beauty, Eliza was not living up to her reputation. She looked miserable.

Her husband, Richard, tall and sinewy, with crisp brown hair, was equally unhappy. Yet every time he glanced at his lovely young wife, he could not help but think that he had good reason to rejoice despite their recent ill fortune. Having fled England when his ancestral lands had been confiscated following the execution of King Charles I, Richard had created a new life for himself in the New World colonies, where he had married Eliza and won a responsible position in his father-in-law's company. And he had so distinguished himself in wars with the Indians that he had risen to the rank of lieutenant colonel and field commander of the New Haven militia, second only to the venerable Adam Burrows. Together, Eliza and he lived comfortably, were well off financially, and should have been more than content with their lot. Yet Richard's misery equaled his wife's.

"We thought we were being so wise when we went to France," he said bitterly. "We should have known better."

Eliza, ordinarily calm and courageous, was on the verge of tears. "It serves us right," she replied, "for thinking we could outsmart Cardinal Mazarin. It's no accident that he became first minister of France. He rose to that post because he's the most ruthless and pitiless man in Europe."

"What annoys me," Richard said, "is that I was so sure we could just walk away from our posts as secret agents for France. Of all people, I should have known better."

She gripped his arm so hard that her knuckles turned white. "It infuriates me every time I think of it. Not only did he physically threaten us, making it plain we would die if we didn't go along with his crazy schemes, but he also acted as if he was doing us a favor—as if we wanted or needed his filthy gold!"

Richard shook his head bleakly.

"And to top it all, he even recruited Celeste, right under Papa's nose! And as his colonial master spy! It's almost too much to believe that anyone could be that underhanded."

"For the life of me, I still can't understand how Celeste is qualified to hold that position," Richard said.

"Obviously," Eliza replied, "she's been in the employ of the French for some time. You can be sure that Mazarin didn't just pluck her out of the blue to work for him now. She must be an old hand at his dirty work, and I daresay she thoroughly enjoys it, too." Her tone was acid.

"I'm not so sure about that," Richard said, staring out to sea. He had his own opinions as to Celeste's true loves and loyalties, but he wasn't about to broach that sensitive subject just now. Besides, until he definitely knew otherwise, it would be prudent to assume the worst of Celeste, even though it went against his nature.

Musing on the quirks of fate that had created the untenable situation, the young couple fell silent. It was indeed unfortunate that Colonel Adam Burrows, after spending more than twenty years as a widower, should have unwittingly chosen as his bride the one woman who had the power to place all of the English colonies of North America in the greatest of jeopardy. Celeste Burrows was lovely, as desirable to men as she was sharp-witted, and nearly everyone in New Haven society who had met her felt the colonel was to be envied. The New Haven public, however, was not aware of Celeste's spotted past. Nor had they the slightest inkling of what Richard and Eliza had learned from Cardinal Mazarin himself—that France coveted the English colonies and would use almost any means to gain possession of them during this strange, unsettled period when no king sat on the English throne and when the self-proclaimed English lord protector, Oliver Cromwell, had his hands full with Royalist enemies at home and Dutch enemies abroad.

"If just you and I were involved," Eliza said, breaking the silence, "I wouldn't be as concerned."

"Nor would I," Richard replied. "It's your father we have to worry about. But even though we may not be in Cardinal Mazarin's class as profound or devious thinkers, I'm still reasonably certain we'll be able to handle Celeste. By that I mean we'd be able to pretend to go along with her, while actually looking out for the best interests of New Haven and the other English colonies."

Eliza sighed heavily. "But nevertheless, my father is deeply involved, and I'm afraid of what the news will do to him if he finds out."

"We've got to tell him," Richard said.

"But I just couldn't," she replied. "It would break his heart. In fact, I'd be inclined to go to almost any length to keep the truth from him."

"That would be very wrong," Richard said. "His position in the militia and his standing in the community make it essential he know that one of Mazarin's spies is operating in his own house." Richard shook his head. He knew Celeste well—perhaps too well for his own good—and try as he might, he could not get used to the idea of her being a French spy.

"My father," Eliza replied hotly, "is a proud man. He's never been particularly vain—far from it. But he seemed to take on new life when he married Celeste. I'm afraid that he will be crushed if he learns the truth."

"I'm trying to look at the larger problem," Richard said. "I mean, the damage Celeste can cause if your father isn't told the truth. As a loyal Englishman—even though I've been treated shabbily by Cromwell and his fanatical Roundheads—I wouldn't like to think of what will happen if France gains control of our colonies. The freedom and personal liberties we take for granted will vanish. We'll no longer govern ourselves. Instead we'll be second-rate citizens in a land where the orders are given in French, and we'll be expected to obey without question. I couldn't tolerate that, and neither could you."

"What you say is true, Richie. But still, if we told Papa the truth, and then something terrible happened, I couldn't live with myself. No, I recognize the point you're trying to make, but I think we'll simply have to work around my father and find other ways to neutralize Celeste."

"That's far easier said than done," Richard said, "and we'd be taking frightening risks with the future of the colonies."

"The other way we'd be taking risks with my father's well-being," she replied.

Richard knew how stubborn Eliza could be where her father's welfare was concerned. "I suggest," he said, "that we drop the subject for now. It'll be a few days before we reach New Haven, and maybe by then a solution will occur to us. I certainly hope so, for all our sakes."

Still severely troubled, Eliza nodded her assent.

Long accustomed to crisis in her young life, Celeste Burrows did not grow panicky as she reviewed her precarious situation. Sitting in the master's cabin on board the *Eliza*, she tapped her fingers lightly on the arm of her chair as she analyzed the problem. It had been necessary for her to tell Richard and Eliza of her arrangement with Cardinal Mazarin, because they would be working under her supervision and would be reporting to her. That alone had been difficult enough.

But ultimately, she knew, Richard and Eliza would feel compelled to go to Adam and tell him the truth about his wife. There was nothing she could do to prevent it. The only question was when they would tell him.

Celeste's red lips tightened. If Adam felt that she had deliberately deceived him, he would put her aside at once. He was a man of high principle, and he would not tolerate deception from his own wife.

But her situation was far from hopeless, Celeste assured herself. She had many assets, many weapons—principal among them being her husband's infatuation with her. She stood up and walked across the cabin. Staring at her reflection in the small looking glass set into the bulkhead, she felt infinitely better. Her principal appeal to Adam was erotic, and everything about her appearance confirmed her beauty and sexual attractiveness. She removed her hairpins and shook her head, and her lustrous blue-black hair fell in loose waves down her back. She moved her head closer to the glass, and her striking violet eyes, their appeal intensified by the ring of kohl surrounding them, stared back at her, powerful and alluring. And her figure, she had to admit, was superb: slender, yet feminine, willowy, and supple. She inspected herself critically, feature by feature: She had broad, sloping shoulders; a high, firm bust; an incredibly tiny waist; long, firm hips and thighs; slender, perfectly formed legs. No other woman could compete with her—not even Eliza, who was renowned as one of the greatest beauties in New Haven Colony. Removing her nightgown and donning a lacy black peignoir, which she left mostly unfastened in front, Celeste allowed herself the luxury of a faint smile and approved the shape that her full red lips assumed.

She was back in her chair when the door opened and Adam Burrows returned from the quarterdeck. He stopped short to admire her, but was surprised that she had not yet dressed for the day.

Celeste knew what had to be done and wasted no time. "I must discuss a matter of the gravest importance with you, my dear," she said.

He was surprised by the seriousness of her tone, and he raised an eyebrow.

Moving gracefully to the foot of the feather bed, she positioned herself so that her peignoir fell open to reveal part of her bosom and her long, shapely legs. She waved him to a chair directly opposite her.

As she had hoped, he was fascinated by the tantalizing glimpses of her body.

Adam removed his hat and smoothed his gray hair. Then his blue eyes became troubled. "What's the matter?" he demanded.

Certain that she had his full attention, Celeste began her well-thought-out speech. "As you know, my dear," she said, "I lived at the court of King Charles until he was executed by the Roundheads. I was fortunate enough to flee safely to France, and managed to escape from the enemies of my country, who had put a price on my head. I found temporary refuge at the court in exile of the boy king, Charles the Second."

So far she was not telling him anything that he didn't already know, and Adam nodded complacently.

"I was summoned to an interview by the most powerful man in France—the first minister," she said.

Adam sat bolt upright. "Cardinal Mazarin?" he asked in astonishment.

Celeste sighed plaintively. "He offered me work that was easy to perform and very well paid," she said. "I was penniless and friendless, so I accepted." She saw no reason to tell him that she had been the mistress of a nobleman who had lost his life in battle with the Roundheads, and that it was his death that had left her bereft.

"What kind of work?" Adam wanted to know.

She drew a deep breath, and her tone was tremulous as she replied, "Before I knew what was happening, I was being used as a secret agent—an informant—for France."

Adam was surprised, but quickly recovered his poise. In more than a half century of living, most of it spent in the New World, he had become accustomed to many twists and turns in the lives of friends and acquaintances, and his bride's revelation only momentarily stunned him.

Seeing him taking the news calmly, Celeste was greatly encouraged. "I've been in Mazarin's employ for several years," she continued. "In fact, while we were in Paris—while you were engaged in negotiations with the minister of trade—Mazarin summoned me to his office."

Mazarin was indeed devilishly clever, Adam reflected. "Why the great secrecy?" he asked.

"I've been promoted," she said, "much against my will. I'm now the director of espionage for France in the New World."

Adam whistled under his breath.

"I've learned, to my horror," she went on, "that people have died as a result of my previous efforts for France. I didn't want this new post and tried to refuse it, but Mazarin threatened me with public exposure and complete ruin unless I did his bidding."

"In other words," her husband said, "he blackmailed you into accepting this new position."

She nodded, a pleading, downcast look on her face. "That's exactly what happened. I've had to tell Richard and Eliza, because they're also employed as agents in the French cause—

albeit reluctantly, like me—and I've been living in dread that they would go to you with the truth."

Adam looked at her, thinking that she had never been lovelier than she was at this moment. "You have nothing to fear from me, Celeste," he assured her. "Not now and not ever."

"Then you forgive me?" she murmured.

He rose and crossed the cabin to her. "There's nothing to forgive," he replied.

Hoping to make certain that his mood did not change, she rose to her feet, curled her arms around his neck, and, pressing her body close to his, kissed him soundly. There! she thought. That should insure his constancy.

Adam was breathing hard when they finally drew apart. "I trust that in the future you'll have greater confidence in me," he said.

Her victory was even greater than she had dared to hope. "I promise you I will," she said. "And I don't know how I can ever thank you for showing such faith in me."

He smiled blandly. "I expressed my faith in you when I gave you my name," he said, "and you've done nothing to change my opinion. After all, as commander in chief of the New Haven militia, I consider myself fortunate to have direct, inside knowledge of the intentions of France."

Celeste averted her face to hide her surprised expression. No wonder Adam was not upset by her revelation! He intended to use her position as a means of keeping himself informed of the plans and schemes of the ambitious Mazarin. She should have foreseen that. He was far shrewder than she had expected.

"I assume," he said, "that you'll remain in the employ of the cardinal and will say nothing to anyone about having told me of your position. By acting as a double agent, you can be of great value to England and to the New World colonies."

"I must confess to you," she said, "that after what they did to me, I feel no loyalty to the England of Cromwell and his Roundheads. But I've also discovered that England's colonies in America are not England. It's another world in New Haven—in all of the English colonies. The people think and act differently, not like Englishmen, and I feel fiercely loyal to them, just as I'm fiercely loyal to you, Adam.''

He looked at this lovely, earnest young woman and saw no reason to disbelieve her, no reason to suspect that she was being anything but completely sincere in her declaration.

"For your sake, my dear," she continued, "as well as for the sake of the colonies, I shall do precisely as you suggest. I'll keep my position with the French, but I'll pass along to you everything I learn." Despite the risks involved, she knew she had a great deal to gain by such an arrangement.

Adam took her hands in his. "I hope our marriage will not be influenced by this strange turn of events," he said.

"I swear to you that our marriage won't be touched," Celeste replied, and she was not playacting. She had determined, from the moment that Cardinal Mazarin had pressed this new assignment on her, not to allow her marriage to be damaged. She had gained both wealth and stature as the bride of Adam Burrows, and she had no intention of losing either now.

"There's no time like the present," Adam said, smiling gently, "to learn what's in the mind of Mazarin. It's been troubling me.... Do you know his intentions toward New Netherland?"

Adam certainly wasn't giving her much breathing room, Celeste thought. However, she knew that the status of the Dutch New World colony was of great interest to her husband, especially since the recent Indian uprising, where several New England tribes had been armed and equipped by the Dutch. Adam knew that she had lived in New Amsterdam, the capital of New Netherland, for several years, and that she was well acquainted with Peter Stuyvesant, the Dutch governor there. Maybe, Celeste thought, Adam was testing her, seeing how much information she had previously withheld about Stuyvesant's motives and alliances.

She thought fast. "Well, I myself was only an informant at that time—I kept watch on Stuyvesant. But surely it's no secret," she said, "that the French were eager to obtain possession of New Netherland from the Dutch. I think, though, that Mazarin was mainly trying to stir up as much trouble as he could—

and clearly he succeeded. As for actually taking over the Dutch colony, Mazarin himself has admitted to me in so many words that he's now reconciled to the inevitability of New Netherland's becoming an English colony."

"That's good news, if indeed it is true," Adam said with obvious satisfaction. "I mean, New Netherland's becoming an English colony."

"Mazarin didn't say exactly how it's going to come about," Celeste said, "but he feels that with New England thriving to the north and Virginia to the south, New Netherland is being squeezed, and if it doesn't simply fall into Cromwell's hands, the English will be able to buy it from the Dutch owners for a pittance."

"I hope this particular prophecy comes true," Adam said with a grin; then his smile slowly faded. "But I find it difficult to believe that a man as wildly ambitious for France as Cardinal Mazarin is will be satisfied with that snowbound land to the north they call Canada. The English colonies occupy territory that's far more lucrative and valuable. I'm certain Mazarin covets it."

"Indeed he does," Celeste said, her sexual designs now forgotten. She might as well tell him everything, she decided. She would have to tell him anyway, sooner or later. "Mazarin has a far more ambitious scheme in mind."

"I knew it," Adam said in quiet triumph.

"There's an island that lies alone on the sea routes from the West Indies to Europe, about a thousand miles off the Virginia coast."

"You're referring to Bermuda," he said.

"That's the place. It's a British colony and, as I understand it, mostly unsettled. There are a few tobacco plantations, and one small town, but most of the island is uninhabited."

"Yes, I've been there," Adam told her. "But I fail to see the connection between Bermuda and France."

"That's because you aren't as devious as Cardinal Mazarin," she said. "He always tries to achieve his goals with a minimum of risk and with the least amount of effort necessary. If he tried to confront the English directly, he would need a very large fleet and a huge army, and in all probability France would find herself engaged in a major war with England. Mazarin wants to avoid all that, and I honestly believe he thinks he's found a way. Exactly what he has in mind I'm not quite sure of yet, but I will tell you all that I do know."

Adam was totally absorbed by what she was saying. She was providing him with privileged information that was probably not known by more than a half dozen people in the entire New World. "Please, go on," he said.

"He intends somehow to capture Bermuda and to station a fleet of ships there. Another fleet will be based somewhere to the north, in New France. Between these two fleets, I think, he hopes eventually to intercept all sea traffic among the English colonies themselves, as well as all trade between the colonies and England, and between England and the West Indies."

Adam immediately grasped the French strategy and had to admire its cleverness as well as its boldness. "I suppose," he said, "he will deny all knowledge of any French participation and will claim that the sea traffic is being interrupted by privateers of unknown nationality."

He was marvelously quick, Celeste realized anew. "That seems likely to be his plan," she said. "He feels that once the English colonies are isolated, they'll fall one by one, like ripe apples dropping to the ground."

"And just how does he plan to take Bermuda?"

"I told you, I'm not exactly sure yet," she said. "That was a detail—a major detail—that hadn't been worked out as yet when the cardinal last received me in Paris."

In spite of himself, Adam felt a stab of bitter disappointment. It was frustrating to have learned so much, yet to be thwarted in his attempt to gain an understanding of the entire French plan.

"You look so disappointed, my dear," Celeste said with a wry grin. "But never fear, I'll be in a position to satisfy your curiosity before any overt moves are made."

"What makes you think so?"

"I have the assurances of Mazarin himself that I'll be privy to his scheme. I don't yet know the role that my agents and I will be called on to play, but I do know that Mazarin will be depending on me to arrange the details. He told me as much himself. And you can be certain I will keep nothing from you."

Adam nodded in grim satisfaction. "I could ask for no more."

"Then you're not angry or upset because Mazarin has forced me to continue to work for him?" Celeste said, her lips curled in a tentative pout.

Her husband grinned at her. "I'm grateful to the cardinal for opening a private door into his innermost chamber for me. He doesn't know it, but I'm already in a position to overcome his scheme."

Celeste well realized that she had committed herself to a tricky and possibly dangerous game. She would be continuing to act as the French spy chief for the colonies, while privately passing along to her husband information of vital interest to the English. At least she knew she could count on Adam not to reveal his source of information to anyone. And, just as important to her, she would continue to have a sturdy roof over her head, to eat the best food available, and to be able to afford fine clothes and other luxuries. She was still living by her wits, and living in the style to which she was accustomed. And now that she had confessed the truth to her husband, she was no longer a traitor to the English colonies. Why, she might even consider herself a patriot!

Odd, Celeste reflected momentarily, that such a thought should occur to her.

The Louvre, one of the largest and most ornate palaces in all of Europe, was the home of the French monarchy and hence the heart of France itself. Overlooking the River Seine in the center of busy Paris, the rambling gray structure was patrolled day and night by king's musketeers in their broad-brimmed hats, full blue capes, and long, efficient swords. Visitors customarily approached through the elaborate gardens called the Tuileries, and foreigners and strangers to Paris were invariably awed by the grandeur and sheer size of the edifice.

The pair of men approaching now, however, were not awed. In fact, they did not even turn their heads as their open carriage clattered past the first set of sentries in front of the main entrance. Admiral Antoine de Bosquette, in the front seat, wore his gold and blue uniform with a jaunty air. A suave and slender seafaring man who was as at home in the Paris salons as on the quarterdeck of his own flagship, he paused to inspect his freshly manicured fingernails before pulling on his white gloves. In the rear seat, facing him, was General Etienne de Cluny, the admiral's opposite in every respect. Gruff and hardy, a no-nonsense soldier, the burly general was accustomed to attacking problems with the same force and blunt, direct energy he employed to attack the enemies of his country on the battlefields. This occasion, however, called for forbearance and tact, and the general fidgeted and muttered to himself without cease. As they rode face to face in the open carriage, caught up now in the crawling traffic around the government offices, Admiral de Bosquette absentmindedly stroked his elegantly waxed mustache, then reached over and tapped his companion lightly on the hand. "I have no idea why we're being called in to talk with the first minister," he said, "but it's apparent to me that a coordinated military operation of some sort is being planned."

"Why should it be apparent?" General de Cluny demanded.

"Logic demands it, Etienne," the admiral replied smoothly. "I know of no other reason why you and I should be called together to see Mazarin. He usually prefers to deal with our kind one at a time. The better to keep us in line, you see. He doesn't want any plots being hatched."

General de Cluny thought for a time, was satisfied with his colleague's answer, and grunted. That sound was his indication that he thought Admiral de Bosquette was correct.

The carriage finally drew up in front of the main entrance to the palace, and there a priest in a coarse, dark-gray habit awaited them. He led them up the central staircase of marble, with a huge chandelier of Venetian glass overhead. Milling crowds of courtiers parted before them, in deference to their silent but apparently respected escort. At the second-floor landing the priest paused a moment to whisper something to a colleague, then continued on to the top floor, where he wove down countless corridors until they came to an older, remote wing of the palace. Here, in an ill-lighted chamber off a large anteroom, a half dozen other priests were seated on high stools in front of two rows of small desks, where they industriously copied various orders and lengthy directives. They did not talk, and no sound emanated from the chamber except the steady scratching of their quill pens and an occasional cough. The priests did not even look up as the pair of visitors passed by the door and seated themselves on an upholstered bench in the anteroom.

After a short wait, the visitors were ushered through a pair of gilt doors into a small chamber, where a stark crucifix on the opposite wall momentarily arrested their gaze. To the right, harsh light flooded the room from a row of floor-to-ceiling windows, in front of which stood a simple table of unvarnished wood. Behind the table, silhouetted in the glare, sat a small and, at first glance, insignificant-looking man, whose coloring and features were more Italian than French. Only the scarlet of his biretta and the piping of the same color on his vestments, as well as the huge carved sapphire ring of a prince of the church, identified Jules Cardinal Mazarin, the most powerful and most feared man in France. Retained by the regent, Anne of Austria, Mazarin served as first minister, successor to the great Richelieu, and was destined to hold that position until King Louis XIV came of age in 1661.

The double doors closed behind them, and the visitors squinted into the light, waiting for some acknowledgment of their presence.

At last Mazarin rose to his feet, extended his ring, first to the admiral and then to the general. After they had bowed over his hand, kissing the ring, he resumed his seat, leaned back, and stared at them. "Please, gentlemen, be seated," he said in a surprisingly kind voice.

The visitors settled uncomfortably into the two straight-backed, unpadded chairs facing the desk.

"I presume," he said, "that you already know why I've called you here today."

Admiral de Bosquette and General de Cluny looked at him blankly.

"What a pity," he said with mild sarcasm. "I thought His Majesty's army and navy prided themselves on their knowledge of all things in France that pertained to them."

General de Cluny looked irritated and was on the verge of replying bluntly, but a glance from his colleague silenced him.

Admiral de Bosquette knew what the situation required. "As Your Eminence certainly realizes," he said, "the days when we or our intelligence-gathering organizations were privy to the government's intentions have vanished. Not for years—ever since Your Eminence took office as the first minister—have we been permitted to find out anything in advance."

The cardinal, who delighted in the secrecy of his operations, rewarded them with a deep-throated chuckle. "In that case, gentlemen," he said, "I advise you not to make any plans for the future. I trust that neither of you is currently encumbered with business that makes it necessary for you to remain in France?"

The admiral shook his head. "I'm at the service of Your Eminence," he said.

"Call on me for whatever you wish," General de Cluny growled.

"Good," Mazarin said. "Then I'll be brief. The interests of His Majesty and of France require your being sent, gentlemen, to the island of Martinique in the West Indian Ocean. There, Admiral, you will take command of our West Indies squadron, while you, General, will gather a small force—I leave the exact size up to you—on the island of Guadeloupe or Martinique. I specified a small force because I do not wish, at this particular time, to alarm our British neighbors."

The admiral and the general exchanged crestfallen looks, and Admiral de Bosquette spoke quickly, because he was afraid of what General de Cluny might blurt out. "Is Your Eminence so dissatisfied with our efforts that you see fit to demote us?" he asked.

The cardinal smiled quietly and shook his head. "You're mistaken, gentlemen," he said. "I assure you that neither of you is being demoted. On the contrary, you're being given an opportunity to win great glory for yourselves and for France."

General de Cluny immediately brightened. Admiral de Bosquette, suspicious by nature, waited to hear more before he passed judgment.

"You are familiar with an island called Bermuda?" Mazarin asked.

General de Cluny's expression registered nothing.

Admiral de Bosquette flicked a speck of dust from his uniform sleeve and cleared his throat. "It's an English possession in the Atlantic Ocean about a week's voyage north of the West Indies. It has been of little importance to anyone, save as a navigational aid, and a dangerous one at that, since it is surrounded by treacherous reefs."

The cardinal looked pleased. "I offer you my felicitations, Admiral," he said. "Clearly you know the area under discussion quite well. Therefore I am going to charge you, along with the general here, with the conduct of a joint operation to bring the island of Bermuda under the French flag."

General de Cluny grinned. "Splendid!" he boomed. "We'll land a few spies there, learn the island's fortifications, and then put the admiral's gunners to work blasting the forts into the Atlantic."

"That, General de Cluny, is precisely what you will not do," Mazarin declared in a mildly annoyed tone. "You would cause certain catastrophe for France."

The general looked bewildered.

Admiral de Bosquette waited to hear more.

"The situation is delicate in the extreme," the cardinal said. "Bermuda is a British colony, even though the British stole it from Spain. The Spanish are too weak to dispute the issue, and the island has been settled exclusively by Englishmen. We have no legitimate claim whatsoever to the place."

"I see," the admiral said, although he still had no idea what Mazarin had in mind.

"You would create an impossible situation," Cardinal Mazarin continued. "France cannot afford a war with Cromwell at the moment. As beleaguered as Cromwell may appear, his army and navy are not to be taken lightly. We would almost surely become involved in a full-scale war, which would probably be fought on our own soil. This France must avoid at all costs. But let me add, gentlemen, that I'm certain Oliver Cromwell is as eager as I to avoid all-out hostilities. He has his hands full with the Dutch, as you are well aware. And though he knows we're encouraging the Royalists, he has carefully refrained from making direct accusations. This leads me to conclude that he prefers a period of peace with us. All we have to do is avoid an *open* provocation."

"Then may I presume, Your Eminence," Admiral de Bosquette declared, "that you want us to occupy Bermuda, yet you wish this deed accomplished in such a way that the British public will not know that France was involved—even though Cromwell himself might suspect otherwise?"

"In essence, yes," Mazarin replied. "Cromwell must be able to save face."

The general bristled, and was on the verge of retorting that the first minister was expecting him and his colleagues to perform the impossible.

But once again Admiral de Bosquette averted a crisis by speaking first. "Does Your Eminence suggest a way in which we can accomplish this rather delicate feat?"

The cardinal shook his head. "If I knew of a way, be assured I would not conceal it from you. I realize I'm asking a great deal. Perhaps too much. We shall have to see what develops. All I can tell you now is that I have great faith in your judgments and in your talents. You will be far better able to devise a workable plan once you reach your own headquarters in Martinique. Needless to say, the espionage service that functions for me in the English colonies will be placed at your disposal. And you may call on the Royal Treasury for any reasonable expenditure. All I ask you to do is to remove the English from one tiny, insignificant island."

"Very well, Your Eminence," Admiral de Bosquette replied. "I think your instructions are clear."

"Good," the cardinal said briskly. "I urge you to depart as soon as possible. And one more thing—I don't like to set schedules for operations of this nature, but the political situation in this case will necessitate very precise timing. I want you to go ahead and prepare your plans, but you must wait for a message from me before you proceed with the actual attack. Is that clear?"

"Very clear, Your Eminence," Admiral de Bosquette said. "We shall keep your wishes very much in mind and will do our best to please you."

"Good. You are to report to the Finance Ministry first thing tomorrow. My agent there will be expecting you, and he will provide you with the required written authorization for your assignment."

They knew they were being dismissed and rose to their feet.

The cardinal picked up a tiny crystal bell from his desk and rang it once. The priest who had escorted them in reappeared at the double doors.

"Good day, gentlemen," the cardinal said, without looking up or bothering to rise.

As the doors closed behind the departing pair, Mazarin opened a drawer in his desk and removed a small piece of paper. Taking a quill from the stand in front of him, he paused a moment, pen above paper. Then he seemed to reach a decision, for he dipped the pen in the inkwell and began to write in his small, meticulous hand. A few moments later he replaced the quill in its stand and rang his crystal bell again, this time twice. Another gray-robed priest appeared, and Mazarin handed him the paper.

"Did you listen in as I instructed you, Father?"

"Yes, Your Eminence."

"Well, what do you think?"

"They are very capable and loyal officers, Your Eminence. However, I would not trust Admiral de Bosquette with a secret any longer than absolutely necessary, and I would not depend on General de Cluny to observe the more subtle distinctions of politics."

"My sentiments exactly. That is why I want you to forward that paper to my agent in Virginia. He is now residing in Jamestown, I believe. From this moment on, he will be my new master spy in the English colonies."

"Virginia, Your Eminence? But I thought that Madame Burrows—"

"To Virginia, Father. Madame Celeste Burrows and her friends, the Dunstables, have served their purpose. From now on they will be fed false information. As for De Cluny and De Bosquette, there is an old Italian proverb: 'Keep your dogs hungry, and they will hunt better.' Well, our dogs will not eat Bermuda, even though every English agent will soon be expecting just that."

The priest still looked perplexed.

A sly smile spread across Mazarin's lips. "No, Father. Our dogs will sniff and whine around Bermuda and tug at the leash. But when I finally let them loose, it will be for much bigger game. Be patient. You will see."

Ten days after the admiral and the general held their meeting with the first minister, a squadron of French warships sailed from the naval base at Brest on the west coast of France for the island of Martinique.

The squadron was much smaller than either officer had expected, consisting of an old thirty-six-gun frigate and two small pinnaces. Even though Mazarin had warned them that they should avoid attracting attention, both men had expected a larger, much grander fleet. Upon receiving General de Cluny aboard the frigate, Admiral de Bosquette had simply returned the general's puzzled look and shrugged, as if to declare his innocence.

For a week after the vessels sailed, Admiral de Bosquette, who had assigned himself the relatively spacious and airy captain's cabin, held daily meetings with his staff, while General de Cluny, consigned to a dark, cramped, belowdecks cabin, did the same. Swearing their subordinates to absolute secrecy, both officers confided to their aides the difficult mission they had been assigned by Cardinal Mazarin. The stormy summer seas grew calmer as the ships sailed toward the southwest, and when they were two weeks out of Brest, the wind abruptly died, leaving the convoy drifting listlessly on the mid-Atlantic.

Admiral de Bosquette, mindful that the last of his fresh food would soon spoil, took advantage of the exceptionally calm seas to invite General de Cluny to dine formally with him.

That evening, General de Cluny, in a slightly rumpled gold and white uniform, repaired to the great cabin with his host. The general, who had resented his cramped quarters but had said nothing in deference to the admiral's nominal command at sea, examined the large cabin curiously as a servant handed him a glass of wine. The area in which they were to dine was furnished like a sitting room, except for a serviceable desk and chair, while the rest of the space was outfitted as a rather luxurious bedchamber. "You have very handsome quarters, Admiral," the general said.

Admiral de Bosquette could not conceal a small smile. "Yours, I'm afraid, are the best I could arrange on short notice," he replied. He inspected his wineglass in the candlelight, then put it to his nose to sniff the bouquet.

General de Cluny wanted to say that the admiral could at least have sacrificed half of his own quarters, but he didn't want to appear niggardly and unappreciative. So he bowed slightly, then raised his own glass. "This is a fine wine," he said. "It comes from Provence?"

"I congratulate you on your taste," the admiral replied. "It does indeed."

The general saw an opportunity to win a point for himself. "You must allow me to send you a case of a wine that I discovered in Provence, one that I find superior to all others. Unfortunately, I could not bring any on board, for there wasn't room enough in my quarters, and I wouldn't dare store it anywhere the crew could get at it."

Admiral de Bosquette concealed his annoyance. "You're very generous, General," he murmured.

Having evened the score somewhat, General de Cluny felt more willing to speak freely. "My staff," he said, "has been establishing some interesting figures for me. I'm told that I shall command a sizable force for this part of the world— approximately two thousand men. They are presently stationed at garrisons on a half dozen West Indies islands, but if you'll furnish me with transports, I can assemble them under one command rather quickly."

Admiral de Bosquette was impressed. "Two thousand men is indeed an army of consequence in the West Indies," he said. "I had no idea we had that many troops stationed out there."

"The overwhelming majority of them, I regret to say, are malcontents," General de Cluny said. "Only five hundred are what I would call reliable troops. I'd be far happier, I can assure you, if I had just one of my old regiments. However, I must make do with what I am given. I have no artillery to speak of; but your ships, I am certain, will provide more than sufficient cannon."

"It appears that between us our forces shall be adequate," the admiral said. "Counting the ships of our present squadron, I shall be commanding a small flotilla of island craft, including two sloops of war and a host of small transports. And I'll supply your troops with all the artillery support they'll need, you may rest assured. A force of our size is capable of taking possession of any British port in the entire New World. Doing it under-handedly, however, in the manner the good cardinal suggests, is a different story altogether."

General de Cluny sighed, sipped his wine, and then unexpectedly pounded his fist on the table, rattling the china and silverware. "How I wish that we could mount an expedition in force against Bermuda," he said. "Between us we have the strength to capture the island and make it a French possession in short order."

"I must admit," the admiral said, "that I, too, have been tempted by that idea; but I'm afraid my common sense has prevailed."

"My staff and I have had little enough to occupy us during this infernal voyage," General de Cluny said, sounding somewhat bitter, "so we've discussed the problem thoroughly. In fact, we've been in almost continuous meetings since we left Brest. We've examined in infinite detail the matter of how we can reduce Bermuda and raise our own flag there without resorting to overt force. And frankly, Admiral, I say to you that it cannot be done. The first minister has given us an impossible assignment. That's what comes of having a man of God as the first minister. He seeks peace at all costs, and he ends with absolutely nothing accomplished."

Admiral de Bosquette was sympathetic. "Ordinarily I would agree with you, General," he said. "And as a matter of fact, my entire staff feels the same way as you. We, too, have had a number of meetings; and without exception, my subordinates insist that Bermuda will fall to us only if we use superior force. But I continue to cling to the hope that we shall find some other method of attaining our ends."

General de Cluny gulped the last of his wine. "Do you mind telling me how you intend to perform this magical feat?"

Admiral de Bosquette looked rueful as he refilled his guest's wineglass. "I would save myself from sleepless nights if I could answer your question," he said, "but so far I cannot. I know only that Cardinal Mazarin has given us specific orders, and he expects them to be fulfilled. Therefore we shall continue to strive, you and I, toward the achievement of a goal that ordinary men regard as unattainable."

The general scowled and cursed under his breath.

"The history of human warfare," the admiral said softly, "is filled with surprises. He who undertakes the truly unexpected is almost inevitably victorious."

"Surely you're not suggesting that we resort to the building of a Trojan horse?" the general said contemptuously.

The admiral showed no surprise. "Now you begin to perceive what I have in mind," he said, "although a Trojan horse would not achieve our ends in this particular situation. But there must be scores of other techniques we can employ, dozens of tricks we could conceal up our sleeves."

"I am a troop commander," General de Cluny said, "not a magician. I do not stoop to cheap trickery."

"I've been given the command of a fleet of ships, yet I must not use them," Admiral de Bosquette replied. "I regard that as an enormous challenge, and I shall do my very best to meet it. Don't despair, my friend. We have experienced officers awaiting us in Martinique, and the entire network of French agents in the colonies has been placed at our disposal. I shall put all of these people to work on the problem as soon as we arrive in Martinique, and we shall see what they can come up with. One way or another, we shall live up to the cardinal's expectations, because we must. We will conquer Bermuda, even if not in the name of France. We will persevere, and we will succeed!" The admiral, carried away by his own enthusiasm, had risen to his feet, his glass held high in the air, as if exhorting his fleet into battle.

General de Cluny remained in his seat, unimpressed. "Well, Antoine," he said, "what's for dinner? I could eat a horse."

II

O N the island of Bermuda the sun shone brilliantly in a
cloudless sky, and a gentle breeze blew in off the
waters of the Atlantic Ocean. The residents of George's
Town, the capital and site of the original English settlement,
had dubbed their island "the land of perpetual spring," and this
morning, with the air fragrant with the smell of tropical flowers,
it was easy to see why.

For with the exception of a small stone fort, now dilapidated,
which the settlers had built long ago to protect themselves from
the Spanish, there was little hint of anything but peace and
prosperity. The town itself, overlooking the snug inner harbor,
comprised a few dozen neat, single-story homes, most of them
whitewashed, but a few attractively painted in bright pastel
colors that mimicked the flowers blooming everywhere. There
were also a jail, an inn, and a small school; and just a stone's
throw away, off the main square, stood the old statehouse, atop
of which an English flag flapped lazily in the morning breeze.

Across the square from the statehouse, a bell was clanging
in the belfry of a small whitewashed church, and since it was

not Sunday, the townspeople knew they were being summoned to a town meeting.

Small knots of people moved toward the church at a leisurely pace. Despite the seeming calm, however, a stranger would have noted immediately that something was very much amiss in George's Town. The citizens, most of them heavily tanned tobacco planters in their rough field clothes, moved to either the left or the right side of the church, and those on one side took pains not to acknowledge the presence of the others. The small island, though thousands of miles remote from England, nevertheless mirrored the troubled political climate of the motherland. On the right were the Cavaliers, Royalist supporters of the exiled Charles II and the house of Stuart; and on the left were the somber followers of Oliver Cromwell, commonly called Roundheads, or Puritans.

The island's loyalties were split as a result of the feud between the Cavaliers and the Roundheads. In fact, the political situation had recently degenerated to such an extent that a group of moderates had decided it was necessary to step in and carry on the duties of the island's government until the political rift was either healed or settled in England itself.

One man stood out above the crowd making its way toward the church. Middle-aged and grizzled, with a stocky build, Mark Prescott was called Major by everyone because he was the elected head of the colony's militia. One of the oldest and most distinguished of Bermuda's residents, he had been associated with the late John Rolfe a generation earlier in a project to cultivate tobacco on the island. Rolfe had later moved on to Virginia, where he had married an Indian princess named Pocahontas; but Prescott had remained and, through hard work and sheer persistence, managed to build up one of the largest and most lucrative tobacco plantations in Bermuda.

Walking demurely beside him was a woman almost twenty years his junior. She had strawberry-blond hair, a slim but sturdy figure, and chiseled features. She was his sister, Adella, who ran his house for him and who, partly because of his position and partly because of her own charm, was regarded by many of the settlers as the first lady of Bermuda. Stalking a step or two behind her was a huge black giant clad in knee breeches and shirt. Slung from his shoulder was a wicked-looking curved knife that he himself had fashioned and which bore a strong resemblance to a Turkish scimitar. His name was Zwingli, and he was a Bantu chief who had been captured and sold into slavery in his native Africa. But now he was a free man, thanks to the intervention of Adella Prescott on his behalf, and he was employed as the overseer of the work crews at the Prescott plantation.

Anyone who knew Adella and her brother took Zwingli's presence for granted. Anyplace that Adella was to be found, Zwingli invariably was nearby, ready to use his prodigious strength and his sharp Bantu blade to protect her from harm. And as he had often proved, his devotion to both Prescotts was total.

As the trio approached the front of the church, they were hailed and halted by a wizened, stoop-shouldered old man, Arthur Mossdecker, the proprietor of the local inn. The crotchety-looking Mossdecker belied his appearance, however, and gallantly removed his hat with a flourish and bowed to Adella, acknowledging Zwingli's presence with a cordial nod. Only then did he turn his attention to Mark Prescott. "We're in for big trouble tonight, Major," he said, wagging a finger. "Our problem is that there isn't enough plain common sense on this island. No matter how long since they've come out here from England, people still take their politics seriously. Me, I wouldn't give you a shark's tooth for either a Cavalier or a Roundhead."

"What makes you think we're in trouble?" the major asked.

"It's a question of simple arithmetic," Mossdecker replied curtly. "You see, Major—" He looked to the left and to the right, then motioned Prescott closer, as if about to impart information of the utmost secrecy. "I've heard it said that the Cavaliers and the Roundheads are actually going to band together to take a stand against us."

Adella, who overheard, laughed, and her brother grinned broadly.

"If we've succeeded in placing the Roundheads and the

Cavaliers on the same side of any question, I'd say we've accomplished a near miracle, Arthur."

Mossdecker was not amused. "There's too much at stake, I tell you. Speaking for myself, I've had enough of this squabbling. I'm hoping that before this year is out someone will buy my inn, and good riddance, I'll say. I've already had two good offers, you know."

"You hadn't told us about that, Arthur," Adella said politely.

"There isn't much to tell," Mossdecker replied. "I'm just waiting for the right buyer. Can't sell to just anyone, you know. But once I do sell, mind you, I'm going to shake the coral dust of Bermuda from my boots once and for all. I intend to migrate to America, where there's room to breathe, and the feuds of the Old World aren't carried to the New."

"Don't depend on that, my friend," Mark told him. "Men usually cling to their prejudices, you know. Well, shall we go inside?"

He stood aside to let Adella, still closely followed by Zwingli, precede him into the church. Arthur Mossdecker looked with disgust at the group that was assembling inside. "The Roundheads act as though they own all the pews on the left side," he said, "and the Cavaliers know very well that the pews on the right belong to them. Where that leaves those of us who don't hold with either group, I don't know."

Major Prescott was equal to the occasion. "I suggest, Adella," he said, "that you move right down to the front of the church. We'll see what can be done from there."

Mossdecker, who had long served as the chairman of the town meeting, moved up to the pulpit, where he demanded order.

Aware that the session was about to begin, those who had been loitering outside hastened into the building and took their seats.

The church was crowded now, as had been expected. The issue to be debated had been a heated subject of discussion for several weeks, and virtually everyone in Bermuda had already made up his mind on how to vote.

Arthur Mossdecker called the meeting to order and quickly

recognized Major Mark Prescott. Mark rose to his feet and surveyed the audience. "Ladies and gentlemen," he said, "I see no need for formality. I know all of you by your first names, and you know my sister and me equally well. What's more, you know the issue that is being brought to a final vote tonight. I've been elected by you to head your militia, and in the absence of any troops from England, I alone am in charge of our defenses. I intend to live up to my responsibilities. That's why I tell you flatly that our weapons are antiquated and that our defenses, through our neglect, have become inadequate."

Several men on both sides of the aisle raised their voices and called, "No! No!"

"I'm sure you are already aware of this," Mark said patiently, "but I'll tell you again. The fort in its present condition cannot offer Saint George adequate protection."

"It ain't Saint George, it's George's Town!" someone yelled.

Major Prescott refused to lose his temper. "Saint George or George's Town—I don't care what you call it—we still have to defend it. Can't you see? Just one enemy ship could level this entire town in a matter of minutes, and its crew could take every island here with a minimum of effort."

Some of his listeners stirred uncomfortably, but the majority continued to glare at him, their hostility undisguised. It was painfully apparent that the people of Bermuda did not agree with his estimate.

"The cost of improving the town's defenses will be negligible," Mark went on. "We have sufficient cannon, and once they are properly deployed, we'll be strong enough to repel an invader by sea and to hold an invader by land at bay. What we desperately need is a demonstration of the same spirit that the early settlers showed a generation ago when they sacrificed their time and effort to build the fort. We need the brawn of manpower, no more and no less, to enlarge and strengthen the fort." He looked slowly around the audience and then took his seat.

Several of the spectators clamored for the right to be heard. Mossdecker selected a plantation owner who sat at the back of the hall, mistakenly thinking that he shared the major's sentiments.

"Major Prescott," the man said, "has neglected to mention his reasons for wanting our fortifications reconstructed and strengthened. Does he have any information that leads him to believe an enemy is about to attack us? Certainly no one in England holds any such belief. If the government there felt as Major Prescott feels, funds would be supplied for the strengthening of the fort, and manpower, also, would be provided. But London knows nothing about any threats to the security of the island, and neither do I."

There was a buzz of excited comment, and Mossdecker rapped his gavel furiously, but another speaker leaped to his feet and began to address the assemblage before Mossdecker could halt him. "Bermuda is safe," he shouted. "Friends and neighbors, use your heads! Use the good sense that the Lord gave you. Who is going to attack this island, and what reason would an enemy have for such an assault? Bermuda is small and poor. We have no gold. We have no military importance, stuck out here in the middle of nowhere. Sure, we have a little tobacco, but Virginia has a hundred times more. I can't imagine anyone in his right mind trying to capture this island."

The first speaker stood again and continued the argument. "If danger threatened us, I'd be willing to work day and night on the construction of new fortifications," he said. "Under the circumstances, however, I have no desire to spend needless hours laboring under the hot sun for no good reason. Therefore, I propose a formal resolution to the effect that the present state of the fort be left unchanged."

Another man jumped up and seconded the motion, and there was a roar of approval.

Mossdecker saw no reason to prolong the discussion, and in a weary voice he put the question to a vote. He had been correct all along, he told himself, as the Cavaliers and the Roundheads alike voted overwhelmingly in favor of leaving the fortifications in their present state. Not one man in ten stood with Mark Prescott.

When the meeting ended, Arthur Mossdecker intercepted

the major as he was following his sister and Zwingli up the center aisle of the church. "Why is everyone so shortsighted?" the innkeeper said, shaking his head.

Mark nodded somberly. "You were right, Arthur," he said. "I just hope they won't have cause to regret their vote today. We would be virtually helpless in the event someone should attack."

A short time later, as Mark and Adella walked back to their nearby plantation house, followed closely by Zwingli, the girl looked up at her brother inquiringly. "Were you exaggerating for the sake of making a point, Mark, or are we really so very vulnerable to an attack?"

He wanted to soothe her, but was aware that his sister knew him too well and would easily be able to tell if he were lying. "We are helpless in the event of an attack," he told her. "The fort is too small, the cannon are emplaced in such a way that they don't offer a full sweep of the harbor, and I'm not sure that the stone fortifications would last very long if they were bombarded by enemy cannon on board a warship."

Adella absently picked a brilliant red flower growing by the side of the road. "I must be frank with you," she said. "I think that your opponents made a great deal of sense. As they pointed out, Bermuda is poor and remote, and has no military importance to anyone. So why would an enemy want to gain possession of it? And who might such an enemy be in the first place?"

He shook his head. "I wouldn't have expected you to be as blind as all the rest," he said. "The coastal waters of North America and the West Indies are badly infested with pirates. How a band of corsairs would love to have a permanent base here they could call their home."

Her expression began to darken.

"Next," Mark continued, "consider the international situation. The absence of a monarch on the British throne makes us more vulnerable and a more attractive target for foreign adventurers. Spain, for one, has established a number of thriving colonies in the Americas and no doubt would find Bermuda very useful. In case you have forgotten, it was a Spaniard who discovered this island, and there is no telling when the king of Spain may wish to renew his original claim. Must I remind you that the Spanish alone have lost scores of ships on the reefs surrounding this so-called worthless island? Ships loaded with thousands of pounds of silver and gold." He frowned at his sister. "And then there are the Dutch, whom Cromwell is at war with, and the French, who are probably the most dangerous enemy of all. Do you wish me to go on?"

The girl was wide-eyed. "If all that's true," she said, "why isn't England offering us proper protection?"

"The Roundheads have their hands full at home in England," Mark explained. "They have had to rebuild the navy because there were so many Cavalier officers in it; and because of the naval war with the Dutch, they have no ships to spare for the defense of Bermuda these days. Plus they need to keep a large army on hand in the event the Cavaliers try to rally the people to the cause of Charles the Second. What it all means, I'm afraid, is that we're on our own—strictly on our own." He looked down at her, his face grim. "But I truly hope you are right, dear Sister, and that there really is no danger, because I, for one, shudder to think of what may happen to us if some foreign power has designs on these islands!"

Saint Pierre, the capital of the French island colony of Martinique, had obvious advantages as a military stronghold. Perched between the shore and the jungle below towering Mount Pelée, the town boasted a large, sheltered, deepwater harbor, at either end of which rose promontories on which forts had been constructed. And the slopes of Mount Pelée to the north and Mount Carbet to the south, along with the nearly impenetrable jungle that blanketed the rest of the island, provided ample protection from any overland attacks. In short, the town was as impregnable as the forces of nature and the ingenuity of the French could make it.

Admiral Antoine de Bosquette, however, was not concerned about the island's defenses. Defense, after all, was not his specialty. Shortly after arriving, he had commandeered a large, airy house that afforded him views of both the sea and Mount

Pelée. Attended by a staff of well-trained servants—including the chef he had brought with him from Paris—he now spent most of his time pacing in his garden, scheming. He had already come up with a plan to reduce Bermuda—a plan that even he had to admit was a stroke of genius.

A servant boy entered the garden with news that General de Cluny had just arrived and was waiting to see the admiral. "Bring the good general to me, then," the admiral said impatiently. "I shall receive him on the veranda."

General Etienne de Cluny suppressed his feelings of envy as he was escorted to the shady veranda of the dwelling overlooking the twin forts of the harbor. "You navy men know how to live, Antoine," he said as he greeted his host. "You have a superb house here. If I were you, I'd vigorously resist all efforts to transfer me elsewhere."

"I'm expecting no transfers for a long time to come, Etienne," the admiral replied. "I understand that your new home has its own, ah, unique rustic charm."

The general made a wry face. "Rustic isn't exactly how I would describe it. It overlooks a dusty parade ground hacked out of the trees and scrub in the heart of the jungle. During the daylight hours the weather becomes as hot as the very hinges of Hades, and there is no breeze of any kind until the blasted sun finally goes down at night. Then, of course, the insects come swarming out of the jungle. Some fly, some are on foot, and some both crawl and travel through the air. I'll be glad to return to France at the earliest possible moment, thanks very much."

Admiral de Bosquette chuckled. "Surely, Etienne, you can have a new home erected almost anywhere you wish," he said. "Select your site and assign your troops to build it. The problem is easily solved. Or simply take someone else's, as I did."

"I'm looking into it," General de Cluny admitted. "I haven't yet made up my mind, although I am considering several sites." He cleared his throat self-consciously. "I've appointed a young lady of the town as my adviser in the matter."

The admiral gave no sign that he had already been informed General de Cluny had recently taken a liberated slave girl as his mistress. "Good for you," he said. "I'm sure you'll soon find more enjoyable accommodations."

There were matters of far greater import that the general was eager to discuss. "I've read your confidential note to me several times," he said, "and I must admit that I can see no other alternative. Your plan to capture Bermuda is actually quite ingenious—even though a bit complicated for my taste. Still, if all of the elements mesh properly, and if everything proceeds according to your plans, it might work. In any case, I must congratulate you on your resourcefulness, Antoine."

The admiral bowed. "Thank you very much," he said modestly.

Neither spoke while a barefooted serving maid brought them a pitcher filled with coconut milk and fruit juice mixed with a locally made rum. Bottles of the concoction had been immersed in the waters of a stream that descended from the heights of Mount Pelée, and as a result, the drink was surprisingly cold. The maid poured out two glasses of the cloudy liquid, then padded back into the house.

General de Cluny raised his glass to his host, sipped at it suspiciously, then drank avidly. "As I said, Antoine," he declared, smacking his lips, "all of the various elements need to mesh in order for the plan to be effective. Unfortunately, I find the probability of that happening very remote."

Admiral de Bosquette's feeling of comradeship began to dissipate. "I don't believe that the possibilities of the plan's being effective are in the least remote," he said. "I'll grant that we need good fortune to attend us at all times, and the success of the plan certainly will depend on the personnel involved. But that's true of any venture."

General de Cluny again tasted his delicious drink. "You exercise control—absolute control—over the ships under your command," he said, "just as I control my regiments. We know what to expect from them. But the personnel involved in your plan for the reduction of Bermuda I view as highly questionable, as I view your recruiting methods."

"Perhaps," the admiral said distantly, "you are in a position to concoct a better scheme that will nevertheless abide by the first minister's rather stringent directives in this matter."

General de Cluny shook his head. "On the contrary, my dear Antoine. My mind has been blank on the subject, and it remains blank. I think we know each other well enough for me to tell you in confidence, as I already have once before, that I believe Cardinal Mazarin has given us a totally impossible assignment."

"That may well be so, my dear Etienne," the admiral replied, "and I urge you to keep that in mind when you examine my proposed plan. I will grant you that we are taking a number of calculated risks. But this is the only scheme I could think of that had any chance of succeeding. Therefore, I intend to go ahead with it at once. In fact, I've already put the initial stages into operation."

"In that case, I hope it is not too late for me to wish you the best of good luck," General de Cluny said gloomily. "I fear we will need it. Because if your plan should not come to a happy conclusion, both of us will face an exceedingly unhappy Cardinal Mazarin."

Richard Dunstable had grown accustomed to thinking of New Haven as home and was delighted to be there after his journey to France. The house he and Eliza shared was snug and comfortable, and though he preferred the life of the wilderness, Richard happily resumed the routine of his work at the warehouse offices of Burrows and Clayton.

Papers had grown to thick piles on his desk during his absence, and he now attacked them with great vigor, arriving at the office early every morning and not bothering to take time for a leisurely meal at noon, returning home only when darkness came at night.

Richard was thus immersed in his work one morning soon after his return when a clerk came to him with word that Adam Burrows wanted to see him at once. Replacing his quill pen in its stand, Richard rose and walked across the warehouse and up the stairway to his father-in-law's office.

There he was surprised to find Celeste Burrows seated in a

visitor's chair, looking unusually demure in a short jacket and long skirt of ivory-colored cotton trimmed in black.

Celeste greeted him warmly, and Richard returned the gesture in kind. He had not seen her since they had returned to New Haven, and now he found himself pleasantly surprised to be near her again. He also felt certain from Celeste's expression that his feelings were reciprocated. Yet there seemed to be nothing hidden, nothing untoward in her attentions. She loved her husband—of this Richard was certain.

Eliza, to be sure, disagreed with him rather violently. She held a highly prejudiced view of Celeste, and not without good reason, Richard reminded himself. He could understand Eliza's feelings. After all, when she had been absent in New Amsterdam, in the days prior to Celeste's marriage to Adam, Richard had engaged in a furious but very brief affair with Celeste. Of course he had confessed it all to Eliza, and had explained to her that he loved her and no one else, that he had been drawn to Celeste only by a strong, masculine passion that had temporarily robbed him of his reason. And since that time, he had kept his emotions under strict control. Eliza, however, remained highly suspicious of Celeste. Perhaps it would be just as well if he didn't mention this meeting when he returned home tonight.

"I know how eager you are to get back to your work, Richard," Adam said, "so we'll bother you only for a moment."

"We were anxious to see you," Celeste said in calm, measured tones, "because we wanted to inform you—and Eliza, too—that Adam now knows of my appointment by Cardinal Mazarin."

Richard was dumbfounded.

"She told me about it on board ship coming home from France," Adam said. "My wife is a woman of great courage."

Richard had to agree, but he remained speechless.

"As a matter of fact," Adam said, "this situation works to the benefit of New Haven as well as the other English colonies. We have our own impeccable source of information direct from Mazarin's office, so to speak."

Richard had to concede Adam's claim. After all, he himself

had used the same argument to justify his own actions as a double agent. Why should Celeste be any different? Surprisingly, Richard found his admiration for Celeste growing. She could have concealed her status from her husband, who would have been none the wiser. Instead, she had told him the truth and was offering her complete cooperation. Indeed, she was a courageous woman.

"My position in working for France is the same as yours and Eliza's," Celeste said. "I had no choice. But maybe between us we'll be able to neutralize Mazarin's schemes, and perhaps even turn the tables on France."

Her expression was serious, and Richard was convinced she was telling the truth. His own expression relaxed, and he grinned at her. "I'd like nothing better," he said, "and I'm sure Eliza will agree with me."

Celeste extended her hand to him, and he took it.

Adam Burrows stood up and clapped his son-in-law on the back. "Good man, Richard. And I almost forgot—on our recent voyage to France, I purchased a cask of the best French brandy, from Mazarin's personal vineyard, I was told. So if you two will follow me downstairs, we can all toast the cardinal's downfall with his own brandy!"

Later, when Richard returned to his own office, he was filled with wonder at what he had just learned, and the feeling persisted for the rest of the day. The news continued to occupy his thoughts when he returned home that evening.

Eliza met him at the door, and they kissed and embraced. Inside, Richard poured them each a glass of sack, then sat down and described at length his visit to Adam's office. He beamed as he revealed to her what he had learned there.

Eliza flicked a long, thick strand of blond hair off her forehead. "You make it sound," she said, "as though Celeste has done something rather wonderful."

"Certainly she has," Richard replied. "It took a rare brand of courage for her to admit to your father that she's Mazarin's principal spy here in the English colonies."

Eliza was expressionless. "Why shouldn't she tell him?" she demanded. "She's only fulfilling her duty as his wife!"

Too late, Richard remembered that he had warned himself against praising Celeste in Eliza's presence.

"That may be so," he told her. "Still, the fact that your father knows of her delicate position makes it far easier for all of us to act as agents for France when we're required to do so. This simplifies matters considerably; and as Adam stressed to me this afternoon, it's going to be very helpful to New Haven and to the other English colonies to have direct access to Cardinal Mazarin's thinking."

"It will be helpful, indeed, if Celeste chooses to tell the truth at all times," Eliza replied. "But she's in a position to do us great harm if she wishes. Either she can lie—which she does convincingly—or she can cause us much harm by failing to tell the whole truth."

"We have no reason to believe that she's going to dissemble when she reports to Adam," Richard said. "Give her credit for a courageous move in the right direction."

"I give her credit," Eliza said, her voice tight, "for maneuvering to protect herself from possible exposure. She knows my father well enough to realize that he'd throw her out of his house and take steps to have their marriage annulled if she hadn't confessed to him that she's in Mazarin's employ."

"We don't know," Richard said patiently, "and I doubt if we'll ever know, what was responsible for her telling him the truth. But I'm pleased that she did, and I'm especially glad because it makes our own positions much more tenable."

Eliza sighed and turned to stare into the fire.

Richard swallowed more of his sack than he had intended, and much to his annoyance, he began to cough.

Eliza neither moved nor took her eyes from the fire.

When Richard recovered his voice, he said, after a long silence, "You do hate her, don't you?"

"I dislike her strongly," Eliza said, "because she thinks all she needs to do is snap her fingers to get any man, as she got my father and as she had you before him."

For some reason Richard felt he had to defend Celeste. "She didn't snap her fingers," he replied. "On the contrary. I initiated our affair, as I have taken pains to tell you in the past."

"I know what you told me," Eliza said, "and I've observed Celeste in action often enough that I know her, too. She set her cap for you and she got you. Any woman would recognize her techniques, just as any man would be too stupid to see through her."

"I suggest," Richard said, "that we adjourn for dinner, and I heartily recommend that we drop this subject before we begin to say things we will regret."

"By all means," Eliza agreed. She rose and went to the kitchen, where their maidservant had left a pot of stew warming on the hearth.

Richard joined her at the table, and they were silent during the better part of the meal. What conversation they had was strained and required a great effort from both of them.

The atmosphere in the Dunstable house had changed almost in an instant, and the young couple, who had been so loving, so close, now drew apart. The almost palpable presence of Celeste Burrows had come between them and created a rift that, although they papered over it, continued to grow.

Hispaniola, next to Cuba the largest island in the West Indies, was a pirate's paradise. Although a small Spanish enclave on the southern coast had managed to survive for more than a century and a half, the greater part of the island was unoccupied and owed allegiance to no European power. It was a land of violent contrasts—of dense, steaming tropical jungles, high grassy plateaus, and rugged chains of mountains, the highest and wildest in all of the tropical lands of the West Indies.

Fierce bands of Carib Indians roamed the interior, but even they took care to vanish whenever one of the great ships filled with white men put into one of the island's many coves. The Indians were wise, for these vessels were the dreaded pirate ships that were the scourge of the West Indies and sailed far beyond into the Atlantic. Their crews, who bore allegiance to no one except their captain, were a ragtag assortment of Englishmen, Frenchmen, Dutchmen, Swedes, and Portuguese.

Only Spaniards were rare—mainly because vessels flying the flag of Spain were a pirate ship's favorite victims.

Most of these pirates made their home port somewhere on Hispaniola because the island offered nearly everything they needed. It was remote and mostly unoccupied; the jungle provided the hardwoods necessary for ship repairs; and, most important, there was food enough for everyone, free for the taking. There were fish, tropical fruits and vegetables, and huge sea turtles, as well as large herds of wild cattle that roamed the highlands, waiting to be slaughtered. No one knew how these cattle had come to Hispaniola, and certainly the pirates did not care. It was enough for them that they had an inexhaustible supply of meat, which they dried over low fires on a grill, or *boucan*, and carried out to sea with them. The French called these men *boucaniers*, or buccaneers—but they were known by many other names—none of them good.

One of the largest and best equipped of these pirate ships lay at anchor now in an otherwise deserted cove, and the surrounding cliffs made the ship invisible from the open sea beyond. The late summer sun beat down on the placid water, and the tropical humidity was almost unbearable. The members of the crew, men of several nationalities, lounged listlessly on deck. Few could swim, and those who did enjoy an occasional cooling dip were taking no chances because of the presence of sharks and barracuda in the seemingly innocent waters of the cove.

Such indolence, however, was unusual on board this particular ship. Her master and owner, Roger Stephens, was one of the more notorious pirate captains of the West Indies. He was a hard, unyielding taskmaster who drove his men unmercifully, but who was generous and fair when dividing the spoils. He was ashore at the moment on urgent, unexplained business, and hence the atmosphere on board was relaxed, particularly as the bo'sun, Wee Willie Walker, was nowhere to be seen.

Completely devoted to Captain Stephens, Walker was a hulking giant of a man endowed with prodigious strength, which he seldom hesitated to use when enforcing the discipline that the ship's master demanded. Everyone in the company was afraid of Walker, and with good reason. He was brutal in dealing with cases of disloyalty to the captain, not even bothering to summon the grudging mercy he often showed to the unfortunate passengers and crew members of ships captured by the corsairs.

Only one person on board the ship dared to flout the will of Wee Willie Walker. Gabrielle, a half-English, half-French green-eyed vixen with flame-colored hair, was the captain's mistress, and hence enjoyed something of a privileged status. Nevertheless, she thought of herself as an equal member of the ship's company, and whenever the pirates went into combat, she tied up her long hair, donned men's attire, and fought side by side with the corsairs, wielding a cutlass or a pistol with ruthless efficiency—though usually against an old man or an unarmed passenger.

When there were no battles to look forward to, however, Gabrielle grew easily bored, and in order to relieve the monotony of shipboard life, she always resorted to the same amusement—flirting with the crew, especially during Captain Stephens's absences from the vessel. No one quite knew how serious these flirtations were, because nothing ever came of them. The crew members were too afraid of the captain's wrath—and of the anger of Wee Willie Walker—to experiment, and Gabrielle herself usually knew when to call a halt. One way or another, she had managed to stay out of trouble—so far.

The afternoon sun in the secluded harbor was so intense, with heat waves shimmering up from the deck planking in the relentless glare of the sunlight, that the members of the crew lolling in the few shaded corners of the deck neither moved nor conversed. They stared dully out at the placid, clear green waters in which the vessel rested, and watched the small fish that darted about just below the surface. Suddenly there was a flurry of underwater excitement. A larger fish, lean and about two feet long, drifted lazily into view. He was silvery-gray in color, and something in his appearance was menacing.

"Barracuda," one of the crew members said with a slight chuckle. "Watch him stir things up."

Even as he spoke, the killer fish flashed into action, striking so rapidly that those who watched from the deck of the ship were unable to keep track of its movements. Several of the smaller fish, trying frantically to escape, were caught and devoured in a matter of three or four seconds. Then, as suddenly as the incident had erupted, the scene again became tranquil.

The quarterdeck door opened, and a figure that looked quite at home on board a pirate ship stepped into view. Gabrielle, her face daubed with cosmetics but her features still heavy with sleep, sauntered slowly across the deck. It was obvious, at a glance, that she was naked beneath the off-the-shoulder gown of thin silk that clung to her. The only other item of clothing she wore was a pair of high-heeled slippers she had taken as booty in the ship's last adventure. Now, showing off this latest acquisition to her wardrobe, she clopped her heels loudly on the deck as she paraded languidly, her hips swaying, a pout on her full lips.

The crew members stirred, their attention riveted on her. Of the dozen or so men on deck, every last one lusted after Gabrielle. Several of them were beginning to rise to their feet when all at once a huge shadow appeared behind her on the deck. Wee Willie Walker, a belaying pin in one huge clenched fist, towered nearly two feet over Gabrielle. One by one, the seamen dropped back into their shady nooks. They shifted their gaze away from the girl and stared off innocently into space. A few of the men would have risen to their feet and gone belowdecks quickly, but they were afraid that any motion on their part would be certain to attract Walker's direct attention and thus indicate their guilt. Looking guilty was in itself a capital offense to the bo'sun.

Gabrielle slowly turned and raised her face to return the bo'sun's cold stare, her attitude insolent but at the same time provocative. Even though he had caught her flaunting herself shamelessly, she appeared to be challenging him, daring him to deny his own interest in her as a woman.

"Cap'n Stephens told me to keep an eye on ye, and that's what I be doin'," Willie boomed. "What think ye that ye be doin'?"

Gabrielle gathered her long red hair in a bunch and held it above her head, craning her neck this way and that, as if cooling herself in a refreshing breeze. "What does it look like I'm doing?" she demanded. "Instead of staying in my cabin, which is an inferno, I elected to come up to the deck in search of a breath of air. Would you deny me that right, Walker?"

Willie glowered at her. "I deny ye nothin'," he said, "but if ye be all that innocent, how does it happen that ye've dressed and made up your face like a slut?"

His words infuriated the girl. "Call me a slut, will you?" she hissed, and from nowhere produced a tiny, needlelike bodkin, with a blade no longer than her little finger. She waved the weapon threateningly as she advanced toward him.

The bo'sun held his ground. "I watched ye struttin' and cavortin' for the benefit of these here louts," he said. "It was plain what ye were trying to do, trying to get them to lust after ye." He raised his voice and spoke clearly and slowly for the benefit of the men, who continued to pretend they had no interest in the exchange. "I'll remind ye of Cap'n Stephens's orders, lads. Any man in this crew who as much as touches Gabrielle will be hanged from the yardarm. There will be no exceptions to this rule."

Her threats having made no visible effect on the bo'sun, Gabrielle hesitated, and then her temper seemed to subside. Roger Stephens, though a generous, considerate lover, could be violently jealous, as she was well aware, and she knew he would be only too willing to listen to the bo'sun's tale of how she had deliberately underdressed, then strutted around the deck to tease the crew.

She retreated a step or two, and the bodkin disappeared from her hand and vanished into the folds of her skirt. Her stance became less belligerent, and there was a sly appeal in her eyes as she gazed up at the bo'sun. "Surely you won't deny that Hispaniola is the hottest place on earth, Willie, and that the heat today is fierce."

"If ye ask me," he replied evenly, "some of that heat seeped into your loins. I warn ye, wench, mend your ways and behave, or Cap'n Stephens will thrash ye within an inch of your life."

His insults were more than Gabrielle could tolerate. The tiny bodkin materialized in her hand again, and she sprang at the man, the blade upraised. She was a tigress in action, indifferent to her own fate and intent only upon doing away with the man whose insults irritated her so much.

It would have been simple enough for Walker to sidestep her blow or to catch hold of her wrist, but he did neither. Instead, nonchalantly flicking her blade away with his belaying pin, he raised his free hand and cuffed her hard across the head where the blow would leave no mark.

So great was his strength that Gabrielle staggered backward, then lost her balance and collapsed onto the deck with a thud.

Walker's expression indicated that he took no satisfaction in striking a woman whose weight was considerably less than half of his own. Paying no further attention to Gabrielle, he looked at each of the seamen in turn, then wandered off and disappeared down the amidships hatch.

It remained very silent on deck.

The sprawling Gabrielle realized that her skirt had risen, exposing her thighs. She pulled it down, then slowly hauled herself to her feet. She rubbed the side of her head, bitterly aware that Walker's blow would leave no mark she could complain about to Captain Stephens. Well, maybe she could find a way to vent her ire on him instead. After all, it was Stephens who had instructed Walker to keep an eye on her. But Roger was too powerful and far too clever, and only under the most extraordinary of circumstances could she even hope for a chance to strike back at him.

Wee Willie Walker, however, was another matter entirely. His physical strength was fearful, but she felt certain there were many chinks in his armor, and she intended to find and exploit one of them. No man could make a fool of Gabrielle and rest easy thereafter.

As she retreated toward her cabin, she heard the sound of splashing oars, and looking over the starboard rail toward the shore, she saw the captain's gig, manned by eight seamen, being rowed to the ship. Seated in the stern was Roger Stephens, easily recognizable by his wavy black hair, drooping mustache, and long, scraggly beard. Even at this distance, she knew something was afoot. Stephens looked alert, excited, and, in spite of the intense heat, ready for action.

A bo'sun's mate, his silver whistle sounding shrilly, piped the captain aboard.

Gabrielle threw herself at him as he stepped on deck. He caught her with one arm, and as he kissed her, his hand fondled her buttocks.

Simulating great pleasure, she nestled closer to him. Let his bo'sun say what he pleased, she thought. Her sexual power over Roger was far greater than the strength of any words against her that Walker might employ.

Still caressing her, the captain ordered all hands on deck.

Gabrielle continued to lean against him as the crew assembled. He loved mauling and fondling her in the presence of his men, and she didn't mind in the least. These gestures showed the company in no uncertain terms what he thought of her and, as far as she was concerned, demonstrated her power over him.

His arm still encircling the woman, Stephens waited until his entire crew had assembled. Then he addressed the men, his powerful voice rising and falling and working the crew into a fever pitch of excitement and greed.

"It's no secret to any of you," he began, "that we have by far the most successful corsair operation in the West Indies. Every last one of you has become wealthy sailing under my command—just look at the gold on your fingers and hanging from your ears. It's also no secret *why* we are successful—we always have accurate information on the movements of richly laden galleons. I pay for that information, you know. I pay dearly, and I never stint. I never cheat my sources. That's why I've been able to depend on them, and you've been able to depend on me. I tell you this now for a reason. In a few hours we are going to make the largest and most lucrative strike in our history. A Spanish treasure ship virtually dripping with the gold and jewels of the Incas is due to appear off the coast of Hispaniola this very night, en route from Cuba to Santo Domingo. She is only lightly armed, I have learned. In fact, there's so much gold and jewels in her, lads, that there's no room for any cannon!"

The men's eyes were wide with greed, and wild shouts began to erupt from the crowd on deck.

Stephens took off his floppy plumed hat and waved it in the air, shouting his last few words so loudly that the sound echoed from the cliffs surrounding the cove: "We shall take her tonight, and tomorrow we shall all be filthy rich, wealthier than we've ever dreamed possible!"

The men cheered and whooped and danced around one another until Wee Willie Walker brought them to their senses by ordering them to prepare to get under way.

Roger pulled Gabrielle closer. "As for you, my sweet," he murmured, "you will dance and perform for me in a victory celebration tonight, doing the things that you know will delight me. In return, you shall have a trunk of your own filled with gold and gems." He kissed her with a loud smack.

Rubbing her body against his with calculated abandon, Gabrielle was delighted. At last she was going to acquire the huge wealth of which she had dreamed when she had first joined Roger Stephens.

As soon as the ship left the cove, cruising close to shore in order to stay out of sight, Gabrielle went to her cabin and changed into her battle clothes. These consisted of a man's shirt left carelessly unbuttoned, a snug-fitting pair of black breeches, and supple, calf-high boots. She buckled on a sword, stuck two loaded pistols into her breeches, then returned outside to join Captain Stephens at his post on the quarterdeck.

By dusk the crew was fully armed and the cannon were all loaded and ready to be run out. All hands were at battle stations, where they were served a meal of smoked beef and a special treat, cold roasted yams.

As was her custom, Gabrielle insisted on bringing Roger Stephens's food to him from the galley, and she stayed beside him as he ate. But she was incapable of sitting for more than a few minutes at a time, and periodically she jumped to her feet, searching the horizon for a sign of their prey.

Captain Stephens, however, calmly finished his meal, rinsed

it down with a beakerful of rum, then licked his fingers clean. Later, when the moon came out, he rose to his feet and scanned the horizon to the north through his glass. After a half hour his patience was rewarded. "Willie," he shouted, and handed the glass to the dour, silent bo'sun as he approached. Walker peered through the slender black tube, nodded, then returned it to the captain.

It was unnecessary for Gabrielle to ask. She merely looked up at Roger in silent appeal, and he handed her the glass. Through it she studied the galleon—a huge, ungainly vessel, she thought, with a billowing sea of canvas unfurled above her broad deck. Judging from her size, she had to be carrying a huge treasure of gold and gems. Gabrielle's heart beat faster.

Stephens put his arm around her and fondled her roughly, while she directed a triumphant, hateful glare at the bo'sun.

"For luck," Roger murmured, whacking her soundly on the rump.

"For luck," she replied, and drew her sword.

The belligerence of her gesture delighted him, and he roared with laughter.

The pirate vessel continued to cruise under reduced sail in the shadow of the shoreline until the galleon was close enough to be seen plainly. Then an order from the captain sent the remaining canvas aloft and brought the ship about, sending her hurtling straight at the Spanish treasure ship.

As the corsair vessel bore down on her victim, Captain Stephens ordered the ship's identifying banner, a square of unrelieved black, hoisted to the masthead. A few seconds later he ordered the gunports raised and the cannon run out.

Before the Spaniard could react to the sight of the black flag, however, the pirate ship opened fire with her portside guns, raking the larger vessel from stem to stern. The gunnery on most pirate ships was deplorable, but Stephens's vessel was an exception. His men were well drilled in gunnery, and their aim was surprisingly accurate. A number of cannonballs slammed into the sides of the Spanish vessel, sending a murderous hail of splinters across the galleon's deck.

"Prepare to board," Stephens shouted above the roar of the

guns as his ship neared her victim. Several pirates climbed to the rail with grappling hooks dangling from their hands, and when the two vessels were nearly alongside, the men twirled the hooks two or three times and let fly. Most of the hooks took hold, and the two vessels were locked together.

"Boarders, away!" Stephens screamed, waving a cutlass above his head.

"Boarders, away!" Wee Willie Walker roared as he bounded forward.

Gabrielle drew one of her pistols and followed the men into action, the prospect of booty and bloodletting transforming her to a hissing, snarling fury.

The galleon's defenders proved unusually well disciplined, however, and more numerous than any of the pirates had expected. Captain Stephens immediately sensed something was wrong, but in the heat of battle he didn't give the matter a second thought, being too occupied with preserving his own skin.

Bo'sun Walker, always an awesome figure as he laid about him with a cutlass, was in the vanguard of the boarders, and had already fought his way almost to the quarterdeck of the galleon. But then, as if by plan, a half dozen uniformed men, each armed with a heavy saber, formed a circle around the giant and cut him off from the rest of the boarding party.

In the meantime, Gabrielle eagerly searched for a victim of her own. She had already discharged both her pistols to no effect, and now, armed with just a sword, she preferred to pick out a safe target. Perhaps an old sailor or a passenger, whom she would humiliate first by cutting off his breeches and then by demanding, quite seriously, that he make love to her then and there.

The man, as she well knew from past experience, invariably would not know what to do or say, and she would then force him to jump overboard to his death. She had played this scene many times, much to the delight of Stephens and his crew, and she thought that she had found the right party when she saw a slim, pale young man in elegant clothes who was taking no part in the battle.

"En garde!" she shouted to him.

He smiled slightly and drew a light rapier, swishing it tentatively in the air.

Gabrielle decided to make short work of him, but to her surprise, he parried her thrusts with ease and, suddenly going onto the offensive, forced her to retreat across the deck.

Then, with a flick of the wrist, he somehow disarmed her, flipping her blade from her grasp so that it flew into the air and then vanished over the rail into the dark water below.

Gabrielle was stunned. She was not prepared to die.

Her opponent astonished her a second time, however, by signaling to some associates, who raced forward and grasped her by the arms.

The pale young man sheathed his rapier and pulled a handkerchief from his sleeve, dabbing it on his forehead. "Bind the woman's wrists behind her and guard her closely," he said in a language Gabrielle immediately recognized as French.

"Yes, Lieutenant," one of the men replied crisply.

"If she tries to flirt with you or to say anything at all, gag and blindfold her."

"Yes, sir," the two men replied in chorus as Gabrielle's arms were jerked behind her back and made secure with a leather thong.

It occurred to the stunned girl that her opponent was definitely a military officer—but a French lieutenant? On a Spanish galleon?

Once Gabrielle recovered from the surprise and dismay of having been made prisoner, however, she noticed for the first time that a strange silence had fallen over the ship. She began to wonder what had happened to her comrades and craned her neck to get a better view of the main deck. A series of further shocks awaited her:

Wee Willie Walker had been subdued by a whole band of opponents and was propped against a bulkhead, bound hand and foot, with a gag stuffed into his mouth.

Everywhere the girl looked, corsairs had been taken prisoner.

She felt her heart sink when she saw that Roger Stephens,

too, had been taken captive. Not only were his hands tied, but a noose had been looped around his neck. A grinning young man was leading him, as one would lead a dog on a leash, toward the quarterdeck.

The girl's two captors propelled her in the same direction, and she noticed several men carrying a helpless Willie Walker, who was red-faced with impotent rage.

A series of further swift-moving events stunned the pirate prisoners. A prize crew was sent to board their ship, and as they watched in wonder, the black buccaneer flag was lowered, and in its place was raised the gold and white fleur-de-lis of the French Navy. A similar banner was run up the masthead of the treasure galleon, and painted canvas coverings were pulled up from the gunwales to reveal seventeen gunports on each side of the hull. In a matter of minutes, the hulking Spanish ship was transformed before their eyes into a sleek, well-armed French warship.

A number of crew members and two officers now appeared in what Gabrielle assumed was the uniform of the French Navy. One of them was the officer with whom she had fought her unsuccessful duel. When he noticed her staring at him, he grinned broadly and lowered one eyelid in a wink.

This was all the encouragement Gabrielle needed. Even though she had been taken captive, she decided that all was not yet lost, and proceeded to flirt energetically with the lieutenant.

He responded by turning his back to her and moving away.

The officer apparently in command, a gray-wigged captain, shouted a number of orders in a voice of crisp authority.

Stephens, who did not understand French and hence didn't know what had been said, looked imploringly to Gabrielle for a translation.

Gabrielle, however, remembered the lieutenant's order to have her gagged if she said anything, so she could not tell Stephens what little she did know—namely, that both ships were setting sail for "home"—wherever that might be.

Once the two ships were on course, the captain transferred his attention to Roger Stephens, addressing him rather frostily in English. "I must congratulate you on the discipline of your company," he said. "You gave us a somewhat more difficult time than we anticipated. You wounded a number of my men, and I regret to say it was necessary to dispatch a number of your subordinates."

In spite of his bonds, Roger stood proudly erect. "Then I gather correctly that a trap was set for me."

The French captain chuckled. "That is a very fair assumption, Captain Stephens," he said. "Not only was a trap set, but you swallowed the bait without hesitation. The rest was quite easy for us."

"Then could you possibly tell me," Roger asked, "why you went to such lengths just to capture a buccaneer? Why not just kill us?"

"The reasons for your capture were not revealed to me," the Frenchman replied, "and I do not make it a habit to inquire of an admiral regarding his motives."

So an admiral was involved! The mystery deepened, and Roger cast a quick glance at Gabrielle.

Like him, she remained impassive, her face devoid of all expression.

"I daresay," the French captain continued, "that you will learn your fate from the admiral himself. He gave instructions that you and this rather unusual young woman be brought before him as soon as we land."

"Land where?" Roger asked.

The Frenchman was amused. "Why, Martinique, of course. You are to be accompanied by your second-in-command, who, I assume, is that great brute of a boatswain over there. I must ask you to speak with reason to him and urge him to behave, or I shall be compelled to present him to the admiral trussed like a wild beast. It will do him no good, I can assure you, to rebel against his fate."

"Is it our fate to be prisoners of France, then?" Gabrielle asked, addressing the officer in perfect French.

He was agreeably surprised by her ability to speak his language, and his pleasure was evident. "So it appears," he said, smiling.

"Since I have been totally disarmed," she began, her tone sugary, "surely the victorious navy of His Christian Majesty is not so afraid of the powers of a woman that I, too, must remain trussed."

The captain flushed deep red and immediately ordered her bonds severed.

Gabrielle concealed her elation. She had no idea why the unnamed admiral had gone to such lengths to capture Roger and his entire band, as well as his ship, but she was certain of one thing: Her own future was looking much brighter. Her destiny was being determined by mere men, and she had yet to meet the man she could not handle.

Why should an admiral be any different?

A week later the three captives were rowed ashore in a gig. Captain Stephens's and Willie Walker's hands were still securely tied behind their backs. They attracted considerable attention on the wharf, where a number of residents of Saint Pierre were fishing, but a contingent of French soldiers in green and gold uniforms promptly dispersed the crowd. The prisoners were bundled into a waiting carriage, and the French captain climbed in with them. The blinds were drawn, which made the heat inside the vehicle suffocating.

Gabrielle's shirt, damp with perspiration, clung to her body, revealing the fact that she wore no undergarments. That, she reflected, was all to the good. She hoped the admiral, whoever he might be, would prove to be as susceptible to her charm as the French captain had been. As the carriage clattered through the streets of Saint Pierre, she found herself daydreaming about this great French leader.

Armed sentries were stationed at the entrance gate to Admiral de Bosquette's house, and the new arrivals were subjected to a close scrutiny before being allowed to pass. Then, when they descended from the carriage, other sentinels armed with muskets and swords were stationed every few yards. The captain led them to a broad veranda, where Antoine de Bosquette was relaxing in a wicker chair.

Resplendent in his uniform of blue and gold, he sipped a drink as he looked at each of the captives in turn.

His gaze lingered on Gabrielle, and she preened subtly as he inspected her from head to toe, then from toe to head.

At a nod from the admiral, the captain cut the bonds of Roger Stephens and Wee Willie Walker.

The admiral was polite, almost jovial. He addressed them in perfect English. "Won't you sit down?" he asked, waving them to chairs. "I must apologize for any inconvenience I've caused you."

"I'd call it something more than an inconvenience," Roger Stephens replied dryly.

Antoine de Bosquette laughed.

Gabrielle risked her lover's displeasure by smiling broadly to indicate she was joining in the admiral's amusement at Stephens's helplessness.

A manservant entered and proceeded to pour a cloudy, pale yellow beverage into four glasses and handed them to the three prisoners and the French captain. "You are no doubt wondering," the admiral said, "why I have gone to so much trouble to bring you here."

"The thought has crossed my mind," Stephens replied.

The admiral smiled. "I have something of an obsession for demanding complete control at all times," he said. "I confess it freely. I suppose I could have approached you at your anchorage at Hispaniola and made a business offer to you. Even if you had accepted it, however, you would have remained independent of me and could have changed your mind or altered the terms as you pleased. This way, having made you my prisoners, you are dependent on me for your freedom, your lives—everything. If you employ treachery in your dealings with me, I can have you executed, and I assure you that that is exactly what I would do, without a moment of regret." His glance flicked toward Gabrielle, and he stroked the ends of his mustache.

Gabrielle tried to look as innocent as she could. He would indeed regret giving such an order in her own case, she thought—at least until such time as he had bedded her.

"Are you familiar with the island of Bermuda, Captain Stephens?" the admiral asked, almost offhandedly.

"I know where it is, if that's what you mean; but I've never paid the place a visit," Stephens replied. "The people there aren't particularly wealthy, and I've no interest in a shipful of tobacco. My crew is accustomed to a richer fare."

The admiral nodded absently, as if in deep thought.

Wee Willie Walker had been watching for his chance, and suddenly he sprang to his feet, intending to lay hands on the admiral. Before he could get halfway to his objective, however, three sentries bore down on him, two of them brandishing bayonets at the ends of their muskets, the third aiming a brace of cocked pistols.

Gabrielle was outraged. He was undoing all her efforts to please the admiral. "Behave yourself, Walker!" she screamed. "Have you gone mad?"

Roger Stephens spoke a few words to his subordinate in a calm, low tone, and the giant promptly subsided. Rising and bowing to the admiral, Stephens said smoothly, "On behalf of my bo'sun, I offer you an abject apology, sir. His loyalty to me is considerably greater than his discretion, and he has the commendable trait of looking out for what he regards as my interests to the exclusion of everything else. However, I assure you he'll behave himself from now on."

Antoine de Bosquette replied coldly. "I sincerely hope you're right, Captain," he said, "because the next time he puts on an exhibition like that, my subordinates will shoot first and express their regrets later."

"You hear that, Walker?" the still furious Gabrielle demanded. "Perhaps you don't value your own life and skin, but I have a rather high regard for mine."

The admiral turned to her, and there was no mistaking his gaze or the meaning of his words. "Well, you should appreciate your skin," he said softly.

Stephens clenched his fists but knew better than to express his feelings openly.

"To return to the business at hand," the admiral said briskly. "Allow me to explain the Bermuda situation quickly, Captain

Stephens. For reasons that are no concern of yours, my government is interested in acquiring possession of the island. But the state of international affairs is such that France cannot intervene directly. Therefore, I have elected to act through you, and that is why you are here now."

Stephens listened intently. The reason he and his company had been captured rather than killed was finally beginning to make sense.

"I am dispatching my agents to the island," the admiral said, "in order to determine the exact state of the English defenses there. This information will be forwarded to me as soon as it is acquired, and then you and I shall sit down together again and make our precise plans."

Stephens's thoughts raced far ahead of the conversation. "Granted this is premature, sir," he said, "but I don't think my company is sufficiently strong at present to capture a fortified island."

"You may be right," the admiral replied. "In which case the problem can be solved by simply augmenting your force. The tactics I employed to gain your services can be used again. I'm sure that, one way or another, we can gather together as many of your fellows as are necessary to gain our ends."

"You realize, of course, that my crew and I will be taking all of the risks," Stephens said. "If there are casualties, as probably there will be, we'll suffer them. What do we gain for our efforts?"

The admiral placed his fingertips together, studied them for a time, and smiled. "For one thing," he said, "you'll regain your freedom. I shall release you unconditionally."

As a bargainer, Stephens was not shy, and although he knew he was at a disadvantage, he nevertheless spoke boldly. "If you knew corsairs, Admiral, you'd realize that they are motivated in battle by one thing and one thing only—gold. They find the lure of gold irresistible and will fight to the death for it. They will fight for nothing else."

The admiral did not seem surprised. "I anticipated your request, Captain," he said, "and I can assure you that a considerable sum of money will be made available to you and your companions in return for accomplishing the necessary feat."

"How much?" Stephens demanded brusquely.

Gabrielle saw Antoine de Bosquette frown, and she intervened quickly before he could speak. "I think that it is premature to talk about exact sums of payment now," she said. "I believe we should rely on the natural generosity of the admiral. I, for one, am sure we can depend on him to satisfy our needs."

The admiral's expression showed his pleasure at Gabrielle's little speech.

"I quite agree," Stephens said. "But until your agents report and we determine what size force we need to capture the island, I believe we should settle one detail, as a matter of principle."

Admiral de Bosquette admired Stephens's gall. Although the pirate chief was in no position to bargain, that was exactly what he was doing.

"Let us assume that we carry out the mission successfully, in a way that meets your requirements, Admiral," Stephens said. "What is to assure us that you don't go back on your word and keep us prisoner—or even kill us to keep our mouths shut?"

Again the admiral chuckled. "You will just have to accept my word as a gentleman," he said. "I'm afraid you have no choice. Besides, why would I want to kill you to keep you quiet? No one believes the word of a pirate, anyway." He seemed amused at his own joke and glanced at Gabrielle again for an instant, then turned back to the pirate leader. "No, Captain, you can trust me. And I think that certain higher authorities in Paris would share my feelings of gratitude to you for winning Bermuda for us. Maybe something can be arranged—permanent employment, perhaps, if you prove your competence."

Stephens was more than satisfied. He knew there was no way he could be totally assured that the French would keep their word. In his business, treachery was unavoidable—you just had to stay one step ahead of your friends and double-cross them before they double-crossed you. "We have a meeting of minds, Admiral," he said. "My crew and I shall be at your service."

"Indeed," the admiral said as he rose to his feet, "I intend to see that you remain so, until such time as Bermuda is ours. Your crew shall be transferred back to their ship, where they will stay, under guard, until you are ready to sail. The three of you will be allowed limited freedom in Saint Pierre, and quarters in town have been prepared for you. But understand one thing: If anyone attempts to escape, or steps out of line for so much as a moment—well, on your way back into town, you'll see a bluff off to your left. At the top of the hill you'll see a gibbet and a graveyard. I trust I make myself clear."

"Very clear," Stephens replied.

"Aye, clear as bilge water," Wee Willie Walker muttered to himself.

The admiral laughed at the giant's frustrated expression, then extended his hand to Roger Stephens. "I'm glad to find you so cooperative, Captain."

He turned to Gabrielle and took her small hand. As their fingers met, Gabrielle exerted a slight, but insistent, pressure. She looked straight into the admiral's eyes and indicated to him not very subtly that if he wanted her, she was available.

His look told her everything she needed to know.

The French naval captain did not ride in the carriage with the trio as they returned to the waterfront to collect their belongings. It was the first time since their capture that they were able to speak freely.

"Well, we've been left with little choice," Stephens said. "What do you two think of the admiral's offer?"

Gabrielle shrugged. "I know nothing about this place called Bermuda. But as you say, we have little choice in the matter, so I say we cooperate. If we produce the results he wants, he's more likely to be generous in his dealings with us. It's as simple as that."

Wee Willie Walker, who had not said a word during the interview, could contain himself no longer. "I don't trust no Frenchman!" he said bitterly. "Even if this here one is an admiral, he'll lie and cheat and break his word to us."

Captain Stephens was amused. "You're a typical English-man, Willie," he said. "You'd have a higher opinion of the head devil in hell than you'd have of a Frenchman."

"What if I did?" the bo'sun demanded. "I may not have any reason to be loyal to England, but I don't have no call to be a traitor, neither. It don't sit good on my conscience to attack a British colony."

"You'll do exactly what Roger tells you to do," Gabrielle said, "because if you don't, you'll cause trouble for all of us."

"She's right," Roger Stephens said flatly. "We're caught in a trap, Willie, and we're obliged to do as the admiral wishes."

Had anybody else given Walker such a directive, he would have rebelled openly. But he respected Captain Stephens, and despite serious misgivings, he nodded glumly.

Gabrielle raised the blind beside her a fraction of an inch, and seeing that they were nearing the waterfront, she spoke quickly. "I assume you're going to explain our situation to the crew, Roger."

He nodded.

"Then you won't need me for the next hour or two," she said.

"Why?" he demanded. "Where are you going?"

"To take a bath, if you remember what that is. You men might not mind being filthy for weeks on end, but I, for one, would like to take advantage of being in civilization for a change. And since we're going to be here for what appears to be quite a time, I want to find a dressmaker, too."

Stephens nodded vaguely, having no interest at all in the subject of the woman's self-indulgences.

When they reached the waterfront, Stephens and Walker descended from the carriage and were joined by a small escort of soldiers, who apparently had been waiting for them. Gabrielle remained in the carriage and waited until her companions had moved out of earshot before she addressed the coachman.

"Take me back to the admiral's house," she said softly.

As soon as the carriage was in motion again, she began to primp in the privacy of the enclosed cabin. She bit her lips and pinched her cheeks until they were bright red, and without thinking opened another button on her shirt. She looked down and inspected herself and sighed—then opened another button. The admiral, she felt certain, would notice nothing now except her breasts.

When the carriage drew to a halt, she saw that the coachman was letting her out not at the front gate as before, but at a secluded side entrance.

The sentries immediately passed her into the property.

Gabrielle strolled slowly toward the house, pausing long enough to pick a flaming scarlet flower and fix it in her hair above one ear. She knew the admiral was watching her from the veranda, so she exaggerated her movements for his benefit, walking slowly and provocatively, her hips swaying as she took small, mincing steps. As she approached the veranda, her lips formed into a sultry half pout.

Antoine de Bosquette rose from his wicker chair. She had returned even sooner than he had anticipated. He had known she would find some excuse to return, but the speed with which she had arranged the visit was a welcome surprise.

But he was pleased for more reasons than one. Clearly she would willingly go to bed with him. Far more important, though, was the fact that through her he could keep closer track of Roger Stephens. Yes, there were natural advantages to a liaison with Stephens's mistress, and he was prepared to make the most of the situation.

III

CELESTE Burrows was puzzled when a stranger stepped in front of her on a side street in New Haven, handed her a small letter, then disappeared. She called after the mysterious man to ask him for an explanation, but he ignored her and hurried away. As she stood there and broke the seal on the communication, she felt slightly indignant; but as she unfolded the paper, she realized this was no ordinary letter.

Inside the folded sheet, which appeared to be a bill from a milliner she had never heard of, was a single sheet of rice paper. She opened it, and there, in a finely lettered hand, were special instructions for her. She was to proceed to the island of Martinique, she was informed, accompanying her husband on a business journey he would soon make there. Once she reached Saint Pierre, she would receive detailed instructions regarding the forthcoming Bermuda campaign. The communication was unsigned, but she entertained no doubts regarding its source. The instructions had come from Cardinal Mazarin.

What perplexed Celeste was that she had been directed to accompany her husband to Martinique, yet to the best of her knowledge, Adam had no plans to go there. She wanted to show him the communication but thought better of it. Adam might resent the fact that he was being manipulated by a foreign power, and it would be more diplomatic to wait until after he himself learned that his presence in Martinique was desired.

Four days passed before Adam brought up the subject. When he returned home from the dockside office for noon dinner, he was in bubbling spirits, and his face was wreathed in a smile as he said to her, "I realize, of course, that you were the real cause of our recent summons to Paris. Nevertheless, my arrangements with the French minister of trade are beginning to pay off. I learned today that there's a large and extremely valuable cargo of French silks waiting for me in a warehouse in Saint Pierre, and I've got to make a journey there and fetch it home."

He was so pleased with the prospective business transaction that Celeste didn't have the heart to tell him the truth—that her situation was again responsible for the forthcoming journey. "Where is Saint Pierre?" she asked, trying to think of a way to break the news to him.

"It's on the island of Martinique, in the West Indies. Saint Pierre is a very exotic port, as I understand it, much like a Mediterranean city in France itself. I assume you would like to make the voyage with me, and if it's all right with you, we'll set sail the day after tomorrow, weather permitting. Can you be ready to go by then?"

"Of course." She put her arms around his neck and kissed him. "How thoughtful of you to include me, Adam."

He grinned at her a trifle sheepishly. "It will soon be winter, and the weather here is so cold and raw," he said, "that I thought you'd welcome an opportunity to visit a tropical land. I'm sorry to rush you, but I'm eager to take possession of the silks as soon as possible. I have never done business in Saint Pierre before, so I don't know how safe the warehouse there will be."

They adjourned to the dining room, and as the meal progressed Celeste lost her resolve to reveal to her husband her prior knowledge of their coming journey. If she had confessed to him from the start that she had received a secret communication from Cardinal Mazarin, it would have been possible for her to tell him the rest. Now, however, it would be extremely difficult, and she knew she would be depriving him of the pleasure he was feeling.

It would do no harm, she decided, to keep her information to herself, at least for now. Once she learned what was expected of her in connection with the Bermuda campaign, she could reveal the whole truth to him, and little harm would be done. Until then, however, she would say nothing.

General Etienne de Cluny was disturbed. As a blunt-spoken military man, he scarcely knew the meaning of tact, and he was afraid he might make an enemy of his closest associate.

He had learned on impeccable authority that Antoine de Bosquette was having a secret affair with the mistress of the notorious pirate, Roger Stephens, whom he had taken under his protection. That was carrying matters too far.

Unfortunately, General de Cluny knew he was open to criticism himself, since his own mistress was a Saint Pierre native. But at least he did not mix business with pleasure.

He glanced at his distinguished dinner guest as a servant carved the roast pig, then ladled out the boiled yams and papaya. The general moistened his lips in anticipation.

Admiral Antoine de Bosquette sat with a frown frozen on his face. Not only was the heat in the dining room of the general's house insufferable, but the unimaginative meals that Etienne served were more suitable for a peasant household than for the table of a gentleman.

The native servant continued to pile the plates high, then plopped one in front of the admiral, who wondered how he could avoid eating the better part of it.

General de Cluny himself poured generous quantities of a dark red wine into two goblets and waited until the servant had departed before he spoke. Raising his glass, he took a larger swallow than politeness dictated, then cleared his throat. "Antoine," he said, "I hope you don't mind if I speak to you frankly."

"By all means, my dear Etienne. I know of no other way that we should ever converse."

Again General de Cluny swallowed some wine. "I'm not prying into your private affairs. Believe me, that is not my intention. But it has been brought to my notice that you've been engaging in a liaison with a young woman of—well, of certain notoriety."

Admiral de Bosquette smiled. "Ah, Etienne, you're not jealous now, are you? After all, I've heard that you yourself—"

"Unfortunately," the general said, plowing ahead, "this young woman is also rather intimately connected with Captain Stephens, the corsair leader."

The admiral's smile faded slightly. "So much the better," he said. "She keeps me informed of Stephens's plans, and nothing serves my purposes better."

"I also think you're wrong to depend so heavily on this Stephens fellow," the general said. "I've always found that in battle it does nothing but harm to assign surrogates to attend to vital matters. I've always done my own fighting, and that principle has never failed me."

The admiral twirled his glass and sipped his wine, as if he had not heard a word the general said.

"I am well aware of your motives in assigning the task of taking Bermuda to Stephens," the general went on. "The deed could be attributed to a band of unscrupulous cutthroat pirates, and France could plead innocence. Cardinal Mazarin would be delighted, and a war with England could be neatly avoided."

"Precisely," the admiral replied as he cut a small piece of pork from the huge slab he had been served.

"There's only one thing wrong with your scheme, though— the likelihood of failure."

There was a long moment of silence.

"Why should it fail?" Antoine de Bosquette demanded at last.

Etienne de Cluny finished chewing a mouthful of food, then rinsed it down with another swallow of wine. "The capture of a fortified island is no laughing matter. It requires great military skill and considerable planning. This is no simple attack, like a pirate ship's assault on a helpless merchant ship. You assume Stephens is trustworthy and equal to the task you've given him, when that may not be the case."

The admiral tried to interrupt the flow of words, but the general was warming to the theme, and nothing would halt him. "I feel you're taking a terrible risk," he continued. "If Stephens does fail, the defenders would be alerted to future danger, and it would then become virtually impossible for us to take the island except in an open attack." The general seemed to hesitate, as if he didn't like where his argument was leading. "Of course, if that should become necessary," he said quietly, "we're practically guaranteeing that the English would declare war on us."

The admiral wondered why dolts were so attracted to army life. A man like Etienne de Cluny would never have risen to a high rank in the navy. "Are you through with your little speech, Etienne?" he asked, with more than a tinge of sarcasm in his voice.

De Cluny nodded and spread his hands to indicate he had said all that needed to be said on the subject. Then he devoted himself to his meal and began to devour it rapidly.

"What you fail to take into consideration," the admiral told him, "is that we're not going to be attacking Bermuda blindfolded. Quite the contrary—when Stephens conducts his assault, he will know the precise nature of the island's defenses and will be prepared to counter them."

"How can you be so sure of that?" the general demanded, scowling fiercely.

The admiral directed a triumphant smile at his colleague. "Because I happen to know that Mazarin's director of espionage operations in the New World—who I am sure is vastly experienced in such matters—is en route to Martinique at this very moment."

The general looked up briefly from his plate.

"And I assure you," the admiral continued, "that I am quite aware of the hazards of employing Roger Stephens to perform this task for us. No, Etienne, I give you my word—I intend to reduce the risks of this enterprise to an absolute minimum."

It was a crisp November day, and Richard Dunstable and his wife made their way down a narrow path through a seemingly endless expanse of trees and bushes. Richard, a superb marksman, kept his rifle ready for instant use, and even Eliza carried a loaded pistol, concealed in a specially made pocket of her traveling cape. Neither had spoken a word since setting foot on shore; they were not particularly worried about Indians, but both of them knew it was better not to attract undue attention in the wilderness.

Periodically Richard would whistle ahead to his good friend Roaring Wolf, a Pequot warrior who appeared much younger than his more than forty years. The Indian brave would then trot far out in front of the couple to make sure the trail was clear of danger.

Earlier that morning, a small boat from the brig *Eliza* had rowed Richard, his wife, and Roaring Wolf ashore to a beach near the head of Narragansett Bay; then the *Eliza* had sailed away, toward the mouth of the bay and her ultimate destination, the West Indies. The three had wasted no time in striking north through the woods to their own destination, and they had now been walking for nearly five hours.

When they reached a relatively open area on the trail, Richard at last felt free to speak to his wife.

"I think we should have no trouble reaching Taunton before nightfall," he said. "The trail seems much better than I had expected."

"It seems much *longer* than I had expected," Eliza replied. "It seems never to end."

Richard grinned at her and nodded. "That's what I like best about the New World. In England, the royal game preserve that was my domain was perhaps twelve leagues long and half as wide. Here the wilderness is endless. Why, between New Haven and the town of Taunton, there's nothing but a solid sea of trees, and it's the same between every town and every city and every village. It's a world unlike any other."

"Well, I grew up in these forests," Eliza replied, "and I don't find them at all unusual."

Richard waved in the direction of Roaring Wolf, who stood perhaps a hundred yards up the trail. The Indian was listening intently to something, then turned abruptly and resumed his loping stride.

"But you've been to the Old World," Richard continued, "so you must know what I mean. Roaring Wolf's a perfect example. I'm as familiar with the wilderness as is any outsider who wasn't born to it, and yet I can't compare with him. He hears things that are inaudible to ordinary men—large animals, bands of Indian hunters, perhaps even enemies trying to stalk us."

"Well, I surely hope he doesn't hear any such things today. But it's true," she said, "that we take the wilderness for granted. It's so much a part of our lives that we don't really give it much thought."

"That's the quality I know will make this a great nation one day," Richard said. "*And* a free nation—beholden to no one, except the land."

The little group encountered no difficulties on the rest of its journey. When they arrived in Taunton, they proceeded directly to the farmhouse of Aunt Hester Browne, an elderly widow who had formed a partnership with a young couple, Dempster and Robbin Chaney, and shared her home with them.

Like Richard, the Chaneys were Royalist refugees from England, and like him, they had adapted quickly to the New World and its ways. Dempster, whose family had owned a farm of considerable size in England, had labored day after day with fierce determination and had been eminently successful in growing a variety of crops.

Robbin, too, had proved her mettle. Although she had been spoiled as a young girl and had seldom done a day's work, she now scrubbed and sewed, cooked and baked, fed the livestock, made her own soap from leftover fats, and even chopped and split firewood.

Now the Chaneys had become parents of a son, and Dempster had sent an invitation to Richard and Eliza to come to the

Taunton farm for a feast of thanksgiving and celebration. When Richard read in the same letter that the boy had been named after him, he knew he could not turn down the invitation.

Aunt Hester made her justly famous meat pie in honor of the new arrivals, and even Roaring Wolf, who did not care much for the dishes of the settlers, happily accepted a second serving. Robbin demonstrated her own expertise in the kitchen by producing pumpkin and raisin pies for her guests.

A special thanksgiving service was conducted by the local clergyman in the Taunton meetinghouse, the most impressive structure in the village, and a large group adjourned to the home of the baby's parents for a celebratory meal, with each of the ladies of the community providing a dish for the occasion.

Richard, accustomed to the more metropolitan customs of New Haven, was experiencing something new in colonial living, and he was somewhat taken aback at first. Never since leaving England had he seen so much food or such a variety of dishes. For that matter, he had rarely encountered such ravenous appetites, and he discovered that he, too, was hungrier than usual.

Dempster, who was captain of the local militia and had served with distinction under Richard in two previous Indian campaigns, carried his plate to the corner where his friend was sitting and joined him. Several other veteran officers of the Indian wars also made their way to the corner table, and inevitably the conversation turned to military affairs.

"Most of the Indian tribes hereabouts," Dempster said, "don't understand the meaning of treaties and don't feel under any obligation to keep their pledges. When they're forced into a corner, they'll promise to establish and maintain peaceful relations with us; but as soon as we turn our backs, they go on the warpath again. So it seems to me that we need to be prepared for trouble at all times and to keep our militia up to full strength."

His companions nodded vehemently.

Richard listened but said nothing.

"The best way to meet our needs," Dempster said, "is the old way. Require every man who lives in a district to drill in the militia there. The length of service should depend, I'd say, on the state of relations with the nearby Indian tribes."

Again his companions agreed.

At last Dempster became aware of Richard's silence and looked at him questioningly. "It appears, gentlemen," he said, "that my friend here doesn't agree with my analysis."

"Oh, I agree that a citizens' army of volunteers is necessary," Richard replied. "But that is just the beginning of the solution. What happens if, say, the French should attack us from Canada, using regular troops that they've sent here from France?"

The men argued over this for some time, and finally Dempster said, "Clearly we can't count on England for help, especially on short notice. The Roundheads have enough of a problem ferreting out Cavaliers and Royalist sympathizers. I very much doubt if Oliver Cromwell can spare any regiments for overseas service."

"And even if he could," one of the militia officers added, "they'd be totally lost trying to fight a war in our wilderness. A few Indians could pick them off and scalp every last one of them at their leisure."

"That is exactly the point I intended to make," Richard declared. "In my opinion, the danger we face from France is very real. Any French troops sent to the New World will have Indian allies waiting for them here. The French high command is very shrewd, and you can be sure they will take full advantage of the goodwill they've established trading with the Indians. They've used the Indians before to fight their battles, and they'll use them again."

"It seems to me," Dempster replied slowly, "that we'll just have to rely on our militia in the event of a war with France. There's little else we could do."

Richard shook his head. "I'd go one step further, and I urge you to give my thoughts serious consideration, gentlemen. As we all know, wilderness fighting requires special techniques and special training. An experienced and well-trained force, even a small one, is worth ten European regiments. Therefore I'd recommend that every militia unit in every colony provide a corps of trained, battle-wise veterans who could make up, on short notice, a kind of emergency force. I haven't quite worked out the details yet, but I don't see why it couldn't be done."

Dempster frowned and looked dubious. "That's a splendid idea, Richard," he said. "But you're assuming that a group of stubborn, independent frontiersmen are going to be willing to leave their own homes and families to go off and fight someone else's war. We all know from experience that such an assumption is often at odds with the facts."

"I am afraid Captain Chaney is right," one of the officers said. "Militiamen will fight like demons to defend their own homes, but they're inclined to balk when asked to fight even a day or two's march from home. As for coming to the assistance of a sister colony—well, they can be as stubborn as mules, Colonel, as I'm sure you know. Massachusetts Bay wants nothing to do with Rhode Island; Rhode Island would just as soon turn its back on Connecticut; and Connecticut wouldn't care a whit if Plymouth fell into the sea. To persuade them to work together for the common good is a feat beyond the talents of ordinary mortals."

"In that event," Richard said somberly, "I'm afraid we may suffer a major disaster before the truth sinks in. For all our sakes, I only hope that the French don't realize how divided we truly are, because if they do, we may well lose a colony or two before the rest of us come to our senses."

The clear green sea was glassy, virtually motionless, and heat waves danced on the surface of the water. The slight breeze that drifted out to sea from Mount Pelée carried with it the mixture of odors typical of the tropics, a combination of lush vegetation, flowers, and spices, and the moist scent of rotting foliage.

Celeste Burrows, her raven hair pinned high on her head, managed to look coolly composed in spite of the intense heat. Wearing a lightweight indigo-linen gown with a low-cut neckline and wide, airy sleeves, she stood beside her husband as the brig *Eliza* tacked slowly into the harbor of Saint Pierre.

Although apprehensive of what the day might bring, she managed to conceal her feelings, her long experience as a political agent standing her in good stead. She smiled up at Adam and placed a hand on his arm.

"I hope," she said, "that it doesn't get much hotter than this once we're ashore."

"I doubt it," Adam replied. "We'll be out of the sun, and I'm sure our accommodations will be quite comfortable. We're to be quartered, the pilot's informed me, near the government compound, and if there's any breeze at all, that portion of the island should be cool." He pointed to a wooded area atop a cliff, beyond one of the twin forts guarding the harbor entrance.

Celeste nodded and fell silent. She found herself nervously fingering the fleur-de-lis ring on her right hand—Mazarin's ring. He had given it to her in Paris, in order to identify her as his New World master spy, and until today she had kept it safely hidden. Now, as she furtively glanced at the purple stone, she felt slightly queasy. No, she thought, even under the most luxurious of circumstances, she was not looking forward to her sojourn in Saint Pierre.

When the couple stepped ashore an hour later, a carriage awaited them, and after a few minutes' drive, they arrived at the house where they would be staying for the next few days. It was spacious and cool, with large windows on all four sides to catch any breeze. The surrounding gardens were in full bloom, adding a burst of color to the ever-present dark green of the island's vegetation.

An experienced majordomo introduced them to the household staff, and after inspecting all the rooms, Celeste had to admit she was impressed. Either Adam's business warranted unusually special consideration, or her own position as Mazarin's agent was far more prestigious than even she had dreamed possible.

The servants unpacked her trunks, leaving her with little to do. After Adam went off to meet with the French port officials, she wandered out to a corner of the garden that stood high on a cliff overlooking the sea. Rare and exotic plants were everywhere, and Celeste was delighted by their colors and variety.

She recognized the tropical passion flower she had heard so much about, with its ten green and lavender petals; but the rest of the brilliantly colored blossoms were new and strange to her, and she marveled at their luxuriance.

"Forgive my intrusion," a man with a smooth, musical voice said somewhere behind her.

Startled, Celeste turned and found herself being admired by a tall, lean man with gray hair and an elegantly waxed mustache. He was wearing the blue-and-gold uniform of an admiral of France, and as she took in his appearance, he bowed deeply.

"You are Madame Burrows, I presume. Permit me to present myself. I am Admiral Antoine de Bosquette."

She quickly recovered her manners and extended her hand. "You took me by surprise, m'sieur," she murmured.

He kissed her hand and, noticing the ring, grinned knowingly at her. Then, unexpectedly, he turned her hand palm upward and kissed it. The gesture was rude and strictly unnecessary, and Celeste knew there was trouble ahead for her. She did not lose her composure, however, and smiled tight-lipped at him.

"I thought we could become acquainted," he said, "while Colonel Burrows is busily engaged with the port officials. You can be certain he'll be kept occupied for a considerable length of time. Therefore, if you please—" He offered her his arm.

Celeste had no idea where he might be taking her, but as Mazarin's agent she had no alternative except to show her complete confidence in this representative of France. Her expression did not falter as she slipped her hand through his arm.

He conducted her to a bench overlooking the sea, and almost miraculously, there was a strong, cool breeze that blew down from Mount Pelée.

"This is very pleasant," Celeste said, and unpinning her blue-black hair, she let the wind ripple through it.

She quickly realized her error. The admiral had regarded the gesture as flirtatious and was sidling closer to her on the bench. Immediately assuming a businesslike attitude, Celeste stared straight ahead, avoiding his gaze.

The problems facing her were being unexpectedly compounded. Not only was she risking her life by acting as a double agent, but now the French admiral she would be reporting to wanted her as a woman as well. She had been faithful to Adam since the day she had married him, she reminded herself, and had no intention of disregarding her marriage vows now, whatever the reason. Besides, she didn't find the admiral at all attractive.

The admiral sensed her withdrawal and adopted a brisk attitude himself. "You'll be pleased to hear," he said, "that our basic plan for the conquest of Bermuda has been completed."

Celeste allowed herself to show only slight interest. "Is that so?" she said.

"Our forces will not be directly involved," he explained. "I have reached an agreement with a notorious buccaneer—who fortunately is of English descent—and his company, supplemented by a number of volunteers who cannot resist the lure of gold, will attack the island. Before that happens, however, there is work for you to do."

"Could you be more specific, please?" she said.

"Certainly," he replied. "You and your associates, whoever they may be, will make a thorough survey of George's Town and its fortifications. I want specific information on the location and size of the British forts there, the number and size of their cannon, and the strength of their garrisons. That is not all—but I'll let Captain Stephens himself explain to you what he requires."

"Captain Stephens?" she asked.

He nodded. "You shall meet him tomorrow, when Colonel Burrows will again be occupied with matters of business." He glanced at his pocket watch, then slid even closer to her on the bench. "He will be occupied for at least two more hours today."

Celeste knew what was coming next.

"I believe one should take advantage of one's opportunities as they arise in this world," Antoine de Bosquette said blandly. "To advance in this life it is necessary to recognize an opportunity and grasp it enthusiastically." He put a hand over hers and squeezed roughly.

"I quite agree," Celeste replied sweetly, removing her hand from beneath his. "But on the other hand, only a fool places himself or herself in needless jeopardy."

The admiral frowned. "But in this instance," he said, "I fail to see how you would be jeopardizing your future. In fact, a laudatory report from me to Cardinal Mazarin could do a great deal to advance your career."

Celeste sighed to herself. The last thing in the world she wanted was to rise in the cardinal's service, but of course she could never tell the admiral that. Perhaps a subtly worded warning would suffice.

"When a younger woman is married to an older man," she said, "and particularly when that older man is well-to-do and has a certain renown, then that younger woman is closely watched. I'm not saying that my dear Adam is jealous—I give him no reason to be. But he is very quick to note when something is not quite right; and if he questioned my fidelity, that would be the end of my marriage. It would also be the end of my usefulness to Cardinal Mazarin. I'm of value to him now only because I am the wife of a prominent merchant and soldier of New England." That, she hoped, would be enough to put the admiral in his place.

Antoine de Bosquette looked faintly regretful, and drew his hand away from her. "I learned long ago, when planning a naval campaign, to exercise patience," he said. "I apply that principle to every phase of my life, and I find that it succeeds far more often than it fails." He grinned at her, then stood and took her hand. Deliberately kissing her palm again, he looked her full in the face. "Until tomorrow, madame," he said. He bowed gallantly and took his leave.

Celeste spent an uneasy evening and night. Ordinarily, she would have hastened to recount the conversation to Adam. But Antoine de Bosquette's behavior had made her unusually wary, and she knew it would be necessary to tread carefully so as not to arouse her husband's jealousy. After giving the matter considerable thought, she decided the safest course would indeed be to divulge everything to Adam—but only after they had departed from Saint Pierre.

When Adam returned, she listened as he described in detail his negotiations for the delivery of the French silk and other goods being held for him. She feigned an interest in the topic, although it was difficult for her to concentrate her full attention on it.

He also gave her some information that lifted her spirits somewhat. "I had occasion to walk through the town this afternoon," he said, "and I'm sure you would find some of the shops there very interesting. But I was advised at the customs office that the best time to go there is in the morning. They said if you're interested in picking up any cloth or in seeing any of Saint Pierre's dressmakers, you should do it before noon, because after that the heat becomes too intense."

Accordingly, early the following morning, after spending a restless night, Celeste investigated the surprisingly busy commercial district of Saint Pierre. Although there were relatively few Frenchmen and even fewer Frenchwomen evident in town, Saint Pierre seemed to attract representatives of every native tribe and every nationality in the West Indies. The shops were all crowded, and Celeste temporarily forgot her troubles as she indulged herself, loading down the two servants who accompanied her with exotic trifles and gaily colored bolts of cloth she intended to take with her to a dressmaker.

At noon, feeling lighthearted for the first time since she had arrived in Martinique, Celeste returned to the house she and Adam were occupying, expecting the staff there to have prepared a light midday meal. Instead she found a young French officer awaiting her with a note. It was unsigned, but obviously written by the admiral, and directed her to accompany the lieutenant.

The young officer led her through the gardens on the property she and Adam were occupying, then through some adjoining gardens and up to a large house, where armed, uniformed sentries stood on duty. As she climbed the steps to the veranda, Admiral de Bosquette, accompanied by three raffish-looking strangers, suddenly appeared before her. The admiral bowed, then introduced her to Roger Stephens, Wee Willie Walker, and Gabrielle.

Stephens, a hairy but devilishly handsome man, looked her over with evident appreciation, stroking his beard all the while. Walker was sleepy-eyed and showed no particular interest in her. Gabrielle seemed downright hostile, perhaps gauging her as a dangerous rival, Celeste thought.

Captain Stephens spoke frankly. "The admiral has told me that you are already familiar with our requirements, madam," he said.

Celeste looked at Admiral de Bosquette, who nodded. "You want a report on the forts of Bermuda, their location, their armaments, and the size of the defending force," she replied.

"Yes, of course," Stephens replied. "But that's not all." He turned to the admiral. "Do I gather you haven't discussed my most urgent need with her?"

Antoine de Bosquette shook his head. "I thought that you could offer a far more thorough explanation."

Celeste had a feeling that she was going to be asked to do something she would dislike.

"My men," Stephens said, "know how to fight a sea battle. They are sailors—the best sailors in the West Indies. But most of them completely lack military training, and few of them have ever landed under fire from shore batteries or attempted to storm a fortress. The admiral here has told me that he will supply additional men; but he's also told me not to inquire too closely as to their background and training, so I'm not sure what I can expect of them."

Admiral de Bosquette nodded faintly in approval, obviously pleased by subordinates who obeyed orders without question.

"The brunt of the assault, therefore," Stephens went on, "will have to depend almost exclusively on my men." He turned his gaze to the admiral. "I have, however, been given to understand that I may be offered some subsequent relief—"

"That depends on circumstances," the admiral interrupted. "Buccaneers are noted for being an undisciplined lot, and if they run amok after they capture Bermuda, killing innocent women and children, the British will be forced to take retaliatory measures, which we must avoid at all costs. Therefore, my comrade-in-arms, General Etienne de Cluny, will be prepared to intervene with his troops, should that become necessary. I mention this only as a possibility, however. I am sure Captain Stephens will be able to keep his men under control."

Captain Stephens knew he was being held at arm's length by the admiral, but there was little he could do about it. "In any event, madam," he said, again addressing Celeste, "if my men are not to be slaughtered like swine, it's essential that I reduce the risks of our operation somewhat. Therefore I must count on you and your agents to weaken the defenses of Bermuda. I don't care how you do it—divert their attention, destroy their supplies, spike their cannon—it doesn't matter to me. That's your business, and I have been assured you can be counted on."

His confidence in her was flattering, Celeste thought wryly.

"And once you have accomplished your mission," Stephens continued, "you can send me a prearranged signal. I could then land my men; and if everyone has done his job properly, I'm sure our casualties will be negligible."

In other words, any casualties suffered would be her responsibility, Celeste thought, amused at the man's subtlety. Not only was she being given the most dangerous task, but Stephens would be able to place the blame on her if the assault failed. He was more clever than he appeared, she realized.

To her surprise, the admiral came to her defense.

"Of course we don't expect Madame Burrows to produce a complete and foolproof plan as soon as the idea has been suggested to her," he said, turning to Celeste. "My dear lady, you must understand that Captain Stephens is extremely apprehensive for the safety of his crew—though I am sure he has not given one single thought to his own well-being." The admiral directed an icy look at Stephens, who grinned widely and bowed, as if taking the compliment seriously. "No, Madame Burrows," the admiral continued, "I urge you to take your time in deciding the best course of action. Once you've developed a plan— which will not be possible, of course, until you actually go to Bermuda and see the terrain and fortifications there for yourself—you will get in touch with me here. Before you leave, I shall acquaint you with the means of communication we shall employ."

Stephens stepped forward and extended his hand. "I gather we're in this boat together," he said to Celeste. "Let's see if we can keep it afloat."

As she gave him her hand, she deduced from his careful comment and his expression that he, too, was cooperating with the French under duress.

Celeste began to wonder. She had also noticed that the big pirate, the one called Walker, didn't seem at all happy with the French. And he had been secretly scrutinizing her all the while.

The pirate woman, on the other hand, seemed to want to ingratiate herself with the admiral, but without being too obvious about it in Stephens's presence. She had moved closer and closer to the Frenchman, and now, Celeste noticed, she reached out a hand, intending to place it on his arm.

The proprietary gesture annoyed the admiral, who reacted, to Celeste's surprise, by firmly encircling her own waist with one arm.

Stephens and Walker pretended not to notice, but Gabrielle was far less subtle. She glared at Celeste, then glowered at the admiral and proceeded to stamp out into the yard in a fury.

The admiral did not release his grip on Celeste.

She knew better than to create a scene, so she stood there expressionless, as though tolerating, if not enjoying, the intimacy. Stephens and Walker took their leave, and as the admiral bade them farewell, he tightened his grip on Celeste's waist.

"In my business," Celeste said frigidly, "I have found it best to devote my time exclusively to business matters. I find that personal affairs and business are not at all compatible."

The admiral laughed as he pulled her still closer, showing surprising strength for a man of his build. "I've found quite the contrary to be true," he said, "particularly when dealing with a beautiful lady. Besides, we don't have much business to attend to. All you have to know is how to get in touch with me from Bermuda, and that's simple enough—see the chambermaid at the inn. There is only one chambermaid, a girl named Marie, and only one inn, so you will have no problem. So much for business. And now, my dear, as we have at least an hour and a half until Colonel Burrows returns from his present meeting, I suggest we retire to the privacy of the house." He started toward the door, dragging the reluctant Celeste with him.

Celeste quickly figured that she could scream or protest loudly and probably force the admiral to drop his attentions by embarrassing him in front of his sentries and servants. Such conduct, however, would be sure to earn his enmity, and might result in her being excluded from the planning for the Bermuda invasion. No, she decided, she had to go along with the admiral—at least up to a point. Therefore, with great reluctance, she allowed him to lead her toward the house.

Suddenly a huge form stepped in front of them.

"Excuse me, your honor," Wee Willie Walker boomed, "but I was wonderin' if ye happened to see my cap."

Celeste took advantage of the unexpected interruption to pull free of the admiral.

"Ah, there it is," Walker said, and retrieved a huge, ragged seaman's cap, which was hooked over the back of a chair on the porch. "I've got this here bad habit," he said cheerfully. "The hat ain't none too comfortable in the hot sun, so I get to takin' it off and forgettin' it." He chuckled as though he were unaware of the tensions between the other two. "I suppose it's all right, though, long as I don't lose it permanent-like. I could never find me another just like it."

"Indeed, it's a handsome cap," Celeste said, grateful beyond measure to him for providing her with this unexpected respite.

Willie grinned at her, his eyes reflecting his seemingly total innocence. "If ye be headin' anywheres, ma'am, I'll be glad to be your escort."

"That's very kind of you, Mr. Walker," she said. "As it happens, I'm going back to the house where my husband and I are staying, and I'll be very grateful to you for your company."

Willie Walker immediately moved up to a place beside her and offered his massive forearm.

Celeste took it, then looked back at Antoine de Bosquette. "Thank you for a most instructive meeting, Admiral," she said. "We shall be in touch with each other through your friend. And who knows? After this Bermuda business is over, perhaps we shall meet again." She smiled and half curtsied to him, then accompanied the giant buccaneer onto the lawn.

The admiral was powerless to prevent her departure and tried to make the best of the situation by bowing ironically.

Celeste did not speak until she and her escort had made their way through the admiral's garden and had crossed to the property of the adjoining house. "Thank you very much, Mr. Walker," she said warmly. "I don't know what I'd have done without you."

The giant reddened and was embarrassed. "I didn't do nothin' special, ma'am," he said. "I knew what was in the admiral's mind, and it was plain as this big ugly nose on my face that ye weren't liking it. So I deliberately left my cap behind and hurried back as fast as I could."

She halted and looked up at him. "You were wonderful," she said, "and it was the last thing on earth I expected."

He chuckled heartily. "I have learned that when I'm with men who can read and write and such-like," he said, "I gain a heap more than I lose by actin' stupid. I've sounded dull and looked dull for so long that it's no great shakes for me to act dull."

"You certainly had me fooled," Celeste told him, and looked at him curiously. "Why did you come to my aid, Willie? It could have been very unpleasant for you if the admiral had realized what you were doing. You were taking a considerable risk on my behalf. Why?"

He shuffled his feet and looked at the ground. "I'm none too sure," he said, "except I've been around long enough to know a lady when I see one, and ye ain't at all like that Gabrielle. She's been playin' some private games with the admiral, and if Cap'n Stephens ever catches her at it, he'll hang her from the bowsprit and use her for a figurehead. And the no-good lyin', cheatin' wench deserves it! But ye ain't that kind, and I knew it right off. Matter of fact, I know a lot more about ye than ye think."

Celeste was intrigued. "Really? What else?"

His smile vanished. "Seein' as how I'm English," he said, "I haven't liked the idea of bein' a traitor to my country and sellin' out Bermuda to the French. I got the strong notion that ye be feelin' exactly the way I do."

"Perhaps I do," she admitted, instantly recognizing the possibility of acquiring a secret ally in the camp of the enemy.

He spread his hands in a gesture of finality. "There ye are, ma'am," he said. "Now ye know why I helped ye." He removed his cap, then bowed awkwardly and departed, vanishing around the bend in the garden path.

Shaken by the events of the day, Celeste returned to the house and locked herself into the bedchamber she shared with her husband. She had lost her appetite and wanted neither food nor drink. She even refused access to the servants, who tapped politely at the door from time to time. Not until Adam returned at the end of the afternoon did she breathe easier.

He took one look at her and said, "What's wrong?"

She countered with a question of her own. "How soon do we leave Martinique to sail for home?"

"The bolts of silk and some leather goods and dyes that I've also accepted are being loaded in the hold right now," he said, "so we can pack tonight and sail on the early morning tide."

"Good!" she exclaimed. "We can't leave Martinique soon enough to suit me." Aware that she sounded distressed and mysterious, she looked at Adam apologetically. "Be patient with me, my dear, and in due time I'll explain everything."

His confidence in her was sufficiently great that he asked no questions and instead began to pack his wooden sea chest.

Celeste began to gather her own belongings, and her feeling of apprehension lifted somewhat as she watched a pair of man-servants carry two small trunks to a waiting carriage that would transport them to the brig.

She concealed her anxieties at supper and chatted pleasantly with her husband. Adam noted, however, that she was still very nervous and ate virtually nothing.

Her spirits improved markedly the next morning on the ride to the waterfront, and when Adam helped her across the gangplank onto the *Eliza*, she turned suddenly and, flinging her arms around his neck, kissed him soundly. "Thank heaven we're free of this place," she said.

He made no comment and waited until the ship cast off her moorings and the master ordered the topsails unfurled. As the brig slowly picked up speed, Celeste and Adam stood side by side on the starboard rail, staring at a just awakening Saint Pierre in the distance and the dark mass of tropical jungle surrounding the town.

"Well?" he asked at last, speaking with utmost gentleness.

Celeste drew a deep breath and told him the whole story, beginning with the instructions she had received from a stranger on the streets of New Haven. She recounted her two meetings with Admiral de Bosquette, omitting no painful or embarrassing detail, and gave full credit to Wee Willie Walker for saving her from a compromising episode with the admiral.

When she was finished, Adam clasped his hands behind his back and shook his head. "I don't like this," he said. "I don't like it in the least. It's plain that the French are in dead earnest about gaining possession of Bermuda, which I still find hard to believe."

He was so lost in thought that Celeste did not want to interrupt him.

"The French apparently have a hold of some kind on Roger Stephens," Adam said, speaking more to himself than to his wife. "I've heard about him from all of our captains who sail the West Indies, and they agree he's a clever rogue. As for the woman with him, she's quite notorious. I've heard stories about her that would curdle your blood."

Celeste was willing to believe anything she heard about Gabrielle.

"How the French have caught those two in a noose and are holding them there is beyond me," he said. "But that really does not matter. What counts is that they're in the employ of France now, and that they're vicious, bloodthirsty people." He turned to his wife and stared into her eyes.

Celeste's heart sank. "I realize now," she said, "that I should have confided in you from the very beginning, Adam; but I was convinced I could learn more if I acted on my own, without your having to worry about me constantly. If I erred, I'm sorry."

"You've done well," he told her. "All too well, in fact. That isn't what bothers me. I wasn't too concerned about your being forced to work for Mazarin, because I could not envisage a situation in which you could be harmed. But this matter alters everything drastically. You've been in grave danger the last two days, and I never realized it." He took her hand and squeezed it softly.

Celeste looked at this slightly overweight, middle-aged man she had married, and her heart overflowed with deep gratitude.

She had no idea what he intended to do next—and indeed, she wouldn't even blame him if he never trusted her again. But she did know one thing: She was glad to have him beside her now, whatever the future might bring.

IV

A SNOWSTORM slowed the *Eliza* as she entered the Great Bay off Block Island, but the weather turned to heavy sleet before the brig reached her home port of New Haven. In spite of the inclement weather, Richard Dunstable was on hand to greet his father-in-law and wife when they debarked at the wharf adjoining the Burrows and Clayton warehouse.

"Eliza and I would like you to join us for supper tonight," Richard said. He refrained from adding that his wife had agreed to extend the invitation only after a bitter argument. She had pleaded that the maidservant was indisposed and that the dinner could be postponed a few days, but Richard strongly suspected that she simply wanted to avoid Celeste's company.

Adam and Celeste seemed pleased. "That will suit us just fine," the colonel said. "There's no one else coming, I hope."

Richard was puzzled by the remark. "No, sir," he said.

"Good," Colonel Burrows replied. "We're anxious to speak with you and Eliza about an urgent matter."

Several hours later the two couples sat down together in the

Dunstables' parlor over glasses of sack. Celeste related the recent directions she had received in her capacity as Mazarin's head agent in the New World.

Eliza grew pale as she listened. She turned her gaze away from Celeste and stared gloomily into the fire.

Richard, who was habitually coolheaded in a crisis, asked a number of questions.

Celeste answered as best she could, omitting to mention only the advances Admiral de Bosquette had made to her. She saw no need to embarrass her husband or herself by revealing this personal matter.

"I assume," Richard said calmly, "that you're passing this information on to Eliza and me in our capacities as agents for France."

There was a twinkle in Celeste's eyes as she murmured, "Of course."

He nodded and turned to his father-in-law. "This is going to be interesting, Colonel," he said. "There is an expression Roaring Wolf often uses that I think is rather appropriate. There are many ways, he says, to remove the scalp of one's enemies."

Adam laughed aloud. "You're taking this in precisely the spirit I hoped you would."

Richard chuckled and then sobered. "I don't want to shoot until I line up my target in my sights," he said. "Let me think about the matter overnight, and we'll talk again first thing tomorrow morning at the office, if it's all right with you."

Adam readily agreed.

After the guests had gone, Richard went out to the well to fetch water for his wife, then added wood to the fire and made himself comfortable in a kitchen chair while Eliza heated the water in which to wash the dishes. "I'm delighted Celeste is being so frank," he said. "She is taking a rather large risk, I think."

Eliza nodded slowly. "I've never been one of Celeste's admirers, as you know," she said. "But in this instance I must reluctantly salute her. She's showing great courage."

"We'll have to think of some way to protect her so the French don't learn she's revealed their secret military plans to

English colonials. Mazarin can be very ruthless, as we have seen with our own eyes."

"You think Celeste realizes the extent of her danger?" Eliza asked.

He nodded. "I'm sure she does," he said. "If she's been in the employ of France as long as she says she has, she must know Mazarin and his ways."

Eliza put the dishes into a large cauldron, to which she added soft, yellow soap, and then poured in a liberal quantity of hot water. "It seems you have an idea to counter the French moves," she said. "What do you have in mind?"

"I'm not exactly sure just yet," he replied. "I want to perfect the plan in my own mind, then discuss it with your father. But I'll say this much: We're going to give the French and their pirate friends the surprise of their lives!"

Richard slept fitfully that night, and when Eliza awakened in the morning to prepare breakfast, she found him already shaved and dressed, seated in a chair before a window that overlooked New Haven harbor. Oblivious of the cold, he sat staring out at the early morning mist. Occasionally he closed his eyes and rubbed his chin, as if lost in deep thought.

She had come to know him well enough to ask no questions. He would tell her what was on his mind when he was ready.

Richard hurriedly ate his breakfast of broiled fish and freshly baked biscuits, then donned his greatcoat. After kissing Eliza good-bye, he walked quickly to the dockside offices of Burrows and Clayton. He was not surprised to find Adam Burrows already there, seated before a fire burning in his office hearth.

"Are you ready to talk, Richard?" he asked.

The younger man nodded. "Let me preface what I'm going to say by pointing out that we must exercise great caution to keep our plans secret. If word should leak out to the French that we know what they're intending, they're certain to suspect that Celeste has talked out of turn, and her life won't be worth a ha'penny."

The older man looked relieved. "I was very worried for her myself, but I didn't want to allow my personal concern to interfere with whatever course of action we see fit to pursue."

"There's also a valid strategic reason for keeping Celeste's revelations quiet," Richard said. "If the French should find out we've learned of their plans, they'll undoubtedly drop them and develop others."

The colonel nodded in silent agreement.

"For quite some time now," Richard said, "I've entertained the idea of forming a special corps of veterans from the militia units of every New England colony—men who can make themselves available in an emergency. It just seemed like common sense that experienced soldiers would be best able to meet a crisis. Now, however, we're faced with a real crisis, and we need more than ideas to deal with it."

"Under normal circumstances," Colonel Burrows said as he stared into the fire, "I would call this situation to the attention of the king or the Parliament in London and trust that they would act accordingly. Unfortunately, however, the king is in exile, and Oliver Cromwell is in no position to help us. Anyway, we would simply be losing time that we desperately need to prepare for this invasion."

"Explain one thing to me," Richard said, "because we're going to have to explain it again and again in the next few weeks to anyone whom we ask for help. Just why is a small island in the Atlantic so important to the New England colonies?"

"For one very good reason," Adam replied. "Every colony in New England has grown to depend on trade with the West Indies, especially in the past few years. If any enemy of England's—Frenchmen, privateers, pirates, or whoever—were to gain control of an island from which they could interrupt that trade, well, none of us would like to find out what would happen. It would certainly wipe out New Haven, for one."

"You've answered my question, sir," Richard said. "Very well. With your permission, I shall leave tomorrow and make my way up the coast. I shall ask each colony for experienced militiamen as volunteers, preferably men who've served with me in the New Amsterdam campaign or in Indian wars elsewhere. Unless absolutely necessary, I won't tell them where we're going or why. I think they know me well enough to trust me this once. For now I'll simply say that the colonies face a very grave threat. I'll not ask for that many volunteers—only a few experienced men who can give us maybe six months of their time. The rest who stay behind can help out the families of the volunteers—that's the least they can do. I can tell them our destination and reveal the French plans to them once we're on the high seas. Presumably Burrows and Clayton can furnish the ships necessary to transport us to Bermuda?"

"Of course," the colonel murmured. "You intend to land these men in Bermuda with no warning? What will you tell the English settlers there?"

"The situation is far too delicate," Richard said, "to permit any such notification of the people of the island. Of course, we'll have to take the military commander there into our confidence, but I'm sure he'll agree that we must keep absolutely silent as to the reasons for our preparations."

The colonel turned in his chair and faced his son-in-law. "In other words," he said, "you're proposing that Celeste give the French the signal to attack, and you'll be waiting for them with this corps of yours."

"Precisely," Richard replied. "Let them expect that the island will be loosely defended and will fall to them quickly. They'll sail right into our trap, and we'll give them a far warmer welcome than they anticipated."

A slow smile spread across the colonel's face. "It sounds good to me," he said, "provided you are sufficiently persuasive to round up a corps of competent men."

"I must succeed," Richard replied grimly. "There is no other alternative."

No Burrows and Clayton ships were readily available for the journey, so Richard, accompanied by the faithful Roaring Wolf, set off on foot. Following the trail that ran parallel to the Great Bay, he paused briefly in two other Connecticut towns, Saybrook and New London. Evading the questions of the curious militia leaders of the two communities, he obtained promises for the service of a total of eight volunteers for his expedition.

Hurrying along the coast to Rhode Island, Richard continued his quest, recruiting a few grudging, though competent, volunteers everywhere he stopped. Finally he reached Boston, where for once he was overwhelmed by the eagerness of veteran militiamen to join him. The city dwellers, it soon became apparent, didn't have to worry about being away from their homes come planting time. A grizzled longshoreman spoke for many of his colleagues when he said, "Colonel Dunstable, gettin' out of Boston for a spell ain't going to overly upset no one, and we don't need to know nothin' you don't see fit to tell us. It's enough for us that you're headin' the expedition and that you need us."

Richard's spirits were buoyed by the results of his efforts. By the time he and Roaring Wolf left the environs of Boston, he had acquired the services of nearly sixty experienced wilderness fighters, all of whom had previously served under his command. Without exception, they were first-rate marksmen, and he knew he could depend on them in battle. Now he had but one errand left.

He went home by way of Taunton, where he knew he would be welcome to stay the night with Dempster and Robbin Chaney. Roaring Wolf, to Richard's surprise, immediately struck up a long, rambling conversation with Aunt Hester Browne, who took the fierce-looking Indian brave in tow for a tour of a new barn. Apparently they had become fast friends on Richard's last visit to Taunton.

Later, as Richard and his hosts sat down to a supper of turkey accompanied by Aunt Hester's special relishes, Dempster grew more and more concerned about Richard's unaccustomed gravity. Richard had not yet mentioned why he was passing through the area, and Dempster, who usually respected his friend's privacy, at last asked if anything was wrong.

Richard, looking dead serious, nodded his head. "Do you remember," he said, "when not too long ago you and I had a talk about forming an elite corps of militiamen? Well, there's a crisis impending, which I assure you is very real, and I've been traveling throughout New England to gather recruits for just such a corps."

"What results have you had?" Dempster asked.

"I'm very pleased to say," Richard replied, "that fifty-nine veterans are meeting in New Haven in a fortnight's time. They've all agreed to give me four to six months of their time."

"Where will they serve?" Robbin asked.

"I hate to sound mysterious," Richard told her, "but I'm not permitted to say."

"This crisis you mention is grave, I gather," Dempster said.

"Extremely," Richard assured him. "If we don't react firmly and promptly, the English colonies will be seriously damaged. I have no doubt of this."

Aunt Hester and Robbin looked at each other, both of them deeply concerned. Dempster leaned back in his chair, his lips set in a tight line. "I assume, then," he said, "that the enemy is some European power."

Richard said nothing.

Dempster interpreted this as agreement. He brooded in silence for a few moments. "Have you enlisted any officers?" he said at last.

"Two lieutenants have agreed to serve again," Richard replied. "One of them is from Boston and the other is from Providence."

Dempster appealed silently to his wife. She nodded solemnly in reply to his unspoken question.

He exhaled slowly. "We're doing well on the farm these days. Well enough that we have a full-time hired hand. So if you have any use for me, Richard, count me in."

Richard was delighted. "I was hoping you would volunteer," he said, "but I didn't want to ask you, what with your new son and your large property here. Are you sure your hired hand can handle it all?"

"There's no need for that," Aunt Hester snapped waspishly. "There's nothing wrong with my health, you know. I'm still capable of doing a day's work."

"And I can pitch in, too," Robbin said. "After all, the baby spends hours every day sleeping, and a bit more outdoor work won't hurt me. It's not as if I hadn't done it before."

Richard still seemed reluctant.

Aunt Hester leaned across the table and wagged a finger in front of his face. "You heed my words, Richard Dunstable," she said. "We've known you for quite a spell, and you're not one to exaggerate. If you say that the colonies are facing a crisis, I take you at your word. Robbin and I enjoy the life we lead. We love the freedoms that we've been granted in this colony, and we aim to keep them."

"And not just for ourselves," Robbin added firmly. "My son was born free, and I want him to grow to manhood in freedom. So if my husband is willing to make sacrifices for the sake of our family's future, I'm not much of a wife or a mother unless I'm willing to pitch in and do my share."

"You heard the ladies, Richard," Dempster said with a smile. "They've settled the issue. When do you want me to report to you in New Haven?"

"Two weeks from today," Richard replied, and added fervently, "You have no idea how much this means to me and to the expedition. You'll be my second-in-command, and at the appropriate time I'll be telling you where we are going and why."

On their way back to New Haven, Richard noted that Roaring Wolf had become taciturn and sullen, which was very unusual. At first Richard thought he was imagining things, but ultimately he was forced to conclude that the Indian was angry for some reason.

Trying to humor him, Richard addressed him in the language of the Mohegan, a tongue familiar to most of the tribes of the southern New England area.

Roaring Wolf, however, replied only in curt monosyllables.

As Richard well knew, the ways of Indians were not those of white men, and he realized he would be wise to say nothing until Roaring Wolf voluntarily revealed the cause of his disturbance. But it was not like Richard to turn his back on a friend, and he determined to bring matters to a head.

They caught two large fish through a hole they chopped in the ice of a small lake, and when they paused to make a fire and cook their meal, Richard seized his opportunity. "My friend," he said, "is as silent as the wolf that stalks a deer. Why is Roaring Wolf so silent?"

"Richard call himself friend of Roaring Wolf," the warrior replied. "Richard not friend."

Concealing his surprise, Richard asked, "What makes you think that?"

"Richard travel to many towns of white men," Roaring Wolf replied. "In every town Richard ask for soldiers who fight beside Richard. Roaring Wolf shoot arrows with bow and also use firestick of white man. But Richard no ask Roaring Wolf if he go, too."

At last the truth dawned on Richard, and he earnestly tried to make amends. "I didn't ask you to join me," he said, "because we're going to be traveling a very great distance from New Haven, and the journey would take you far from home."

"There will be fighting where you go?" the warrior demanded.

"I believe so," Richard replied.

"Where Richard go, Roaring Wolf go," the Indian said flatly. "When Richard fight, Roaring Wolf fight." The issue was settled as far as he was concerned.

Richard grinned at him, then clasped his forearm in the Indian gesture of brotherly affection. "Thank you, Roaring Wolf," he said, "for offering to come with me. I gladly accept. I was mistaken not to have asked you in the first place."

The warrior appeared to weigh the remark carefully, and after a slight hesitation he clasped Richard's forearm in return, the ghost of a smile appearing on his stolid face. "Together," he said, "we kill many enemies." That ended the matter, and the Indian brave cheerfully built up the fire under the cooking fish.

They arrived in New Haven a week later, and Richard, invited along with Eliza to his father-in-law's house for supper, reported on the success he had enjoyed in his travels.

"We seem to be all set," Adam said. "I've ordered the *Eliza* and another, smaller brig readied to carry us all to Bermuda, and we'll load the holds with provisions for your troops so that we'll be no burden on the Bermuda colonists. And Celeste has some news, too."

Celeste smiled. "While you were gone, Richard," she said, "I received a message ordering me to proceed at once with several assistants to Bermuda, and I sent a reply stating that you, Eliza, and I were going there without delay."

Richard and Eliza looked at each other.

"Then it appears," Richard said, "that our special force will be ready none too soon. I just hope that we are enough."

The volunteers for the expedition began to arrive in New Haven two days before the planned sailing date, and Celeste and Eliza were kept busy providing meals for the newcomers, who were quartered in an empty Burrows and Clayton warehouse.

New Haven's citizens were intensely curious about the appearance of the strange men, but Adam Burrows said that all he knew was that the men had paid well to hire his brigs. Their destination and their business, he insisted, were none of his business. Soon a rumor began circulating that the men were mercenaries who had been hired by rich tobacco planters in Virginia to fight Indians there, and that seemed a fabulous enough explanation to put an end to further questions.

Early in the morning on the day the brigs were to depart, barrels of jerked beef, salted codfish, beans, and parched corn were loaded in the holds. Just before sailing time, several barrels of gunpowder were also taken on board.

Adam and Richard were sharing the cost of these supplies and expected no recompense from anyone. They both, however, took great satisfaction from the fact that Mazarin's own gold — from Celeste's, Eliza's, and Richard's wages as French agents — paid for most of the expenses.

Together, Celeste and Eliza boarded the larger of the brigs — the *Eliza* — and to Richard it appeared that they had worked out a temporary truce of sorts. At least they seemed to tolerate each other's company.

Adam followed them on board, as did Roaring Wolf. But Richard arranged to join the others later, deciding to begin the voyage on the smaller brig with the bulk of his company of militiamen.

When they were a few hours out of New Haven, Richard delivered a short speech in which he told the men that the French were planning to use mercenaries—probably buccaneers—to attack Bermuda, and that since almost all colonial shipping to the West Indies skirted Bermuda, the island had to be defended at all costs. "I must stress to you," he said, "that the information I have just now given you is a military secret that you must guard closely. Under no circumstances are you to speak of an impending attack once we land in Bermuda. The colonists there know nothing about what's in store for them, and for their own protection, we prefer that they remain in the dark. If the French should learn that we're planning a special welcoming committee for them, they might well change their minds and plan some mischief elsewhere. So your silence will contribute as much as your expertise with muskets, and you'll have ample opportunity to demonstrate both."

The midwinter voyage was rough. The winds were icy, the sea was choppy, and a number of the men soon became ill. Roaring Wolf was terrified, and swore that once he returned to New England he would never leave it again.

Richard and Eliza were veteran sailors, however, and spent long hours on deck, particularly when the weather grew a bit milder as they sailed farther south.

"I must confess to you, darling, that I feel rather uneasy about this whole venture," Eliza said.

Richard placed an arm around her shoulders. "The time just before an actual battle is always the most difficult," he said. "It doesn't matter how many times you've been through it."

"No, Richie, it's not that. At least not exactly. I've tried to analyze my feelings a hundred times, and as nearly as I can figure it, what really bothers me is that we're challenging the might and power of France. Who are we, mere colonials, to challenge perhaps the most powerful nation in Europe?"

Richard tightened his hold on her and spoke gently. "We may be mere colonials, and France may be the most powerful nation in Europe," he said, "but they're as human as we are, and we have one great advantage: We're not servants or slaves, forced to fight for harsh masters, but free men, fighting for our own freedom. And that makes all the difference in the world."

The men of Richard's volunteer company sprawled in the sun behind the main house on Mark Prescott's Bermuda estate. They had not expected such warmth and luxury. A half hour earlier, they had feasted on freshly caught fish cooked over open fires, a local specialty called mussel pie, and a stew made of vegetables that had been picked from the Prescott kitchen gardens under Adella's supervision. Now Richard, Adam Burrows, and their wives partook of the same fare in the formal dining room of the Prescott house, where Mark presided and Adella acted as hostess.

"I can't for the life of me express my gratitude for these men who've traveled so far from their homes and are risking their lives for us, complete strangers to them," Mark said in wonder.

"It's truly generous," Adella agreed.

"What's important," Richard said, "is that we not become a burden on you. We've brought along enough supplies for ourselves for at least ninety days, and we can't live off you. It's too much to expect you to supply food for sixty men."

"What's more," Adam added, "you're being far too hospitable. There's no reason for you to feel obliged to house the men indoors in your tobacco barns. We have tents, and we're perfectly capable of using them."

Mark shook his head. "Begging your pardon, Colonel Burrows," he said, "but it's apparent you're none too familiar with our Bermuda weather. I don't know whether you've noticed it, but the winds have died away almost completely, the air is very still, and the sky is growing hazy."

"Then there's the dampness," Adella added. "The air is so sticky that it becomes hard to breathe."

Celeste smiled at Adella. "We're so pleased to be in this warm, springlike climate," she said, "that the nuances have escaped us."

"What we're trying to tell you," Mark Prescott said, "is that a storm is blowing up. I urge you, Colonel Burrows, to have your captains anchor their ships out in the inner harbor and take down all sail. The gales here are some of the worst you will ever encounter anywhere."

"That's true, unfortunately," his sister added. "And since we're on the principal shipping route between Europe and the New World, one or more ships are washed up on our reefs and beaches every month or so, usually total wrecks. I hate to admit it, but there are people on the island who make their living salvaging whatever they can find on these unfortunate vessels."

"In any event," Mark said, "your troops deserve our thanks and the best treatment that we can give them. They certainly don't deserve to be exposed to the elements in some flimsy tent that would be certain to blow away in no time at all. The very least we can do for them is to give them shelter in our barns, which are secure."

"There's something else to be considered as well," Adella said. "If your men stay out of sight behind our house or in the barns, we'll all be better off. We were lucky enough to land them on the north shore and get them here in the first place without anyone noticing. If we put up a dozen or so large tents that could be seen from miles away, we'd just be asking for trouble. It would be sure to cause a great deal of local comment, and word might get back to the French that we're onto them."

Eliza felt certain that the girl's point was valid, and was about to say as much, but Celeste spoke first.

"You're probably quite right, Adella," Celeste said. "And there's no way we could ever be sure that we knew the identity of every French agent or sympathizer in the area. In fact, when dealing with a man as cunning as Cardinal Mazarin, you can never be quite sure of anything."

Mark was curious. "I've always felt that his reputation was somewhat exaggerated. I take it you don't agree, Mistress Burrows?"

Celeste's manner became solemn. "I can assure you any stories you've heard about the deviousness of the first minister of France are not in the least exaggerated," she said. "I don't think anyone has ever outsmarted him and lived very long to brag about it."

Richard's jaw clenched tight, and although he did not know it, his eyes blazed. He had witnessed the cardinal's brutality firsthand, and wanted nothing more than the opportunity to humiliate Mazarin—to defeat him so soundly that he would never venture to interfere with the English colonies again.

Mark glanced out an open window and rose to his feet. "Well, you'll have to excuse me. The storm is beginning, and I'll need to check the outbuildings and make sure everything is secure."

The New Englanders were surprised, especially at his matter-of-fact tone.

"Atlantic gales always begin very gently in Bermuda," he said. "They start as slight rains and consistently build in intensity for hour after hour."

Mark proved to be an accurate weather forecaster. The rain gradually became more intense, forcing the troops to retire into the tobacco barns. The winds blew in heavier gusts and eventually became so wild that, at Adella's instigation, Zwingli checked every window in the house and nailed extra planks over the shutters where necessary.

Eliza, sharing a guest room with her husband, heard the rain driving through the cracks in the shutters and against the windowpanes, and the wind shaking the very foundations of the solidly built dwelling. She shivered slightly and nestled closer to her husband. "I don't mind the storms in New Haven," she said, "but this is so much more furious, so powerful. And knowing that we're on a small island, surrounded by the ocean, makes me uneasy."

Richard tried in vain to comfort her, and both of them remained awake for hours before they finally drifted off to sleep.

When they awoke in the morning, the storm had still not abated, but Mark and Adella were calm when their guests collected in the dining room for breakfast.

"Just be glad that we're on dry land now," Adella said.

"The only thing that makes me nervous in weather like this is the thought of being at sea in a ship."

"I've been aboard ships in gales like this," Adam said, "and I must confess that I'm thankful I'm here right now."

There was little that they could do but wait for the foul weather to subside. Richard went out to the tobacco barns to make certain that his men were dry and that they had enough food. When he returned to the house, even though he had been out in the open for only a few moments, he was so soaked that he had to change his clothes.

The weather did not begin to clear until the following afternoon. In all, the gale had lasted for more than forty hours.

The sun came out in midafternoon, and waterlogged Bermuda began to struggle back to life. Zwingli appeared and conferred hurriedly in low tones with Mark, who promptly approached Adam and Richard.

"A ship has foundered on the reefs about a league from here," he said. "Ordinarily, she'd be overrun and stripped clean in an hour or two by scavengers; but to get to her by land they'd have to cross my property. And I've given Zwingli orders to let no one through, and to post a guard aboard in case someone tries to get at her from the ocean side. But I still think we'd better hurry."

Exchanging a quick glance, Richard and Adam fell in beside Mark, who had set off at a brisk pace.

"She appears to be a sloop of war," Mark said, "and the name on her prow identifies her as the *Dauphin*."

"French?" Adam said.

"Quite possibly," Richard replied. "They call their crown prince the Dauphin. Is she armed?" he asked Mark.

"We'll soon find out," Mark said.

When the three men reached the harbor of Saint George, they boarded a small skiff Mark kept there.

They wasted no time hoisting the sail, and quickly left the harbor, doubling back toward the coral reef once they reached the open Atlantic. After a half hour's sail they came alongside the storm-battered vessel.

Boarding her, the trio found everything eerily silent. Her

crew, consisting of three officers and eleven seamen, lay exhausted on the deck, more dead than alive. From her master, himself barely able to speak, it was learned that they had lost several other men overboard during the storm, and that most of the crew were badly ill, as well as exhausted.

But Adam's guess had been correct: The sloop was a vessel of the French Navy. And apparently she had been on a special mission. In the one passenger cabin on board, a youthful civilian was sprawled unconscious on the deck, a bad gash on his forehead. Suspended from his waist was a locked leather pouch, which Richard removed.

"We'll do what we can to help these poor devils," he said. "But in the meantime we'll help ourselves, perhaps, by learning what's in this pouch."

They returned to Mark Prescott's house to find that Adella had already organized a rescue team, pressing Celeste and Eliza into service with her.

While the women were off helping to unload the crew from the battered ship, Richard went to work on the lock of the pouch, finally managing to open it with one of Eliza's hairpins. "We seem to be in luck," he said. "It's two letters—one to Admiral de Bosquette, and the other to General de Cluny." Both, Richard noted, bore the wax seal of Mazarin.

Excited by the discovery, Richard nevertheless decided to wait until Celeste returned before opening the letters. Her experience in such matters was vastly greater than his, and perhaps she could remove the seals unobtrusively.

Celeste, it developed, was able to do just that. She asked Adella for a sharp knife and then heated the blade over a candle. She managed to slide it under the seal with sufficient delicacy that the entire blob of wax could be lifted up without breaking. She then repeated the operation, and both of the letters were opened. She scanned them hurriedly and passed them to Richard, who also knew enough French to read them. Adam and Mark waited patiently to learn what, if anything, had been discovered.

Celeste, a worried look on her face, methodically refolded the letters and returned the seals to their original positions.

Richard, who stood staring out a window, his back to the others, at last turned and spoke. "We are indeed very lucky. Bermuda, it appears, was at no time Cardinal Mazarin's target."

Adam Burrows gasped and paled.

"I told you Mazarin was clever," Celeste said as she carefully put the resealed letters aside. "He explains to his subordinates in so many words that he has placed no trust in me, in Richard, or in Eliza. All of us, he has felt certain from the outset, would betray France and reveal his plans to the English colonials. Therefore he deliberately created a ruse, in order to mislead the colonials."

Richard nodded. "The real attack," he said, "is to be against Virginia, about one thousand miles west of where we stand this very moment."

Adam lowered himself into an armchair, as if still in shock from the news.

Richard continued, his expression grim: "And his plan is as simple as it is ruthless: As we well know, Virginia, even more so than Bermuda, depends on one crop for its livelihood— tobacco. Mazarin wants De Bosquette to send his pirates up the coast and burn out every plantation on every tidewater river, starting with the Toppahanock."

"Which would ruin the colony," Adam said, his voice lifeless. "Yes, I see his logic. But burning out innocent farmers— that's not even warfare, it's sheer barbarity."

"That it is," Richard agreed.

"In the meantime," Celeste said ruefully, "we're a thousand miles from the scene of action, and the volunteer force Richard has assembled serves no useful purpose."

"That isn't necessarily true," Adam said. "If the letters are never delivered to the admiral and the general in Martinique, the attack will take place precisely as they planned it, against Bermuda."

"I don't think so," Celeste replied. "It's clear from those letters that De Bosquette and De Cluny were not to proceed with any attack until ordered by Mazarin to do so. If we keep the letters, they will simply do nothing until they hear from Mazarin again."

"I'm afraid she's right," Richard said. "We'd just be post-poning the attack on Virginia, in effect. Unless, of course, Mazarin suspected that his orders had been intercepted—in which case there's no telling what he'd do next."

Mark Prescott shook his head in confusion. "Then why don't we just show these letters to the Virginia settlers, to warn them of the possible danger?"

Richard's eyes met Celeste's. They exchanged no words but were of one mind.

"Celeste and I disagree," Richard said flatly. "At least now we know exactly where the attack is coming. We have an opportunity at last to accomplish the impossible. We have the opportunity of beating Mazarin at his own game!"

"How?" Adam Burrows demanded.

"It's very simple," Richard said. "We turn the ship and her crew over to the benevolent residents of Bermuda, who will nurse them back to health and even perform the good deed of repairing their ship for them—at a steep price, just to make it look good. They will then be allowed to resume their voyage, and the messenger—" Richard stopped, suddenly reminded of something. "The messenger—the young gentleman in the passenger cabin—is he all right?"

Adella and Eliza looked at each other, and Eliza spoke first. "He's still unconscious, but I think there's a good chance he'll survive."

"I agree," Adella added. "His heartbeat was strong."

"Good," Richard said. "Let's hope and pray that he does recover. In the meantime, let's get that pouch back to him, so if and when he wakes up, he'll assume his letters were untouched."

Adam Burrows still looked perplexed.

"Don't you see it, Adam?" Celeste demanded eagerly. "We'll sail without delay to Virginia, and as soon as we arrive, Richard's troops can go to work putting the defenses there in good order. The French will have no way of suspecting we know their plans. And I can write to Admiral de Bosquette before we leave Bermuda, giving him a great deal of misinformation about the strength of the local garrison here. Of course by then he'll know I'm a double agent, but he'll figure I've fallen for Mazarin's trap."

"Then," Richard continued with a slight smile, "we'll have a real surprise awaiting Admiral de Bosquette's mercenaries when they sail up the Toppahanock."

"And in addition to that," Celeste added, unable to resist smiling broadly, "we'll be free of our obligations to France for all time. The first minister has already dismissed us as untrustworthy. So be it! We return the compliment, and we leave the service of France without regrets."

"You're right!" Richard said. "Mazarin no longer has any hold on us, and we no longer have any reason to continue this farce. We can now openly express our loyalty to the English colonies—and to the devil with France and her first minister!"

He and Celeste grinned at each other. Not only was their plan sound, but they were being relieved of an onerous obligation that had weighed heavily on their consciences. With one accord, they turned to Adam, whose approval they needed in order to put their counterscheme into operation.

As he always did when making a major decision, Adam Burrows took his time. After much pacing and frowning and head scratching, he finally nodded. "Very well," he said. "Your thinking is sound, and I approve. How soon should we be ready to sail?"

"That, sir, depends on you and your ships," Richard said. "I assure you my men will be prepared to embark immediately."

"Twenty-four hours would be enough," Colonel Burrows said, "to take on supplies and water, and for the provisions that have been moved ashore to be reloaded."

The plan was put into operation immediately.

Mark made arrangements with several leading Bermuda families to nurse back to health the injured French officers, seamen, and the first minister's messenger—with his courier pouch intact. The sloop was freed from the reef and towed ashore, and a team of ships' carpenters was put to work repairing the vessel. And Arthur Mossdecker's young chambermaid, who was secretly working for Admiral de Bosquette, was watched closely night and day.

In the meantime, while all these arrangements were being made, Richard went out to the tobacco barns and spoke in private with Dempster Chaney and Roaring Wolf. Then he called the rest of his men together and broke the news to them.

"All of you have served with me before," he began, "so I don't have to remind you that being in the militia is nine-tenths marching and one-tenth fighting."

The men knew what was coming next, and there was a chorus of groans.

"But the good news," Richard continued, "is that instead of marching, we'll be heading back to the mainland, so all we'll have to do is take another little cruise."

There was a rising murmur, but Richard held up his hands.

"I know you men are eager to get the fighting over with and go home. Well, we've just discovered that the enemy was expecting to be met by you fellows all along, so they were planning to attack Virginia instead. And I fell for their trap— almost. So tomorrow night we're all going to slip back on board just as quietly as we got off, and then we're weighing anchor for Virginia. And if we get there fast enough to arrange things properly, we can still welcome them ashore, just as we had planned."

His troops cheered lustily. The subtleties of the enemy's schemings meant little to these veteran wilderness fighters, whose one desire was to meet the representatives of France in combat and teach them a lesson they would never forget.

The Prescotts' cook prepared a gala dinner that evening. Mark brought up a cask of his best wine, which he saved for festive occasions; and Adella, more than anyone, seemed to be enjoying herself, smiling as though she had a secret she was sharing with no one.

As the meal drew to an end, Mark rose to his feet. "You'll be leaving this island in less than twenty-four hours," he said, "and ordinarily we'd be sad to see you depart. But we are less than unhappy, because Adella, Zwingli, and I are going to sail with you to Virginia."

The others stared at him in openmouthed surprise.

"You appeared here out of the blue," he said, "bringing

with you a corps of militiamen devoted to the defense of Bermuda—men willing to sacrifice their lives for people too blind to defend themselves. This was a gesture that I cannot and shall not forget. I can repay you in only one way, and that is by offering my services and those of Zwingli. Besides, I'm sure you gentlemen could use a couple of our nine-pounders, seeing as they're not doing much good here. As for my sister, she refuses to miss the excitement, and she insists that as Mistress Burrows and Mistress Dunstable are going to Virginia, she will go there too."

Richard was deeply touched. "I well understand what motivates you, Major Prescott," he said, "and on behalf of my company I welcome you and Zwingli—and your cannon—to our ranks. As for you, ma'am," he said to Adella as he turned to her, his eyes twinkling, "I can't necessarily promise you an exciting stay in Virginia. Eliza and Celeste are going there with us because we can't spare the time to take them back to New Haven first. I don't believe in ladies taking an active part in battles, and I can assure you that Eliza and Celeste will be kept far away from the action and will be sent packing at the first opportunity. And I must warn you that you, too, can expect the same treatment."

Adella was on the verge of retorting that she would do what she wished, not what he wanted, but Celeste caught her eye, and one eyelid fluttered in a subtle hint of a wink.

Adella promptly subsided and understood why the other two young women accepted Richard's dictum so calmly. They intended to do what they wished and were seemingly bowing to his will only for the sake of convenience.

The winds were blustery and the weather was raw when the brigs entered the mouth of the Chesapeake Bay and skirted the southern shore. As they approached the mouth of the James River, Adam pointed out to Richard a small sloop in the distance flying the English union flag.

"Those are Cromwell's men, most likely on the lookout for Dutch warships," Adam said. "And that, I suspect, is why Mazarin has chosen the Toppahanock instead of the James or the York rivers as his target. He probably figures it would be a whole lot easier to chip away at the edges of the colony, where there would be little if any resistance, and where the local Indians might be persuaded to finish what he has begun."

The ships continued past the James and up the bay, and early the next morning they rounded the dangerous shoals off a headland Adam called Stingray Point. The water turned a muddy brown now, and as the *Eliza* and her companion tacked a zigzag course slowly up the Toppahanock, Richard and Adam carefully observed the lay of the land on either shore. So did Mark Prescott, who joined them at the rail a little while later.

Just before noon, the brigs entered a narrower section of the river, where a point of land jutting out from the northern shore constricted the channel considerably. Across from the point rose a bluff, perhaps fifty feet high, at the base of which clustered a few small wooden buildings and a dilapidated wharf. The men exchanged glances, and Mark Prescott nodded vigorously.

"That's the place," he said. "My nine-pounders on those bluffs could almost reach the opposite shore. Together with the six-pounders from our ships, we could plug up the channel to everyone excepting the fish."

Adam Burrows was impressed. "You sound as though you know something about gunnery, Mark," he said.

Prescott nodded and bowed modestly. "I served as an officer in the royal artillery corps before I migrated to Bermuda and became a planter," he said. "I've remembered enough of my old trade to make life fairly miserable for an enemy."

Wharf space beneath the bluffs was limited, and there was barely enough room for both vessels. But with the help of a few eager boys on shore who apparently knew what they were doing, both ships finally managed to tie up, one in front of the other.

An exceptionally tall, spare, gray-haired man, his face leathery from long exposure to the sun, stood on the wharf waiting to greet the newcomers. His breeches, shirt, and boots were worn and dusty, indicating that he spent the better part of his time in the fields, but he nevertheless exuded an air of authority that was immediately recognizable.

Adam Burrows was delighted and waved to the waiting man. "That's Kevin Nettleton," he told his son-in-law and Mark. "He's a former commander of the Jamestown militia and the very man we want to see."

Within a few minutes' time the trio went ashore, and Adam, who had met Colonel Nettleton on a number of occasions in Jamestown, was warmly greeted.

"I'm delighted to see you gentlemen," Colonel Nettleton said in his slow, methodical drawl after Richard and Mark had been presented to him. "We don't get many visitors here this time of year, before the tobacco harvest. No reason for any, especially since Virginia ain't Cromwell's favorite colony nowadays." He looked in turn at the three serious faces, then said, "I hope there's no trouble."

"I'm afraid there is, Kevin," Adam said, and speaking succinctly, told him about the French plot and how it was uncovered after the Bermuda shipwreck.

Nettleton listened carefully, an annoyed expression settling on his face. "You mean to say that the French are going to use buccaneers to burn us out of Virginia? That old Cardinal Mazarin must be crazy!"

"That may well be, sir," Richard declared, "but he's a determined madman. And since he believes that we've been misled and are awaiting his mercenaries in Bermuda, he thinks nothing stands in his way."

Nettleton scratched his head as he absorbed the information.

Richard went on to explain that he was accompanied by a force of sixty New England veterans, all of whom had served under him in a previous campaign, and that they had volunteered to meet the mercenaries and were determined to vanquish them.

Nettleton looked relieved. "Well, at least that's good news," he said. "I, for one, surely wasn't expecting anything of this sort. I moved out here thinking I could retire in peace, do a little farming, and not worry about anything but an occasional tangle with the red men hereabouts—but I reckon I was mistaken. Anyway, things could be worse, I guess. The militia in this area was just organized fairly recently, and we do have near fifty men in our unit. And with your volunteers added to the total, maybe we'll stand a chance of holding the enemy at bay."

"Are any of your fifty men experienced in handling cannon?" Mark Prescott interjected.

Nettleton thought awhile and nodded. "Half a dozen or so, I reckon. We have four beat-up old demiculverins we salvaged last year from a shipwreck down at Stingray Point, and the boys shoot 'em off now and again, just to remind the Indians we have 'em. Throw nine-pound shot a fair distance, they do."

Mark did some quick figuring in his head. "Counting me and the brigs' crewmen, that gives us about three experienced artillerymen per nine-pounder, including my two guns," he said. "We could do far worse."

That evening, Colonel Nettleton assembled the local militia officers and apprised them of the emergency. He had already sent out messengers to call up all fifty of the local militiamen to full-time duty, and the troops were expected to be fully assembled by late the next day.

Meanwhile, a prominent local family had taken Eliza, Celeste, and Adella into their home, for it was assumed that the men would be conferring late into the evening.

There were no facilities near the landing suitable for the corps of sixty New England volunteers, so they pitched their tents atop the bluff, instinctively occupying the high ground overlooking the river. Colonel Nettleton's wife saw to it that they were well fed, and the local women quickly set up an improvised mess tent, where a supper of smoked ham and venison haunches and dried corn and beans was served up in heaping portions. The men, tired of the simple rations they had brought with them, were delighted at the change of diet; and as Dempster Chaney said, with a broad smile, the food was as varied and as good as that served in their own homes.

As they settled in for the night, most of the volunteers agreed they were relieved they had returned to the mainland for their engagement with the French mercenaries. Roaring Wolf, for one, was especially delighted. "Better to fight here than on island," he told his companions. "Enemy ships cannot sail into forest."

His view summed up the situation. The return of the expedition to the mainland meant that the battle against the mercenaries would take place in the wilderness, and that would enable the men to take advantage of the fighting techniques with which they were familiar.

In the succeeding days, plans for the forthcoming battle were worked out in detail. It was agreed that a lookout be posted downriver to warn of any approaching enemy ships, and Roaring Wolf and one of Nettleton's militiamen promptly volunteered for that post. They would communicate with Richard by means of smoke signals during the daylight hours and by drums after dark. As soon as they saw a suspicious vessel heading upriver, they would give the alarm.

Major Mark Prescott took command of the artillery contingent, superseding the lieutenant of Virginia militia who had been in charge. The situation with regard to the guns was very promising, he said. The six nine-pounders—the two he had brought with him, and Nettleton's four demiculverins—had all been hauled to the top of the bluff, and they were capable of inflicting severe damage on any foe who dared to approach upriver. He was pleased to discover, too, that two of Nettleton's six artillerymen had also served in the royal artillery during the reign of the late King Charles. The others, although less experienced, were nevertheless familiar with nine-pounders and their use. And the remainder of the militiamen had already fashioned a defensive redoubt of earth and logs, behind which they had placed the guns so that they were hardly visible from the river. One of the tents pitched nearby was designated as the command post, and the entire area was being hastily enclosed by a palisade of logs.

But the question that occupied Richard's mind was how he could best deploy the members of his corps of infantry and the bulk of the Virginia militiamen. He discussed the problem at length with Dempster Chaney, and his father-in-law and Colonel Nettleton agreed with the two younger men's final plan, which Richard presented at a meeting of all the officers.

A small force of infantrymen would be deployed in the redoubt alongside the gunners, he explained. The bulk of the force, however, would go on board the *Eliza*, which would be armed with its own two small cannon and the two from the other brig. These guns were only six-pounders, but at close enough range were capable of inflicting considerable damage on an enemy.

The other, unarmed, brig would be sent upriver to the narrowest point in the channel. Manned by only a skeleton crew, it would be sunk in the middle of the channel should the buccaneers break through the main defenses.

Meanwhile, the *Eliza* would be moved some two thousand yards downriver from the bluffs, where it could be hidden close to shore, behind a spit of land overgrown with tall pine trees. Any ship sailing past up the river would not notice her presence and would probably not bother to investigate the inlet for fear of running aground.

"When the cannon on the bluff open their bombardment of the enemy," Richard said, "that will be the signal to the brig to attack the corsairs from the rear. Not only will the enemy thus be subjected to a heavy crossfire, but we can block their escape down the river and come alongside and board them if they try."

"The overall scheme involves certain risks," Adam said, "but since the other brig can block the channel upriver if we fail, we'll at least have a second chance to stop them. The military doctrine is sound, and I approve of the plan."

"So do I," Colonel Nettleton said. "The enemy won't be expecting a trap, so he won't be looking for one. And what's the first thing any man does when he's ambushed? He either stops or turns around and retreats. Either way we got him dead to rights."

"Precisely," Richard said. "I want to use our advantage of surprise to the fullest extent, and I think this is the best way to do it. Let the corsairs attack, and we'll send them limping all the way back to Martinique!"

* * *

The arrival in Martinique of the sloop of war carrying secret communications to the French commanders created a considerable stir. Antoine de Bosquette at first reacted violently because Cardinal Mazarin had not seen fit to confide in him all along; but after repeatedly questioning the first minister's messenger, the admiral finally resigned himself to the new state of affairs. After all, his meticulously laid plans could still be used. Only the objective differed.

The messenger and his companions told the admiral of their deep gratitude to the citizens of Bermuda, who had nursed them back to health and had repaired their ship. And the messenger swore that the secret letters had never been out of his possession. Certainly the seals on the communications had not been broken; and the sturdy leather pouch, the messenger insisted, had never been unlocked during the voyage. The admiral marveled at the naivete of the English, who could have learned the true French plans had they shown a little initiative.

Captain Roger Stephens was not overly disturbed by the change in the French plans, particularly when he learned that his force was to be augmented by an additional fifty buccaneers recently captured and pressed into service by De Bosquette's lieutenants. And in addition to his own sturdy ship, Stephens learned, he was being supplied with two small pinnaces, each armed with a pair of six-pounder cannon.

His one concern was whether the Toppahanock River was safe for oceangoing ships to navigate for any appreciable distance. Admiral de Bosquette, however, provided him with a number of accurate charts of the river—English charts, copies of which had fallen into French hands years ago, thanks to Cardinal Mazarin's ever-active network of spies.

Of all the pirate company, only Wee Willie Walker voiced any reservations about the forthcoming campaign. "I don't like it," the bo'sun said emphatically. "Virginia is an English colony, and the French have no claim to it. They know that, so the cowards are going to try to burn the English out, then pick the carcass like the scurvy hyenas they are."

Gabrielle adopted an attitude of superiority toward the giant.

"The whole point of this enterprise," she told him scornfully, "is that France will be making no claims of any kind to Virginia or any portion of Virginia. As far as England is concerned, Virginia will have been attacked by pirates interested in nothing more than booty. If French traders move in once the English settlers decide they've had enough, that's none of our business. We're just doing what we have to do to regain our freedom."

Walker did not argue the point with her. He well understood Admiral de Bosquette's purpose in forcing the cooperation of Captain Stephens and his crew. The results, however, would be the same for the Virginia settlers regardless of who attacked them: They would lose their crops, their farms, their homes—everything for which they had labored their entire lives. And England would lose possession of a colony that had struggled for almost a half century to survive and, finally, to prosper. Now all of that would come to an end, and he wanted no part in it.

V

MARK Prescott, Adam Burrows, and Richard Dunstable were given quarters in a small house conveniently located near the fort. Celeste, Eliza, and Adella Prescott, however, were quartered in a farmhouse a half mile away from the probable scene of future hostilities. Colonel Nettleton considered this a safer arrangement, and the men all agreed.

Zwingli continued to shadow Adella, offering her protection she didn't really need. The giant's activity, however, gave Richard an idea. At his request, the former slave also took Eliza and Celeste under his wing.

"It will be some little time before we're able to arrange passage for the ladies back to New Haven," Richard said, "and until then, they're somewhat in the way here. I don't want to see them endangered when hostilities break out, so I commend them to your care, Zwingli."

The giant nodded and smiled, and assured Richard he would guard the women closely.

He kept his word scrupulously. The few local inhabitants, as well as Indians of nearby tribes who came by on trading missions, took one look at the gigantic black man with a huge scimitar slung over his shoulder and gave him and his charges a wide berth. The three women were unusually striking, and ordinarily they would have attracted the attention of every restless young man in the county; but under the circumstances they were left strictly alone. No one wanted an altercation with Zwingli.

Eliza, however, chafed at the restriction of her freedom. And she did not at all like the idea of being separated from Richard. But as long as Celeste was in the same position and bore the hardship without complaint, she herself would not protest. She would just have to be patient, along with the others. At least she could keep herself busy helping out with the chores on the farm where they were staying, and that would keep her thoughts on other matters.

Early one morning, however, Eliza's enforced separation was rudely and abruptly brought to her attention.

Richard Dunstable had risen before dawn, as was his habit. But this morning, after three days of pouring rain, the sun had broken through at last and he had decided to ride over to the house where Eliza was staying, to see if all was well. He was just tying his horse's reins to a tree in the front yard when Celeste suddenly appeared from around the side of the house.

"Richard," she called out, approaching him. "If you're looking for Eliza, she's still in bed. We were all up late last night, helping our host with a sick calf in the barn, and Eliza was the last of us to get to bed."

Richard, slightly ill at ease to be alone with his father-in-law's beautiful young wife, unwound the reins and held them in his hand. "Well," he said, "in that case I'll be moving on to the fort. I just stopped to say hello, but I wouldn't want to wake her. Good morning to you, Celeste. Tell Eliza I was here."

Richard was about to remount when Celeste halted him.

"Richard," she said, "I've been meaning to talk to you alone for quite some time now, but I haven't had a chance."

Richard's first impulse was to get on his horse and ride away as fast as he could, but he forced himself to hear Celeste out.

"It's just that I'd like to apologize for that night aboard ship when we were together. Not that I didn't enjoy myself thoroughly, mind you. On the contrary—I've never had a better time."

Richard, his face averted, was speechless.

Celeste prodded him. "You do remember, don't you?"

He remembered all too well, and turned bright red, but forced himself to remain calm. "Of course," he said. "But what is there to apologize for? It was my fault more than yours, and I've told you as much before." Richard regretted that his words sounded so harsh, but he had too much respect for Eliza to absolve himself of even the slightest guilt for his one-night affair with Celeste.

Celeste seemed to sense his intense discomfort and was mercifully short. "Well, I wanted you to know that, regardless of what you say, I am sorry. I love Adam deeply; and for his sake as well as my own, I had to tell you that. And I hope you can convince Eliza that I no longer have my hooks out for you, as she still seems to believe. That's all I wanted to say."

Richard was relieved as well as surprised, and his respect for Celeste grew immeasurably. She was indeed a remarkable woman. "Thank you for telling me that," he said, regaining his accustomed good humor. "I'll tell Eliza. And I'm glad for you and Adam." He impulsively took Celeste's hand and kissed it, then mounted his borrowed horse and rode off.

Neither Celeste nor Richard realized that Eliza had witnessed the end of the scene from the window of her upstairs bedchamber. Unfortunately, she did not hear what had been said; and all that she saw was Richard kissing Celeste's hand.

Eliza, however, had little time to think about the incident—and no time to confront Richard with it—because later that same day the soldier assigned to keep watch for signals from Roaring Wolf raised a cry that carried through the entire fort. "Pirates!" he yelled. Gaining control of himself, he called Captain Chaney's attention to the puffs of smoke rising above the forest downriver. Dempster promptly notified his lieutenants that an enemy was approaching, then sent word to Richard, Adam, and Colonel Nettleton.

Thanks to the repeated practice sessions that Richard had instituted, the deployment of the militiamen was smooth. The guns of the fort were loaded, run out, and aimed toward the center of the river. The bulk of the militia force, both the New Englanders and the local Virginians, marched unseen through the thick forest to the camouflaged *Eliza*, which they boarded over a plank bridge. The crew made ready to sail, waiting for the word to be given. Everyone kept close watch for the arrival of the enemy.

They did not have long to wait. Soon the observers on the bluff could see the three buccaneer vessels sailing up the river in single file, with the larger ship, under reduced sail, between the two smaller pinnaces. The pinnaces each mounted two cannon, one forward and one aft, and the gunports on the large ship were open, the cannon muzzles protruding. The decks of all three ships were lined with armed men.

"It appears," Richard said, "that the corsair commander has plans for our little settlement here. And apparently he is intending to launch his attack at dusk, when it will be more difficult for anyone on shore to see what he's up to—otherwise he wouldn't be taking his time the way he seems to be."

Adam Burrows smiled. "They can attack at midnight for all we care—we'll still have a surprise or two in store for them," he said.

He and Richard left the fort with Colonel Nettleton in charge and Major Prescott in command of the artillery unit. Richard led the way to the inlet where the *Eliza* was hidden, and as they came on board they found the militiamen eager for battle.

Suddenly there was a rustling noise in the woods behind them, and several muskets were immediately trained in that direction. To Richard's surprise, however, it was Roaring Wolf. Apparently the Pequot brave had run all the way upriver, racing the enemy ships, in order not to miss the fighting. Without pausing, he agilely crossed the narrow plank bridge and took a place at the rail.

A few minutes later, still panting from his exertions, he raised a hand in warning.

Richard immediately ordered absolute silence.

The men made no sound and peered through the trees and underbrush of the concealing spit of land as the three corsair vessels quietly slid past on their way upriver. Then, when all three had moved around a bend in the river and were out of sight, Adam Burrows gave a quiet order and the converted merchant vessel moved from her place of refuge out into the middle of the river, where her gunports were raised and her cannon rolled out.

Meanwhile, word had spread through the surrounding areas that the long-awaited battle was about to break out. The settlers accepted the news with their customary calm. People who had resisted innumerable Indian attacks and withstood the threat of still more were not overly disturbed by the prospect of combat with a motley band of river raiders. The frontier had taught the Virginians what the New Englanders, too, had learned — that those who stood on their own feet had the best chance of survival in this primitive land. Here, as in every frontier town, men were endowed with spirit and courage that were not common elsewhere. "The wilderness has its own way of giving men backbone," Captain John Smith, the onetime governor of Jamestown, had said.

Unfortunately — at least as far as Zwingli was concerned — it had given the women backbone, too.

Eliza Dunstable, safe in the house a half mile from the scene of the impending battle, suddenly rebelled against her lot. "For months," she said, "we've done nothing but plan for a confrontation with the French. Now the day has finally arrived, and I'm certainly not going to sit here like a stump, listening to the sound of artillery in the distance, and then wait until tonight to get a secondhand report of what happened from Richard. I intend to see this battle for myself."

Celeste smiled approvingly. "I quite agree," she said and, emulating Eliza, went to a wall peg for her own cloak.

Adella hesitated for a moment, then followed the example set by the other two women.

Zwingli had received instructions from Richard and did his best to obey them. He stood towering before the doorway, his arms crossed. "You ladies are to stay away from the fight," he said.

Eliza smiled at him sweetly. "I appreciate your desire to protect us, Zwingli," she told the giant African, "but my curiosity has gotten the better of me, and I shall take full responsibility with my husband for our behavior." She approached the door, but the giant did not budge.

"I've waited a very long time for the humiliation of Cardinal Mazarin," Celeste said, "and I certainly do not intend to miss this occasion." She stood beside Eliza, her arms also crossed, in challenge to the black man.

But it was not until Adella approached, a determined look in her eyes, that Zwingli sighed ponderously and stood aside to let all three women past. He worked for Adella and would do whatever she desired, regardless of Richard's orders, so it appeared there was no way he could stop these stubborn young women from doing what they wanted to do.

Reduced to the role of a helpless chaperon, Zwingli followed the women as they hurried down the dirt road toward the river, halting at last on a rise just downriver from the fort. They were far too close for comfort to the scene of combat, but the officers in the fort who noticed them had other, more important, matters in mind than the safety of three headstrong young sightseers.

Mark Prescott patiently watched the flotilla sail closer. "We are in luck," he said. "Apparently they are intending to land directly on the wharf, under cover of their guns. They must not see us; their commander is not even elevating his cannon toward our positions."

"It seems to me," Colonel Nettleton replied, "that he's either blind or simply a fool. Is he close enough yet for us to blow him clean out of the water?"

"I'm not certain, Colonel, but I'd sure like to try," Mark answered.

"Permission granted," Nettleton replied. "You may fire at will."

Mark hastily checked the elevation of his six nine-pounders, then ordered a salvo fired. "Aim for the mainmast on the flagship, boys," he said. "Ready."

The gun crews scurried from behind the cannon, and a flaming torch was held near the touchhole of each gun.

"Fire!" he called softly.

The six cannon roared in unison, lurching back several feet from the power of the recoil.

On the *Eliza*, more than a quarter of a mile away, the militiamen grinned as they heard the shots. They had been waiting a long time for the arrival of this moment.

"Hold your fire, lads," Richard called. "We don't want to waste our ammunition. Let him take a beating on his front before we drill his backside!"

The six guns boomed again, and then again, the crews reloading and firing as fast as they could.

Mark was proud of his men, and they did not disappoint him.

The pinnace in the rear had moved in front of the larger ship, apparently trying to join the other smaller vessel and run past the fort, probably to put their men ashore upriver. But three shots hit her as she entered the line of fire, and suddenly the small ship was literally torn asunder as an explosion that was heard for miles echoed through the forest.

It was evident to Major Prescott and Colonel Nettleton, even before the smoke cleared away, that one or more shots had penetrated to the pinnace's powder magazine.

In a moment the remnants of the vessel slipped to the bottom of the river, the few surviving crew members swimming for their lives.

Captain Stephens cursed loudly. He had been led to believe that the English colonists had no idea they were going to be assaulted, but obviously that was not the case. They had been awaiting his approach, lying in ambush, and now they were tearing his force to pieces.

Signaling his remaining pinnace to pick up the survivors, he abandoned all thought of landing at the wharf below the bluff. It would have to wait for another time. He had to get out of range before the deadly guns on shore destroyed his remaining ships. He yelled the order to come about and head back downriver.

Richard's plan was working to perfection, and he was elated. "Now," he told his militiamen, "open fire, lads!" The small six-pounders on the converted merchantman boomed their own greeting to the corsairs.

Clad in her customary battle attire, Gabrielle rushed past Willie Walker toward the side of Captain Stephens. "We're trapped," she shouted.

"And it serves us right," Willie said to himself gloomily.

But Captain Stephens, staring through his glass at the new enemy, refused to panic. "I'm not ready to give up yet," he shouted, then roared with laughter. "These tobacco farmers are clever, I'll hand 'em that. How they learned of our attack is beyond me, but they should've finished us off. Now it's too late." He handed the glass to Gabrielle, then looked at the anxious faces of the crew members who stared up at him from the main deck. "Don't you see it, boys?" he yelled.

They remained silent and confused.

He laughed again. "What are you afraid of? We're nearly out of range of the fort now, and that ship downriver is equipped only with small six-pounders," he said. "We'll stand off long enough to tear her to shreds, then make our escape. Now all hands back to your guns!"

After maneuvering his ship broadside to the channel, Stephens ordered his starboard battery to open fire on the *Eliza*.

There were those who later claimed that the pirate gunners were the equal of the militiamen, but that was not an accurate observation. One of the six-pounders on the *Eliza*, the one farthest aft, was an ancient weapon, unfit for rapid fire. The gunman had just ignited the powder in the touchhole when the gun exploded with a mighty roar, setting off the powder keg next to it as well and instantly killing the gunner.

Eliza, from the bluff, was able to make out what she thought were the figures of Richard and Adam, both standing on the quarterdeck. Then, after the explosion, both of them had vanished from sight. Afraid they had been killed or at the very least badly wounded, she became frantic. It was too much for her to contemplate that she had lost both her husband and her father in the same tragic instant.

Scarcely aware of what she was doing, she picked up her skirts and half ran, half stumbled the short distance down the bluff to the landing. There she climbed into a rowboat and began to wrestle desperately with the heavy oars, trying to get them into position.

She succeeded, but the giant Zwingli appeared and leaped into the boat just as she was casting off. "Where are you going?" he demanded. "Turn back."

Eliza paused, but the current in the rain-swollen river was strong and swift, and the small craft began to move downstream with greater speed.

Although she was the daughter of a shipowner and had spent much of her life on the water, Eliza was confused and half hysterical and could not prevent the drift of the little boat.

By the time Zwingli took the oars, fitted them back into the locks, and seated himself amidships, the craft had moved well out into the river and had increased its speed. Knowing little about the sea and even less about how to control the movements of a boat, Zwingli struggled furiously to turn the little boat around, only to lose one of the oars overboard.

In the meantime, Stephens's nine-pounders were still raking the colonial brig, and the sea battle was drifting downriver from the fort. The remaining pinnace, following in the larger ship's wake, was less fortunate and was still being pounded by Mark Prescott's guns.

The men on board Stephens's ship were concentrating so hard on the battle that they failed to notice the small rowboat that was overtaking them.

But Gabrielle, who happened to look back toward the fort, spotted the craft, and was intrigued by the presence of the blond woman and the giant black man on board. She called Roger's attention to the craft, tugging at his arm and shouting insistently until he turned around.

Stephens realized immediately that the distraught young woman in the boat was intent on reaching the converted merchantman, and it occurred to him that she might be a hostage worth the taking. Besides, his opponent was crippled, and it would be no trouble finishing him off later. So he gave orders to the helmsman, then to Bo'sun Walker. A boat was quickly lowered, and in a matter of minutes the two rowboats were riding side by side, several pirate muskets trained on the two helpless passengers.

In the meantime, the pirate pinnace had managed to escape the guns of the fort and was now rejoining the sea battle downriver, and it also converged on the tiny craft.

To the horror of Mark Prescott and Colonel Nettleton, who watched the incident through their telescopes, Eliza and Zwingli appeared to have been taken on board one of the pirate ships.

Now Stephens signaled to the pinnace to close on the crippled colonial brig and board her. But the colonists' ship, though badly damaged, had three of her guns still in service. Now, when the smaller corsair ship came within her range, she poured out a deadly stream of fire from her remaining six-pounders.

The marksmanship of the militiamen was unerring, and a cheer went up on board as the second pinnace listed heavily to port and began to founder.

Captain Stephens, noting the fate of his companions, decided he had better make his way back downriver with his own vessel intact before it was too dark to navigate. He ordered his crew to crowd on full sail. The ship picked up speed and, beating a course to the far bank of the river, managed to avoid being hit.

In the meantime, the pinnace heeled over onto its side.

Richard Dunstable, who had been knocked off his feet and stunned by the explosion of the defective cannon, had recovered his wits sufficiently to take charge. Some men were about to lower a small boat to pick up survivors from the pirate wreck, but Richard interceded. "First take care of our own wounded," he said. "They should be rowed ashore as soon as possible."

The hull of the pinnace bobbed in the water briefly; then the small vessel slid and sank with a soft, whooshing noise, and all was quiet.

The pirate flagship disappeared around a bend down the river.

Richard watched her as she escaped, and was helpless to pursue. He had won a notable victory, but his heart was heavy because the cost had been high. He himself had received a nasty head wound, and had survived the explosion only because he had been shielded by the mainmast. Adam Burrows, his father-in-law, was not so lucky. He lay dead on the shattered quarterdeck, his sightless eyes staring up at the stars that began to appear in the Virginia sky.

Richard, his head still throbbing from his wound, listened as Mark Prescott explained how Eliza had seemingly lost her wits and run down the bluff toward the river. Relating the story in a matter-of-fact voice, Mark recounted how the woman had boarded the rowboat and had been joined by Zwingli. He told how the pair had started out toward the scene of the tragedy, only to be picked up by the current and swept toward the pirate vessels.

"The pinnace picked them up," Mark said, "a matter of minutes before she was struck by your batteries and foundered."

"You're quite certain it was the pinnace and not the larger corsair ship that took them in?" Richard demanded.

Mark thought for a moment before replying. "If my life depended on my answer," he said, "I'd say I believed it was the pinnace that took them in. The distance was deceptive, what with the smoke of battle and the coming of dusk, but as nearly as I can judge what happened, they were captured and taken on board the pinnace."

Colonel Nettleton, who had been silent, felt compelled to add his opinion. "To the best of my belief," he said, "you've been given an accurate account of what happened, Richard. I was standing next to Mark in the fort, and I had the same view he had. I remember seeing the rowboat being approached by a boatful of pirates, then the pinnace temporarily blocked the view. When it moved past, I did not see them again. I can only assume they were brought on board."

Adella Prescott was wide-eyed and solemn. "They were in a far better position to judge than Celeste and I were," she said. "We were on top of the bluff, pressing close behind some trees to avoid being hit by gunfire from the ships. Then Eliza screamed and began to race down to the water. We didn't have a clear view of her after she and Zwingli put out in the boat."

Richard was silent and pressed a hand over his eyes.

"I know how you must feel," Adella said. "You're blaming yourself because you saw to your own wounded first instead of searching for survivors."

Richard nodded.

The girl looked at him sympathetically, her gaze unwavering and her voice gentle. "All my life," she said, "I've heard of the strange and terrible things that happen in battle. It seems to me what took place today was just that—something no one could foresee and certainly no one could help. It's wrong of you to blame yourself, Richard. We all would have done the same thing in your place."

Richard knew the advice was good, and tried hard to accept it. It was wrong, he realized, for him to shoulder the blame for the death of Eliza, and he knew that nothing would be accomplished by torturing himself.

He found Dempster Chaney and asked him to round up some volunteers to search the riverbanks for Eliza's and Zwingli's bodies. But he had little hope that either would be found; by now their lifeless bodies would have been carried out to sea.

Though numbed by grief and shock, Richard knew he still had a duty to perform. He walked to the commander's tent, where he was told Celeste was waiting.

Sitting erect in a straight-backed chair, she was wet-eyed but composed. During the brief months of her marriage to Adam Burrows, she had learned to appreciate his wisdom, his forthright nature, and the gentleness that lay behind his stern devotion to duty. She had always admired and respected him, and in the past few weeks she had even come to love him. It was an emotion that, despite her worldly experience, was still new to her—and now she felt cut off, adrift.

She looked up at Richard as he entered, and managed a wan smile. "I've been expecting you," she said. "I guess all we can do is exchange condolences."

He felt responsible for her, and replied quietly. "What can I do for you, Celeste?"

She shrugged weakly. "I can think of nothing," she said. "Even though Adam was much older than I, somehow I never thought of what I'd do when he died. I suppose I've inherited the house in New Haven; but I can't even think of that now, any more than I can think of what will happen to the business."

"The Claytons and I will operate the company," he told her. "There'll be nothing for you to do other than collect your share of the profits. And don't worry—I'll see to it that you get what's coming to you."

"Thank you," she said, bowing her head. "I knew I could depend on you."

He cleared his throat. "Do you feel strong enough to attend the funeral tomorrow?"

"Of course," Celeste replied without hesitation. "I'd be derelict in my duty if I failed to give him the respect that he deserves."

Admiring her strength, but unable to put his feelings into words, Richard reached out and touched her shoulder.

As she felt his touch, she looked up at him, then slowly rose to her feet. "We didn't plan it this way," she said. "It never crossed my mind that the day would come when I'd be forced to lean on you."

"Lean," he said. "That's why I'm here."

"I hope you won't be afraid to lean on me in return," she said softly. "It's the very least I can do for you. And by helping, I'll feel less useless."

They stood close together, and both were comforted by the knowledge that the other was not grieving alone.

Richard squared his shoulders, and then his strong arm encircled Celeste's tiny waist. They emerged together from the tent, solemn but in control of their feelings. Their whole world had changed in a matter of a few short hours.

Contrary to the belief of those who had viewed the incident from the shore, Eliza Dunstable and Zwingli were very much alive. After having been taken on board Stephens's vessel, both had immediately been put in chains and thrown into the dark, filthy hold. Now, late the next afternoon, both were shepherded to the quarterdeck, where Captain Stephens was guiding his vessel down Chesapeake Bay toward the safe, open waters of the Atlantic.

At first he paid no attention to the pair; but then a huge, red-haired man — apparently the bo'sun, Eliza thought — broke his concentration.

"Here be the prisoners we took, Cap'n," he said.

Stephens looked at Eliza and smiled, his white teeth sparkling through his black, scraggly beard. Then he quickly surveyed Zwingli and nodded in approval. "I never thought I'd see another man your size, Willie," he said. "Treat him well and see if you can't persuade him to join us. You'd make a ferocious pair in battle."

Willie grinned and gestured to Zwingli. "Come along to my quarters, and we'll have us a little talk."

Zwingli, however, made no move and planted his feet apart stubbornly, as far as the chains would allow.

Eliza felt nothing but numbness and a vague sense of hatred. She did not care about her own fate. "Go with him, Zwingli," she urged, "and hear what he has to offer. It may be to your advantage."

The giant accepted her word, nodded, and accompanied Walker down to the main deck.

Roger Stephens now studied her in earnest. Her blond hair was tousled, and her dress was dirty and water-soaked, but in spite of these disadvantages, he realized, she was exceptionally attractive. Her figure, although fuller than Gabrielle's, was equally pleasing, and she seemed endowed with a natural grace that was completely lacking in the other woman. "You sound like a woman with brains," he said. "I applaud your decision."

She felt his eyes traveling slowly up and down her body, pausing to examine her breasts. For an instant she wanted to lunge forward and strike him, but her chains weighed heavily around her ankles and wrists, and her anger quickly faded to a dull, helpless ache.

When he reached out a brawny hand to stroke her shoulder

and arm, she did not flinch, but instead stared straight back at him, her expression stonelike. Though still numb with the shock of battle, the deaths of her husband and father, and her own capture, Eliza felt a dizzying rush of memories fill her head as she returned the pirate's gaze. For some reason she thought of New Haven and her father. Then, painfully, she thought of Richard, and shut her eyes against the tears. His memory did not matter now, she told herself, for it was all too apparent he had died loving another woman. She tried to dismiss the image of his kissing Celeste's hand, but the scene kept returning vividly to her mind. She *would* rid herself of that memory, she vowed, and from now on focus all her attentions on survival.

When she opened her eyes, she returned Roger's gaze with renewed determination.

Stephens was at first puzzled, then heartened by her reaction. Rarely had he encountered such a fearlessly practical woman. She seemed to recognize the price she would be required to pay in return for her life, and she seemed prepared to pay it. He'd grown tired of Gabrielle and her moodiness, her pouting, and the scenes that she so enjoyed making. Perhaps it was time for him to replace her with another woman.

Stephens grinned, then deliberately hauled Eliza closer.

Silently gritting her teeth, she made no objection. All she saw was Richard lying dead on the deck of the converted merchantman. And her father—dead, too.

"You know how I earn my living?" Stephens demanded roughly.

"I can guess," Eliza replied.

"And you don't mind?" he wanted to know.

She shrugged. "Why should I?"

Stephens chuckled. "If you live up to your promise," he said, "there's a good chance you and I could form a very interesting partnership. You'd like that, wouldn't you?"

Again she shrugged. She was a hard wench, he told himself. He was in luck. "Remove her chains," he ordered.

Turning over the watch to his mate, Stephens took the woman's arm and escorted her to his cabin. Eliza, quickly regaining her wits, was astonished by the size and luxury of the cabin.

Stephens slept in a huge four-poster bed, the tops of the posts having been cut off so the bed could fit in the low-ceilinged room. A section of the cabin toward the stern windows was used as a parlor, and another area was obviously for dining. Although she had seen many captain's cabins on her father's various ships, she had never imagined anything as sumptuous as this could exist.

Roger Stephens was watching her carefully, and he chuckled. "You like all this, eh?"

"I—I've never seen anything like it," she answered.

"If you please me, woman, you can share these quarters," he said. "I'm needed on the quarterdeck now, and can't return here until we're safely in the open sea. That will give you plenty of time to get ready for me." He gestured toward a wardrobe that stood against a far bulkhead. "You'll find everything you'll need in there," he said. "The rest is up to you— and your imagination."

Before she could reply, he was gone. She heard a bolt clank, and knew she had been locked into the cabin.

Alone now, Eliza shuddered, then stood still for a long time, her fingernails digging into the flesh of her hands as she curbed a desire to break into tears.

It would avail her nothing to cry, she told herself. She had to face reality. But what could she do?

She was on the verge of becoming a pirate captain's trollop, she thought bitterly. But was that so bad? She did not have to expect him to be faithful, or even kind.

Eliza stared at the stern windows. It would be easy enough to slip out, and end her problems that way. . . .

She dismissed the thought and looked around the cabin, and her gaze settled on the wardrobe. Out of curiosity she opened the door and inspected the contents. Apparently she was not the first woman Captain Stephens had tried as a partner. There were dozens of silk dresses lying in a neat pile, and boxes of cosmetics in every imaginable variety. No doubt it had all been taken from the wardrobes of his ship's victims; yet it was clear everything had been chosen with great care. All the dresses were the most daring fashions—not a single high neckline among the lot—and there were dozens of lacy peignoirs, most of them quite indecent.

Eliza shrank from the thought of donning such attire, but it was an indescribable pleasure just to be out of the wet, stinking dress she had worn in the ship's hold. She picked out the least daring dress in the wardrobe. That, however, was the wrong approach, she realized. She had been around seamen all of her life, and well knew what her fate would be if Captain Stephens chose not to protect her: she would be handed over to his crew and passed from one sailor to the next like a common slut— if she wasn't fast enough to jump overboard first.

Eliza delayed the inevitable by tinkering with the cosmetics. She painted her face carefully, paying special attention to her eyes and her lips.

Then, steeling herself, she donned a black peignoir surrounded by a froth of lace and slipped her feet into a pair of absurdly high-heeled slippers she found on the floor of the wardrobe. When she put them on, however, she realized that she could not walk naturally in them. She was forced to take tiny, mincing steps in order to keep her balance. That, she reflected as she discarded the shoes, should satisfy Captain Stephens, but it would not suit her purposes.

She was thunderstruck when she stared at her reflection in a looking glass attached to the bulkhead. The brazen creature who stared at her in wide-eyed astonishment bore scant resemblance to the Eliza Dunstable she had been. When she started to laugh hysterically, the scarlet-lipped hussy in the glass seemed to mock her, and she hastily turned away.

But she quickly composed herself, not forgetting she still had one task left. Methodically searching the cosmetic boxes, she at last found what she wanted—a small, heavy perfume bottle. Splashing a little of the liquid on her forearms, she poured the remainder into another bottle, then placed the empty bottle on the floor. Using one of the wooden cosmetic boxes as a hammer, she struck the bottle, breaking it into several pieces. She chose one piece and carefully slit open a seam in the cuff of her peignoir. Then she inserted the glass shard snugly into the cuff, making sure she could remove it quickly if necessary. After she had finished this, she picked up the rest of the broken glass and deposited it in the back of the wardrobe.

She was giving herself to Captain Stephens because she had no real choice, she reminded herself—but she would never trust any man again, for as long as she lived. She fingered the deadly sliver in her cuff, assured that she could kill him whenever she chose.

Moving to the stern windows, she looked into the half light of early evening. She could not see land anywhere, and the roll of the vessel told her that the ship had entered the open waters of the Atlantic.

All she could do now was wait. She took a bottle of rum she had noticed earlier and, finding two large goblets, poured generous quantities of the pale liquor into both. She sat on the bed and forced herself to drink. Shuddering as the raw liquor warmed her insides, she swallowed again.

A short time later, when she heard the sound of Captain Stephens's key unlocking the cabin door, she was drunk enough to kill him and not regret it for a moment. She realized she was desperate and probably foolish, but she had no one else to look after her interests. She fingered the glass shard and braced herself.

Stephens turned and locked the door behind him as he entered. Smiling at her, he walked over to the dining table and picked up the goblet of rum she had poured him. Sniffing at it first, he emptied it in two gulps, then offered her the bottle.

"No, thank you," Eliza said. "I've already helped myself."

Stephens laughed heartily. "Aye, you're a hard wench," he said. "I can tell by looking at you. Tell me, have you ever killed a man?"

Eliza, perhaps because of the rum, answered truthfully. "Yes, I killed an Indian once."

"I knew it," he said. "I never should have picked you up. Or else I should toss you overboard to the sharks now, before you put a knife in my back."

Eliza averted her eyes from his searching gaze. She heard his footsteps approach across the cabin, then stop. She looked up.

He was holding a cocked pistol in front of her face. But he was offering it to her, handle first.

"Here," he said. "It's loaded, I assure you. And primed. If you're going to kill me, do it now."

Eliza looked up at him. He was not joking, it appeared.

"Take it," he said.

She took the pistol and slowly raised it, aiming at his chest.

"But before you shoot me," he said, "you had better think of what you'll do next."

Eliza realized he was right. She might just as well shoot herself. The result would be the same—and probably a lot quicker and less painful. She lowered the pistol.

"Ah, I see you've come to your senses," he said. "Now, listen to me, wench—"

"My name is Eliza," she whispered.

"Eliza. I'm willing to make life very easy for you."

The day's tensions finally overwhelming her, Eliza burst into tears. She fell into Stephens's arms, and he held her.

"There now," he said. "You'll not come to harm—I'll make sure of that. And who knows? You may even come to like it here."

"You'll do very nicely, Eliza," Stephens muttered early the next morning. "Give you a week or two, and you'll be right at home." He chuckled as he sat up in bed. "And we've got to get you some more clothes so I can show you off to the crew. I want my buccaneers to turn green with envy when they see the wench who is all mine."

He turned toward her. His large, hairy hand stroked her hair, her cheek, then moved down to her neck, where it lingered. The fingers spread, then tightened.

"Stop! You're choking me!" Eliza gasped.

The pressure eased, but only slightly.

"I almost forgot," Stephens said, his tone deceptively kind. "You wouldn't happen to know why my ships sailed into a trap the other day, would you?"

"I—I know nothing," Eliza lied. "I'm only a woman. I was just trying to help my husband. They didn't tell me anything."

The pressure increased again.

"Who didn't tell you anything?"

"The—the commanders of the militia," Eliza gasped. "All they told us was that they knew there was going to be an attack. They didn't even say by whom."

Stephens released his grip. "I didn't think you knew anything," he said. "And to tell you the truth, I don't care. But still, if I find out you're lying—"

He didn't finish the sentence. Eliza breathed a secret sigh of relief that she and Zwingli had agreed they would both plead ignorance if questioned by the pirates.

Stephens dressed hurriedly and stamped out of the cabin, announcing as he left that he was going to the quarterdeck and that he'd see to it she was served breakfast.

Eliza managed to doze for a time, and when she heard the cabin door open and shut, she assumed it was a crew member bringing her breakfast. She opened her eyes and suddenly sat bolt upright, drawing the silken sheets around her to conceal her nakedness. Standing inside the closed door was a slender, red-haired woman in an off-the-shoulder scarlet dress. Her eyes blazing, she held a long, curved knife in one hand.

"Damn you," Gabrielle cried angrily. "You think you're so clever, don't you, stealing my man from me. I'll show you what I do to a thief!"

Before Eliza had a chance to understand what was happening, the woman threw herself at the bed, the sharp knife blade pointing directly at her victim.

At the last instant, life suddenly returned to Eliza's body, and she rolled out of the way of the dangerous blade. Then, all at once, the danger was ended.

To Eliza's astonishment, Gabrielle dangled in midair, squirming and cursing as she was held in the firm grasp of Zwingli, her knife-hand pinned behind her back.

"I was sent here with your breakfast," the giant said, "fortunately for you." He continued to hold the thrashing, furiously angry Gabrielle.

The uproar was so great that Captain Stephens returned to the cabin himself to find out the cause of the disturbance.

Zwingli explained how he had arrived just in time to rescue Eliza. In the meantime, Gabrielle redoubled her loud cursing, and Eliza, rather than compete, fell silent.

Roger Stephens was so amused that he laughed until tears came to his eyes. "I knew you'd be useful," he told Zwingli. "Learn all you can about ships, and you will be bo'sun before you know it. For the present, put the wench down, but keep an eye on her. I wouldn't put it past her to try to knife me."

Zwingli, keeping the knife, reluctantly released his grip on Gabrielle, who made no attempt to straighten her dress, but glared first at Eliza and then at Roger as she pushed back a mop of unruly red hair.

"I never knew you were the jealous type," Roger said.

Gabrielle replied with a string of violent oaths, then spat on the floor of the cabin. "If you will not let me murder her, I challenge her to a pirate duel. By your own rules, she cannot refuse."

Stephens was silent for a moment, staring at Eliza. He had been secretly worried about the morale of his crew, afraid that they would become mutinous because of the defeat they had suffered at the hands of the English colonists. Certain that Admiral de Bosquette would order another assault, he knew that the spirits of his men had to be restored, and that a thwarted Gabrielle would do nothing but provoke trouble. Besides, she was right: By the rules of his ship, any officer—and Gabrielle was considered one of his mates—had the right to challenge any of the crew to a duel, and to pick the weapons. Stephens had found this a very effective way to promote discipline and prevent insubordination, and had taken advantage of it many times himself. He made up his mind.

"She is right," he said to Eliza. "On this ship there is only one way to settle an affair of honor, and that is through a duel."

Eliza stared at him in anger, but he simply shrugged.

Gabrielle stopped cursing and smiled maliciously at Eliza. "I choose knives, to the death."

The cabin was silent for a moment, as if everyone was waiting for Eliza's reply. But she said nothing.

"The sea is calm today," Stephens said, "so you'll fight this afternoon. Be prepared."

Eliza felt sure she had sunk into a nightmare from which there was no escape. Within a matter of hours she had been made a widow, slept with a pirate, been nearly choked to death, and now she was being forced to defend her life in a duel with a reckless vixen.

The events of the day became increasingly curious. Wee Willie Walker came to the cabin, accompanied by Zwingli, and urged her to wear the tight-fitting breeches and the shirt he had brought with him. "It be this way, ma'am," he told her. "I know Gabrielle, and she's a witch incarnate. If ye wear them breeches and the shirt, with the sleeves and the collar cut off, there will be nothin' for her to grab and twist when she gets to wrestlin' with ye. I know her, see, and I put nothin' past her."

The pair waited expectantly.

"Turn around," Eliza ordered, surprised at the authority in her own voice.

She quickly discarded her clothes and donned the shirt and breeches. The breeches fitted snugly, and the shirt was so tight that she had to leave the top buttons open in order to allow her arms to move. So much for modesty, she told herself cynically.

The two giants inspected her critically, and Willie nodded approvingly.

"That's it," he said. "Be sure ye get rid of your earrings and bracelet, because she could get her claws on those and do ye real damage."

She quickly removed the earrings and the bracelet.

"Don't wear shoes," Zwingli said. "Shoes make you slip on the deck."

"That's good advice," Willie added. "See that ye heed it."

"Why are you being so kind to me?" Eliza asked him.

"Because I hate that she-devil as though she were Beelzebub himself," Wee Willie Walker replied vigorously. "And I'll do blame near anything to see her beaten. Now listen and heed what I say to ye. She's goin' to be in a mighty rush to strike the first blows. Let her. See to it that ye dodge and move aside and stay out of reach of her knife. Watch for your chance, and when the time comes, put your blade into her, hilt-deep."

The thought of committing cold-blooded murder disturbed Eliza, and her look said as much.

"It's either kill or be killed," the bo'sun said. "That's the way o' things in the corsair world."

Zwingli nodded in solemn agreement.

The attitude of the African convinced Eliza that she was being given sound advice. She had known Zwingli only as a faithful retainer of Mark Prescott's, who had devoted himself to the protection of Adella. Now, apparently, he had transferred that devotion to her. And being well accustomed to the ways of the world, he had neither protested nor tried to struggle against his captivity by the buccaneers. Accepting the twists and turns of fate as normal and natural, he did what he could to improve his own lot. There was a lesson to be learned from him, Eliza told herself.

When he and Willie withdrew, she tested her footing on the deck in the cabin, and discovering that she was inclined to slip somewhat, she searched the cabin for something sticky. The tarry oakum between the deck planks overhead served her purpose, and she rubbed some of it on the soles of her feet. Then, strictly for the sake of her own morale, she washed off the cosmetics she had applied the night before and splashed her face with cold water from a washbasin. Then she carefully combed out her hair and tied it in a queue behind her neck.

She drank a small quantity of water but touched no alcohol and ate no food, in accordance with the advice Wee Willie Walker and Zwingli had given her.

Then, as she waited to be summoned to the deck, a subtle transformation began to take place within her. She was no longer a lady, the daughter of New Haven's most prominent merchant, nor was she the wife of a Cavalier baronet who had made a glittering name for himself in the New World. She was a woman of flesh and blood, and her identity, her social standing, her entire past life, did not matter. Only one thing had any importance to her now—the desire to stay alive.

She thought of her numerous trips into the wilderness. She had grown up on the edge of the forest and felt at home there. Funny she had never thought of it this way before. The many dangers that lurked in the wilderness were second nature to her. That attitude, she now knew, was what had preserved her thus far. She was engaging in just such a journey now, on board the pirate ship—a journey through the wilderness. She could not afford the luxury of thinking or acting like a lady. She had to remember the corsair creed, the law of the wilderness, at all times: kill or be killed.

A tap sounded at the door, and Wee Willie Walker stood in the frame. "They be ready for ye now," he said, "and don't be scared none by them animals." He grinned at her and extended a huge hand.

Eliza unhesitatingly held out her own small hand in return, and in some mysterious way that she didn't recognize, their friendship was sealed.

Willie reached into his belt and drew out a pearl-handled knife. The point was very sharp, and the straight blade was about six to eight inches in length. "Here," he said, "use this knife. It has a good balance, and your grip won't slip from the hilt. Those things are important."

Eliza was familiar with hunting knives, and as she took the weapon from him, she weighed and balanced it in her hand. It seemed very light, and she was pleased. "Thanks, Willie," she said. "I'll try not to disgrace you or your knife."

"Ye shall win the day from that witch," he said. "I'm sure of it." Not waiting for a reply, he started toward the main deck.

She followed him, her bare feet silent on the wooden planking.

The ship was sailing southwest and had covered a good distance since its flight from Virginia. Now a warm sun shone in a cloudless sky, and a balmy breeze blew from the southeast.

As Eliza made her appearance on deck, pandemonium broke loose. The crew members who had heard of her but not yet seen her instantly decided that she was well worth their captain's attentions. Her tight-fitting sailor's trousers and shirt left little to their imagination, and her golden yellow hair, pulled tight behind her head, shone brilliantly in the bright sunlight.

The roars of approval and the shrill whistles of the men sent a chill up the back of Eliza's neck. She noticed Roger Stephens, looking dead serious as he watched the scene from his quarterdeck; then she riveted her full attention on her opponent.

Gabrielle had not bothered to change out of the off-the-shoulder flounced red dress she had worn that morning. She gripped her long knife in her hand, and her face was twisted into an expression of venomous hatred. She spat contemptuously when she saw the other woman.

Roger Stephens stepped forward. "Hear me out," he said. "This is a duel to the death. No quarter will be given, and none will be allowed. The fight will end only when one of the combatants is driven overboard or killed. Am I understood?"

"Every word is clear," Gabrielle replied in a hissing voice. "I heed you now as I heed you in all things."

The members of the crew realized she was mocking him and dared to roar with laughter.

Eliza waited until the laughter subsided. "I understand," she said quietly.

The tone of her response startled the crew. She sounded confident, absolutely sure of herself, and the men gaped at her and studied her more intently. Here was a woman to marvel at—beautiful, silent, and fearless. The wiser of the crewmen immediately understood the reasons for Gabrielle's jealousy.

Wee Willie Walker and Zwingli stood together near the mainmast. Both were armed with belaying pins, and it occurred to Eliza that they were prepared to intervene in the event that the crew became unruly. But she had other things to think of.

"You may begin whenever you please," Stephens said.

The words scarcely passed his lips before Gabrielle sprang into action. Her features contorted with rage so that she resembled a wild animal more than a young woman, she sprang forward, bounding across the deck toward her opponent, her knife poised in one upraised hand.

Eliza felt remarkably calm. In the back of her mind she remembered the advice Richard had given her: "If you become involved in a fight, always keep your head. Your enemies are more likely than not to lose their tempers, and when they do, they lose their judgment at the same time." Now, standing unmoving, Eliza watched the other woman racing toward her.

Timing her response with the expertise of one long accustomed to swordplay, Eliza waited until it was almost too late, then nimbly stepped to one side just as Gabrielle reached for her with one hand and swept her knife in a downward arc with the other.

The knife cut harmlessly through the air, and Eliza gave the woman a little shove as she rushed past, sending her sprawling.

The corsairs cheered lustily.

That sound aroused Gabrielle's ire still more. Her face flushed, she rose to her feet and twirled, expecting to find her opponent directly behind her. Instead, Eliza stood fifteen feet away, her hands on her hips, smiling quietly.

The superiority she expressed in that smile was maddening, and Gabrielle, already out of control, responded exactly as her opponent had hoped she would.

Cursing loudly, the red-haired woman lunged forward again, heedless of her own safety and bent only on destroying her foe.

Again Eliza sidestepped, and again the audience cheered her.

Gabrielle, snarling like a wounded wild animal, stopped for a moment and glared at Eliza. She charged again, this time flailing the knife through the air before her, back and forth, up and down, while her free hand worked convulsively, groping for her foe's eyes and hair.

Eliza, backing and dodging, decided she had waited long enough.

Steadying herself, she avoided one more wild slash by her opponent, then lunged forward and caught hold of Gabrielle's knife hand at the wrist. At the same time, gripping her own knife hard, she took a deep breath and struck.

She felt the blade cutting into flesh.

Gabrielle's scream of pain and rage sounded like the cry of a demon from hell. The knife dropped from her hand onto the deck. Wrenching her own weapon free, Eliza relaxed her grip with her other hand.

Gabrielle staggered backward, the blood hardly visible on her dress. Her eyes glazed, she stumbled against the railing that surrounded the deck. For a moment it seemed as if she would collapse right there; then she turned and, before anyone could reach her side, toppled overboard.

As she struck the water, the entire crew ran to the rail. Then, seemingly out of nowhere, two long, silver-gray shapes appeared and the water thrashed noisily. But the moving ship had already left the grisly sight far astern, and all that could be heard was the creaking of the masts, and the wind in the rigging.

Numbed by the shock of the experience, Eliza stood on the deck and stared at the spot at the rail where her foe had disappeared.

The crew members were silent, too. The tragedy had developed so swiftly, so unexpectedly, that it had caught them unawares, and no man was cheering now.

Wee Willie Walker moved forward and took the knife from Eliza's hand.

His motion broke the spell. Captain Stephens descended from the quarterdeck and lifted Eliza off her feet, giving her a hard, lingering kiss.

Roger's display of raw passion in the presence of his crew, coming on the heels of her victory over Gabrielle, caught Eliza by surprise. Somehow it didn't seem to bother her, though. The one thought that filled her mind was the realization that she had survived the ordeal and was still alive. After spending a lifetime of weighing the consequences of everything she did and accepting responsibility for all of her acts, Eliza found herself giving in to the sheer release, the sheer exhilaration of the moment. A flood of feelings surged through her. It was a beautiful, warm day, and she was alive!

Roger Stephens quickly realized the change that had come over her. She seemed to collapse in his arms, as if surrendering to him. Still holding her off her feet, he turned and started toward the cabin.

The men came to life and cheered loudly. The blond woman's triumph over Gabrielle was all that was needed to make her a heroine in their eyes. They had had a good day's entertainment, and the dramatic outcome of the duel had wiped away all thought of the crushing defeat they had suffered in Virginia.

Spurred by Adella Prescott, who had conceived the idea, volunteers cut and shaped logs with which they built a long, narrow building that contained a small room at one end, a kitchen at the other, and a long open space in between. Located within the stockade on the bluff, this crude structure was the county's first hospital.

Eleven militiamen had been wounded in the battle with the corsairs, and all of them were moved from the tents into the new building, where they were placed under the care of Robert Barnes, a physician who had retired the previous year to his son's nearby plantation.

Adella immediately volunteered her services as a nurse to assist the capable but overworked doctor, and Celeste Burrows promptly joined her there.

That night Richard tried to dissuade Celeste from accepting these new responsibilities.

"There was a small brig docked at one of the plantations upriver. We're sending her up the coast to alert every colony to the danger of possible attack by French mercenaries," he said. "If you wish, you may go home to New Haven on board her."

Celeste shook her head. "New Haven may be home to you," she said, "but I don't yet regard it as such, even though I've inherited the house in which Adam and I lived. I don't know the Claytons all that well, even though Tom Clayton was my husband's partner; and although I've met a great many residents of the town, I didn't live there long enough to become really friendly with any of them. You're my one real tie to New Haven, Richard. When you decide to go there, I'll go, too. Until then, I prefer to stay where you are."

She was clinging to him, Richard knew, but he sympathized with her and was willing to accept the responsibility for her welfare. Still loyal to the memory of his father-in-law, he owed it to Adam to take care of her, he told himself. But there was more to his motives than that.

He felt lost without Eliza, and for the first time in his life he knew the meaning of loneliness. Celeste was a lovely woman, warm and sympathetic, and Richard had felt close to her ever since they had engaged in their brief affair more than two years ago. That bond, combined with the family ties they had formed, brought them closer together in this time of sorrow.

To the surprise of the Virginians, who had thought of her as a great lady, above soiling her hands with hard, physical labor, Celeste attended to her duties at the hospital with great diligence. Splitting the hours between early morning and mid-evening with Adella so that one or the other was always on duty, she looked after her patients with an almost fiercely attentive care. No chore was too menial for her, and at no time did she complain about the work or the long hours she spent at the hospital. As Adella pointed out to Richard when he came to visit his wounded comrades, Celeste seemed almost possessed by her work.

For all practical purposes Richard had now assumed full command of the New Haven militia. In this capacity he held long conferences with Colonel Nettleton and Major Prescott, often stopping to drink a glass of sack with Adella at the conclusion of their meetings. The contrasts between Adella and Celeste were marked. Adella was shy, almost retiring, in his presence; and although it was evident that she admired him and enjoyed his company, at no time did she take the initiative in their conversations. He suspected, however, that she was more like her brother than it appeared on the surface. Mark was aggressive and firm, and surely Adella's crusading fervor on behalf of the hospital revealed a similar tough-mindedness. And the expression that appeared in her eyes, particularly when the subject of the pirate raids was raised, led Richard to believe that there was a fierce fire smoldering within her.

Most of Richard's waking hours were now devoted to his military duties, and he met daily with the garrison's officers. "From what I know of the temperament of the French," he said, "they won't accept the defeat of their mercenaries calmly. Their pride will demand that the buccaneers raid us again, and they will assume that we will meet them the same way again."

"That's all the more reason," Colonel Nettleton replied, "why we must not relax our vigilance."

"As I review the tactics we employed on the last occasion," Richard said, "I am convinced that we made one crucial error. We assumed that a lightly armed brig converted to a warship would be able to halt the enemy. That was a mistake, as our casualty list shows, and as is further evidenced by the fact that the corsairs escaped."

"What do you suggest we do instead?" Mark asked.

"Our basic thinking was accurate, it seems to me," Richard said. "But we failed because we didn't fully exploit our natural advantages."

Those present looked at one another blankly.

"I'm not sure I understand the point you're trying to make," Colonel Nettleton said.

"The forest itself is our greatest ally," Richard said. "Not only would we be able to conceal our limited number of cannon in it, but it could also provide a perfect cover for our troops. And it can't be sunk or blown up or even damaged by enemy fire."

Mark chuckled. "That's certainly true," he said.

"Are you suggesting," Colonel Nettleton said in his slow drawl, "that instead of stationing one of our ships behind the enemy, we deploy our artillery in the forest itself?"

"Exactly," Richard replied. "It's such an obvious solution that it didn't occur to us earlier. But I think that was mainly because the last time the pirates attacked, the river was abnormally high; we knew they could stay near the opposite shore and avoid sailing too close to our guns. The next time it probably won't be so high. And even if it is, we can block the channel opposite our guns so that they have to come within range."

"That's easy enough," said one of Nettleton's lieutenants. "Just anchor a few snags out there. They'd never know the difference."

"That's an excellent idea," Richard said. "Furthermore, I propose that we try to beg or borrow some additional cannon from any colony that's willing to part with them."

"That won't be easy, I can assure you," Colonel Nettleton said. "They're hard enough to get under normal circumstances. And the brig we're sending out to spread the word is going to create alarm in every city up and down the coast. Every commander worth his salt is going to assume that he himself will be the object of the next attack by French mercenaries. No, sir. Guns are just too scarce this side of the Atlantic, and every militia unit that has one is going to hold on to it."

"But surely we could reason with them," Richard said. "The French aren't going to attack any of the cities up north—that would accomplish nothing. If they sailed into Boston harbor, say, they'd immediately arouse the opposition of every other colony, every other town in the area, like a hive of bees. That's why they'll attack Virginia again. The people and the towns here are spread far apart, so they can stamp them out one at a time, using a relatively small force. And Virginia is sufficiently remote from New England that the people up north aren't likely to be seriously concerned when they learn of an attack here."

"And for that very reason," Colonel Nettleton persisted, "they're unlikely to give up any of their precious cannon for the defense of a bunch of tobacco farmers."

Mark Prescott sighed. "If only the colonies could be taught to stand together against a common foe," he said.

"The day will come," Richard told him, "when a clear danger will threaten all of us. In the meantime, unfortunately, I suppose Colonel Nettleton is right. We'll have to plan our defense here with the cannon we already have."

The Virginia lieutenant who had spoken earlier coughed and stood up. "Sir," he said, "assuming, then, that the buccaneers will attack Virginia, how can we be sure that it will be here again, and not somewhere else?"

Richard ran his fingers through his hair and exhaled a deep breath. "We can't be sure," he said. "But I'm betting it will be here. Other than Jamestown, which is too well guarded by sea, we're the only obstacle standing in their way; so if they get rid of us, they'll have clear sailing. But that's not my main reason for believing we'll be their target again."

All eyes in the room were on Richard.

"If my guess is right," he continued, "the French commander, who we have excellent reason to believe has been ordered by Cardinal Mazarin to attack here, will try more than once before he'll admit to Mazarin that he's failed. Mazarin does not accept failure like a gentleman."

For the rest of the meeting, the officers weighed and discussed at length Richard's plan to station a force in the forest along the riverbank. Ultimately the idea was adopted to move the guns from the brig to the heavy underbrush near the narrowest part of the river, and to block the channel opposite the guns, as Colonel Nettleton's lieutenant had suggested.

"I'm afraid the scheme isn't foolproof," Richard told Adella one night as they sat over glasses of sack following a meeting, "but it's the best we're able to manage."

"You seem very certain that we're going to be attacked again," she said, "and I'm sure you have good reason to think so. But we haven't very many men, and some of the Virginia militia have gone home for the spring planting. Do you really think we have a good chance of achieving another victory?"

Richard shrugged and smiled. "War," he said, "is something of a game—a deadly, bloody game played for very high stakes, and a game whose outcome is often in doubt until the last shot is fired. I hope we'll win, and we're doing our best with the limited forces we have to ensure that we do win. But I wouldn't even attempt to answer your question until I see how large a force the enemy commits to battle, and how he intends to use that force."

VI

"**Y**OU deserve a reward," Roger Stephens told Eliza as they sat together at supper in his cabin one evening. "You've not only rid me and this ship of Gabrielle, but you've revitalized the crew."

Eliza thought she had already been amply rewarded. She had been given Gabrielle's old cabin—although she now spent most of her time in the much more spacious captain's quarters—and had been somewhat shocked when Stephens had presented her with all the other woman's belongings, including her appreciable wardrobe and substantial quantities of expensive jewelry.

Eliza felt only a twinge of guilt at acquiring this property, despite the fact that she was directly responsible for Gabrielle's death. After all, she told herself, Gabrielle had begun the fight.

Even so, Eliza recognized that her outlook toward life was changing drastically. She now lived simply to survive to the next moment and to keep herself from going crazy. She refused to burden her soul with regrets and feelings of guilt. The gold and diamonds she had acquired may have been worth a small fortune to anyone else on the ship, but to her they were worthless, and she treated them as no more than cheap toys. As for the clothing she had acquired, it was far more flamboyant and revealing than anything she had ever owned, but on a pirate ship modesty and propriety were meaningless. The old Eliza would have been shocked, but the new Eliza calmly accepted what had to be.

She had never in her life been greedy and, if anything, was even less selfish now, mainly because nothing except her life had any worth to her. Gifts were but useless tokens, and for that reason she made no protest when Stephens told her that she deserved a reward.

But Eliza did not suspect that Stephens had unusual ideas of how to go about acquiring a suitable reward. Summoning his mates to a meeting that evening, he spoke to them succinctly. "We're back on the shipping routes to Europe, lads," he said, "and all of you are familiar with these waters. Though eventually we'll have to return to Martinique—or have the whole blasted French Navy on our tails—I'm not in any great rush. The admiral can wait another few days for the bad news; and besides, I have me a hunch that the fishing is good off of Hispaniola this time of year—especially for Spanish galleons."

The corsairs roared their approval, as he had known they would. He was offering them a chance to fill their pockets on the way home, and, like their captain, they were not in a particular hurry to return to Saint Pierre. They all agreed—the opportunity was too great to resist.

Stephens took the watch himself that night, as he wanted to select the cove in which his ship would hide and establish a lookout for a suitable victim.

Eliza, alone for the evening, lolled in her own cabin. They had been at sea for over a week, and the inactivity made her uneasy. She went repeatedly to the windows in Stephens's cabin, but saw only the palm trees and the clumps of bamboo growing in the surrounding jungle. For a moment she thought of slipping overboard and swimming to shore, but suddenly the ship started to move again. She heard bare feet thudding on the deck overhead as the crew hastened to their stations.

She was tempted to go on deck herself to see what was happening, but refrained. She had heard from various crew members of Gabrielle's exploits during and after battles, but she herself certainly had no intention or desire to follow in the other woman's footsteps.

So she returned to her cabin and occupied herself by combing out her long blond hair. Ever since the duel with Gabrielle, she had taken to wearing it in a queue. Now, as she worked the comb, she daydreamed of her former life and of Richard. Maybe he had always loved Celeste, she thought, as she recalled, for the hundredth time, the scene she had witnessed from the upstairs window. But did it matter now?

Her thoughts were interrupted by a sudden clatter—gunports being raised, she realized with a start. At almost the same moment she heard the cannon being rolled out. Then the entire ship shuddered as salvo after salvo was fired, followed by a jarring thud as the vessel came up alongside her prey. She heard the insistent crackle of small arms fire, but it was no longer overhead, but off to the side.

Eliza remained in her cabin for more than an hour and wondered what was happening when the sounds of battle faded and were followed by a long, deep silence broken by an occasional shout. She did not venture to find out, however, and sat in suspense until Zwingli appeared. He carried his scimitar in one hand and a pistol in the other; a glance at his face and body was sufficient to determine that he had been in the thick of the action.

"Cap'n says you can come out now," he said.

Eliza followed him to the main deck, where the heavily armed crew had assembled.

Stephens stood before a number of cases and leather boxes, all of them taken from the Spanish galleon. They had been opened, and a single glance was enough to reveal that they contained a king's fortune in gold and gems and expensive clothing. Lined up against the rail were a half dozen seamen— the only surviving members of the galleon's crew—and three passengers also unfortunate enough to have been taken captive. As she could gather from the shouted comments of the buccaneers, the fate of these prisoners was not in doubt. They would be put to death, one by one, after mock trials and other entertainments devised for the amusement of the crew. She could not help feeling sorry for these Spaniards, and she turned her gaze away from them.

They were none of her affair, she kept telling herself. Life was unfair, as she knew all too well, and the fruits of victory belonged to the strong and unscrupulous.

"Ah, you're here," Roger Stephens bellowed. "Look at these cases and select the one you want. Any one you choose will become your property."

Eliza hesitated briefly, and then, as if in a dream, she walked up to one of the cases and pointed to it. It appeared to be filled with a lady's attire; she saw laces and silks, and caught a glimpse of gold bracelets, necklaces, and other jewelry.

First one man, then two, then the entire crew began to chant, "Earn your booty! Earn your booty!"

Eliza was somewhat bewildered, not understanding what they meant. Then all at once she remembered what she had been told the previous day about Gabrielle's conduct after a battle, and realized with a sinking feeling that the crew was demanding her participation in the grisly entertainment that followed a victory.

She glanced again at the surviving Spaniards, and one in particular caught her eye. He was tall, swarthy, and bearded, and his expression of arrogant pride made him stand out from the rest.

He returned Eliza's look, and the hateful scorn in his eyes was plain for all to see.

Eliza stood frozen. She knew the masquerade was over now, that she could never do what was required of her. She could not kill a defenseless man in cold blood, and if it meant sacrificing her own life instead, so be it.

The chant continued, filling her ears: "Earn your booty! Earn your booty!" She was about to turn away when Willie Walker, sensing her plight, came quickly to her side.

"Pipe down, you scum!" he shouted.

The chant stopped abruptly.

Eliza watched with growing horror as Walker stared down the crew, waiting for someone to defy him openly. But no one spoke, and the big man, wasting no time, strode over to the line of prisoners.

"Up with ye," he grunted as he spun the first man around, grabbing him by the collar and the seat of the trousers and lifting him atop the rail with one effortless motion. The man stood perched there, quaking, as Willie moved down the line to the next prisoner.

"Up with ye, ye spaniel!" The giant buccaneer proceeded down the line, using the tip of his cutlass to prod the reluctant Spaniards onto the rail. Soon they were standing all in a line, facing the water below and, in the distance, the dark, inhospitable shore of Hispaniola.

Willie sheathed his cutlass and, with no further ado, strode back down the line, pushing each man overboard with one shove of his huge arm. Before he was halfway back, the rest had got the hint and had jumped out into the water below.

At first there was silence, then a chorus of angry growls rose from the crew. They had been denied their evening's entertainment.

Captain Stephens, to Eliza's surprise, was leaning nonchalantly against the opposite rail, seemingly enjoying the confrontation.

Willie glanced at Stephens, then turned his attention back to the restless crew. "If any of ye have any argument," he said, "I be ready to hear ye out." He stood in the middle of the deck, his arms crossed.

The crowd parted, and in three huge strides, Zwingli was standing at Willie's side, his fierce Bantu scimitar in hand. The two men nodded in silent understanding and stood back to back, daring any comers.

Captain Stephens had watched long enough. He collared two of the crewmen standing near him and pushed them toward the chest Eliza had chosen, directing them to carry it to her cabin.

"Well, do any of you wish to argue the point formally with the bo'sun and his friend here?" he shouted.

There was absolute silence. Captain Stephens spat in disgust on the deck. "I didn't think so," he said. He turned to Willie. "Divide the spoils, Bo'sun. I doubt if any of them will argue the size of their share with you. And when you finish, set course for Saint Pierre. I'll be in my cabin."

Willie was relieved that the incident had ended without further trouble. The unfortunate prisoners would at least have a chance to swim to shore or to the hulk of their ship, and the crew would soon forget everything, of that he was sure. Captain Stephens, however, was a different story. It was hard to tell what he was thinking or feeling.

Willie shrugged. He had done his part to protect the woman, he told himself; now he only hoped that she had enough sense to take care of herself once she was alone with Stephens.

A carriage awaited Captain Stephens at the inner end of the wharf in Saint Pierre, but Eliza felt that everyone in the vicinity was staring at her, not at him. She was also aware of the fact that she was well worth their stares.

Her gaudy jewelry was worth a fortune, and she had plastered a heavy layer of cosmetics on her face. She wore a skintight laced bodice she had inherited from Gabrielle, and the silk skirt that hung snugly over her hips was fit more for a trollop than for a fine lady. Still, she did not hang her head as Stephens led her through the crowd to the carriage. There had once been a time when she had thought herself a fine lady, and would have been ashamed to appear in public in such a way—but all that was over now.

Stephens was glum and silent on the carriage ride, and Eliza realized he was worried about his confrontation with his French overlords. She knew better than to bother him when he was in such a mood, so she also remained silent, staring at the passing scenery.

On the whole she considered herself lucky. She was still alive, after all, and that was something to be thankful for. And Stephens had at least turned out to be a tolerable master—not tender or caring, surely, but not brutal or thoughtless, either.

And the bo'sun, Wee Willie Walker, would probably sacrifice his life for her. . . .

The carriage drew to a halt, and she and Stephens were escorted by a group of soldiers into the presence of two high-ranking French officers.

The one called De Bosquette admired her openly and immediately began to flirt with her surreptitiously.

The other, General de Cluny, was more circumspect. He eyed her quietly whenever he thought Stephens was not looking.

Eliza tried to avoid their gazes. She had enough trouble already without asking for more.

Stephens explained his failure to complete his mission, relating to the admiral and the general a somewhat twisted account of the battle he had fought and lost. He did not mention that he had sailed into a trap, and this puzzled Eliza. Instead he led the officers to believe that the colonials had simply been fortunate in having one of their ships appear just in time.

Stephens's imaginary account of the fighting was so vivid that Eliza soon found herself reliving the battle in all its horror. And when she thought of Richard and her father again, lying dead on the quarterdeck, a sudden surge of revulsion swelled up within her, breaking through her surface calm. How could she tolerate, even for a minute, a cutthroat like Stephens? A burning hatred for him, and for the two Frenchmen as well, took possession of her. How she would like to kill them all, she thought, here and now!

Eliza listened in mute anger as Stephens droned on about the battle. He again surprised her, however, by concluding his account with an abject apology, stressing that the overall strategy had been correct, and that he had failed merely because of bad luck and his own inexperience in conducting river assaults.

Admiral de Bosquette, seemingly satisfied with Stephens's account—even obviously pleased by the pirate's appraisal of the correctness of the overall strategy—was nevertheless upset. When the pirate finally finished speaking, the admiral leaned forward and asked in a sneering tone, "Well, what next, Captain?"

Stephens had his answer ready, and replied without hesitation. "With your permission, I will return to Virginia with a stronger force, and this time I'll reduce the garrison and complete my mission. I very much dislike to admit a failure."

General de Cluny heartily approved of this attitude.

The men now launched into an earnest discussion of how to strengthen the corsair forces in order to make certain they would be victorious when they next assaulted the garrison. The conversation centered on the number of ships required, the additional men needed, and the number and type of cannon necessary to ensure victory.

Eliza was surprised that the men did not even consider attacking elsewhere. They were like proud boys who, deprived of some toy, wanted it all the more. Apparently Stephens had counted on this stubborn pride to save his own neck. And now she understood why he had not blamed his failure on the fact that his ships had sailed into a trap. That would have implied the defeat was the fault of the French, who had not kept the plan secret. No, the admiral would not have liked that at all, she thought.

As Eliza continued to listen, she slowly realized she was attending a conference whose sole object was the destruction of the English colony of Virginia. This was a rude awakening, and she became shamefully aware that she had thought of nothing and no one but herself ever since her captivity. Now, conscious of the dogged resolve of the French leaders, she knew without a doubt that Virginia and ultimately every English colony in the New World was in grave peril. In spite of her desire to close the door permanently on her past, to harden her heart to every memory in order to ensure her survival, she could not forget that she was still a British subject, still a citizen of New Haven Colony. She could no longer suppress her feelings of loyalty, and she knew that her duty required her to report what she had learned to Colonel Nettleton and Mark Prescott.

Perhaps this had been the reason she had fought to stay alive all this time, she thought. Perhaps she really did have something to live for.

The possibilities raced through her mind, distracting her, but Eliza forced herself to listen carefully to the men. This was not the time to ponder the question of how she might transmit what she had learned to the commanders in Virginia. That would require thought and careful planning, for the slightest slip would mean the immediate loss of her life and ruin any chances of the English for another victory. Her duty now was to listen and to learn, and not raise a single glimmer of suspicion. Now that she had a good reason to survive, she would play her part to the hilt; and she would start right now.

More than an hour later, near the end of the conference, Admiral de Bosquette rose and scratched his head. Stephens's new mistress certainly was odd—not at all like Gabrielle, he thought bitterly. As much as he had tried to gain her attention, she had ignored him—him, a French admiral!—instead leaning her lovely blond head dreamily on that pirate's shoulder. Just like a harlot, he thought, with nothing but sexual pleasure on her mind.

The militiamen who had been wounded in the battle with the corsairs recovered one by one, and as they regained their health, there was less work to occupy Celeste and Adella at the hospital. Finally the doctor discharged the last of his patients, and the services of the women as nurses were no longer required.

Richard repeated his desire to send them off to New Haven, where they would be out of danger if the buccaneers attacked again. But Celeste remained adamant in her refusal to leave. "I've already told you," she said, "I have no friends and only a few acquaintances in New Haven, and I'll feel much more comfortable staying near you."

Adella echoed the other woman's reasoning. "My brother is here," she told Richard, "and you're here. So is Celeste, to whom I've grown close. I don't know a living soul in New Haven, and I see no good reason for going there."

Celeste added an argument that was unanswerable. "The

women and children who live along the river here have nowhere to go," she said. "They're staying right in their homes, no matter what may happen. Are we any less courageous and resolute than they? I should say not!"

Richard could not disagree, so he gave up in his attempt to persuade the women to leave for New Haven.

Spring came early to Virginia, and with the dramatic improvement in the weather, Celeste and Adella began to explore the surrounding countryside.

"I don't want to alarm you, ladies," Colonel Nettleton told them, "but you'd be wise not to stray beyond the limits of the houses and cabins of the settlers. The Chickahominy Indians have been restless for some months, and although they've been peaceful enough, there's no telling when they might turn ugly. It would be wise if you took no chances."

The young women heeded his advice and exercised great caution in their strolls beyond the farms spread around the fort. But they saw no sign of Indians other than the few braves who came through the area to barter with the settlers, and gradually the women became increasingly careless. So when the unexpected happened, Richard was shocked.

Adella hurried to the fort and into the tent the officers used as a headquarters and began to babble excitedly. "Celeste has been captured by Indians!" she announced breathlessly. "They appeared out of nowhere and grabbed her! I ran for my life, and I was lucky to get away from them. Although, in all honesty, they didn't seem very interested in me."

Her brother forced her to sit down, and when she became calmer, Colonel Nettleton and Richard began to question her.

"How many warriors were there?" the colonel asked.

"There were about five of them," she replied. "I really didn't stop to count them. I was too terrified."

"You're sure they took Celeste prisoner and didn't merely take hold of her and then kill her?" Richard said.

"Oh, no," she replied emphatically. "I'm quite sure they made off with her. That seemed to be the whole point of what they were doing. They went straight for her, picked her up before she had a chance to run away, then made off with her.

They disappeared into the forest almost faster than I can tell you about it."

Richard exchanged a long, thoughtful glance with the colonel. "What tribe were they?" he asked.

Adella shrugged helplessly. "I have no idea," she replied. "They looked like the Indians we sometimes see on the streets here in town, but I really didn't notice any distinguishing characteristics."

Richard persisted. "They wore paint?"

The girl nodded.

"What color was it?"

"Brown," she said. "A dark, chocolate brown."

"They were Chickahominy, then," Colonel Nettleton said firmly. "There can be no question about that."

Adella, who had held up well, began to weep.

Her brother went to her, but she waved him away, ashamed of her display of weakness.

"It was our own fault," she said. "We were warned, but we became careless."

"What do you think, Colonel?" Richard asked.

Colonel Nettleton shrugged. "It beats me," he said. "It sounds as though the incident was well planned, and I'd guess that the Chickahominy had been keeping the women under observation for some time and finally decided—for whatever their reasons—that they wanted to take Celeste as a prisoner."

"But why?" Richard demanded. "This makes no sense!"

"I'm afraid," Nettleton replied slowly, "that I'm as much in the dark as you are."

"That raises the immediate question of what we're going to do about it," Richard said.

The head of the Virginia militia raised an eyebrow. "Ordinarily," he said, "the abduction of a settler, particularly a woman, would be a cause for war, and the Chickahominy well know it. We've taken up arms against them on a number of occasions for just this reason and trounced them severely every time. I had thought—or at least I had reason to hope—that the day had ended when our people would be kidnapped by the warriors, but apparently I was wrong. Unfortunately, this is the worst of all possible times for us to go to war with the Chickahominy. We're preparing for another attack from the French mercenaries, and we can't waste our men and powder in a fight with the Indians."

It was true, Richard reflected, that the settlers would be hard pressed from both sides if Celeste's abduction should lead to a protracted war with the Chickahominy. "It appears," he said quietly, "that I will have to take my chances and go off to the land of the Chickahominy alone."

Colonel Nettleton shook his head slowly, and Mark Prescott rose to his feet in anger. He was about to say something, but Adella grabbed his arm to restrain him.

"Seems to me," Nettleton said, "that what you'd be doing is nothing better than a form of suicide."

"I think not," Richard said. "I'm thoroughly familiar with the Mohegan and their customs, and the Conestoga, too, for that matter. And I've fought nearly a half dozen other Indian nations at one time or another. I'm not totally ignorant of the ways of the redskins."

"They're still savages, and you'd be taking a big risk," Prescott told him.

Richard shrugged. "Roaring Wolf's a savage, and I'd trust my life to him over any white man. Besides, there comes a time in the life of every man when he's faced with a clear choice. He may either think and think and do nothing, or he may act. All we know for certain is that Celeste has been abducted. There could be dozens of reasons for the Chickahominy doing what they've done, and we could twiddle our thumbs and never find out. But by that time, Celeste could be dead—or worse." He did not elaborate.

It was just as well that he stopped short. As it was, Adella shuddered.

"I can't and won't abandon Celeste," he said. "She desperately needs help, and I'm going to help her."

Roaring Wolf, when he learned of Richard's plan, insisted on going along. So both of them, clad in buckskins and moccasins, made their way silently through the deep forest of Virginia with the Pequot brave in the lead. Roaring Wolf carried a quiver of arrows and a bow, and Richard was armed with the rifle that had been made for him some years earlier in London. Designed to his precise specifications, it was infinitely more accurate than the muskets most colonists owned.

The tidewater countryside was less austere than the New England wilderness Richard had come to know so well. It was flatter, for one thing. And the spring weather was much milder, as was evident from the already lush vegetation. Everywhere were rolling meadows and clearings covered with bushes, tall grasses, and flowers, instead of the never-ending forests that predominated up north. But the red clay soil made Richard feel right at home, for it reminded him of the reddish soil common around New Haven. And as in New England, deer were everywhere. Richard spotted a large buck before they had been gone an hour, and was sorry he had no time to go hunting.

Roaring Wolf set a quick pace, pausing every now and again and standing very silently as he listened intently.

Richard relied implicitly on the Pequot, but at the same time used his own senses and his knowledge of the deep forest. Hearing a faint sound off to the right—perhaps the snapping of a twig under the weight of a man's foot—he motioned to Roaring Wolf and inclined his head toward the right.

Roaring Wolf listened, then nodded and silently dropped to the ground, making himself invisible in the tall grass.

Richard followed his example, then carefully checked the priming on his already loaded rifle and the pair of pistols he carried in his belt. Now he was ready for any crisis that might arise.

The pair did not have long to wait. Three warriors were cautiously advancing through the forest, spread out so that each was separated from his fellows by about fifteen feet. Apparently they had heard the approaching pair and were searching for them. The braves were young and burly, dark-headed men with deep copper skin. The brown paint they had smeared on their faces and torsos made them look even darker and more menacing. Two of the trio carried bows and arrows, but the warrior in the center was armed with only a tomahawk, which he clutched in his right hand. Presumably he was the leader, for he was making hand signals to his comrades, who nodded and proceeded in the direction he had indicated.

Richard knew at once what had to be done. Indians, he knew from experience, responded best to bold, dramatic acts.

Silently removing one of his pistols, he waited until the leader was no more than fifty feet away. Then, as the brave raised his tomahawk to motion to one of his fellows, Richard quickly sighted the pistol and fired. His aim was true, and the upraised tomahawk flew out of the surprised warrior's grasp. Even as the sound echoed and reechoed through the wilderness, Richard leaped to his feet, holding his rifle across his chest and raising his right hand in salute. "Hear me, O Chickahominy. I appeal to you in the name of friendship and peace!" His expertise with the dreaded firestick of the settlers spoke for itself, as did the fact that he did not fire again. Obviously he was sparing the life of the warrior, and consequently he deserved to be heard. And Roaring Wolf was standing beside him, his bow at the ready. "We seek a woman with fair skin who was stolen from the land of our people by your warriors," Richard said. "Return her to us and all will be well. Fail us in this, and there will be blood on the moon." He hoped they would understand English, but in case they didn't, he accompanied his words with hand signals to make his meaning clear.

The Chickahominy, however, were perfectly aware of what this bold white man was looking for. The leader glanced down at his empty hand, where the tomahawk had been. "The chief of our people will hear you and will decide what is to be done," he said. "You must come with us."

"Take us to him, then," Richard demanded.

Without another word, the trio turned and began to trot through the forest.

Roaring Wolf smiled at Richard in acknowledgment of his excellent marksmanship, then set off after the other Indian braves. Richard followed close behind.

They trotted tirelessly for more than two hours, maintaining the same even pace. Richard knew that the warriors were testing

him, gauging his ability to keep up with them without showing
any sign of discomfort or distress.

At last they came to a cleared field where corn, squash, and
beans had been planted. Beyond the field was a circular log
palisade similar to that which the Virginians had recently erected.
Inside the palisade was the town, where the Indians lived in
houses made of log frames with woven reed walls and animal
skins over the door and window openings.

Startled by the sight of a white man and a strange Indian
entering the village, the townspeople gathered around Richard
and Roaring Wolf and followed them as they made their way
behind their guides through the town. Young warriors, wearing
only loincloths, stared stonily at them, while squaws with braided
hair and buckskin skirts giggled and smiled openly at the
strangers. Small children, almost all of them naked, raced back
and forth, chased and circled all the while by barking dogs.

Richard paid no attention to the stir he created. The Mohegan
up north had reacted in much the same way until they had
become accustomed to his visits, so he ignored the confusion
around him and continued to trot, his expression and bearing
dignified.

At last they came to a rectangular building with a rounded
roof, much smaller than the main lodges that evidently housed
most of the tribe. This was apparently a private dwelling. A
warrior posted in front pushed aside the animal skin covering
the doorway and vanished within.

Richard and Roaring Wolf halted at the signal of their guides.
The leader also disappeared inside the hut, and his two com-
panions squatted in front of the door. Richard and Roaring
Wolf stood and waited. Neither spoke nor displayed any sign
of impatience at the delay. Their manner demonstrated to the
Indians that they were long accustomed to such treatment.

At last the lead warrior reappeared and beckoned.

The pair entered the house, and as they became accustomed
to the gloom, relieved only by the cracks of light that filtered
in at the windows where the skins did not fit properly, they
became aware of a young man, probably in his twenties, who
sat cross-legged on the ground. He was wearing a cape of

feathers, and on his head was an elaborate headgear, also fashioned of feathers.

"I am No-mi-ma, the chieftain of the Chickahominy," he said in halting but perfectly understandable English.

Familiar with the history of the nation, Richard assumed that this was the grandson of Powhatan and the nephew of his daughter, Pocahontas, who had married John Rolfe and had gone off to England with him.

Speaking in the same unemotional tone, Richard introduced his companion and himself.

"What brings you to the land of the Chickahominy?" No-mi-ma demanded.

Speaking quietly and slowly, Richard explained that they were seeking a young woman who had been abducted by several warriors wearing the identifying paint of the Chickahominy.

The leader of the tribe listened, his face expressionless. When he spoke, his voice was matter-of-fact, displaying neither anger nor animosity. "If it is true that this woman is here," he said, "why should she be returned to you?"

Richard thought rapidly, then beckoned. "Perhaps No-mi-ma would accompany me outside," he said, "where I can show him the reasons better than I can explain them."

Richard figured his approach was probably sound, based on the lively curiosity of all Indians for the mysterious. He was not disappointed, for No-mi-ma rose quickly to his feet and led the way into the open.

Richard inspected the sizable crowd that had gathered, and his attention was caught by a burly warrior, taller and more broad-shouldered than the rest, who wore a single feather that protruded vertically from his scalp lock.

The brave, aware of the white man's interest, bristled, stared back arrogantly and, muttering something to those around him, spat into the dirt.

Richard knew he had been insulted, but paid no attention. "May I ask this brave to assist me for purposes of illustration, No-mi-ma?" he asked, pointing to the man.

The chieftain was somewhat bewildered but nodded his consent.

Richard issued instructions to Roaring Wolf in a low voice.

The Pequot grinned, walked up to the burly warrior and, saying something to him, led him down the narrow street to a point about one hundred feet away. There he stood the man against the log palisade and signaled to Richard that all was ready.

Richard knew that the Chickahominy traded extensively with the settlers and that many of the braves could understand English. Nevertheless, he realized that whatever he said would be of no avail unless he backed it up with a demonstration of his prowess as a warrior.

"I came to this place," he said loudly, speaking so that all who were present could hear him, "seeking a woman of my people who was taken from the white man's town on the river you call the Toppahanock. Your chieftain has asked why she should be returned to me, if indeed she is here." He pointed a finger at the brave, who stood with folded arms one hundred feet away. "Observe, O Chickahominy, and think well on what you see." He raised his rifle, and as he did, he hoped the warrior had the sense to stand still. Looking down the long barrel, Richard took quick but careful aim and then slowly squeezed the trigger. The sound of the shot seemed to fill the entire village, and a number of the women gasped, while several of the children began to cry. They were immediately silenced by their elders.

Richard was relieved beyond measure when he saw that the feather had been shot away no more than an inch or two above the warrior's scalp. His aim had been perfect.

An excited buzz of comment followed the shot. The braves who had witnessed it were clearly impressed, and their faces reflected their incredulity as they discussed the remarkable shooting.

"You have been told," Richard said, "that a large band of white men has come to the shores of the Toppahanock. All of these men are fearless warriors, and all of them are armed with firesticks like this firestick." That was a gross exaggeration, Richard knew, inasmuch as his rifle was unique, but it was necessary to get his point across. "All of them can shoot as true as I shoot." Again there was an excited buzz.

No-mi-ma tried to look impassive, but his expression nonetheless indicated that he was deeply impressed.

"Your white brothers," Richard said, "wish to live beside you in peace. Here the forests are very large, and there is game and other food for all. Your white brothers do not wish to go on the warpath against the Chickahominy. But if the squaw who has been taken from us by force is not returned to us at once, you will leave us no choice. We will take to the warpath against you, and one hundred firesticks will speak as one. Every time they are fired, one hundred warriors will die. Their squaws will weep and tear their hair, but that will not bring their husbands back to life ever again."

His words were received in silence, but his meaning was very clear: Either the young woman who had been abducted would be handed into his custody without delay, or the white warriors would make war on the Chickahominy, exacting a fearful vengeance on the tribe.

Somehow No-mi-ma was able to keep his dignity. Beckoning with an imperious gesture, he started off through the town.

Richard and Roaring Wolf fell in behind him, their senses alert to danger and possible trickery. Both were acutely conscious of the burly warrior whose feather had been shot off, for the man glared at them with undisguised hatred as he joined the crowd that followed.

The chieftain reached a building on the far side of the town, and pulling aside the animal skin that covered the entrance, he again beckoned as he entered the dwelling.

Richard, with Roaring Wolf at his heels, followed him inside, then halted in surprise at the unexpected scene before him.

The window coverings had been thrown back, and in the light that streamed into the dwelling, Richard saw an Indian woman kneeling over a small child who was stretched out on a raised pallet of woven reeds. The child's flushed face indicated he was suffering from a high fever.

The kneeling woman turned her head and glanced up at Richard, and only then did he realize it was Celeste.

Richard stood there in shocked silence, taking in the marvelous transformation Celeste had undergone. Her long, blue-black hair had been twisted into braids that fell forward across the shoulders of her Indian-style doeskin dress. Her feet were bare, and all trace of cosmetics had disappeared from her face. Her only adornment consisted of a simple necklace of shells.

Richard was about to speak, but Celeste gestured for quiet. She turned back to the child, and dipping a cloth into a basin of water, she applied the compress to his forehead. Then she gracefully rose from her kneeling position and moved to the far side of the single-room dwelling.

"Speak softly," she said. "The child is still feverish, but I think he is sleeping at last."

Richard was about to tell Celeste how relieved he was that she was alive, when No-mi-ma, obviously more concerned about the child than about the white couple's reunion, inquired anxiously, "Is your magic curing him?"

"I do not know yet," Celeste said calmly. "I told you when I was brought here and when you commanded me to attend to your child that I was no physician. I have known such sicknesses as this in London, and I am treating him as the doctors there treat their patients. I do no more and no less."

The little boy, who had been silent a moment before, began tossing and breathing in quick, wheezing gasps. Celeste frowned and shook her head in evident concern.

Richard turned to her and spoke in a low voice, so that No-mi-ma would not overhear. "What disease does this boy have?" he said. "I have never seen such symptoms before."

"There are many names for his illness," she replied calmly. "The physicians, however, call it pneumonia."

His fear for her increased rapidly. "I have heard it is possible to communicate such an illness," he said. "You're mad to allow yourself to be cooped up here with that boy."

Celeste shook her head. "I have no fear," she said, "and I will continue to do all I can to see that this child recovers. He's the great-nephew of the Princess Pocahontas, a woman much revered by this tribe, and I must do what I can to help him."

No-mi-ma turned to Richard and spread out his arms. "Now you know," he said, "why this woman was brought to town of Chickahominy. The child is my only offspring. His mother died when he was born, and he means more to me than life itself. I know this squaw worked in the white man's house of the sick, so I brought her here. She will cure my son, as she cured many others."

Richard did not want to alarm the chief, so he simply nodded. Again he turned to Celeste. "How soon will it be," he whispered, "before the child passes the crisis of his illness?" Richard had heard that if a person suffering from pneumonia were to recover, the fever must burn itself out according to a schedule that physicians and others familiar with the disease could predict in advance.

"By dawn tomorrow morning, I think," Celeste said. "If the fever subsides by then, he will recover."

"It is my wish," Richard said, speaking again to No-mi-ma, "to talk with this woman in private." His voice was firm, allowing no room for dissension or argument.

No-mi-ma hesitated for a moment and then withdrew, with Roaring Wolf following him.

The moment Richard was alone with Celeste, he took hold of her shoulders, and his fingers dug into her flesh. "Are you mad?" he demanded. "The child's ailment is contagious, and you know it. Many people who contract it die!"

She smiled wanly and appeared unruffled. "When I was brought here," she said, "I was given no choice. If I had refused to attend to the child, I would have been put to death at once. But even if I had come here of my own free will, I still would not have refused to help. You cannot refuse help to a sick child!"

"Even at the extreme risk of your own life?" Richard said hotly.

Celeste began to look annoyed. "Your fingers are cutting into my shoulders," she said.

Richard immediately released his grip and murmured an apology.

"I don't know what you've heard about this sickness," Celeste said, "but I myself had it once, about six years ago in London. The physicians who attended me then knew very little about it, but they did tell me that the disease is not as dangerous to a strong adult as it is to a small child or an aged person. And despite what you may have heard, it is not easy to communicate. It has been known to happen, but only rarely."

A great weight fell from Richard's shoulders as he looked at her. "You're sure of this?" he said. "You aren't making it up to quiet me down?"

"I swear that every word I've spoken is the truth," Celeste assured him.

He was so relieved that in his exuberance he swept her into his arms and kissed her.

She clung to him for a moment, then gently disengaged herself. "I must look after my patient," she said. "And I should shoo you out of here right now, Richard Dunstable, and I would if I weren't so happy to see you. For a while, I must admit, I thought I'd never see another white man again."

Richard smiled at Celeste's matter-of-fact expression of gratitude. "You seem to have managed quite well without my help," he said, returning his attention to the feverish child. "I only hope that your patient here is as hardy as the Indian braves who led Roaring Wolf and me to this village. Will you really know by morning whether he will live or die?"

"Yes," she said. "But I expect him to live. He's improved considerably since I began to apply poultices. It's a far more effective treatment, I can assure you, than having half the Chickahominy marching around his bed, chanting and screaming. I threw them all out when I arrived here. I only hope none of them caught the disease. I don't think so, since it would have shown up by now, and I've been checking on all of them daily."

In spite of himself, Richard chuckled. He had been deeply concerned about Celeste, and his imagination had run wild as he pictured the hazards to which she had been exposed. But he should have known better: Of all the women he had ever met, she was the most unflappable and the most resourceful. Nevertheless, he intended to take no risks. "I'll remain here, then. I'll not leave unless you are with me."

Celeste wanted to protest that he was placing his own life in jeopardy for her sake, but nevertheless she was vastly relieved. After all, she didn't even know for certain that she'd be released if and when she pronounced her patient well. She hadn't liked the look in No-mi-ma's eyes when he had examined her, and the mere fact that he had insisted she dress like a Chickahominy had made her apprehensive.

"I'll remain within earshot," Richard said firmly. "Call out if you need me for anything."

Not waiting for a reply, he stalked out of the hut. There No-mi-ma awaited him, and Roaring Wolf sat nearby on the ground.

Richard saw no point in continuing his discussion with No-mi-ma. He wanted to tell the Chickahominy chieftain that a simple request to the colonists would have produced the same results. But the Indians simply did not understand such behavior. "I have decided," he said, "to spend the night here, outside this door. I will remain here until your child is recovered and the woman is ready to return with me to her own people." He made the statement as a fact that could not be denied, and No-mi-ma resigned himself to acceding to the stubborn white man's demands.

Richard and Roaring Wolf began their vigil outside the dwelling. Richard sat with his back against the front wall of the hut, his rifle across his knees, and Roaring Wolf sat cross-legged a few feet away. The people of the town, intensely curious, wandered back and forth in front of the hut. At dusk, some squaws brought gourds filled with a stew of fish, corn, and beans, and later they even provided the strangers with straw mats to recline upon.

In spite of the great temptation he felt, Richard did not disturb Celeste again. He recognized her need to be able to devote all of her time and thought to the boy in her care. Her life, as well as the lives of the two men who had followed her to this remote community, depended on the recovery of the child from an illness that in Europe was fatal almost as often as not. And Richard was well aware that the Indians of various nations, because they had suffered so few diseases before the coming of the white men, were extremely susceptible to epidemics of many kinds.

The night was unexpectedly warm, but Richard did not sleep. When the stars came out, filling a cloudless sky, he found himself wondering at his own conduct in following Celeste to this remote place. He had never even considered any other course of action, he realized. Certainly this was strange behavior for a recently widowed man who was also personally responsible for the lives and welfare of sixty militiamen.

He thought again of the recent battle, then of Eliza. He tried to imagine her lovely face, but somehow he couldn't. She seemed far away now, almost as if she had always been a dream. He shook his head and deliberately put the painful memories behind him. His duty now was to remain alert, not to mull over his misfortunes.

At last dawn came, and he and Roaring Wolf arose simultaneously. Richard refreshed himself in a small lake nearby and, after shaving with his knife, returned to the hut. There a middle-aged squaw awaited with a breakfast of broiled fish and coarse corn bread, which he ate in spite of his growing apprehensions.

At last, an hour after dawn, the flap over the door opened, and Celeste appeared, blinking in the light of day. There were circles beneath her eyes, and she looked very tired. But her voice was strong and confident when she said, "You may inform No-mi-ma that his son is going to live."

Roaring Wolf raced off through the town to give the good news to the Chickahominy chieftain, and within a very short time, No-mi-ma returned with him, his face wreathed in a smile.

Celeste had been anticipating his appearance and immediately returned to the entrance, where she blocked his effort to move past her.

"Your son is sleeping," she said, "and I will permit him to

have no visitors until later in the day. It is vital that he sleep now."

No-mi-ma looked confused. "How can my people and I celebrate his recovery unless he is present?"

Celeste looked quickly at Richard, who frowned.

"Will the celebration be noisy?" she asked.

No-mi-ma shrugged. "We must summon the Great Spirit by beating our drums," he said. "As He hears many things from many people at all times of the day and night, we must speak to Him in unison so that He hears our voices and is aware of our thanks."

In spite of her own weariness, she tapped a foot impatiently. The illness had been grueling, and her young patient was undoubtedly exhausted, worn out by his struggle. His one need now was for rest, and under no circumstances should he be forced to undergo the ordeal of listening to the beating of drums and the chanting of his people. She was uncertain how to tell the ruler of the Chickahominy that she disapproved of his plan, and she looked at Richard for guidance.

He knew what was on her mind without being told, and he spoke swiftly. "The evil spirit that this woman has dispelled is very potent," he said, "but it is also very tricky. It has been driven away, but it has not gone far yet. If it hears any noise, it will surely return, for it is very fond of noise. Therefore everyone must be very quiet for—" He glanced at Celeste for help.

"For two days," she said. "Then it will be safe to celebrate. What this man has spoken is true. I have fought very hard, and the spirit of the illness that attacked your son is now on its way to the nether world. But if the demon is aroused by the sounding of the Chickahominy drums or the chanting of the Chickahominy people, it may return."

No-mi-ma withdrew hastily, and soon a half dozen warriors appeared and surrounded the house, obviously under instructions to make certain that no loud noises were made anywhere in the vicinity.

Celeste grinned at Richard. "Thanks for your help," she

said. "I'm sure there will be plenty of peace and quiet around here now—even if they have to shoot someone."

Richard chuckled. "If I were you," he said, "I'd get some rest, too, while you have a chance. The Chickahominy have postponed their celebration, but ultimately they'll feel compelled to have it, and I can't see them waiting a minute more than the two days you requested."

Roaring Wolf nodded solemnly. "When the sun sets tomorrow," he said, "Chickahominy will hold great feast, where many wise men will speak. Leaders of tribe will praise the squaw who has driven away the evil spirits."

Celeste decided that Richard was right, and after eating she retired into the dwelling to catch up on her own much-needed sleep.

Under no circumstances would Richard consider returning without Celeste. However, he was sure she was safe now, so when he learned that a hunting expedition was being formed to get meat for the banquet set for the next night, he volunteered to join it. His offer was accepted, and during the hours that he and the braves roamed through the forest, he again added to his already formidable image in the eyes of the tribe. Twice he spotted the hoofprints of deer, twice he tracked the animals, and twice he felled his prey with a single rifle shot. The Chickahominy were in awe of his marksmanship.

The next day the squaws of the Chickahominy dug a large oblong pit, which they lined with stones; the children filled it with wood, and soon a large fire was blazing. The deer carcasses had been butchered the previous evening, and the venison was placed on spits, while other meats, including rabbit, squirrel, and many varieties of bird, were stewing slowly in earthenware pots.

The preparations for the evening's festivities went on all afternoon, and the women and girls of the Chickahominy were particularly busy as they prepared spring vegetables and baked corn cakes, which they soaked in honey, and otherwise readied the feast. The braves, however, all of whom had painted themselves in bright colors for the occasion, mostly sat around and smoked pipe after pipe of tobacco, chatting amiably with one

another. Richard noticed that even Roaring Wolf had joined in
the festivities, painting his own face and torso and puffing
vigorously on a large wooden pipe.

Gradually the natural amphitheater that surrounded the cooking fire began to fill as groups of braves made their way to the
site. Everyone was in a joyous, celebratory mood, and Richard
felt none of the underlying tensions he had been aware of when
he had first arrived in the town. He was wondering whether
he should go to the small dwelling and fetch Celeste, when a
roar of approval signaled her arrival.

She walked slowly toward the scene of the celebration,
carrying in her arms a little boy of about two or three years,
who smiled up at her.

Still wearing an Indian dress of doeskin, with her blue-black
hair in twin braids, she looked more like a Chickahominy than
did some of the women of the tribe. The previous day's rest
had apparently been good for her, because the shadows beneath
her eyes had vanished.

Richard, who was accustomed to seeing Celeste dressed in
only the most expensive and fashionable clothes, thought she
had never looked more attractive.

No-mi-ma rushed to her side, and she finally relinquished
his son to him. He held the little boy in his arms, and for a
moment his Indian reserve threatened to break down. Then he
recovered and, hugging the child, carried him to a small pallet
at the front of the assemblage.

Richard and Roaring Wolf, flanking Celeste, accompanied
her to the place No-mi-ma had assigned them nearby.

"His son is much stronger now," she said, "and I have no
doubt he'll be able to survive any entertainment the Chickahominy devise this evening. I insisted that they have a resting
place here for him, though, and I'm glad to see that his father
heeded my advice."

Grinning at her, Richard reflected that she was a remarkable
young woman, who not only knew her own mind, but also saw
to it that others obeyed her will.

The friendliness of the Chickahominy to the woman who
had cured their chieftain's son was readily apparent. The squaws

of the tribe came up to Celeste in twos and threes, and timidly reaching out their hands, they touched her on the arms and shoulders. The braves kept their distance but treated her with great respect, raising their right arms in rigid salute to her whenever she happened to glance in their direction. The children were in awe of her, and those who sat near her with their parents were silent and far better behaved than was their custom.

Drums began to beat near the top of the amphitheater, slowly at first. Then the throbbing became more rapid, more insistent, and Richard was surprised to discover that the sound was influencing even him. A glance at Celeste indicated that she, too, was affected by it. Their eyes met and held, and they regarded each other gravely and in silence. Conversation was impossible when the drums were being pounded so loudly, so the couple made no attempt to talk. But there was no need for words between them: They had been drawn together by the adventure they had experienced, and both now enjoyed the relief and simple happiness of the occasion.

At last the drums stopped, and squaws who had prepared the meat moved through the throng, holding out large wooden platters while the Chickahominy helped themselves. Richard took a smoking joint of venison for Celeste and another for himself. Soon they were served gourds containing a mixture of corn and beans that had been cooked with an unfamiliar but deliciously pungent spice.

Later, more squaws appeared with the corn cakes sweetened with honey, and the couple ate their fill.

"I don't suppose," Celeste murmured to Richard, "that it's possible for us to wash. I've never felt so greasy."

Roaring Wolf, used to the strange desires of white people, heard her comment and quietly slipped away, returning moments later with some large, fragrant green leaves he had soaked in cold water. They proved to be remarkably effective in ridding the couple's hands and mouths of grease.

All at once the drums began to beat again, and the crowd, having eaten, now got down to the serious business of the evening and began to chant in unison.

Celeste looked at Richard for an explanation.

Richard, familiar with such ceremonies, related the gist of the chant for her. "They're thanking their gods of sky and earth and water," he said, "for the magic you performed on behalf of the chief's son. They're calling you greater than the most powerful of medicine men in the history of their tribe."

Flattered and amused, Celeste smiled broadly.

A medicine man, his head and shoulders concealed by a weird mask of animal skins stretched on a frame of wood, appeared in front of the fire and began to harangue the crowd. He spoke interminably, and from time to time when he began to chant in a singsong voice, the entire assemblage joined in.

"He's literally singing your praises," Richard muttered. "He hasn't said anything that wasn't said previously, just repeating himself endlessly."

Somehow Celeste managed to keep a straight face.

The speaker was followed by another medicine man, similarly attired, and he, too, delivered a long, rambling speech, in which he repeated almost word for word what his colleague had already said.

The Chickahominy, long accustomed to such occasions, displayed no signs of weariness or boredom.

Celeste, however, began to grow tired of sitting cross-legged on the ground. Nevertheless, she forced herself to remain still.

Finally it was No-mi-ma's turn to speak, and he also delivered an oration that seemed to last forever. He dwelled at length on his love for his son, and praised the fair-skinned woman who had responded so nobly to the crisis and had saved the child's life.

"He's now swearing by all of the gods of the Chickahominy," Richard said in a low voice, "that he and his people will be your friends for all time. Of course, that means if there's anything you want from them, they will do all in their power to grant your wish."

Celeste's violet eyes became thoughtful. "Is it customary for me to reply to this address?" she asked.

Richard was uncertain and conferred with Roaring Wolf.

"You may reply if there is some favor you think the Chickahominy can grant you," Richard told her, "but it isn't necessary. You can simply stand and acknowledge the praise you have received with a smile and a bow, and nothing else will be necessary."

"But there is something I want," she replied. "May I address the entire tribe directly?"

"Of course," Richard said, and before he could say another word, she had risen to her feet. Richard had no idea how she had learned the appropriate Indian style of greeting, but her gestures were so smooth that it appeared she had been doing it all of her life.

She folded her arms across her breasts, and bowed her head, first to No-mi-ma, then to the two medicine men who had spoken, and finally to the crowd.

The Chickahominy responded with loud cries as they roared their approval.

Richard was apprehensive, wishing she had consulted him before expressing a desire for whatever it was she wanted from the Chickahominy. Indians were often unpredictable, and she could unwittingly offend them.

Celeste smiled and began to speak loudly and clearly, her voice low and resonant.

"The English colonists of Virginia," she said, "have been the good friends of the Chickahominy for almost fifty years. Your princess, Pocahontas, knew this, and that is why she gave herself in marriage to him who is called John Rolfe. I will not lie to you, though. It is true the Chickahominy and the English have sometimes argued—but it has been as brother argues with brother, not as enemies. And as brothers we have also lived in peace and harmony for many years. The magic deed I performed for the son of your chief was a token of the goodwill I feel in my heart for the Chickahominy. It was not necessary to abduct me for this purpose. Had the warriors asked me to come here to help this child, I would gladly have come."

One of the Indians translated her remarks for the sake of the braves who did not understand English. As Celeste waited for him to finish, Richard grew increasingly curious. Her arguments surely were persuasive, but he still had no idea what she had in mind.

Celeste began again. "Not all who come to these shores and the great forests of this land are the friends of the Chickahominy and the other Indian nations who have lived here for so many years," she said. "There is one nation whose warriors are greedy and selfish. They are called the French."

Richard at last understood, and almost simultaneously grew angry at himself for not coming up with the idea himself. Celeste had apparently thought it through some time ago, and he had remained totally oblivious all the while.

Celeste warmed to her theme and spoke with the emotion and expertise of an accomplished actress. "We have no secrets from the Chickahominy," she said. "Certainly the Chickahominy already know that the French sent three warships up the river and attacked the English with their huge firesticks that make a noise like the thunder in the sky."

The warriors in the throng exchanged glances and seemed impressed by her candor.

"The French will attack again!" she cried. "If they defeat the English who now live in Virginia, life will be very different for the Chickahominy. The French will enslave them. They will kill the warriors and shame the women. The children will be taken to the land of the French in their great ships and will work for them as slaves. All the Chickahominy who survive, women and children alike, will live in chains."

Richard smiled to himself in sheer wonder at her cunning. She was wildly exaggerating the dangers to the Indians, of course, but he knew now what she had in mind and approved wholeheartedly.

"I ask no favors of the Chickahominy for driving out the demon who inhabited the son of No-mi-ma. I ask the Chickahominy to help themselves. I ask them to preserve the lives of their warriors, the honor of their women, and the futures of their children. I ask them to join with their brothers of Virginia and send a strong force of warriors to help fight the French, who would enslave us all."

The crowd was quiet. The threat she had described was indeed grave, and the nation took her words to heart.

No-mi-ma hastily conferred with the two medicine men and with two older warriors, apparently his war chiefs. Then he turned to the assemblage. "She who saved the life of No-mi-ma's son," he declared, "has no reason to lie to the Chickahominy. I believe she speaks words of truth. The council that advises me in all things agrees that it is right that the warriors of our land stand shoulder to shoulder with their brothers of Virginia to fight the invaders. What say the warriors?"

The response was immediate and dramatic. The braves leaped to their feet and emitted ear-shattering war cries.

Richard smiled at Celeste and shook his head in wonder. "You've performed a second miracle," he said. "You've assured us of a staunch ally in our coming confrontation with the buccaneers!"

No-mi-ma asked for volunteers, and so many men offered to join the expedition that Richard had to intervene. He didn't want too many men, for the enthusiastic warriors would no doubt be difficult to control. "Ten times ten warriors will be all we will need," he said. "You must keep the others here so they may hunt in the forests and provide the food that the Chickahominy need."

No-mi-ma was pleasantly surprised. In his experience, allies always demanded larger and larger numbers of braves to take part in an expedition. This white warrior, however, seemed as unusual as the woman herself.

At last the hubbub subsided, and it was agreed that the Chickahominy would supply one hundred warriors, and that they would leave for the fort on the Toppahanock in two days' time.

Rather than wait to accompany the Indians, Richard decided it would be a wise precaution to leave with Celeste the next morning to prepare his companions back at the fort for the sight of one hundred fierce Indian braves in war paint.

The evening's ceremonies, which had lasted for a very long time, ended abruptly, and the people returned to their lodges.

No-mi-ma took his son with him, carrying the sleeping child gently in his arms.

Richard fell in beside Celeste as she started back toward the small dwelling where she had stayed since her abduction.

"The Chickahominy aren't alone in being indebted to you," he said. "I am also in your debt, and so is every English colonist in Virginia. It took me some time before I realized what you were up to in your speech, and even then I wasn't so sure you would succeed. But your idea was brilliant, and you've won us allies we'll badly need."

"I'm sorry I didn't discuss the idea with you earlier," Celeste said, "but I simply didn't have an opportunity. But I could imagine no reason why you'd fail to give your approval."

"I give it with all my heart," he replied. "When Mazarin washed his hands of you as an agent for France, he and his country suffered a severe loss."

"Why, thank you, Richard," she said, "even though you exaggerate."

"I do not," he replied firmly. "You're the most extraordinary woman I've ever known."

They fell silent as they continued to walk toward the little house. Perhaps because they were alone in a strange land, or perhaps because they had both successfully undergone a harrowing ordeal, they drew together. Their shoulders touched, their arms brushed, and they made no effort to move apart.

As they walked on, they both realized there was far more involved in their relationship than mere camaraderie. Not only had they been intimate in the past, but they still felt a strong physical attraction to each other, an attraction that had in no way been diminished by their marriages. But now Celeste was a widow, and Richard's wife had been lost and almost certainly drowned. There were no impediments in their path now, and only their loyalty to the memories of Adam and Eliza held them back.

They reached the little hut, and Celeste pushed back the flap that covered the doorway. "You're coming in with me, aren't you?" she asked.

He paused at the threshold. "I'm not sure," he said. "We might have cause to regret it if I do."

She deliberately made no move until he preceded her into the building. Inside, she walked to the window opening and stared out at the sky overhead filled with stars.

In the soft moonlight, she had never looked more feminine, more appealing, Richard thought.

"I haven't wanted to rush you or to rush myself, Richard," she said. "The memories of Eliza must be very fresh in your mind. I have no illusions that I could ever take her place, and I would also have to admit that my own memories of Adam are still fresh. But I've learned one thing in the years that I've spent floating from England to France to the New World: Life must be lived by the living, for the living."

He knew she was right. "Memories of the past," he said, "make certain circumstances more bearable and sometimes help ease the pain of the present. But they're no replacement for one's needs from the living."

She slowly turned and faced him. "When I was kidnapped, I expected every moment to be my last. And when I learned why I had been brought here, I wondered whether I'd be safe even if the chief's son recovered from his illness. Then you showed up, and somehow everything has worked out for the best from there."

"Yes," he said with a smile. "It seems that way, doesn't it? But I'm afraid I wasn't much help. It was you who cured the child, and it was you who persuaded the Chickahominy to help us fight our battles. You're an amazing woman, Celeste."

They stared at each other, and neither looked away. Finally Celeste spoke. "We've wanted each other for a long time, a very long time," she said softly. "Now, here, in this heathen, alien place, I say for the sake of our own sanity that we must banish the ghosts of those who are no longer with us and can never return to us."

Richard sensed that she was right, that this was the right time and the right place. At last he stepped forward, took her firmly into his arms, and kissed her.

All the feeling that had been pent up within both of them

for so long was suddenly released, and their mutual desire erased all further cares from their minds. All that mattered now was that they were together, they wanted each other, and the night was theirs.

VII

RICHARD and Celeste created a sensation when, accompanied by Roaring Wolf, they returned to the fort on the river and related their experiences in the land of the Chickahominy. The militia leaders were elated by the news that their force would be augmented by one hundred Indian warriors.

"I know nothing about the qualities of the Chickahominy as fighting men," Dempster Chaney said, "but if they're anywhere near as fierce as the Indians up north, I wouldn't want to tangle with them to find out."

The Chickahominy kept their word, and when their braves arrived in the town a few days later, Richard counted exactly one hundred men. And to his surprise, the force was commanded by No-mi-ma himself.

He was immediately made welcome to the war councils of the leaders of the defense force. The biggest question that faced the planners now was how they could best deploy the Indians.

Richard devoted considerable time and thought to the subject, and eventually produced a solution, which he presented to his fellow officers. "It seems to me," he said, "that if we're going to station the militia, armed with cannon, in the forest on one side of the river, we might be wise to conceal the Chickahominy on the far bank."

There was a gleam of recognition in No-mi-ma's eyes as he nodded emphatically. "That is good," he said. "Then enemy ships must run the gauntlet."

Colonel Nettleton rose slowly to his feet. "I may be wrong," he said, "but it seems to me that if we block the far channel as we said we would, the ships will be forced to stay near this side of the river. That would take them out of accurate range of the heathen arrows, I suspect."

His words made a great deal of sense, and a silence fell on the group.

Richard nodded. "You're absolutely right, if the arrows are aimed at the crewmen. But a sail is a much bigger target."

The others looked perplexed, so Richard continued.

"In New England," he said, "the Mohegan have been known to set fire to arrows before sending them at their foes. Are you familiar with the practice, No-mi-ma?"

The Chickahominy drew himself up proudly. "Warriors of all tribes know this trick," he said.

"So you see," Richard said, "if we station the braves, with fire arrows, on the opposite bank, they can follow the ships up and down the river, making sure they stay in range of our guns and preventing them from landing anywhere unmolested."

Even the conservative Mark Prescott agreed that the tactics were sound, and the group adjourned, deciding to weigh the plan overnight and meet again the following day to work out the details.

A relieved Richard recounted the meeting to Celeste when he joined her that night for supper. They were circumspect in their public behavior, continuing to live in separate houses, but they ate their meals together now, and more often than not, Richard stayed late into the night at the women's quarters. Adella Prescott immediately sensed the changed relationship, but said nothing.

Celeste listened carefully to Richard's explanation of the

military tactics that had been devised. "I'm no expert on battle plans," she said, "but what you've worked out seems foolproof to me. The only question in my mind is whether our forces will be able to cripple the buccaneer vessels severely enough to prevent them from escaping again."

Richard nodded somberly. "That's our ultimate goal," he said. "If we had more nine-pounder cannon available, we'd be in a much better position. But as it is, we'll have to do the best we can with our six-pounders. If our luck is good, the Chickahominy may set fire to the sails or parts of the rigging, and that, combined with the fire from our artillery at short range, should be enough to put the corsairs permanently out of commission."

Celeste concentrated on the fish stew she herself had cooked, and neither spoke for a few minutes as they thought of the coming battle. "It will be such a good feeling," she said finally, "when we know for certain that the French threat to the English colonies has been ended."

"I hope you're right," he replied. "I only wish Cardinal Mazarin was not so persistent, or that his subordinates did not feel so obliged to please him. But you know him far better than I do. Do you think he'll become sufficiently discouraged to give up his plans to gain control of the English colonies after we beat his mercenaries here? Assuming, of course, that we do win," he added with a self-deprecating laugh.

Celeste weighed his question for a time. "I don't believe that the first minister of France ever abandons a goal," she said. "Once he has his mind set on something, he moves heaven and earth to achieve it. But if his mercenaries are decisively beaten, it seems that he'll have few courses of action left. The only choice still open to him will be a direct French attack, and he's afraid to take that step, because he knows that Oliver Cromwell will be compelled to go to war with him when he does."

Richard listened carefully.

"I'm inclined to believe," she said, "that France will follow the course of least resistance and concentrate on controlling young Charles the Second. He's living in exile in France, after all, and if and when he's restored to the throne, he's certain to be grateful to those who gave him refuge and hospitality during his time of trial."

"I hope the French do follow such a course," Richard said slowly, "because it means they'll be misjudging the character of the English—particularly the English colonists. Not even another Charles sitting on the throne at Whitehall could persuade or direct the settlers here to give up the land they've cleared and put to work for them."

"I know," she replied. "I almost feel as though I'm a colonist myself these days, and I can understand how such an order would be taken."

"You and I *are* colonists now," he reminded her.

She shook her head. "You, perhaps. You've fought in two campaigns for the English colonies. But I'm still an interloper. It's true that I have inherited a house in New Haven and an interest in a shipping company, but I somehow don't feel quite at home here yet. I feel I've only been given these things, not that I've earned them."

"That's nonsense," Richard told her briskly. "You're directly responsible for bringing the Chickahominy braves to our aid. You have contributed more than any woman can be expected to contribute."

Celeste shrugged. "Perhaps I'm being foolish," she said, "but I can only tell you what I honestly feel."

"What will it take to change your feelings and make you realize you truly belong on this side of the Atlantic?"

"I don't know," she said.

Richard was silent for a moment. "You lost your husband," he said, "as I lost my wife, only a short time ago. For that reason, I've hesitated to propose marriage to you. I don't think it would be seemly. I also believe we should send the mercenaries of the French to the bottom of the river and make the colonies secure before we even think of our personal welfare. But at the proper time, if you'll agree to marry me, perhaps you will feel that you belong here."

Celeste laughed aloud. "That, sir, is the most convoluted

and complicated proposal of marriage I've ever heard. However, I accept it gladly, qualifications and all."

He leaned toward her across the table, and she raised her face for his kiss.

They thought no more that night about the coming battle with the French mercenaries.

The task of obtaining reinforcements for the buccaneer force that would return to Virginia proved to be a relatively simple matter. Employing the tactics he had used to ensnare Roger Stephens and his men, Admiral de Bosquette set traps for several smaller buccaneer crews and succeeded in capturing a number of them. He promised them French gold in return for their services, and they were further tempted by Roger Stephens's descriptions of the booty they would enjoy when they plundered the Virginia settlements.

"Every town and every village will be yours," he said. "And the women, too. The plantation homes and household goods, the warehouses and their contents—everything—will belong to only you."

The new crews needed no further persuasion—especially when they saw the two swift sloops of war that had been "lent" to the buccaneers by Admiral de Bosquette. These vessels were larger, faster, and more heavily armed than the pinnaces they were replacing.

Stephens was determined not to fail again, and therefore he drilled his new crews day after day, making certain they learned to sail together and fight together. His task was not easy, since many of the new men were not English and could not understand his orders. But he simplified the problem by putting all the foreigners on the two sloops of war, with officers and mates of their own nationality.

While the buccaneers prepared for the invasion, Eliza found herself with little to occupy her time. The knowledge that she possessed information of great importance to the English colonists preyed on her mind and weighed on her soul. If she could convey what she knew about the size and makeup of the buccaneer force to the colonists, they would be far better prepared to defeat the corsairs. But she had no way of communicating with them. It was impossible to send a letter to Virginia, even secretly, since there was no delivery of mail from Martinique to the English colonies. She thought of trying to escape, but even if she managed to elude Stephens and evade recapture, she still had no means of transportation to Virginia.

When she was alone, she brooded over the problem, but could find no solution. She needed help, and was uncertain where to turn for it.

Finally she decided to take a great risk and confide in Zwingli and Wee Willie Walker. Zwingli, she knew, would not betray her to Roger Stephens. And Walker had already come to her aid once. The two men were fast friends; perhaps together they could help her.

She saw her chance one morning when Roger went off to spend the day on the sloops of war, training their crews in the mysteries of handling the sensitive, fast-moving vessels. She and the rest of the crew were confined to the ship, and Stephens hadn't bothered to lock her in her cabin.

The keen interest that her appearance aroused in members of the crew made Eliza acutely conscious of her off-the-shoulder blouse, her skimpy skirt, and the cosmetics thick on her face. She looked like what she had become, what Stephens desired—a pirate's trollop; and she knew that every seaman who saw her wanted her. But she had enough dignity left that she was able to hold herself somewhat aloof as she approached a knot of seamen. "Where's the bo'sun?" she demanded.

The sailors knew she was different from Gabrielle and never flirted with any of them, so they kept a guard on their tongues. "He's on the fo'c'sle, the last I saw of him," one of the men replied politely.

Thanking him, Eliza hurried down the deck, conscious of the eyes that followed her every movement.

She found Wee Willie Walker and Zwingli on their knees, inspecting a new set of canvas just made for the ship by a sailmaker in Saint Pierre. The two giants, always glad to see her, grinned at her and rose to their feet as she approached. Willie doffed his ragged seaman's cap.

"I would like to speak with both of you, if you please," she said. "In private."

Her tone was as serious as her expression, and their smiles faded as they followed her to her own cabin.

Walker was privately relieved that Zwingli was present. The crew invariably knew everything that happened on board, and he didn't need any spiteful seamen reporting to Captain Stephens that the bo'sun had gone alone to the quarters of the captain's mistress.

The heat in the harbor was intense and unrelenting, but Eliza insisted on closing the cabin door after the two big men had crowded inside with her. "I want to speak with you in strictest confidence," she said, "and I trust that what's said here will be repeated to no one."

Zwingli agreed at once and nodded willingly.

Walker was more reluctant, but his curiosity was so great that he also nodded, accepting the woman's terms.

"Zwingli," she said, "until you and I were captured, you were unswervingly loyal to Mark and Adella Prescott. Do you still feel toward them as you did?"

The huge African looked at her unblinkingly. "My feelings have not changed," he said.

She lowered her voice. "What of your loyalty to England? Has that changed?"

The man was surprised by her question, but shook his head. "No," he said solidly.

She turned to the bo'sun. "What about you, Willie?" she demanded. "I know that the life you've led does not promote a great affection toward authority of any kind, but you haven't completely lost your fidelity to your homeland, have you?"

Willie stirred uneasily. "Ye've no call askin' questions like that," he said, "and I'm damned if I'm goin' to answer."

The vehemence of his response told her all she wanted to know, and she continued. "Loyalty to England," she said softly, "also includes loyalty to the English colonies." She stared at him without blinking.

He stood with one arm braced to a beam overhead, his head inclined beneath the low ceiling. The conversation was far too

personal for his taste, and he shook his head as if he didn't
want to hear what she was saying.

"I am not trying to trick you, Willie," Eliza said earnestly.
"Believe me, I feel precisely as you and Zwingli feel. The
loyalties of a lifetime have not been swept away and ended by
the life I'm now forced to lead."

Gradually, Willie's suspicions subsided, and he looked at
the woman curiously. She had made a dangerous admission
that incriminated her, just as the questions she had asked had
incriminated Zwingli and him.

"I grieve," Eliza said, "and my heart is heavy within me
when I think of what awaits the poor people of Virginia. It is
only the whim of the first minister of France that Virginia is
the buccaneer target, rather than my own home of New Haven,
or your home in Bermuda, Zwingli. It is true," she continued,
examining the rings that sparkled on her fingers, "that I will
benefit from what has been planned. I'm sure I'll be given
much new jewelry and many new clothes; but the blood of my
fellow colonists will stain my soul."

Both of her listeners reacted uncomfortably, precisely as
she had hoped they would. Zwingli shifted his feet and stared
at the floor; Willie continued to shake his head slowly, back
and forth, his eyes blank.

"If there were some way, somehow, to warn the settlers in
Virginia of what lies in store for them before the attack takes
place, I would be much relieved," Eliza said.

"But how would that be possible?" Willie demanded in an
angry whisper. "Cap'n Stephens would have the head of any
man who dared betray him."

"I'm confiding in you two," Eliza said, "because I know
you are honorable men and I can rely on you. By myself I can
do nothing. Please, I need your help." Both men seemed deeply
affected by her emotional appeal.

Willie stared hard at her. "Would ye be having any sug-
gestions?"

She shrugged resignedly. "No. I have come to you and
Zwingli because I believed you could help me devise some sort
of plan—anything."

"Maybe you can get away," Zwingli said.

The girl's laugh was bitter. "Stephens often locks me in my cabin or his after dark. And if I did get away from him, how would I get ashore? I can't swim very far; and if I were to take a boat and try to row it ashore, it would be very easy for some men to catch me in the captain's gig. And even if I got ashore, what would I do then? Where would I go?"

Zwingli exchanged a long, hard look with Willie, and in that look many things were left unsaid. Neither would betray the woman's trust—that much was very clear—and Zwingli's expression told Willie that if he changed his mind and warned Captain Stephens of Eliza, he would make an implacable enemy of the man he now regarded as his friend.

But Walker had no intention of saying anything to Stephens. His almost imperceptible nod assured Zwingli that he would stand behind Eliza and do what he could to help her.

Reassured by the expression on his friend's face, Zwingli turned back to Eliza with a grin. "We'll try," he assured her. "We'll do all we can."

Admiral de Bosquette, looking in turn at the three men who sat with him on his veranda, reflected that never had a senior French naval officer commanded such riffraff. However, he was too deeply immersed in his plan of attack on Virginia to back down now.

Directly across from him sat Roger Stephens, and on either side were the two pirate officers commanding the sloops of war. He could not remember their names, and didn't care to. They appeared even more scraggly and grizzled than Stephens, if that was possible, he thought.

"Our plan of attack, gentlemen, is very direct," he began, and he failed to add that it was purposely simple in order to avoid confusion. Even stupid buccaneers, he told himself, should be able to follow these instructions. "As you know, the principal vessel, under Captain Stephens's command, is equipped with twenty nine-pounders and various smaller ordnance."

"The nine-pounders," Roger Stephens added, "will enable us to meet the guns of the garrison on even terms. This means we'll have as good a chance of destroying their fort as they'll have of blowing us to bits." He grinned from ear to ear.

"The element of surprise is all-important," Admiral de Bosquette said, and motioned the others to look at a map that was spread out on the table. "You'll note, gentlemen, that just south of where the Toppahanock flows into the Chesapeake Bay is a large estuary with an island at its mouth. On the east side of this island is an inlet. The area is uninhabited, and any ship that anchors there will be safe from notice."

Roger Stephens continued the briefing of the two other pirate captains. "We will sail from Martinique one at a time," he said, "so as not to attract attention. We will need to pick up extra powder and shot in Guadeloupe, and that will be the job of you two men. Your sloops can make much better time than my ship, and you will leave first, a day apart. After Guadeloupe, you will keep lookouts at your mastheads at all hours, and if you see any other craft—*any* craft—you will run from it. I don't care if it's the richest Spanish treasure ship ever to sail the Indies. We can't afford to take any chances of being spotted."

Admiral de Bosquette nodded. "And just to be safe, you will also fly these when necessary." He motioned to a sentry, who brought over three cloth bundles and gave one to each captain.

The pirates immediately recognized them as English naval ensigns.

"For the sake of security," the admiral continued, "you also will not allow anyone ashore when you reach the rendezvous point. Captain Stephens will probably arrive first, and you will all proceed under his direction to your destination. Is that clear?"

The two newly recruited captains looked at each other, then at Stephens, and nodded their understanding.

"As to the particulars of battle," Admiral de Bosquette said, "I have left that to Captain Stephens. I strongly suggest, however, that you assign a specific objective to each of your ships in advance, and that you concentrate all the efforts of your ship on that objective. In my experience, that is the best way to bring about a successful conclusion to any enterprise."

"I'll work out the details on my own journey north," Stephens said, "and I'll make the individual assignments after we reach the rendezvous."

The matter was settled, and it was agreed that the first sloop would sail the next evening. The plan allowed a generous two weeks for the voyage northward to the Virginia coast, with the attack scheduled to take place as soon as possible so that the rivers would still be high from the spring rains and therefore more easily navigable.

At Stephens's direction, he and his fellow captains kept the plans they had discussed to themselves, revealing no details to any subordinate. The first sloop was provisioned late at night, when the waterfront was normally deserted. Its crew was not allowed ashore the following day, and late the next evening it weighed anchor and quietly slipped out of the harbor. The other sloop followed exactly twenty-four hours later.

Eliza, forced to remain on board Stephens's flagship, did not fail to notice the absence of the two sloops. And when she heard the crew bringing supplies on board her own vessel late after midnight, she knew Stephens would soon set sail. But contrary to her expectations, Wee Willie Walker and Zwingli said nothing to her, and even avoided her when she came on deck in the morning.

Gradually her hopes faded, and she even feared she might have been betrayed by the two giants. Becoming increasingly desperate in her desire to warn the Virginia settlers, Eliza resorted to the dangerous expedient of pumping Roger Stephens for information. When he came below to his cabin for dinner, she tried to ply him with rum to encourage him to talk, but to no avail. He was unusually quiet and preoccupied, and immediately after the meal he went back on deck, locking her in her cabin.

Later that night Eliza heard the rush of bare feet on the deck planking overhead and knew that the crew was preparing to get under way. There was nothing she could do, she realized, and she consoled herself with the knowledge that once they were at sea, she would at least have the freedom of the ship.

The next morning she finally got a chance to speak alone

with Wee Willie Walker for a few seconds. As he put it, "We sneaked out of Martinique." There had been no ceremonies, no farewells, and Admiral de Bosquette had not been present, he said. Quickly returning to his duties, the big bo'sun gruffly warned Eliza to watch her step and to avoid him and Zwingli unless absolutely necessary.

Later in the day, Roger Stephens summoned his crew to the main deck and ordered Eliza to go to her cabin. She was well aware of his motive for sending her away—he wanted the crew's undivided attention, and she was too much of a distraction. But it did not matter as far as she was concerned, for by standing on her bunk and putting her ear to the planking she could hear every word being said on deck.

"We're sailing on an adventure that's going to fill our pockets with French gold and English loot," Stephens began, then went on to explain the coming attack in detail.

His presentation, as always, was forceful and emotional, and he made the coming adventure sound so exciting that the crew interrupted him every few sentences with loud cheers.

Eliza's mind raced as she absorbed the information Stephens was disclosing at last. When he finished and she sat down on her bunk, a glimmer of hope sparked within her. She saw a possible way to outwit the French at last—provided that she, Walker, and Zwingli worked together closely. She was perfectly willing to do her part, whatever the risk. Everything now depended on the willingness of the two giants to cooperate with her.

Eliza's better judgment told her not to go prematurely to Zwingli and Walker with her ideas. If she spoke to them now, they would have two weeks to think and brood before it would become necessary for them to do their part. They were men of action, not thinkers, who might well get cold feet if approached prematurely. So if her plan had any hope of succeeding, she would need to be patient.

The militiamen, Virginians and New Englanders alike, worked hard and steadily, moving the heavy cannon from the brig to their carefully chosen places of concealment in the forest near the riverbank. There the guns were placed behind earthen embankments and camouflaged with underbrush, vines, and tree branches. After this was accomplished, a road was cleared through the woods from the new emplacements to the fort on the bluff.

Meanwhile, several large trees were uprooted and floated downriver to a point opposite the riverbank guns. There the trees were anchored in place so that they appeared to be snagged on a hidden sandbar. Any ship sailing upriver would thus be forced to sail around the trees, well into range of the hidden guns.

Last of all, the battered *Eliza*, manned by a skeleton crew, was moved upriver and anchored in a narrow point of the channel alongside the other Burrows and Clayton brig.

When all these arrangements had been completed, the military leaders made a voyage downriver in a small boat in order to assure themselves that none of the guns was visible from the water.

Colonel Nettleton and Richard thought it would be wise for the gun crews to stay near their cannon at all times, and Mark Prescott agreed that such a precaution was sensible. So the gunners lived and slept in the forest, never straying far from their posts, and their meals were prepared at a camp deeper in the forest, where the smoke from the cooking fires could not be seen from the river.

Celeste Burrows and Adella Prescott volunteered their services to help prepare and serve the food for the crews, and the men gladly accepted.

The infantry and the gunners stationed at the fort on the bluff had less to do and grew restless. Colonel Nettleton, however, put them to work strengthening their own fortifications, adding another wall of logs in front of the cannon and filling in the space between the old and new walls with dirt.

It was far more difficult, however, to convince the Chickahominy of the gravity of the situation. Although the warriors agreed to take their places in the forest on the opposite riverbank, they could not be persuaded to cross the river yet, insisting they would stay with the militiamen until the enemy approached.

Richard sought the advice of Roaring Wolf, who promptly told him the solution. The Pequot chuckled quietly as he declared, "Tell Chickahominy they are afraid to fight in the wilderness. Tell warriors they fear evil spirits of the river and forest. Tell braves they are cowards, and they will do as Richard wishes."

Richard heeded the advice of his friend, and the plan was immediately successful. No-mi-ma proudly led the first boatload of braves across the river, and the rest of his warriors quickly followed.

Richard stayed near the riverbank gun emplacements with his own troops, feeling it would not be right for him to sleep in a bed and eat at a table while the militiamen were forced to endure the hardships of the wilderness. As a result, he and Celeste saw little of each other. She occasionally brought him his meals and took the time to exchange a few words with him. But they were content to see each other even for a few minutes during this time of impending danger. They knew they were together—or at least near to each other—and would share the same fate, so both of them were satisfied.

Celeste, Richard reflected, had responded superbly in this time of emergency. She had grown in stature as a woman, and he knew he had lost his heart to her.

Stephens's buccaneer ship entered Chesapeake Bay near dusk after thirteen days at sea. Taking no chances that he might be spotted by an English ship, he stayed out of sight of shore until well into the bay. Then, flying the English ensign supplied by Admiral de Bosquette, he set course up the sparsely populated eastern shore until just before sunrise, when he turned abruptly away from shore and headed across the bay to the western shore.

Shortly after noon the ship dropped anchor in the secluded harbor that had been designated as the rendezvous. As Stephens had expected, neither of the sloops had yet arrived, and at dusk he left the crew with orders to remain silent and vigilant, then retired to his cabin.

He celebrated the completion of the first stage of his journey by carousing the entire night with Eliza. He was in buoyant spirits, and at his urging she was forced to drink far more rum than she wanted.

Her head ached dully and she was lethargic the following day, but at least she could not remember what had happened the previous night. To her relief, she gained a respite late in the afternoon when the first of the sloops of war arrived and dropped anchor nearby. Captain Stephens promptly ordered his gig lowered and had himself rowed to the sloop so he could confer with its captain. This was the opportunity Eliza had awaited, and she immediately sought the bo'sun.

"Go to your cabin," Willie Walker muttered uneasily. "We'll meet you there."

He and Zwingli soon arrived, their nervousness making it evident that they wanted no prolonged meeting.

Eliza had rehearsed any number of arguments to present to them, but aware of their apprehensions, she cut her speech short. "One of the sloops is here," she said, "and the other, I presume, will arrive tomorrow or the next day at the latest. They will be busy transferring ammunition to our ship, so this is the right time for you to take a boat and row up the river to the fort to warn them. If you hurry, you can return here before Roger moves his whole fleet upriver."

Willie was unconvinced and shook his head. "That's all well and good," he said, "but what excuse do we make to Cap'n Stephens when we return? He's nobody's fool, and he's sure to expect the worst of it when he sees we ain't here."

Eliza had expected this objection. "Leave him a message that you and Zwingli have gone out to reconnoiter," she said. "You can tell him you went to see for yourselves what preparations, if any, the English colonists had made for the battle. I promise you, he'll believe you."

Willie still shook his head, and even Zwingli looked dubious. "Why do you think Cap'n would believe a big lie like that?" the African asked.

Eliza's smile was tight-lipped. "Because I intend," she said, "to keep him so occupied that he'll have no time or desire to think about it. You'll just have to leave that aspect of it to me."

Zwingli still looked a little wary but seemed satisfied.

Willie Walker, however, hesitated. "You seem mighty sure o' yourself, ma'am," he said.

"I have to be," she said, "if I want to stay alive. I'll do my job; don't worry about that." Eliza knew everything depended on her being able to convince Willie to proceed with the plan, and if she had to resort to questioning his courage, so be it. "Besides," she said, carefully watching the bo'sun's expression, "you don't have to return to the ship. You'd be in no danger that way."

Willie, the man of action, was torn, and he hesitated. "I'm no coward, if that's what ye be implyin'," he said. "If I did go, I wouldn't be afraid of comin' back. That is if I *did* go; but I'm not saying as I would."

Eliza knew he was wavering, and she pressed her advantage. "If you're content to have the blood of fellow Englishmen on your conscience for the rest of your days," she said scornfully, "then continue to do nothing. Zwingli, will you go alone if necessary?"

"I will go," the African replied.

"And leave me behind?" Willie demanded indignantly. "No, sir—not on your life. All right, I'll go."

"Good," Eliza said. "Then I wish you both Godspeed. We have no time to waste." She embraced them both briefly before they left the cabin. Then, aware of the task she had set for herself, she steeled her nerves for the night of drunken debauchery ahead, by which means she planned to distract Roger Stephens from his duties. She lavished cosmetics on her face and extravagantly splashed on a strong perfume Roger had given her recently when he had been particularly pleased with her conduct. Then she selected her most seductive dress and, after donning it, examined her reflection in the looking glass by the light of an oil lamp.

The hard-faced young woman who so insolently returned

her stare bore scant resemblance to the demure Eliza Dunstable of New Haven Colony. The respectable wife of a prominent colonial citizen had disappeared, and in her place stood a woman whom any man would be certain to recognize as a bold strumpet.

Continuing to study herself, Eliza grimly reflected that she looked like a debauched trollop because that was precisely what she had become. At least Richard was no longer alive, she told herself, to see her downfall. But she dismissed the thought, telling herself that he wouldn't have cared, that he had never cared.

Well, at least she would be warning the innocent settlers of Virginia of the coming attack; that was the least she could do for the sake of the person she had once been. That alone was something to cling to.

She felt certain that after suffering a second defeat, Stephens would retreat to his pirate haunts and not dare to return to Martinique. He would have to stay clear of the French for some time to come, and she could remain with him for a while. Perhaps she could escape to some island someday. One thing was certain, though: She could never return to New Haven. That life was dead forever.

Hearing the gig return, Eliza quickly applied another layer of scarlet rouge to her cheeks, then hurried to the stern cabin so she would be there when Stephens arrived. She had not heard the departure of Willie and Zwingli, and could only hope they had succeeded in leaving the ship in good time.

In the captain's cabin, she quickly poured two large glassfuls of rum, then seated herself in a chair, artfully adjusting her bodice to expose her breasts and arranging her skirts and petticoats so that they fell away to bare one long, slender leg.

When Roger Stephens entered the cabin, slamming the door hard behind him, it was immediately apparent to her that he was in a vicious mood.

Pretending to be unaware of his temper, she sat absent-mindedly twirling a strand of her long blond hair around a finger.

"Damn that Walker!" he shouted. "He's been with me long

enough to know that when I want him to do something, I'll damn well tell him! He knows better than to go traipsing off in the shallop and to take that bloody giant friend of his with him. I'll have both their hides for this!"

Eliza's heart leaped. So Willie and Zwingli had indeed left the ship, and had even taken the shallop, which had a small sail as well as oars. If the wind was right, they could reach the fort by morning. "When are they coming back?" she asked innocently.

"All that idiot crew of mine told me was that Willie said he'd return in plenty of time to see action with us." He shook his head, clenched his fists, and muttered inarticulately.

"I hope you're not going to let this spoil your evening," she said. "I was hoping we could take up where we left off last night."

His mood was so foul that he failed to respond to her.

Eliza rose, went to him, and stroking him with one hand, held his drink to his lips with the other.

Stephens waved her away. He was not interested in drink at the moment.

She persisted. She pouted seductively and did not lower the glass from the vicinity of his lips, as her other hand traveled from his face and neck down his body.

Impatient and irritated, he took the glass from her and gulped the contents.

That left her other hand free, and she began to stroke him with it, too. She pressed closer to him, rubbing her body against his. "I refuse to believe," she murmured, "that you forgot what you promised me last night."

"Huh?" he said. "What are you talking about?"

"Don't you remember?" she whined, a pretty sulk on her lips. She stood on her tiptoes and whispered something in his ear, and grinned slyly.

"Now that you mention it," he said, "my memory is awakening."

She curled her arms around his neck and kissed him lingeringly, finally drawing away from him just enough to pick up the other glass of rum and feed it to him.

Stephens swallowed the contents before he realized what was happening. Only then did he protest. "That was very unfair," he said. "You gave me your drink."

Eliza laughed as though he had made the wittiest of remarks. "That's easily remedied," she said and, refilling both glasses, picked one up and downed the contents. The raw rum burned in her throat, and after a few seconds she felt an almost uncontrollable urge to throw up. But the unpleasant sensation passed just as quickly, and she was relieved to discover that the alcohol was at work already, making her feel slightly numb.

Stephens followed her example and drained the contents of the other glass.

"I'll make you an agreement," he said, now in a jolly mood. "I'll undress you if you'll undress me."

"That sounds like the best idea I've heard in a long time," she told him.

Picking her up, he carried her to the bed. There he stretched her out, and as he fumbled with her buttons and bows, Eliza knew she had succeeded. Roger Stephens was so absorbed in her that he had completely forgotten about the trip that his bo'sun was making in the little craft. And if she had her way, many hours would pass and many glasses of rum would be emptied before his thoughts reverted to Willie Walker and Zwingli.

It was Sunday, and Adella Prescott and Celeste Burrows had risen an hour before dawn and walked together to the fort, then down the forest road to the riverbank encampment. Between them they carried a dozen loaves of corn bread and an entire smoked shoulder of ham.

The artillerymen, most of them roused out of a sound sleep, greeted the two women pleasantly. As a gray-bearded sergeant observed, had the "serving wenches" been less attractive, they no doubt would have been met with surly curses.

Celeste laughed at this comment, and after all of the men had been served, she left to take a portion of the food to Richard and the remaining men, who had encamped a hundred yards farther back in the woods, around a stream in a wooded hollow.

Meanwhile, the sergeant had begun to tease Adella, asking her to marry him then and there so that she could spend the rest of her life waking him up with a similar breakfast.

She answered him in kind, and in the midst of their joking, she happened to glance toward the river, where a sail in the distance caught her eye.

In the early morning breeze, the small craft moved smartly up the river toward the wharf below the bluff. Sitting at the tiller was a huge, brawny man in a ragged sailor's cap, but it was his black-skinned companion, who was attending to the sail, who attracted Adella's notice.

She stared at him hard for a moment, and before any of the others could say a word, she had raced toward the water, calling "Zwingli!"

The African heard her shouting his name and immediately recognized her voice. He turned and said something to his companion, who obligingly headed the boat toward the near bank of the river.

When Zwingli stepped ashore, Adella Prescott was waiting impatiently and hurled herself at him. He hugged her tightly.

"I'd given you up for dead," she told him, alternately sobbing and laughing. "I thought for sure you had died at the hands of the buccaneers."

"Zwingli is a hard man to kill," he replied with a broad grin.

Adella's shouts had attracted the men from the other encampment, and no sooner had Willie Walker also stepped ashore than he was surrounded by men armed with muskets.

Richard Dunstable stepped forward. "Haul that boat up onto shore and conceal it in the reeds," he directed. "Make certain it can't be seen from the river."

He spoke with natural authority, Willie noticed, and several of the men hastened to obey him. Only after the boat was well hidden did Richard turn his attention fully to the two men—and only then did he recognize the black man standing next to Adella: Zwingli! The man Mark Prescott said had been with Eliza when she had disappeared!

Zwingli had also noticed Richard and, anticipating his question, said simply, "Yes, she is alive."

Richard felt his head spinning, and for a moment he could not speak. Finally he turned to the man next to him and said in a low, strangled voice, "Take these two up to the fort, to Colonel Nettleton and Major Prescott. I will be along shortly."

At first Richard just stood still. He didn't know whether to laugh or cry, to rejoice or to damn the cruelty of the fate that was mocking him. Then, unconscious of his surroundings, he began to walk slowly back to the encampment where he had left Celeste. Suddenly the approach of a pair of footsteps jerked him from his anguished reverie. He looked up and saw her coming toward him. One glance at her pale face and shocked eyes told him that she, too, had learned the truth about Eliza— or had seen Zwingli and surmised it.

"One of the men just told me," she said, "that Eliza is alive and well on board the buccaneer vessel."

Richard nodded dully.

There was deep concern in her violet eyes. "Are you all right?" she asked anxiously.

He grimaced. "Let's say," he replied, "that I'm doing as well as can be expected under the circumstances. I don't know what to say, especially to you, nor do I know what to do. I don't even know what to feel anymore."

"I think I know what you mean," Celeste replied, "and I feel the same way. And I'm every bit as much at a loss as to what to do about it." She continued to gaze at him steadily. "It's as if she had come back from the grave."

Richard looked at her and was startled when he realized that he actually wanted her, at this very moment. That, he reflected, was a desire he would have to squelch now and for all time. With Eliza alive, he could not degrade her or Celeste by continuing to behave as he had. He could not as much as hold her in his arms or kiss her again. Those were pleasures of the past, not of the present, and certainly not of the future.

"Are you going to try to rescue Eliza from the pirates?" Celeste asked.

"I don't know," he started to reply, then stopped himself.

"Yes, of course, though I don't quite know how I'll go about it. She is my wife, and I have an obligation to her. I daresay everything will depend on the way the battle progresses. But I'd be a scoundrel if I didn't try to set her free."

"I wish you well," Celeste murmured, and her voice became shaky.

"Thank you," Richard replied, and again he was at a loss for words. This woman, with whom he had slept and in whom he had confided, suddenly had receded beyond his grasp and had become as a stranger to him. The thought that they had no future together sickened him, but he knew he had to stand firm.

It appeared that much the same thoughts were going through Celeste's mind. "I've got to tell you something that should go without saying," she said, "but I feel I must mention it just once. Naturally, I—I release you from your request to marry me. I think it will be best for both of us if we put that conversation out of our minds and act as though it never took place."

"You're right," Richard said hoarsely. "I feel like a cad, though."

"You must not blame yourself, now or ever, for what's happened," Celeste said. "You and I both acted in the best of good faith at the time."

"Yes," he replied bleakly, "I guess we can say that much. But for our own sake, we'll do well to forget that we ever cared for each other." He looked at her as though trying to memorize her features, and shook his head but did not speak.

"I—I wish you the best of good fortune in the battle that lies ahead," Celeste said, "both in defeating the enemy and in recovering your wife."

Richard thanked her with a nod.

"I know you're going to be terribly busy," she said, "and you'll also want time to yourself. So this is good-bye." She held out her hand.

As though in a dream, he extended his own hand.

Their fingers touched and a strange power seemed to pass between them. Without either of them realizing what was happening, they suddenly moved forward and embraced. Their lips met and they clung to each other desperately, their kiss bitter-sweet.

Suddenly, Celeste wrenched free and fled from the wilderness hollow. She did not weep until she was out of sight.

Richard stood there listening to her footsteps fading in the distance. Her decency, her nobility, deeply touched him, and he was more confused than ever. He realized he should rejoice that Eliza was alive, but he was too numb to feel anything.

All he knew was that he had his duty to perform. Colonel Nettleton and Major Prescott were no doubt waiting for him, and the two men from the pirate ship would probably have information on the enemy's plans. So, ruthlessly casting aside his own cares, Richard set out at a brisk pace for the fort, his mind racing forward to the coming battle.

A battle, he thought, was a simple, clear-cut affair. You devoted all your thoughts, all your energies, to one goal: killing the enemy while avoiding death yourself. His own life had become such a turbulent mass of emotions that he doubted he would ever be able to straighten it out again. A battle, he told himself, was just what he needed.

Willie Walker had at one time or another traveled nearly everywhere in the known world, but never had he seen a woman as strikingly beautiful as Adella Prescott. As she stood there, animatedly conversing with Zwingli, he stared at her in open-mouthed wonder. Perhaps, he told himself, he had been at sea too long.

Richard brought him back to the present abruptly. "Suppose you tell us just how you happened to come here?" he said patiently.

Willie, his cap in hand, explained how he and his friend had simply taken the shallop and sailed up the river, away from the buccaneer ships that lay anchored in the hidden harbor off the bay, awaiting the arrival of the third ship.

Zwingli nodded his agreement with his friend's explanation. Mark again looked at the giant African in wonder and affection. "This is truly a miracle, Zwingli," he said. "We'd given you up for lost."

Colonel Nettleton and Richard, however, were far more interested in the strength of the buccaneers and the number of cannon their ships carried, and in what the pair could tell them about the corsair's battle plans.

They listened to the replies with great interest, and finally Colonel Nettleton said slowly, "I don't rightly know whether to believe these boys or not. It may be that we're being hoodwinked good and proper."

Willie and Zwingli protested that they were telling the truth.

"I can't speak for Walker," Mark declared flatly, "but I've known Zwingli as well as I have ever known any man anywhere, and I'll accept what he tells me as truth."

Richard had not yet made up his mind. He had already talked privately with Zwingli to find out what he could about Eliza, and he was fairly certain he could trust the African. But he wasn't quite sure yet about Walker. "What are you planning to do now that you've brought us this information?" he asked the bo'sun.

"We left word for Cap'n Stephens that we'd come back as soon as we scouted out the fort here," he replied.

"And that you've certainly done," Richard said.

"Indeed," Colonel Nettleton added. "You've learned our secret deployments. I daresay your commander would give a great deal to know what you know."

"He's absolutely right," Richard said. "I regret to inform you, but we can't take the chance of allowing you two to return to the expedition under any circumstances. You've already acquired too much vital information."

Willie and Zwingli looked at each other and seemed to reach a silent agreement.

"That settles the problem for us," Willie said. "Me and my friend was talking as we made our way up the river, and we decided that neither of us ain't all that eager to go back to Cap'n Stephens's ship. So, if it be all the same to ye, we'll fight on your side in the battle that's comin'."

The officers were clearly taken aback by the offer, and conferred with one another in murmurs.

"I think that's wonderful," Adella said, clasping her hands as she looked first at Zwingli and then at Willie. As Willie's eyes met hers, she caught her breath, then turned quickly away, a slight blush evident on her cheeks.

"Not so fast," Colonel Nettleton said. "We can use volunteers, it's true enough, but how are we to be sure that these men won't turn on us once the fighting starts?"

"I'm sure they'll do no such thing," Adella said fervently. "You can depend on them, so help me God."

The head of the Virginia militia looked dubious. Dempster Chaney's expression indicated that he shared Colonel Nettleton's reluctance to accept the two volunteers.

Mark Prescott stepped forward. "I'll personally vouch for Zwingli. But as for the other one, we might be safer keeping him well away from the fighting. I suggest that we put—"

"Hold on." It was a female voice, and it came from the back of the room. Everyone turned in unison, and the men in the rear stepped aside as Celeste made her way to the bo'sun's side.

Wee Willie Walker immediately recognized the woman he had rescued from the amorous clutches of Admiral de Bosquette just a few months earlier, and a huge grin spread across his grizzled face.

"You can trust this man, Richard," Celeste said. "I'd stake my life on that." She turned to the other leaders and spoke in a strong, steady voice. "I'm sorry for interrupting you gentlemen like this, but it didn't occur to me until just now that the red-haired giant the men said you had in here was an old acquaintance of mine. In fact, Mr. Walker here just about saved my life once; he even risked his own neck by admitting to be a loyal Englishman when it would have been much safer for him to say nothing."

The officers began to shout questions and argue among themselves, but Celeste again spoke up.

"I say if Major Prescott can vouch for Zwingli, I, the widow of Colonel Burrows, can vouch for this man."

"That's good enough for me," Richard said. He turned to the commander of the Virginia militia. "Colonel Nettleton, I will be personally responsible for this man. Walker, you and Zwingli will report directly to me. And after you get something to eat, you can join my volunteers at the riverbank."

Richard knew he was acting precipitately. But if the pirate ships were already in the bay, there was little time for debate. Besides, the addition of these two giants to the defending force would be invaluable, particularly if hand-to-hand fighting developed.

As to whether they could be trusted, he had Celeste's and Adella's word—and as far as he was concerned, that was all he needed.

VIII

THE wind had picked up during the night, and the waters of the bay had grown choppy. But when dawn came and the sun rose, Eliza and Roger Stephens continued to sleep soundly. Clothes lay strewn all around the cabin, and an empty rum bottle rolled back and forth across the floor as the ship rocked fitfully at her anchorage.

In fact, they did not awaken until the sun began to set in the west and Roger was summoned on deck to meet with the captain of the second sloop of war, which had just arrived at the rendezvous.

Eliza, still groggy and half sick from the amount of rum she had imbibed the previous evening, had no idea whether Willie or Zwingli had returned as yet—or even if they would return at all. As the events of the preceding day began to filter back into her consciousness, she slumped back into the pillows. It was best not to think about what she had done, she decided. Her entire body felt incredibly weary and worn, and finally she had to force herself to get out of bed, to eat something, and to wash and dress. However bad she felt, she knew she must be prepared to distract Stephens again, should that prove necessary.

Stephens remained on deck for most of the evening and returned to the cabin only briefly. "The bo'sun and the African must have run into trouble of some kind," he scowled. "They haven't come back."

"They haven't?" she echoed. She did not know what else to say.

"Whatever may have happened to them," Stephens said, "it serves them right for going off on their own without permission. Wind blew up last night, it seems. They're lucky if they weren't capsized and drowned. But we can't afford to wait for them or go searching every which way. All of our ships are here, and we are going to attack."

"Oh?" Eliza said, as if not interested. The continued absence of Zwingli and Willie might mean that they had succeeded in alerting the defenders, she told herself. But she couldn't be sure, and it occurred to her that she might never know.

"It's too late to move upriver tonight," he said. "We'll wait until morning and weigh anchor at first light. If the wind is favorable, we should reach their fort by noon." He grinned at her. "Aren't you looking forward to seeing your friends again?"

She didn't like his tone, and wondered if he suspected her true loyalties. But what if he did? Now that Zwingli and Willie were gone, she concluded, it didn't much matter what became of her. On the other hand, if she kept up her masquerade just a little longer, perhaps she would be allowed to come on deck during the battle. Then, if the opportunity presented itself, perhaps she could do something else to harm the French cause.

"I have no friends, except you," she replied at last. "As I told you before, my husband was killed in the last attack. I had no one else."

"Gabrielle would have enjoyed joining the men when the looting starts," he said. "But you're not that sort, are you?"

Concealing a shudder, she shook her head, "No, I'm not," she said. "I admit I do not like the sight of blood."

"Well, you'd better get used to it," he said. "In any case, you're entitled to your fair share of booty, and you shall have it. I'll have the men bring their prizes back to this ship and spread them out on deck. Then you can take your choice, like the last time. You'd like that, wouldn't you?"

It would be ironic, Eliza reflected, if the booty included any clothes from her own previous wardrobe. The idea struck her as oddly humorous, and she couldn't help but smile.

Roger, misreading her expression, was pleased, and he gave her a comradely pat on the behind. "I'm going on deck now," he said, "and I won't be coming back down here until the battle is over. So wish me luck." Pulling her to him roughly, he kissed and caressed her.

Eliza was growing accustomed to enduring his crude embraces, but now, for the first time, the thought crossed her mind that if Willie and Zwingli had been successful, Stephens might well not survive the battle. The man who was holding her now might be dead tomorrow. That thought was startling, but the prospect did not dismay her at all. She had become so used to doing what was necessary to stay alive, so adept at playing her role of pirate's mistress, that she had almost begun to think as a pirate, heedless of human life, heedless of death— even her own death, she now realized.

Well, that was all to the good, she thought as she returned Stephens's kiss. Her life was worthless now, and she would just as well be at peace, as Richard and her father were.

Roaring Wolf had arrived, breathless with news that the enemy convoy had been sighted downriver. Now it was late in the afternoon, and in the woods the militiamen waited silently, their eyes all on the river.

"They're coming!" a lookout stationed high in the branches of a pine tree called softly. "They're in single file, with the large ship in the lead, and two sloops following on her heels."

Richard turned to two of his messengers, who were awaiting orders at his side. "Instruct Major Prescott to hold his fire until we open fire," he said. "And give No-mi-ma the alert signal."

The messengers departed at once, one to the fort on the bluffs and the other to signal to the chief of the Chickahominy in accordance with a simple plan worked out with various colored flags.

The wait seemed interminable.

Finally the familiar-looking pirate ship came into view around a bend in the river, its sails partly furled as it moved cautiously toward the fort on the bluffs.

"That's Cap'n Stephens all right," Willie said. "You can prob'ly see him on the quarterdeck through your glass, sir."

Richard raised his glass to his eye and focused it on the elegantly dressed black-bearded figure on the quarterdeck of the buccaneer vessel. The man was tall and, from this distance, looked surprisingly young. It was difficult to envision such a man as Eliza's lover, Richard thought, not being able to forget what Zwingli had disclosed to him—that Eliza had indeed become Stephens's mistress. But he couldn't think of that now. She had, after all, tried to warn them of the attack. Despite all her hardships, she had done her duty; now he must do his. It was imperative that he keep his mind clear for the intricate task of orchestrating the defenses.

"How many nine-pounders?" he asked again, just to make sure.

"Twenty, sir," Willie replied. "Was ten the last time, but the Frenchies in Saint Pierre took off most of the six-pounders and replaced 'em with nine-pounders."

Richard nodded and transferred his attention to the two smaller ships, both of which were riding low in the water— apparently loaded to the gunwales with cannon and men.

Richard shook his head in disbelief at the stupidity of the enemy. Sloops of war were frail craft, their only advantages in battle being their speed and maneuverability. But overloaded as they were, and forced to fight in a narrow river, they were next to useless. As long as they didn't land their men down-river—and obviously that hadn't occurred to them—they would be sitting ducks.

Richard therefore decided to ignore them for the present and concentrate his full efforts on putting Stephens's ship out of commission. With her nine-pounders, she represented the chief danger to the defenders.

"Gunners stand ready," he called, and the men passed his orders down the line.

Zwingli, standing beside Richard behind the brushwood barrier, peered hard at the large ship that was nearly directly opposite the riverbank guns. "I don't see her," he muttered.

Richard felt a sharp twinge as he again realized that his wife, in all probability, was on board the ship he was about to bombard. But his duty was clear, and he could not call off the attack for her sake.

"You may open fire when ready," he directed.

"Fire at will!" Dempster Chaney echoed softly.

The three six-pounders roared almost in unison and marked the start of the engagement. Two of the shots fell short, the iron balls splashing harmlessly into the river, while the third just overshot the mark, the projectile slicing without effect through the rigging of the pirate flagship.

The gun crews needed no instructions and hastily adjusted the elevation of their weapons.

In the meantime, the opening cannonade had served as a signal to the other defenders. The artillerymen stationed in the fort on the bluff had the six nine-pounders at their disposal, and they used them to the best advantage, taking careful aim, firing, and reloading with practiced speed.

By the second barrage they had found their mark. One shot splintered the foremast of the flagship, another carried away parts of the deck railing, and two others sliced into the hardwood planking near the ship's waterline.

The Chickahominy had been eagerly awaiting their opportunity to join in the combat, and the initial booming of cannon served as a welcome signal to them. In less than a minute they had started fires and lighted the mixture of dried leaves and pine tar that they had attached to their arrows, and a flaming barrage soared into the air, descending toward the decks of the pirate vessels.

Most of the Indian arrows fell short of their mark, and those that did actually strike the ship were quickly extinguished. But the fear of fire on any vessel was great, and as a result the buccaneers were forced to stay within range of the cannon on the opposite shore.

To add to the pirates' worries, two enterprising braves had camouflaged themselves in the snags of brushwood anchored in the river, and from their hiding places they slowly but methodically picked off sailors on the deck and in the rigging of the larger vessel.

The two small sloops of war in the buccaneer flotilla had so far remained untouched, for they were still out of range of the guns on the bluff, and the artillerymen in the forest were concentrating their fire on the larger vessel. But there was little or nothing the smaller ships could contribute to the corsair cause. They carried only six-pounders and lesser ordnance, and even though their captains could distinguish the location of the cannons in the forest from the flashes and smoke of the discharges, they didn't dare approach nearer for fear of also coming under the bombardment of the larger cannon on the bluff. For lack of a better target, they directed their fire on the opposite shore, where the Chickahominy braves were hidden.

Roger Stephens, however, was a fighting man, and he refused to retreat from the enemies' guns. Holding steady under the triple barrage his ship was enduring, he used his own nine-pounders to their best advantage, sending round after round of heavy metal balls crashing into the palisades of the fort and ripping into the underbrush of the riverbank in the vicinity of the smoke and flashes. The Indians he ignored as best he could, although the arrow-pierced corpses that already littered the deck forced him to keep a wary distance from the far shore.

Meanwhile, Wee Willie Walker impatiently observed the progress of the battle. The corsair bo'sun was more accustomed to hand-to-hand combat, and he stirred restlessly. Finally he could tolerate no more.

"Colonel Dunstable, sir" he said earnestly, speaking during a lull in the fire, "I can be a help in bringin' this fight to an end in no time at all. I know that ship, and I know the lads on it. And they don't like this kind of fight, not at all."

"What are you getting at?" Richard said.

Willie's expression was deadly earnest. "A lot of the lads

in the crew felt the same way I do," he said. "After all, they're Englishmen. Granted, they've been livin' beyond the law; still, they won't be caring much for this assignment. It's one thing to board a Spanish galleon on the high seas and take her cargo and send her crew to the bottom along with the ship. The Spaniard never was our friend, always bein' at war with England and such. But it's somethin' else again to attack a British colony—and to be doin' it for the French, no less! No, a lot of the lads ain't too happy about workin' for the French, and it wouldn't take much to make 'em change their minds—and fast."

Richard was interested in what he heard and exchanged a quick glance with Dempster Chaney, who was listening in on the conversation. "What exactly do you have in mind, Walker?" Richard said.

"The way I see it," he declared, "the lads on the flagship—my lads—are interested in saving their own necks. Right now they got metal being thrown at them from two directions, and those confounded Indian arrows spurtin' fire don't exactly give 'em no peace of mind, neither. And the cowards sittin' back there out of range in the two sloops, well, they're not especially bosom buddies of the lads. Fact is, most of 'em are foreigners, recruited by the French."

Richard, listening intently, began to understand what the giant had in mind.

"Them two sloops," Willie continued, "ain't been touched. But give the lads a little added incentive, such as knowin' for certain that they can get away with their skins whole, and they'll turn against the wretches on those two sloops and bid Cap'n Stephens and his cockeyed French plans a fond farewell."

"Are you suggesting," Richard asked, "that I send a detachment of infantrymen to board the corsair ship?"

"Hell, no!" Willie replied vehemently. "That's just about the last thing in the world to do. Send men to attack the lads, and they'll fight like demons!"

"Then I'm afraid I don't understand you." Richard said, becoming slightly irritated.

The giant shook his head. "I never yet seen an officer who

has a lick o' common sense," he said. "Every last one of ye has his head in the clouds. Maybe I didn't make myself clear when I said that the lads need persuadin'. There's only one man can do that and can talk them into attackin' the buccaneers on the two sloops of war. That's me."

Richard stared at him in disbelief. "You mean you're offering to go on board and talk the buccaneers into turning on their comrades?" he said. "You'd be killed before you could get halfway to the ship! And even if you did make it on board, your captain would notice you right away and shoot you as a deserter."

"Cap'n Stephens," Willie said dryly, "has a few other things on his mind right now. He is goin' to be too busy to see what I'm up to. And as to gettin' on board in the first place, well, I'll just have to take my chances."

"I think you're crazy," Richard said at last, "but it's your neck. All right, you can go—"

The grinning giant was already turning to leave, but Richard put out a restraining hand.

"Not yet," he said. "You'll have a much better chance if you wait until dark. That won't be long now; and from the looks of things, your captain seems intent on staying right where he is and slugging it out all night."

Richard well knew that Walker was taking a terrible risk, but he understood the giant's attitude. Direct attack was always the most tempting course of action for a military man, and he himself had to fight the urge to jump in a boat and row out to the enemy ships.

"Aye, aye, sir, I'll wait," the giant said. "But ye don't have to worry none about me. I got a mighty big respect for preservin' myself. I only got one skin, and I don't aim to lose it foolishly. But the way I figger it, if I do a fair enough piece o' work in this here battle, maybe the colonists will overlook my being a corsair and all. I'm about ready to settle down to a quiet life, anyhow, and I don't plan to get maimed or crippled, much less killed."

"As far as I'm concerned," Richard said, "if you can do what you say you can, you need have no fear about your future.

I'll personally do all I can to see that your past actions are completely forgotten."

They grinned at each other, and Richard patted Willie on the back, then returned his full attention to the battle.

The six-pounders hidden in the underbrush were firing more intermittently now, their barrels overheated from the unrelenting volleys. The batteries on the bluff and the pirate cannon had also quieted considerably; and Richard took the opportunity to inspect more carefully the damage the enemy ship had sustained. Putting his glass to his eye, he squinted through the thinning smoke at the quarterdeck of the pirate vessel, hoping to catch a glimpse of Captain Stephens.

To his surprise, however, he saw a woman instead. She had shoulder-length honey-blond hair, the same shade as Eliza's— though it was tied behind her neck—but still he failed to recognize her. Eliza had always dressed and carried herself demurely, but this woman's gown left her half naked, and she moved along the deck more like a swaggering salt than a lady of good breeding.

Gradually, however, the awareness grew in Richard that he was indeed looking at his wife. Feeling shaken and somewhat uncertain, he moved closer to the riverbank to get a better look. Then he noticed the big African standing not far away, and he motioned for him and handed him the glass.

Zwingli saw Richard's ghostlike expression and, taking the glass, focused it on the young woman pacing back and forth on the quarterdeck of the buccaneer ship. One glance was all he needed.

Handing the glass back to Richard, he said, "Yes. That is Eliza."

Richard was stunned. The Eliza he had known and cherished had been transformed into what appeared to be a brazen, hardfaced wench. Yet it was not the dramatic change in her appearance that shook him to his soul—rather it was a deep surge of emotions that nearly took his breath away as he recognized this was the Eliza he still loved, the Eliza he had given up for dead but had never truly forgotten. Even though she now appeared almost a total stranger, his heart went out to her. Scarcely aware of what he was doing, he shouted out a quick string of orders.

"Captain Chaney!"

Dempster appeared almost instantly.

"You're in command now," Richard said in a tone that brooked no argument.

"Walker! Zwingli!" he shouted, but the two giants were already at his side. "All right, Walker," he said. "You wanted to board that vessel. It's dark enough; now's your chance. You know her crew best. How do we get on board without being seen?"

Willie was surprised by the "we," but didn't hesitate with his answer. He had already given the problem serious thought, and knew the best course of action. "Get upriver and grab a log, then drift down to her, hidin' behind the log. Climb over the stern, quiet-like, portside. Won't nobody be lookin' there."

Richard was satisfied and acted without hesitation. Relieving his remaining messengers of their horses, he led Willie and Zwingli in a breakneck ride over the forest trail to the fort. But instead of entering the stockade, he skirted the bluff, heading to the wharf directly below the fort.

As the three men dismounted, Willie looked around him in apparent consternation. "This is far enough upriver, sir, but I don't see any logs we could be using."

Zwingli, however, had already solved the problem. Tentatively shaking a sizable dead oak adjacent to the wharf, he rubbed his palms together and smiled broadly. Before it finally dawned on Walker what Zwingli had in mind, the dead wood was creaking and splintering as the African applied his massive shoulder to the trunk.

A few minutes later, almost invisible among the half-submerged branches, three heads bobbed in the water as the dead tree drifted closer and closer to the enemy flagship.

Recalling what had happened to Eliza Dunstable during the previous engagement, Colonel Nettleton was taking no chances and kept Adella and Celeste under close guard. It was impossible, however, to prevent them from at least watching the battle; he had already tried as much—in vain, as it turned out. Both women had protested so long and so vigorously that he had been forced to compromise and allow them to observe the proceedings from an observation post just upriver from the fort, manned by one of the Virginia militiamen. The fact that both women would probably be needed in the nearby hospital had no doubt influenced the colonel's decision. But just to be sure, he had given the soldier strict orders to see that neither woman strayed closer to the fighting—even though both had given their word to stay put.

Absorbed in the developing battle, Celeste had not taken her eyes off the enemy ships since the first shot had been fired. Eventually, though, she could not help but notice her companion's odd behavior. Adella, her eyes riveted not to the ships, but rather to the shore downriver, would periodically cover her face with both hands and rock back and forth, moaning softly to herself.

Celeste looked at her curiously. "Is it Zwingli you're worried about?" she asked. The other woman glanced up dejectedly and shook her head.

"Is it someone else, then?" Celeste said, surprised.

Adella turned red and nodded shyly. "I scarcely understood it myself," she said, "until I suddenly realized that he was in grave danger—Willie Walker, that is. Then, all at once, I knew."

Celeste smiled, recalling the shy giant of a man who had saved her from Admiral de Bosquette. "I'm told it often happens that way," she said, and refrained from adding that she herself felt the same way about Richard. But that wasn't strictly true, she reflected. Her feelings were far more complex. And the fact that she had twice slept with Richard had complicated matters considerably. Richard had the power to arouse her as no other man had ever done; whether this meant she actually loved him, however, was beyond her ability to fathom. Perhaps, she told herself, she was too worldly and had known too many men during the years when she had been forced to fend for herself, to live or perish by her wits and her womanly charm.

Undeniably, she had held something in reserve in her relations with Richard, never quite letting go completely, never giving unstintingly, even though it had seemed so at the time. But it was just as well that she had protected herself, she thought, because the startling news that Eliza was still alive had changed everything. Now, instead of being his probable new wife, she was reduced to the demeaning role of mistress.

For once in her life she was at a loss for what to do. Richard gave every evidence of being genuine in his love for her; and as she again recalled the painful scene when he had confirmed that Eliza was still alive, she could detect no false note in anything he had said or done.

Whether he loved her more than he loved Eliza was a question she could not answer. In fact, she was a sufficiently astute student of human nature to sense that Richard himself probably wasn't sure how he felt. After all, hadn't he admitted as much?

She would just have to wait and let nature take its course. If there was one thing she had learned through the lean years, it was that even the worst problems, given enough time, had a way of solving themselves. She was determined to be patient and, in the meantime, to remain as calm as she could.

Wrenching herself from her reverie, Celeste smiled at the other girl. "I'm sure Willie is quite safe where he is. And you're brave to admit your affection for him. Many women don't even know their own heart. Does he reciprocate your feelings?"

Adella frowned, looking uncertain. "I'm not sure," she said. "I can't point to anything he's said or done." Then she smiled. "But if my feminine instinct isn't betraying me, I'd swear that he indeed cares for me as much as I care for him. I can't tell you how I know it, but I do. It comes from nothing specific, and yet from everything—from the way he looks at me, from the way he talks, from the way his eyes follow me when I move."

"I'm very glad for both of you," Celeste said.

Adella was wide-eyed. "I'm not sure whether to be glad or sorry," she said. "The battle isn't yet finished, and I'm just praying that Willie survives. I—I—" She stopped with a gasp.

"Celeste! Look down there, near the wharf. Those three men—"

Celeste looked in the direction Adella had indicated. From where she was standing, there was a better view of the wharf than could be obtained from the main fort, where the line of sight down the bluff was obscured by ramshackle wooden structures and the haze of smoke from the cannon. Celeste strained her eyes and, in the quickly growing darkness, finally made out the shadowy forms of the three men Adella had pointed to. When she took in the full meaning of the scene, her violet eyes widened in horror.

A few seconds later, when Adella turned to address her companion, she was astonished to find Celeste no longer at her side. Instead, she was racing over the bluff in the direction of the fort, the helpless Virginia militiaman shouting at her to come back.

Scarcely aware of what she was doing, Celeste rushed into the stockade and sought out Mark Prescott, arriving breathless at his side.

"Stop firing!" she panted.

Mark, who had previously regarded her as a sensible, practical woman, stared at her in astonishment. "What on earth are you doing here?" he said. "You gave me your word—"

Celeste did not realize that she was weeping hysterically. "You don't understand," she cried. "Richard is out there in the river. He, Walker, and Zwingli are hiding behind a log, floating toward the buccaneer ship."

Glancing at her incredulously, Mark hurried to the ramparts and studied the river below through his glass. He picked out the floating log, but at first could see no sign of any men. Then, partly concealed behind a branch, a head rose cautiously into sight, then quickly disappeared.

"You say Richard's out there?" he said, still peering through the glass. "What in God's name is he trying to accomplish? Has he gone mad?"

"I—I don't know," Celeste managed. "Please, you must stop firing."

He looked at Celeste, who was trying to blink back the tears that came to her eyes, and suddenly it dawned on him what was happening. He knew from Zwingli that Richard's wife, Eliza, was still alive and on board the pirate vessel. Apparently Richard had abandoned his command in an attempt to save her, and Celeste, from her position at the observation post, had seen him enter the water.

Uncertain what to do, Mark ordered a nearby soldier to fetch Colonel Nettleton.

The colonel, as unaware of Richard's unexpected move as his colleague had been, listened in silent amazement to Mark's revelation. Midway through the conversation, a messenger arrived from Dempster Chaney, confirming Richard's absence and asking for instructions as to how to proceed.

Nettleton, shaking his head slowly from side to side, scratched his stubbly chin and seemed lost in contemplation for a long while. Mark was tempted to interrupt, but thought better of it. This was a decision that could be made only by Colonel Nettleton, and if he wanted advice or help from a subordinate, he would ask for it.

"I sympathize with Colonel Dunstable," the colonel finally said. "But I am sure he would not want us to cease firing so long as the enemy remained under our guns, or as long as we had a single cannonball or an ounce of powder left."

From the expression of the tight-lipped Mark Prescott it was plain that he concurred. The messenger from Captain Chaney nodded his understanding.

"Richard Dunstable," Colonel Nettleton continued, "knew the risk he was taking when he decided to go out to the buccaneer ship. He no doubt felt it was his personal duty. So be it, gentlemen; we also have our duty. You will maintain your fire. If Richard Dunstable should be struck by one of our cannonballs, that is his fate." The old man's face seemed to be carved in stone as he spoke, and his subordinates knew that he had never made a more painful decision in his long military career.

His orders were clear, and the messenger hurried back to Captain Chaney's post to carry them out.

Celeste Burrows remained where she was, grief-stricken.

She was white-faced and trembling, and Colonel Nettleton took her gently by the arm and tried to comfort her.

"Richard will go on board," she said, her voice hollow. "He'll be killed—I know it. He couldn't possibly have a chance against the entire crew."

Her expression was desolate, but Colonel Nettleton decided to remain silent. It was best to let her have her say.

"He must feel just awful," she continued, seemingly talking to herself. "He probably saw her from shore. He must still love her very much to go after her like that, to throw his life away for her."

The old commander pitied her and idly wondered why she cared so deeply for Richard. He patted her hand in sympathy, then reminded himself that he had other matters to attend to. So, leaving Celeste in the care of one of his orderlies, he returned to his command post.

"Keep firing, boys!" he heard Mark Prescott yell. "Colonel Nettleton wants that ship sunk, and he's relying on us to send her to the bottom!"

The three men rested for a moment under the overhang of the ship's stern, then Willie pulled himself around to the port side and reached up for a handhold.

In a moment he was out of the water and halfway up the sloping side of the ship, Richard quickly following.

Willie's cutlass dangled from his side, and Zwingli had his scimitarlike blade clenched firmly between his teeth as he, too, pulled himself from the water. Richard, however, was without a weapon. He would have to try to arm himself as best he could once he got on board.

As Richard cleared the rail he saw the huge, wet bo'sun walking nonchalantly toward a knot of men at the foot of the quarterdeck, as if he had never been away from the ship. Richard peered through the cannon smoke and darkness for some sight of Eliza.

Then he saw her. Not more than ten yards away, she stood half hidden behind the mizzenmast, her attention on the opposite shore. But before Richard could advance two steps, a crewman spotted Zwingli coming over the rail and yelled out a warning.

Then everything seemed to happen at once. Zwingli throttled the loudmouthed crewman with one mighty slam of his fist, flipping the man's cutlass to Richard with a quick, "You're cap'n now, sir. Good luck." Eliza turned, looking at Richard as if he were a ghost. Simultaneously, the black-bearded man beside her thrust her aside with one hand, leveling a pistol at Richard with the other.

"No!" Eliza yelled, grabbing the man's pistol arm. Richard lunged forward, but to his horror he heard the sharp *crack* of the pistol shot and saw Eliza collapse against the mast, the lead ball meant for him lodged in the side of her chest, the blood streaming down her arm.

Enraged and completely out of control, Richard, cutlass gripped tightly, leaped forward and slashed wildly at Stephens.

But the pirate captain dodged behind the mast, moving amazingly quickly for a man of his size. Before Richard could regain his balance, Stephens had drawn his own cutlass, discarding the useless pistol. Richard cursed his own foolhardy rage, which had given the pirate captain the moment he needed to rearm himself.

The short lull, however, had given Zwingli the chance to dart forward and pick up the fallen Eliza.

Richard, out of the corner of his eye, saw the African put her down gently against a coil of rope, safely out of the way, just in time to turn his attention to an approaching pair of pirates.

The two men recognized Zwingli, however, and were in no hurry to cross swords with him. And by now Willie, true to his word, had assembled a loyal group of men and had sealed off the quarterdeck. He called out to Zwingli, and the African, with a menacing snarl and a wave of his blade, drove his two would-be assailants back to the main deck, where he joined forces with Walker.

That left Richard, Stephens, and the collapsed Eliza alone on the quarterdeck, the pirate captain carefully keeping the mizzenmast between him and his opponent.

A deep anger seethed within Richard as an eerie silence settled over the ship. The pirate gunners, now aware of the commotion around the quarterdeck, had turned from their cannon to watch the spectacle. No man had ever defeated Roger Stephens in a duel.

Richard calmed himself and relaxed his grip on his sword. Balancing on the balls of his feet, he awaited the next move of the buccaneer leader.

"Who the hell are you?" Stephens demanded.

Richard gritted his teeth and forced himself to answer, in order to draw his quarry out from behind the mast. "I am the husband of the unarmed woman you just shot. But I'll waste no more talk on cowardly scum like you, who prefer to fight women."

His words had the desired effect. Stephens lunged, and Richard neatly parried the blow. The buccaneer captain was not an unexperienced swordsman, however, and nimbly kept his balance as he fended off Richard's brisk counterattack. Then they separated, and Stephens circled warily, reappraising his opponent.

Richard regarded himself as just an average swordsman, no better or worse than most gentlemen with two or three years of training with a master fencer. But he sensed at once that he was superior to Stephens, who substituted brute strength and quickness for technical skill. Now, parrying expertly, Richard patiently awaited his opportunity to strike. He knew that when he did, he would kill this man without mercy and without compunction.

Stephens, still circling, abruptly changed his tactics. Wielding his cutlass like a sledgehammer, he let out an unearthly scream and struck again and again in quick succession, trying to smash Richard's sword from his hand by sheer strength.

Richard was surprised by the demonic fury of the assault, but he did not panic. His opponent was growing clumsier and slower with each stroke and soon would open himself to a killing thrust.

Suddenly the sound of Zwingli's voice penetrated his consciousness. "Cap'n has knife," the giant African called softly but urgently.

Richard had been so busy watching his foe's sword that he had paid no attention to the man's other hand. Now he saw that Stephens had drawn a short, wide-bladed knife from his belt and, cradling it in the palm of his hand, was preparing to hurl it at his foe.

Almost too late, Richard realized he had been caught in a clever trap set by an unscrupulous opponent. If he lunged for the pirate now, Stephens would surely hurl his knife and, at such close range, could not possibly miss. Only one course of action remained open to him. Still parrying deftly, he drew back slightly and pretended to be unaware of the trick his foe was playing, while closely watching the man's other hand in the corner of his vision.

In a matter of seconds, Stephens's arm drew back and, in one continuous motion, swept forward again.

Richard estimated where the weapon was being aimed and, hoping he was right, swiftly dropped to one knee. The knife streaked over his head and flew overboard into the river.

One glance at Richard's coldly smiling face told Roger Stephens all he needed to know. He had seriously underestimated his opponent. He, who had been responsible for so many deaths in duels, in brawls, and in his raids at sea, knew that the time of retribution had come at last. He began to back away, step by step, his panic growing visibly.

Richard pressed forward, using all of his knowledge, all of his skill, to continue driving his opponent backward. No longer would he be satisfied with a quick victory. Now he wanted his foe to beg, to die like the miserable coward he was.

Richard expertly flicked his blade at his foe's face, then at his heart, then at his abdomen. Never still, the point flickered and feinted dangerously, ever nearer to its prey, but not yet drawing blood. Soon Stephens's brocaded coat and silk shirt hung in tatters, sliced to ribbons by Richard's darting blade.

Stephens silently cursed Eliza for stepping in front of his pistol. Perhaps he could still get to her and finish her off—or use her as a hostage to bargain for his own life from this madman.

But the starboard railing was already touching his back, telling him he could retreat no farther. He had come to the end of the deck and, he knew, to the end of his life.

Mustering all his remaining strength, Stephens prepared to raise his blade for one last mighty slash. But his opponent's point caught him in the wrist before he could raise his sword halfway, and as his hand convulsed in pain, the sword clattered to the deck.

The watching crowd gasped. Richard kicked the blade away, just out of reach.

Stephens saw the cold determination in the eyes of his opponent. "No!" he screamed hoarsely. "Please, no!"

But it was no use. "I give you this," Richard said, "from my wife."

Before Stephens could blink, Richard's sword had run through his heart. A look of terror frozen in his bulging eyes, he tumbled backward over the rail and into the river below.

Richard stood there, the bloody weapon dangling from his hand. Far in the distance, the bombardment from shore abruptly stopped. But Richard was aware of only one sound—his wife's voice, calling his name.

Mark Prescott had ordered his gunners to cease fire a few minutes after the guns from the pirate flagship had fallen silent. Through his glass he watched the battered but still seaworthy vessel drift slowly out of sight, while the smaller sloops of war were still preoccupied with shelling the opposite shore, where the Chickahominy Indians had been hidden.

Colonel Nettleton lowered his own glass, a puzzled look on his face. Celeste Burrows, seemingly composed now, stuck doggedly to his side. "I reckon, Major Prescott," the older man said, "that they'll be back at first light. And I wouldn't be surprised if this time those two other ships did something more than waste ammunition firing at savages in the forest. That's about as smart as throwin' boulders at hummingbirds."

"And about as effective," Mark Prescott added. He was still

troubled by the enemy's movements, however, and was about to say as much, but Celeste spoke first.

"What about Richard?" she said. "Aren't you going to do anything to find him? Can't you go after him?"

Colonel Nettleton shook his head. "For all we know, ma'am, he may be dead. And we can't go runnin' up and down the river all night, just tryin' to find out. If and when those ships come back, we have to be ready for them."

Celeste looked unconvinced.

"And I'll remind you again, ma'am," Colonel Nettleton said, "that this is no place for a lady."

Major Prescott nodded his agreement and tried to reason with Celeste. "We have to assume that Richard, Zwingli, and Walker made it on board that ship," he said. "What happened next we have no way of knowing. But even if Richard did accomplish what he set out to do and somehow made it back to shore with his wife, it would take him a while to get back here anyhow. They might even be safe on the other side of the river. We just can't tell."

Celeste was forced to admit he was right. It would be suicide to try to send men after Richard, who might not even be on board the ship. For the last half hour she had firmly resisted all Colonel Nettleton's efforts to send her back to her quarters at the farmhouse, but now, with the enemy flagship out of sight, it seemed futile to protest further. Still, if there was any hope at all, she would grasp at it.

"I'm sorry I've been so much trouble," she said in a grudging tone, "but I insist on remaining here in case anything happens or if Richard shows up. And I'm sure Adella will need my help in the hospital. So if you don't mind, I'll stay there for the rest of the night. Please notify me if there's any word of Richard."

Neither officer had the will or the desire to argue the point with her. As she turned to depart, the two men looked at each other and shook their heads.

"That's one stubborn female," Colonel Nettleton said when she was out of earshot. "No wonder the Chickahominy sent her back to us."

Major Prescott chuckled. "That may be true, sir," he said. "Nevertheless, I'm sure glad she's on our side."

After dispatching Roger Stephens, Richard, oblivious of all else, had rushed to Eliza's side. He had torn his own shirt into pieces, using it to patch her wound as best he could; and with a silent crew looking on, he had carried her to the captain's cabin, where he had placed her gently on the bed.

"I'm here," he whispered to her. "I wish I'd been sooner, but I came as quickly as I could." Though he could clearly hear the bo'sun shouting oaths and exhortations to the crew, Richard could not take his eyes from Eliza's. Her face was white as marble, and her breathing was weak and fitful, yet she continued to stare at him wide-eyed, saying over and over, "I thought you were dead, Richie. I thought you were dead."

Richard stroked her hair and forehead, trying to calm her. The wound had stopped bleeding, but it was apparent that she had already lost much blood and could not be moved again. "Please, Eliza," he said, "you must try to save your strength. We'll get you ashore and to a doctor soon."

"I'm so sorry," she murmured. "Please forgive me." Her voice was so soft that he had to lean close to her to hear what she was saying. "If I had known you were alive—" She suddenly became conscious of the tawdriness of her appearance, and turned her head away in shame.

Richard spoke to her in a soothing tone. "I, too, thought you were dead," he said, "until I saw Zwingli. And today, when I saw you from shore, I knew that I had to try to save you. Don't worry, you'll be all right now. I'll get you ashore. There's a doctor there."

Eliza shook her head. "No, Richie. There's no time for that. Just stay here so I can look at you. I'm so glad you're alive."

She closed her eyes for a few seconds, and when she opened them again, a peaceful look had settled there, as if she no longer felt any pain. And when she spoke, Richard noticed, all sign of strain seemed to have disappeared from her voice.

"I thought I had lost you forever," she said. "And I tried to convince myself that I didn't care, that you loved Celeste, not me. But it was no use. I still loved you, even though I tried not to."

Richard's throat tightened, and he felt suddenly sick. "But why did you think that I loved Celeste?" he said. "I gave you no reason."

Eliza reached up and put a cold hand to his lips. She was smiling peacefully now. "Do you recall that morning you rode out to the farmhouse, but I was still sleeping? It doesn't matter now, but I—I wasn't asleep. I watched you and Celeste from the upstairs window, and . . ."

Richard wanted to cry out at the cruelty of her fate as he listened to her story. It was true that he had been unfaithful to her, he told himself bitterly—but not the way she thought, and certainly not while he had believed she was alive.

He quieted her and insisted that she listen to him. Then, holding her hands between his, he explained what had actually occurred that morning, how Celeste had expressed regret for her former conduct and had even admitted her deep feelings for Adam Burrows.

Eliza's smile did not change, though a troubled look passed fleetingly over her face. Richard was sure that she believed him, yet he sensed that it no longer mattered to her whether or not he loved Celeste. She had found her own peace and was free from all petty jealousy.

He gathered her gently in his arms, bent his head toward her, and kissed her.

Her lips were cold and dry, but she welcomed his kiss and, with a great effort, curled her arms around his neck.

"Richie, forgive me. I love—"

Her arms fell to her side. Richard frantically felt for a heartbeat, but there was nothing. Slowly he rose to his feet, his eyes closed, the loss too much to bear. At first there was only emptiness. Then, sweeping into the hollow space within him, came an unslakable thirst for vengeance, a need to strike out, to punish someone for her unjust fate.

As if in answer to his angry prayer, Zwingli appeared at the cabin door. "Need you on deck, Cap'n," he said. "Willie's got most of the men on our side, but the rest need some more convincing." His eyes fell on Eliza, then met Richard's.

"Sorry, Cap'n," he said.

But Richard did not hear him. Grasping a loaded pistol offered him by the African, he strode to the quarterdeck rail and discharged the weapon into the air to get the crew's attention.

All eyes turned toward him.

Later, Richard would be unable to recall exactly what he had said, but everyone present would agree that he had appeared like a man possessed, bellowing commands and hurling or kicking overboard any man who hesitated for even a second in obeying his orders. Within minutes the men were back at their battle stations and the ship was brought smartly about, heading straight for the two sloops of war that had lingered behind, still lobbing cannonballs into the forest.

The men on the sloops were obviously making a party of it, and their drunken shouts could be heard clearly as Willie ordered the starboard battery to open fire as each gun came to bear.

The crews of the overloaded sloops, caught totally unprepared by the broadside, cursed and screamed as they tried to bring their vessels about in order to escape down the river. But Willie barked out orders in quick sequence, and the pirate flagship turned and delivered a second broadside, sending the mainmasts of both sloops tumbling to the decks in a tangle of rigging.

On shore, the elusive Chickahominy reappeared at the riverbank, whooping and emitting hair-raising yelps as one of the crippled sloops drifted closer and closer to them. The braves began to loft flaming arrows toward the hapless vessel, and soon several landed in the rigging, igniting the loosely furled sails. The fire spread quickly, and as more arrows landed on the main deck, one of them ignited an open powder keg, which burst into flames with a roar.

Meanwhile, the pirate flagship again bore down on the other sloop. Willie Walker had ordered boarders to the rail, and as the two ships' yardarms brushed each other, Richard clutched his already bloody cutlass, eager for action.

"Grapplin' hooks!" Willie shouted. "You know what we need to do, lads! Do it!"

The buccaneers had been frustrated by the day's long, inconclusive artillery battle. Now was their chance for some real action, to fight the way they knew best, and they didn't stop to ponder the consequences.

The iron hooks sang through the air and clattered to the deck of the smaller vessel, then were instantly pulled tight. The boarders, brandishing pistols, knives, and cutlasses, jumped atop the rail, with Richard leading the way.

"Boarders, away!" Willie Walker roared, following close behind Richard, a grinning Zwingli at his side. In an instant the three men, each fighting as never before, were surrounded by foes. Everywhere he turned there was bloody mayhem, and Richard reveled in it. Pirates were fighting pirates, and no quarter was given, no codes of honor observed. It was the scum of the earth against the dregs of society, and only death would be the winner.

Richard was beyond all reason. He had entered the combat seeking blind vengeance and a merciful oblivion to end his mental torment, and by now his boundless fury had become contagious. The men following him carved a bloody path across the sloop's deck, annihilating everyone in their way.

Soon Richard reached the opposite end of the ship, and turning around to search for more opponents, he suddenly realized there was none. All the men on the sloop had either been killed or had jumped overboard. From shore he could hear the blood-curdling cries of pirates being scalped by Chickahominy braves.

The other sloop, he noticed, had run aground and was blazing fiercely, illuminating the grisly spectacle on the riverbank.

Richard jumped as a hand grabbed his forearm.

"Cap'n, it's over."

Richard shook his head, trying to clear it.

"Cap'n," Zwingli repeated, "the battle's over. You better get off the ship, Cap'n. It's on fire."

Coming to his senses, Richard realized the sloop he was on was also ablaze, no doubt from the Chickahominy arrows. All around him pirates were looting what they could, stripping the ship and its dead of any valuables that could be carried.

Then he remembered Eliza.

Accompanied by Zwingli, he returned to the flagship. Together they lowered Eliza's lifeless body over the side and into the ship's gig, which Willie Walker had manned and brought alongside singlehandedly.

With the two giants at the oars and Richard in the stern, Eliza in his arms, they headed back to the opposite shore, leaving the blazing wrecks behind them in the night.

It was a stunning victory for the English colonists, Richard realized for the first time. But for him the cost had been too high.

IX

As Willie secured the gig to the wharf, Zwingli urged Richard to let him carry Eliza's body to the fort. Exhausted, bruised, and wounded in several places from the hand-to-hand fighting, Richard could barely walk, so he reluctantly agreed.

As he followed the African up the path to the top of the bluff, Willie came to his side, cap in hand.

"What about me, sir?" he asked. "Do ye suppose I have any chance o' stayin' out o' jail?"

Richard smiled weakly. "No jail would hold you, Willie," he said. "But don't worry. I promised I'd do all I could to see that you got a fair hearing, and I mean to keep my word."

As they neared the top of the bluff, Richard was surprised to see Roaring Wolf, and immediately deduced the truth—that the Indian brave, returning to his downriver observation post, had observed the last stages of the battle and had run back to the fort with the news. Dempster Chaney, standing before the gate, waved his hat in greeting. Both men's smiling expressions sobered, however, as Zwingli passed through the gate with his tragic burden.

The New England volunteers and the Virginia militia had gathered inside the stockade, and they stared in wonder as the three men entered the fort.

Adella Prescott and Celeste Burrows watched the scene from the doorway of the hospital. When Adella recognized Willie bringing up the rear, she clasped her hands and murmured, "Thank God he's safe. My prayers have been answered." Not waiting for a reply from her companion, she picked up her petticoats and hurried across the stockade to greet Willie herself.

Celeste continued to linger in the doorway. She was tearful with joy that Richard Dunstable's life had been spared, but at the same time she felt rooted to the spot as she stared at Zwingli carrying Eliza's lifeless body.

She had already heard the unbelievable news that had spread through the fort only minutes ago—that the pirate vessels had turned on one another and that all three had caught fire and run aground, their crews at the mercy of the Chickahominy. It had rekindled her hopes that Richard was still alive, but she wasn't at all prepared for what she now saw.

Richard Dunstable stood across the yard from her, almost unrecognizable. Shirtless, battered, and bruised, his entire body caked with blood, he seemed ready to collapse at any moment. She had never seen any man appear so bereft, so stricken, and her heart ached for him. But she realized there was nothing she could do for him now. He needed to find his own way out of his grief and the jungle of tangled emotions in which he had lost himself.

The full story of Richard's exploits spread quickly as survivors from the pirate ships—those lucky enough not to have been scalped—were ferried back across the river by the Chickahominy braves.

As a result, every Virginian within a day's journey, as well as the militiamen who had taken part in the campaign, attended the funeral service for Richard's wife.

Colonel Nettleton, in recognition of Eliza's efforts to warn the defenders of the attack, delivered a brief eulogy. For Richard's sake, however, he kept his remarks short, seeing no reason to prolong the grieving widower's agony.

Celeste was present at the graveside ceremony, but she remained in the background, her face concealed behind a heavy veil and her eyes fastened on Richard.

He conducted himself with a natural dignity and remained dry-eyed throughout. He had instructed Zwingli and Willie to tell no one of what Eliza had been forced to endure during her captivity, and he saw no need to mention his final conversation with her to anyone. Eliza, he was certain, would have expected as much.

Later that same day, the charred bodies that had been found on board the three ships were buried in a common grave. No one mourned them, and the site remained unmarked.

Out of deference to Colonel Dunstable, the celebration marking the overwhelming victory over the French mercenaries was postponed until two days after Eliza's funeral. Colonel Nettleton had tried to discourage any merrymaking at all, but the Chickahominy braves refused to leave without some sort of celebration.

The mood of the celebrants was strangely subdued. They had won a victory against great odds, but no one besides the Chickahominy felt much like rejoicing. The local militiamen had been forced to interrupt the routine of their lives for a period of months and were relieved just to get back to the chores of their farms. The New Englanders also were anxious to return home now that their task had been completed, and their thoughts turned to their loved ones and the towns and farms they had left behind.

Mark Prescott wanted to return to Bermuda as soon as possible, and Richard dutifully obliged him, arranging to have one of the Burrows and Clayton brigs resume its usual West Indies trade via Bermuda.

Meanwhile, the militia officers and local civil officials met to discuss the situation of Willie Walker, and after a few words in his behalf from Richard, and a brief discussion, they unanimously voted to extend to him a complete pardon for any of his former misdeeds.

The beaming Willie rushed off for a private talk with Adella Prescott, and shortly afterward they came jointly in search of her brother.

Mark was not at all surprised when Adella stood red-faced and mute while Willie stammered and shuffled his feet.

"I been wonderin', Mr. Prescott," he said, "if ye got any use for the likes o' me on your plantation in Bermuda? Zwingli is goin' home with ye, and from what he tells me, there be work aplenty for an able-bodied man who ain't afraid to get his hands dirty."

"I'm sure a suitable position can be arranged," a smiling Mark said. "As a matter of fact, I've been holding a substantial tract that belongs to Adella, sort of looking after it for her. But since it appears that she's going to be a married woman, I'd be delighted to turn responsibility for that land over to her husband, after instructing him in the best ways of getting the most out of it, of course."

The couple looked stunned.

"You guessed," Adella said.

"I'm very good at guessing," her brother replied with mock solemnity, kissing her and shaking Willie's hand.

Willie was relieved. "Are ye tellin' me that I won't have to be one of those 'dentured servants who have to work for seven years before they're free men again? Ye mean that ain't goin' to happen to me?"

"Indeed it won't," Mark assured him. "Thanks in large part to your efforts, we won a decisive victory over a dangerous foe. The very least I can do is try to repay you in the only way I know how."

Willie was so overcome with gratitude that he didn't know how to reply.

Adella, however, reacted just as her brother had anticipated. Reaching up, she kissed first him and then Willie, removing the giant's cap and affectionately tousling his hair. "You'll have your hands full," she said, "adjusting to a life on land after spending so many years at sea. And the first thing you'll have to do, Mr. Walker, is let me wash and mend that cap."

Willie winced good-humoredly. "Ye don't do me justice, ma'am," he replied, rubbing his bare head. "It's goin' to be a heap simpler to adjust than ye seem to think." He emphasized his words by sliding an arm around her waist and drawing her close, hugging her.

Mark Prescott grinned at both of them. A great deal of good, it appeared, had grown out of the abortive attack by the French mercenaries on Virginia.

Arthur Mossdecker had heard that lightning never struck twice in the same place, but the superstition was mistaken. It had struck him twice. Within the space of a month, he had sold his inn in Bermuda for nearly double the price he had expected, then had bought another establishment on the mainland, in New Haven Colony, that had turned into a virtual gold mine. Called the Cat and Mouse, his new inn was on the harbor waterfront, and it had prospered from the start. In fact, it was already far more successful than his inn in Bermuda had ever been.

Mossdecker knew that good fortune had attended his efforts. Not only was his establishment popular with the sailors who came and went on board the merchant ships that visited New Haven, but it had also become a gathering place for the local members of the shipping community. Obviously they liked the quality and quantity of his food and the generous drinks he served.

Genial in his relations with his customers, Mossdecker kept his dislikes to himself. Perhaps that, he mused, was the reason for his success. Everyone was treated courteously, even his most disagreeable customers. Take Horace Lapham, for example—that was surely one man for whom he had little love. A swarthy, burly fellow who was overly fond of fancy clothes and who seemed to have an infinite capacity for rum, Lapham claimed to be a highly successful shipping agent.

Mossdecker, however, had heard that Lapham, who had recently moved to New Haven with his wife and daughter, had left Boston only because he had worn out his welcome in that city. The tavern keeper had no way of verifying the story, but in all justice to the man, he had to admit that Lapham seemed to be plentifully endowed with gold and silver and did not hesitate to spend it freely. Certainly he always paid the bill whenever he entertained Tom Clayton, a partner in the firm of Burrows and Clayton, whom he met fairly regularly in the taproom.

It was not Mossdecker's place to stand in judgment of those who patronized his tavern, he reminded himself, and conquering his instinctive aversion to the man, he made his way across the sawdust-strewn floor to Lapham's table.

"Seeing as how you seem to be friendly with Tom Clayton," he said, "I wonder if you'd heard the news about his partner?"

Horace Lapham raised his head, his heavy-lidded eyes expressionless. He played it safe and did not reply in words, but merely shook his head.

"Colonel Adam Burrows is dead," Mossdecker said sorrowfully, "and the whole colony will go into mourning for him, I'm sure. He was a great man, and I hear tell a loyal citizen."

Lapham replied with great care. "You have no idea how sorry I am to hear that," he said. "What happened to him?"

"No details are available as yet," the tavern keeper replied. "All I know is that he was killed fighting pirates. Down in Virginia, I think it was." He had said more than enough, he decided, and wandered back toward his bar.

Horace Lapham concealed his elation behind a wooden-faced exterior. This was the stroke of good fortune he had been awaiting, the opportunity for which he had prayed! He had long daydreamed about the possibility of buying into Burrows and Clayton, and had even figured a way to blackmail Tom Clayton and take over his share of the business. But now, if what the innkeeper had said was true, he wouldn't have to settle for a mere partnership.

This news called for a celebration. Summoning Arthur Mossdecker imperiously, he ordered a double tot of rum, and when his drink was served, he downed it in a single gulp. He was celebrating prematurely, perhaps, but the shipping company he had long coveted was ripe for the taking, and now he could pluck it down—and all thanks to the timely demise of Adam Burrows.

Richard directed Dempster Chaney to gather enough supplies for the voyage to New Haven, where the *Eliza* could reprovision for additional stops at New London, Providence, and Boston. The task, however, proved far easier than Dempster had expected.

The Virginians, grateful for the unsolicited aid they had received, showed their thanks by literally filling the arms of every New England militiaman with smoked hams, sides of bacon, and as much cornmeal as they could carry. Added to this were pies and pastries baked by the women, loaves of corn bread, and more tobacco and home-brewed liquor than Dempster thought wise.

While the *Eliza* was being made seaworthy in preparation for the departure, Richard paid a long overdue call on Celeste. He had seen her from a distance at the funeral, and had caught an occasional glimpse of her since that time, but they had not spoken.

Celeste was reading in the sun-drenched garden when Richard arrived at the farmhouse where she had been staying. When she saw him approach, her heart went out to him; he looked so gaunt and drawn. But she knew he didn't want pity, so she took great care not to reveal her feelings.

Richard halted several paces from her bench and greeted her, his manner awkward. It was obvious that he was ill at ease.

"I suppose you know," he said, "that we're sailing for New Haven tomorrow."

Celeste nodded. "Yes, of course," she said.

He put on a jovial air and tried to joke for a while, but Celeste could tell he was doing it only for her sake. "Well, I'll be happy to leave," she said. "There's nothing to keep me in Virginia. I have no desire to stay here, and if you're ready to leave for home, so am I."

"I note that you refer to it as home," he said. "That's a good sign."

"Is it?" she demanded, the bleak expression in her eyes belying her quick smile. "I've never known any place that I could really call home in more years than I care to recall."

Richard nodded and fell silent for a minute. "You may think it rude," he said abruptly, "but I've been avoiding you."

"Not at all," she interrupted. "I understand."

"I'm glad you do, because I'm at something of a loss to explain my own conduct," he said. "I've been confused and terribly upset, and all the reasons may not be apparent to you."

"You needn't tell me anything you'd rather keep to yourself," Celeste told him. "Don't feel that you're under any obligation to speak out."

"But I must," he replied. "After all, before we learned that Eliza was still alive, I'd proposed marriage to you, and you'd accepted. I can't forget or dismiss that from my mind."

She knew it would be wiser to remain silent, but could not help saying, "I released you from any obligation you had to me the moment I knew Eliza still lived."

"Then we had different ideas as to the extent and depth of my obligation. I've been wrestling with a terrible weight on my conscience."

Hesitantly and with considerable reluctance he related his problem. He told her he had always loved Eliza deeply, even when he realized that she harbored a bitter jealousy of another woman—Celeste, of course. Yet when he had thought Eliza was dead, he had, perhaps too hastily, fallen in love with that very woman. Did that, then, prove Eliza right, and him wrong?

Celeste was about to comment, but Richard held up a hand.

"You don't have to say anything," he said. "I have already answered that question for myself. But all that is over and done with."

Celeste, nonetheless, wondered how he had answered it.

"What bothers me now," he went on, "is that, on her deathbed, Eliza seemed to put away her jealousy. She asked for *my* forgiveness, as if I were in any position to forgive her."

"We all are in a position to forgive each other, regardless of our own sins," Celeste said, her voice low.

Richard was not prepared for that, or for what she said next.

"When I grew to womanhood," she began, "I found my family life in a shambles. My father and both my brothers had been killed in the war between the Cavaliers and the Round-heads, and I was left with nothing but my wits and my feminine wiles. Naturally I used both. And because I had to live with myself and my own conscience, I even learned to enjoy what I had to do in order to stay alive, in order just to eat. Or if I really did not enjoy it, I managed to convince myself that I did. I honestly can't tell you now which is true."

"Why are you telling me this?" Richard asked.

"Because that is why Eliza was jealous of me. She sensed I could always convince myself that whatever I did was right— even stealing you from her. And she couldn't understand how a woman could be like that. But who knows? She had no easy time of it herself; maybe in the end she did understand."

Richard remembered the look of peace that had been in Eliza's eyes. "You may be right," he said. "And you're very brave to tell me all this."

"I'm being truthful," Celeste replied. "And now I'll tell you something else. You've had a series of terrible shocks, as much as any man could tolerate. I think that when you regain your senses and feel like yourself again, you may discover that you still want me. If I didn't believe that, I wouldn't be here right now. I want you to know that whenever you realize you do want me, I'll be waiting for you."

"I can't ask that of you," Richard said, his voice almost inaudible.

Celeste shook her head. "There's no need for you to ask anything," she replied. "Don't think I'm being noble. Quite the contrary. I need you and I want you, and I'm quite certain that the life we could have together is worth waiting for."

"I'm sincerely flattered," Richard said. "But I can't help wondering what you and I would have done had Eliza lived."

Celeste's composure melted away and she rose angrily to her feet. "She didn't live. That's what you seem incapable of understanding. Adam was killed, too, and I've accepted his passing as a fact of life and of death. If I had nothing better to do in this world, I suppose I could amuse myself by wondering what would have happened had he and Eliza both lived. The answer is simple enough, I'm sure. I would have stayed married to him, and you would have remained married to her. It is all that simple."

"I—I didn't mean to offend you," Richard said slowly.

She glared at him. "I'm not offended," she replied. "I just grow impatient when you are so obstinate. I'm no angel myself, and I freely admit it. But at least I don't fritter my life away pondering what could have been and skulking around wrapped in guilt."

Richard realized she had a point. He squared his shoulders, and couldn't help but smile at her spunk. "I'm grateful to you for your patience," he said.

"Instead of thanking me for my patience," she replied in a forthright tone, "try to be a little less exasperating. You've already grieved twice for Eliza—once when you thought she was dead, and again when she actually died. I'm sure you've been told this before, Richard, but life must go on, whether you want it to or not." She softened her tone. "And you needn't concern yourself about me. I'll be near at hand whenever you want me."

He tried to reply but could not. This was the moment to take her in his arms and kiss her, he knew, but he could not bring himself to take such action. What she had said was true, he realized. Nonetheless, the expression he had seen in Eliza's eyes when she had died still haunted him.

Celeste seemed calmer now and actually smiled at him and patted his arm soothingly. That gesture was by far the most intimate that passed between them for the rest of the visit. But when Richard bowed and took his leave, Celeste noticed, his step was much lighter, and the habitual gloom that had settled over him since his wife's death seemed to have lifted, at least temporarily.

X

CELESTE was quartered in the owner's spacious cabin on board the brig that carried the New Englanders home from their strange adventure, and she spent most of her time alone, even eating many of her meals in the cabin.

Richard shared a cabin with Dempster Chaney. Although Richard was habitually reticent and preferred to work out his problems himself, Dempster was a good listener and persuaded his friend to talk at great length about Eliza and Celeste. Richard was circumspect to a fault, but Dempster, who had known him for years and had been acquainted with both women, was able to use his imagination to fill in the gaps, and ultimately he sorted out the situation to his own satisfaction.

It came to the fore one bright spring afternoon when the brig was off the New Jersey capes. Dempster came on deck and saw Celeste standing at the fantail, watching a flock of seagulls swooping down to the water to scavenge the remains of the noon meal the cook had just thrown overboard.

Dempster stood off awhile, then, deciding this was the perfect opportunity to speak his mind, joined her at the rail.

Celeste smiled at him. "Isn't this glorious weather?" she said.

Dempster had never seen her look more alive, more attractive. Her skin was clear and bright, there was a healthy sparkle in her eyes, and he realized that she was as attractive a woman as he had ever encountered, his wife, Robbin, notwithstanding. "It's a very fine day, indeed," he said. "However, if you don't mind, ma'am, I'd like to discuss something other than the weather with you."

Celeste was somewhat taken aback by his reply, and looked at him curiously. "I'm at your service, sir," she replied.

"We've been at sea for over three days now," he said, "and each night I've listened to Richard's tortured meanderings on the subject of Eliza and you. I know he would rather this remained confidential, but frankly, he's trying to grope his way out of a very deep morass."

"I know," Celeste said.

"He's doing nothing but going in circles, and I feel sorry for him," he said.

"So do I," she replied. "He seems to be deriving very little pleasure out of life these days."

"I must be honest with you, ma'am," Dempster said. "I may be wrong about this, but I think that Richard loves you."

She nodded, her eyes and expression guarded, revealing nothing.

If he had expected her to confirm or deny his observation, he was disappointed. "What holds him back, of course," he continued, "is the feeling that it is too soon after Eliza's death for him to admit his feelings for you."

She nodded, but did not speak.

"So I've been wondering," he went on, "if you can't possibly do something to put him out of his misery."

"And what exactly would you suggest, sir?" she asked gently.

A cool steady breeze was blowing out from the land, yet Dempster felt uncomfortably warm beneath his collar. "I thought," he said, "that if you went to him and had a frank talk, perhaps he'd see the light."

"That," Celeste replied quietly but with considerable force, "is exactly what I must *not* do."

Dempster shifted uncomfortably and stared down at the ship's wake. "Please forgive me," he said, "for interfering in a matter that's really none of my concern."

"On the contrary," she said, "you've made it your concern because of your regard for Richard. Rest assured, sir, that I share that regard, and for that reason I'm grateful for what you call your interference."

Her gracious reply eased his discomfort.

"I don't want to put words into Richard's mouth," Celeste said, "or ideas into his head. He must think for himself and choose his own path. I cannot do that for him."

"You want him to choose the path that leads to you, I trust," Dempster ventured.

Celeste smiled and nodded. "Of course."

The young man frowned. "There's a terrible danger, as I see it," he said. "When we reach New Haven, there will be reminders of Eliza and of her father everywhere. He'll find them at the offices, at home, even on the streets of the city. You'll be fighting a very powerful ghost."

"The problem, sir, is that I cannot fight a ghost," Celeste replied. "There's no Eliza except for the one in Richard's mind; I cannot fight what I cannot see."

Dempster knew she was right, and he pitied her for what she, too, was going through.

"Actually," she said in a low voice, "I'm terrified. My whole world will crumble if Richard rejects me. But surely you must see why it's necessary for me to do nothing and to let him make up his own mind."

"You're being very noble," Dempster told her.

She brushed back a thick strand of blue-black hair that the breeze had worked loose from under her bonnet. "If you knew my feelings," Celeste said, "you wouldn't compliment me for my nobility. I'm just a woman. My happiness for the rest of my life is at stake. So is Richard's. I could interfere now, but anything I achieved would be but a most insubstantial and temporary victory. It's far better that he be very sure of himself

before we come together, because then I'd know for certain
that we'd remain together—forever."

New Haven harbor looked as it always had. Its alternately
swampy and rocky shores narrowed into a long, uneven neck,
where the clapboard warehouses of some of the oldest and
largest shipping companies in the English colonies clustered in
a row. Behind the warehouses rose the city itself, with its
churches and the homes of the more substantial citizens lining
the green, where the livestock of the town's residents grazed
freely.

Roaring Wolf, who observed the scene from the forecastle
of the approaching brig, was quick to notice the familiar presence of Indian braves loitering in the dock area, hoping to
bargain with any merchant or sailor interested in buying furs
from them. Otherwise the scene near the waterfront could have
been European. Sailors and stevedores thronged the wharves,
loading and unloading the ships tied up there; well-dressed men,
all of them somberly attired in the clothes considered appropriate for merchants, bustled from one office or warehouse to
another; and the ladies, many expensively dressed in the fashions that had been popular before the advent of Oliver Cromwell
and the Roundheads, could be seen entering and leaving the
dockside shops. New Haven, as every seaman who visited the
port knew, was a lively place that in no way resembled the
more sedate Boston or the tightly ruled New Amsterdam.

The New World nature of New Haven was impossible to
conceal, however. The streets were still little more than dirt
tracks, though shaded everywhere by the gracefully arching
branches of young elms; and most of the homes were of simple
clapboard, with an occasional larger brick house or a humble
cottage of wattle and daub. And about a mile and a half from
the waterfront, instead of the rolling fields and pastures almost
invariably found in Europe, a palisade marked the limits of the
community and the end of civilization as the white men knew
it. Beyond, brooding and silent, stretched the wilderness. Here
were forests extending as far as the eye could see, where wild
animals and savage Indians roamed, and where an occasional

pioneer tried to wrest a living from the land, often perishing in the attempt.

The New Englanders of the militia force, who now lined the rail of the brig and stared eagerly at the shore, were undismayed by the sight of the endless forest, however. To them it was home, and they had long ago come to terms with it. For it was also a friend, and although they respected it, they did not fear it. After many weeks of being away, first in Bermuda and then in Virginia, after having defeated the mercenaries of France, they were content to return to the more familiar dangers of the New England wilderness.

Celeste Burrows came on deck, and as she moved toward the rail, even the most homesick New Haven veteran turned his eyes from shore. She wore a dress of fine black silk with white collar and cuffs, and a stylish bonnet of the same material framed her ivory-pale face.

She looked every inch the mourning widow of the former leading citizen of New Haven—and perfectly capable of handling the substantial business she had inherited on his demise.

Richard Dunstable, who stood beside Roaring Wolf, removed his hat and bowed to Celeste as he made a place for her beside him at the rail. He, too, was somberly attired in a dark suit of clothes, with a white shirt, and only his plumed Cavalier hat revealed that he was other than a Roundhead. And he, too, appeared fitted for his position as a senior partner in the firm of Burrows and Clayton.

The master of the ship had taken it for granted, as had Richard, that they would dock at one of the slips owned by Burrows and Clayton, and as the brig passed the jetty protecting the wharf area, the crew hurriedly took in sail and the master maneuvered the vessel slowly toward its berth.

Celeste turned to Richard, her manner formal and businesslike. "The master knows his trade, I'm sure, but he seems to have made a mistake," she said.

"Oh?" Richard did not seem overly concerned.

She pointed toward the stone-fronted building that served as the office and principal warehouse for Burrows and Clayton. There, over the entrance, hung a sign:

BOLD DESTINY

HORACE LAPHAM

Shipping Companies

Richard was confused and turned to a sailor standing nearby. "Have I been gone so long that I have forgotten the location of our wharf?" he asked the man.

The sailor, who either could not read or had not seen the sign, did not seem perturbed. "Nope," he said. "You ain't forgotten, sir. This here be the right place. Burrows and Clayton's 'tis indeed."

Richard knew the man was right, and his bewilderment increased. "I find this very odd, to say the least," he said to Celeste. "Who is Horace Lapham?"

"I have absolutely no idea," Celeste replied.

They were silent as lines were thrown ashore to waiting dockhands.

"I suppose," Richard said uneasily, "that we'd be wise to investigate before we did anything else."

"By all means," she replied. "If there's been something odd going on, I want to know about it. And please don't leave me now, Richard. Remember, I'm the major shareholder in the company."

"Never fear, I'll stand by you," he replied.

Instructing Roaring Wolf to attend to their luggage and to wait with it on the dock, Richard offered Celeste his arm as he led her off the ship. He would have hesitated to touch her at all had he thought about it, but his mind was preoccupied with the puzzle that confronted them, and the gesture was instinctive rather than consciously proprietary.

Celeste, of course, was pleased.

"This is certainly strange," Richard said as they approached the building. He opened the front door, ushered her in, then followed. There was a new desk in the outer room, and there sat a bearded young man writing laboriously in a ledger with a quill pen. He looked up politely at the visitors.

Richard introduced himself and Celeste, and then got right

to the point. "To the best of my knowledge, sir," he said, "these are our offices."

The young man was polite but not obsequious. "I think you'll want to see Mr. Lapham, sir," he said.

"I prefer to see Tom Clayton," Richard replied, referring to Adam Burrows's longtime partner.

The young man hesitated. "I'll tell Mr. Lapham you're here," he said, and departed hastily toward the upstairs office of the building.

Richard and Celeste exchanged blank looks. "This is indeed strange," she said. "Why wouldn't Tom Clayton be here anymore? And what's become of his son, Ezekiel?" Celeste's bewilderment grew.

The clerk returned. "This way, ma'am," he said. "Just follow me, sir." He led them across the warehouse toward the stairs, and when they passed the office Richard himself had occupied, he couldn't help but pause to look inside. The table, chair, and visitors' chairs were still in place, as was the oil lamp that Eliza had given him as a gift when he had first gone to work for her father. But the table was bare, and it was apparent at a glance that no one was currently using the office.

His own confusion growing, Richard fell in silently beside Celeste.

The large upstairs corner office that had been Adam Burrow's headquarters was now occupied by a tall, broad-shouldered man who would have resembled a dockworker or a stonemason had he not been wearing clothes that would have put even a Cavalier fop to shame. He sported a preposterously huge, old-fashioned ruff around his thick neck. His long coat was of canary-colored velvet, with a row of gleaming buttons reaching from top to bottom. Under it he wore a lacy white shirt and breeches of scarlet silk. His stockings were of silk, too, and huge buckles of sparkling silver, embellished with yellow cloth bows, ornamented his shoes.

"I am Horace Lapham," he said, bowing and waving them to chairs. "Your servant, ma'am, and yours, sir." His manner was affable, but his expression betrayed his anxiety. His eyes were guarded, Richard noticed, and he was a trifle too jovial.

"If you'll forgive us, Mr. Lapham," Richard said once they were seated, "but Mistress Burrows and I are confused. She inherited a large interest in this company from her husband, the late Adam Burrows, and I'm also a shareholder through the percentage held by my late wife, who was Adam Burrows's daughter."

"Ah, yes," Lapham replied vaguely in his deep, rumbling voice. "I have a letter that may shed some light on what must appear to you as being very mysterious." He chuckled indulgently.

The sound was unpleasant, and although he obviously expected his visitors to join in his laugh, they remained soberfaced.

His smile faded, and he searched through the papers on the table before him. "Odd, isn't it," he murmured half aloud, "how one always misplaces a document when one requires it most? Ah! Here we are." He drew out two heavy, folded sheets, each bearing a wax seal that kept it closed. One bore Celeste's name, and the other was addressed to Richard.

Richard broke the seal on his and eagerly scanned the contents.

It was from Tom Clayton, and it began by explaining that Horace Lapham was a business associate of his from Boston who had been a trading partner for many years.

Lapham, the letter continued, had bought out the interests of Tom and his son, Ezekiel, in the company, paying them a handsome fee. The money had enabled them, together with their wives, Mary and Mimi, to move to the British island colony of Jamaica in the West Indies, where they intended to establish permanent residences.

In the final paragraph, he related how news of Adam's and Eliza's deaths had reached New Haven, and extended his and his family's sympathy to Richard in his bereavement. Then, without a word of explanation, he urged Richard to sell his interest in the company to Lapham, too: *"He will deal with you as generously as he has dealt with me. I'm sure you'll find it to your best interests to sell to him,"* the letter said.

Obviously disturbed, Celeste handed her letter to Richard, and he gave her his in return.

Tom Clayton had said virtually the same things to her that he had said to Richard, with one significant addition. He revealed that he had taken the liberty of selling Adam's house—which was actually owned by the company—to Horace Lapham "for a very fair and good price," which was to be paid by Lapham to Celeste when she returned, or if she decided to settle elsewhere, to her legal representative.

Richard looked again at Celeste. No wonder she was upset—even her house had been sold!

If Lapham was aware that his visitors were disturbed, he did not indicate it. He took a ring of keys from a drawer and crossed the office to a large, heavy strongbox against the wall. He unlocked it and removed a sum of money, which he carefully counted before closing and locking the box again.

"Here, Mistress Burrows," he said, placing a small cloth bag of gold coins on the edge of his desk in front of Celeste. "That is the sum Master Clayton and I agreed on for the sale of the house you and the late Master Burrows shared. I'm sure you'll agree that the sum is satisfactory; if not, I trust you'll say so."

The dazed Celeste stared at the money, at first not knowing what to do. She quickly glanced inside the bag, but left it on the table before her.

It was obvious to Richard that Celeste was so upset by the turn of events that she was in no condition to make such a crucial transaction, or even to judge whether Lapham had paid her an honest amount or had cheated her.

Lapham went through the motions of being very fair and aboveboard. "I won't press you for an answer now," he said. "Think about it at your leisure, and then let me know whether it's acceptable or if you require a further payment."

Celeste glanced at Richard, and the look of suspicion on his face only increased her own uncertainty.

"Naturally," Horace Lapham said smoothly, "I'm anxious to conclude our business as rapidly as possible. I've been expanding the shipping line, and I have several rather involved deals awaiting completion. So I'm eager to gain total control of the business as soon as I can. Perhaps, if you're not too weary after your long voyage, both of you will come to my house and join my wife and daughter and me for dinner this evening."

The invitation was so unexpected that Celeste did not know what to reply.

Richard, however, welcomed the idea. Though he himself had no intention of being rushed into a sale, and intended to advise Celeste to stand fast and hang on to her shares as well, he was eager to find out more about Horace Lapham. "We will be delighted to dine with you this evening," he said. "As for the sale of our shares, I speak for Mistress Burrows as well as myself when I warn you that we may not be eager to follow the example set by Tom Clayton and his son."

The smile froze on Horace Lapham's coarse features. If he had expected to conclude his business with this couple in a hurry, he had to revise his estimate.

"And I should also tell you, sir," Richard added, "I'm not too sure Mistress Burrows is going to accept the sale of her house. Since the property was jointly held, I think it highly unlikely that Tom Clayton had the right to sell it without the permission of his partner's heirs."

A dark cloud passed across Lapham's face. "I bought that house from Tom Clayton in good faith, and paid good gold coin of the realm for it," he said unpleasantly. "If Mistress Burrows refuses to accept the payment, which I held for her only out of courtesy, then I will forward it to Tom Clayton. It matters not to me; the house is mine."

Richard remained pleasant. "That well may be, sir," he said, "but Tom Clayton may have erred in disposing of a property that was not technically his in the first place. But we shall see; I'm sure the deed to the house will clarify the matter."

A hard note crept into Lapham's voice as he said, "I don't wish to become unpleasant about this, but as I said, I took possession of the house in good faith, and I intend to keep it until such a time as the highest court in New Haven Colony rules that I must relinquish it."

Celeste was too confused to think in terms of whether she did or did not want to keep the house. "I see no need for anyone to resort to threats," she said. "I'm sure that with goodwill on all sides, the problem can be worked out amicably."

"I'm certain it can," Lapham said, immediately recovering his apparent good humor as he drew back Celeste's chair and ushered them down the stairs and across the warehouse to the main entrance. "We'll be expecting you at the house at six o'clock this evening," he said, smiling. "I'm sure you need no one to tell you how to find the place."

It was a tasteless joke, Richard thought, but coming from Lapham it did not surprise him.

When Celeste and Richard returned to the wharf, where Roaring Wolf was waiting with their luggage, Celeste said uncertainly, "It appears that I've been dispossessed."

Richard was relieved that for once he had a practical problem with which to deal. "That's easy enough to settle," he said. "You'll stay at my house."

She started to protest.

He cut her short. "There is no alternative," he said. "The public inns of the town aren't suitable for a lady. So you have no choice in the matter."

She knew it would be difficult enough for him to return to the dwelling he had shared with Eliza. Now he would also have to cope with the presence of a woman with whom he might possibly be in love. But Celeste knew he was right about the unsuitability of the inns, so she reluctantly agreed to accept his generous offer.

Roaring Wolf had borrowed a wheelbarrow, and piling their luggage into it, he led the way toward Richard's small house.

"I find this whole experience quite unsettling," Richard said as he and Celeste followed the Pequot. "There are so many unanswered questions that I scarcely know where to begin. I've never heard of this man Lapham before, and I'm astonished by the speed with which he's moved in and taken over."

"His occupation of my house must surely be illegal," Celeste said. "Tom Clayton had no right to approve of its sale."

"Probably not," he said. "But we don't know for sure whether

Tom actually did approve willingly. Lapham claims that Tom worked out a deal with him, but the letter is strangely vague on the details."

She became thoughtful, and her mind began to function clearly again as her panic subsided. "You're quite right," she said. "I must admit that the conduct he ascribes to Tom certainly doesn't sound at all like him."

"No, it doesn't," Richard agreed. "And for Ezekiel and Mimi to go off with him, without a word of explanation to me, is even stranger. They are both good friends of mine, and at the very least I'd expect a letter of explanation."

"Perhaps there was such a letter," Celeste replied. "I wouldn't put it past a man like Lapham to have gotten hold of such a letter and to have destroyed it."

"That's possible, too," he admitted, and was silent for a time. "I'll have to talk to some people I know in town to see if they can fill me in on just what happened. But regardless of what I learn, I'm very sure in my own mind of one thing: Under no circumstances do I intend to sell my interest in the company to a complete stranger."

"Neither do I," Celeste said firmly, and she knew there was no need to remind him again that she was by far the largest single shareholder in the company.

"By standing together," Richard said, "I don't see how we can fail to keep control of the company. As for your house, we'll have to dig up the deed. And we might have to find a lawyer. But I can't imagine that your displacement is legal under any English law, regardless of the ordinances of New Haven Colony."

"I'm glad to hear it," Celeste said. "When he first brought up the subject, I was at a complete loss as to what to think."

"Well, it's not the kind of news you hear every day," Richard said. "But, legal matters aside, to me it seems a question of pure common sense. Tom can't sell what he doesn't fully own. Unfortunately, that's of little help to you now; but in the meantime, of course, you're welcome to stay here for as long as you please."

They had come to the small house of stone and white-painted

clapboard, and Richard unlocked the door and stood aside to let Celeste precede him into the dwelling. As soon as he followed her, he was flooded with memories of Eliza, and the immediate problem created by the strange Horace Lapham faded from his mind.

There were reminders of her everywhere—in the furniture she had selected, the curtains she had sewn, the chair she had always sat in. Every room was alive with her presence, and Richard would not have been surprised if she had come forward from the kitchen to greet him.

Seeing him standing silently with the color drained from his face, Celeste immediately understood the ordeal he was undergoing, and her heart went out to him. She wanted to take him in her arms and comfort him, but she knew he was not yet ready for that kind of solace.

Fortunately, Richard had little opportunity to dwell on his tragedy. Word of his return to New Haven had spread rapidly throughout the community, and a delegation of prominent citizens soon arrived at the house to welcome him home. Preeminent in the group was the governor of New Haven Colony, who officially expressed his gratitude for "the bold initiative Lieutenant Colonel Dunstable had undertaken and the exploits he had performed in ending the threat to the British possessions in the New World by his prompt action in mustering his corps of New England volunteers and leading them into battle against the French mercenaries."

After each member of the delegation had personally thanked Richard, the governor spoke again. "Because of the sad passing of Adam Burrows," he said, "the position of commander in chief of the New Haven militia is now vacant. However, just last week the militia held an election to determine the appointment of a new colonel in chief, and the vote was unanimous. Therefore I take great pride and pleasure in presenting you with your commission as the new military leader of our colony, Colonel Dunstable."

Richard was surprised and greatly pleased by the honor, and he expressed his thanks.

The opportunity to learn something more about the morning's disturbing events was too good to miss, and Celeste recounted to the governor and the businessmen who had accompanied him what had happened to her and Richard when they had visited what they had believed to be the offices of Burrows and Clayton.

Samuel Giddings, a merchant who specialized in exporting furs to England, frowned and nodded. "I must say," he declared, "that I was a mite surprised when Tom Clayton and his family pulled up stakes and left the colony on such short notice. They'd lived here for a great many years, but Tom Clayton insisted he was doing the right thing. What confused me is that both Tom and his son turned their houses over to this fellow Lapham to sell on their behalf."

"Just who is Horace Lapham?" Richard asked.

The visitors looked at one another, shrugging blankly, and again Giddings acted as spokesman for the group. "Nobody seems to know much about him or his family," he said. "We heard tell that he came from Boston, and I checked with some people up there with whom I do business. They say that Lapham lived in Boston for a number of years and built up a variety of businesses, prospering in all of them. As I gather, there were whispers about his methods being underhanded and maybe illegal, but nobody was ever able to prove any charge against him, and as far as my informants are concerned, he's an honorable man who is everything that he says he is."

The spare, austere Bartram White, reputedly one of the best lawyers in all of the New England colonies, looked down his long nose at Celeste. "Based on what you've just told me, Mistress Burrows," he said, "it doesn't appear to me that this fellow Lapham's seizure of your property without your approval or even your knowledge can be justified under the law, no matter what his alleged agreement with Tom Clayton may have been. There could have been circumstances that will clarify the situation, of course, but if you'd care to call at my office tomorrow, I'll be delighted to explore the matter with you further."

That was exactly what Celeste had in mind, and she felt a

the chamber. A young lady in her early twenties, she was of medium build, with dark-brown hair and remarkably clear blue eyes, which were her most prominent feature. Her figure was trim, and her face reflected both intelligence and strength.

She stopped short as she came into the room and glared at her father looming over her struggling mother. There was undisguised disgust in her voice as she said, "This is too much, Papa. Have you nothing better to do than to treat poor Mama like an animal?"

No one else who was familiar with Horace Lapham would have dreamed of addressing him in such a manner. Indeed, his first instinct was to send his daughter reeling across the room with a well-directed punch. However, the last time he had inflicted physical punishment on her, she had threatened to run away if he ever touched her again, and he knew that, being his daughter as well as Sophie's, she would keep her word. Certainly she needed discipline—and a severe dose, at that, he thought. Right now, however, he had other plans for her.

"Adam Burrows's widow and that man Dunstable are coming for supper tonight," he said, releasing Sophie. "I'm trying to persuade your stupid mother to lay on the hospitality, but she doesn't seem to think we're good enough for them! Me, Horace Lapham, not good enough!"

Barbara Lapham looked her father up and down, and her tone of voice was withering. "Sometimes I think you're mad, Papa," she said, "and right now I'm utterly convinced of it."

He ignored the slur, too absorbed in his own anger even to hear. "I want you to pitch in, too," he said. "You attend to the table settings, because you have a knack for it, and your mother has none. Then look in at the kitchen and see what you can do to help. And make sure that the menu is right. Include that plum pudding from England that set me back a pretty penny."

The girl seemed unimpressed. "Why all the fuss, Papa? Just what are you trying to accomplish, anyway?"

His exasperation increased. "I know you can't bother your pretty little head with such mundane affairs," he said in a mocking tone, "but I, for one, am going to be a blame sight easier in my own mind once I know this house actually belongs to me. Not to mention the chance I have to gain control of the wealthiest shipping company in the English colonies! Of course I want us to exert every effort! If you think I'd pass up an opportunity like this, you're crazy! I've been waiting for Dunstable and Burrows's widow to come back for weeks now, just planning for this day. They played right into my hands at our initial meeting this afternoon, but it'll all go to waste if I fail tonight. No, everything must go just right. Then we'll have no more worries for the rest of our lives."

The young woman put her hands on her hips and shook her head pityingly. "You're not dealing with that hopelessly ignorant widow of a Roundhead clergyman this time, Papa," she said. "In case you don't know it, all New Haven is agog today. This man Dunstable has just been promoted to the rank of colonel in chief of the New Haven militia. He's not only one of the most important men in this community, but he's being hailed as a war hero for destroying a fleet of French mercenaries. I haven't heard the details yet, but I heard enough to know that Richard Dunstable is not the dupe you make him out to be."

Her father looked at her curiously. "Where do you get your information?" he asked.

Barbara had no intention of admitting to her father, now or ever, that she was secretly meeting with a young man in town. Her father would strike her if he learned the truth, and then she would be forced to live up to her threat and walk out.

"I don't spend my days and nights cowering in the house behind closed shutters the way poor Mama does, afraid of my own shadow," she said. "I've made a good many friends since we've moved here from Boston. I know far more than you think. Not only is Richard Dunstable a man of great consequence in this community, but Adam Burrows's widow strikes me as no fool, either."

Her father tapped the toe of his shoe on the floor, his complexion reddening. "I'm listening," he said ominously.

"I've been told on very reliable authority," she said, "that Celeste Burrows is an exceptionally clever woman. She has lived in London and Paris, and was much renowned at the court of the late King Charles."

Despite his anger, Horace Lapham found his curiosity growing. "What was the cause of this renown?" he demanded.

His daughter shrugged. "I have no idea. All I know is that she's very bright, and also that she's inherited considerable wealth from her husband."

Lapham laughed mirthlessly. "I'm doing my utmost," he said, "to make her considerably less wealthy."

Sophie shook her head sadly.

Barbara also did not smile. "You've been very lucky for a great many years, Papa," she said. "You've skirted the edge of disaster rather nimbly. But this time you may lose your balance and fall."

Horace Lapham snorted in derision. "I don't need your little sermons," he said. "Do as you're bidden, no more and no less. Keep your mouth shut, your eyes open, and obey your father." A leer crept into his eye. "Besides, I'm not a complete ogre. I can be very kind and obliging if you behave properly. Wear one of your attractive gowns tonight, and you won't find me lecturing you if you happen to think that Richard Dunstable is sufficiently attractive to warrant your attentions. After all, he is a bachelor."

The contrast between the women at the unusual dinner party was marked. Sophie Lapham, wearing a dress of dark gray wool, said hardly a word and seemed to blend into the background. Her daughter, on the other hand, was too elaborately attired for the occasion in a figure-hugging dress of cream-colored satin and seemed acutely aware of the fact. She spoke too much, too rapidly, and seemed to force herself to address Richard, with whom she flirted clumsily.

Celeste, attired in a simple gown of dark silk, was quiet and seemed very relaxed and in command of herself and the situation.

Richard, who clearly admired his companion, behaved with similar self-assurance.

Horace Lapham, however, seated at the head of the table,

seemed vaguely irritated, attempting without success to get his wife to speak up and his daughter to quiet down.

The meal consisted of far too many courses of far too much food. Lapham alone did it justice, eating plate after plate with obvious relish, despite continually having to interrupt himself to prompt his wife or his daughter.

Richard and Celeste made something of a game of the conversation. Keeping the advice they had been given by Bartram White very much in mind, they avoided talk of business and made cryptic or evasive replies to the host's various remarks about his desire to buy their shares of the shipping company and to reach an immediate settlement with Celeste on the issue of the house.

On lesser topics, however, they were quite long-winded. When Lapham mentioned Boston, Richard embarked on a detailed and somewhat boring account of his last visit there. A mention of London sparked Celeste, and she related one anecdote after another about her life at the court there, surreptitiously winking at Richard as her tales departed further and further from the truth.

Finally, after an underheated plum pudding had been served for dessert, Lapham gave up trying to be tactful. "By the way, Mistress Burrows," he said, "my womenfolk tell me there's a clothes cupboard upstairs that contains a number of your dresses and other belongings. If you'll just tell me where you want it sent, I'll have it delivered to you tomorrow."

Richard was about to intervene, but when he saw Celeste's quiet smile and read the expression in her eyes, he was content to leave the matter in her hands.

"Please don't bother, sir," she said sweetly. "I appreciate your offer, but I'm sure the effort won't be necessary."

Lapham could not accept the rebuff and felt compelled to reply. Simulating astonishment rather crudely, he said, "Surely you want your dresses and your other belongings!"

Celeste's tone and manner remained calm. "Indeed I do," she said. "Some of my favorite things are in that closet, and I miss them terribly."

Lapham grinned expansively. "There you are, then," he

said. "It's all settled. It's no trouble at all to have the cupboard forwarded to you."

Celeste was still smiling. "Oh, I wouldn't think of it," she said. "I couldn't possibly put you through all that bother for what might well turn out to be a wasted effort."

In spite of Lapham's attempt at self-control, his face darkened. "What do you mean by that?" he demanded.

His tone was harsh, and Richard instantly came to Celeste's defense. "Mistress Burrows," he said, his voice icy, "means precisely what you think she means. She sees no need for her clothes to be moved, nor her furniture, for that matter—including, might I add, this very table. She will be returning here to live, and it would be very inconvenient for her to have to move twice." Richard belatedly remembered lawyer White's advice, and forced himself to check his temper. "I'm sorry to put matters so bluntly," he said, "but you've left us no alternative."

Celeste was grateful that Richard had leaped into the breach to defend her, and she patted his hand in thanks.

The issue was now out in the open. The young couple were indicating clearly that they had no intention of accepting the crude scheme of Horace Lapham to rob them of the better part of their inheritances.

Lapham knew better than to bluster. He had no intention of putting Richard Dunstable and Celeste Burrows on their guard any more than he had already. He was furious, however, that he had wasted a good meal on them, and despite an almost supreme effort at self-control, he could not help but glare at them murderously for an instant.

I'll see you both in hell, he said silently, before I'll give up this house and the shipping company. I was willing to treat you decently enough, but if you don't want to accept my bounty, there are other ways of getting your approval. A dead man and a dead woman are in no position to object to anything I choose to do to protect my own interests!

EPILOGUE

CARDINAL Mazarin had found a wealthy nobleman willing to marry another of the five nieces whose causes he favored, and consequently this morning His Eminence was in an unusually good humor.

As he left the small bedchamber he smiled benignly at Brother Peter, the monk who had been assigned as his guide and servant at the monastery where he had spent the night.

"It is a wonderful morning for traveling back to Paris, is it not, Brother?" the cardinal said, briskly descending the stairs to the refectory.

Actually the weather was cold and rainy, and the black-robed brother didn't know quite how to react. Therefore he simply nodded and said, "Yes, Your Eminence."

"If it's not too much trouble, I'll have my breakfast right away," Mazarin said, seating himself. "I must get back to Paris at once."

"Of course, Your Eminence." Brother Peter hurried off to the kitchen and soon returned with a small filet of broiled fish, a slab of toasted bread on which a thin layer of honey had been spread, and a glass of watered wine. With the meal he brought a packet of mail to the table, it being the cardinal's custom to read any correspondence first thing in the morning.

Mazarin smiled in pleasant surprise when he saw that the top letter was from his agent in Jamestown, in the English colony of Virginia. And when he recognized the names of Antoine de Bosquette and Etienne de Cluny in the first sentence, he realized that the good news he had been awaiting for so long had at last arrived. The English colonies in the New World must have suffered a severe defeat, he told himself. Soon, if everything went as planned, the English would be driven from the continent of North America, and he would be able to send in his soldiers and his traders, all for the glory and enrichment of France!

As the cardinal continued reading the letter, he began to cough violently when a bit of fish stuck in his throat.

Brother Peter froze; but when the color of Mazarin's face began to resemble the scarlet of his biretta, the monk summoned his courage and struck His Eminence a violent blow between the shoulder blades.

The cardinal's physical distress ended immediately, but his mental torment had just begun. Thanks to the meddling of Richard Dunstable and Celeste Burrows, France and her agents had suffered a severe defeat. The prize the cardinal had coveted, possession of the English colonies, had again evaded his grasp.

He briefly contemplated the idea of sending a trained agent-assassin to the New World to dispose of the troublemakers once and for all, but then thought better of it. He had more pressing business to attend to at the moment, and the New World would have to wait.

But he would not forget. The time would soon come when he would have the opportunity to dispose of the couple who had thwarted him. Yes, their days were numbered, he thought, as he angrily crumpled the unwelcome letter in his hand.

Brave men and spirited women in a land teeming with promise...they were the AMERICAN PATRIOTS...

THE NEW BREED

When his king is beheaded by Protestant rebels, Sir Richard Dunstable must flee to colonial America. In the wilds of the New World, he is swept up in espionage, intrigue, and Indian wars...and forced to choose between two women, one elegant and unprincipled, the other shrewd and beautiful.

THE GREAT DECEPTION

Double agents against their will, newlyweds Richard and Eliza Dunstable must part ways in a scheme to discredit the unscrupulous Peter Stuyvesant, who is secretly supplying firearms to Indians to drive the British from North America. In a heart-pounding climax, Eliza outwits and Richard outfights the Dutch governor and his bloodthirsty allies.

BOLD DESTINY

Reunited briefly, Richard and Eliza are swiftly parted again as Cardinal Mazarin, wily first minister of France, hires Caribbean pirates to launch a bold naval attack on Bermuda. But the attack is not what it seems, and Richard must act quickly to counter the assault and at the same time rescue his wife, who is caught in the clutches of Mazarin's cutthroats.

Available at your bookstore or use the coupon on the next page.

Ballantine presents another series from
the producers of *The Kent Family Chronicles*
and *Wagons West...*

THE AMERICAN PATRIOT SERIES